M000305531

Baker's Blues

a novel by

Judith Ryan Hendricks

 Chien Bleu Press

First Edition

Designed by Stewart Allison
Cover design by Stewart Allison
Author photo by Jerry Ryan

Library of Congress Control Number: 2015910204

Library of Congress Cataloging-in-Publication Data is available upon request from:
Chien Bleu Press
369 Montezuma Avenue # 544
Santa Fe, NM 87501

ISBN 978-0-9965035-0-1

For Geoff, as always.

Love doesn't sit there like a stone, it has to be made, like bread; remade all of the time, made new.

—Ursula K. LeGuin

PART ONE

NOW

We circle back, learning again what we thought we had known, learning that our map had been incomplete, that vast areas had been only imagined, that our instruments had been insufficient, our chronometer off, our unit of measurement different, our language wrong…once more the coastline had changed. We hadn't been where we thought we were….

— Sheila Nickerson, *Disappearance: A Map*

One

September, 2005

O f all the ways he could have died, drowning was the least likely. He swam almost daily, headed for Matador when the surf was up, learned the Eskimo roll at the age of forty, sailed every chance he got. He couldn't possibly drown.

As we found out later, he didn't. Officially, he died of cardiac arrest. It was cold water that stopped his heart.

It happened on a hot summer day at a lake up in the San Bernardino Mountains. He liked to drive up there to get away from L.A., to swim, to write—his laptop was in the car—or maybe just to be alone.

Whatever his original intention, he ended up diving off a boat dock into the deepest part of the lake. Deep and, in early July, still very cold. Probably he'd been hiking and was overheated, the doctor said. He might have had an undetected heart arrhythmia. It doesn't make any difference, really. Whatever happened that afternoon, it killed him. Two girls in a canoe found him floating in a shallow cove, bravely dragged him ashore and tried CPR. But by then it was too late.

It's been two months since that 5 A.M. call.

I was dressed and working on my first espresso, and before I even picked up the phone I was mulling the possibilities. Could be that the one proofing cabinet we had trouble with last week was acting up again. Hopefully just the thermostat. Or maybe somebody was calling in sick.

As a small business owner, I've learned to start exploring solutions before I even know what the problem is. So I was already thinking about how to adjust for twenty-five under-risen loaves of sprouted wheat bread and who I could call to work an early shift.

At first there was just a sound like someone gasping for breath. Then a vaguely familiar voice said,

"Wynter?"

"Yes…Alan?"

"I…terrible news. It's Mac. He's drowned."

I remember sitting with my elbows on the kitchen table, hands over my eyes, for what seemed a very long time.

At some point I must have called CM, but all I remember about the morning is her materializing on my porch in jeans and her pajama top. She told me later that when she arrived I was drinking espresso and making a list of things to do. It must be true because I still have the list. Just a sticky note that says:

Call Skye. Gabe. Suzanne.
Name of lawyer?
Safe deposit key
Pick up laundry
Call mom

The memorial service was my idea—and one he would have hated. It's at the house in Luna Blanca where we used to live and where he'd lived, alone or otherwise, since I moved out. CM helped me plan every-thing, right down to the priest. To say that Mac was not religious would be to wallow in understatement, but once in an unguarded moment he admitted he'd been an altar boy. I found it sort of touching.

Anyway, CM knows this priest named Father Paul who's a free-wheeling, ecumenical type so I asked him to put together a generic service for an unrepentant lapsed Catholic and he did.

It's a warm, clear September day and the house is full of people, including every woman who crossed Mac's path in the last twenty years, with two notable exceptions:

1. His mother, Suzanne McLeod. When I called to tell her about the accident she sounded appropriately shocked and distressed, but by the time I called her about the memorial she said she couldn't make it because of a special exhibit on New England quilts she was opening at the museum that week.

2. Gillian Welburne, Skye's mother. To be fair, she's still running the farm in New Zealand. She and I have exchanged polite emails over the last few months, mostly concerning the trust and the will and the service and Skye's flight schedule, but the bottom line is, I can't forgive her for having had his child and she can't forgive me for having married him.

I'm at the front door keeping watch for Skye when Kristin French drives up in her Range Rover. She stands by the car for a minute, smoothing her black skirt, pushing her huge sunglasses up on top of her dark hair. She lived here with Mac until this spring when she finally figured out he wasn't going to marry her.

I never understood why he didn't. She's about ten years younger, a successful producer. Beautiful, smart and strong. They rock-climbed together, went backpacking and kayaking, and she produced his screenplay. It looked good on paper.

She comes up to me, takes both my hands in hers and kisses my cheek. Then she walks straight through the house and out the French doors to the patio with the assurance of someone in familiar surroundings.

Liv's here, too. I saw her drinking coffee in the dining room, wearing her stupid rhinestone jeans and a black sweater.

My watch says ten after, but I keep it set a few minutes fast because I hate being late. I also hate other people being late. Wouldn't you think you could manage to be on time for your father's memorial service? Or at least call. It's not like we can start without her.

Just as I'm reaching for my cell phone, a green and white taxi screeches to a halt at the mailbox and Skye unfolds out of the back seat like a young stork hatching. I'd forgotten how tall she is. She drags her roll-aboard up the walk and gives me a careful hug.

"I'm sorry," she says in her wonderful Kiwi accent. "The effing driver got lost." Sunlight on her face shows the traces of dried tears and a tiny smudge of mascara.

We stash her bag in the hall closet and walk out to the patio. Everyone's already seated around the pool. My mother and Richard with CM and Nathan. Alan and Sylvia Lear—Mac's agent and his wife. Willow Maidenhair, his therapist. A couple of writers. A few neighbors. Some studio people that I don't know and who obviously think I'm his sister.

Local blues guy Jim Bozeman is playing his guitar version of "Sometime other than Now", a song Mac liked.

Father Paul thanks everyone for coming. He's wearing a Hawaiian shirt and Dockers and looks more like a UCLA grad student than a priest.

"We are here today to celebrate the life of Matthew Spencer McLeod, known to his friends as Mac." He mispronounces the name, saying *McLee-od* instead of *McLoud*, at which point Skye very politely corrects him.

He talks about Mac as a father, the fact that he never knew about Skye till she was sixteen but how he worked at forging a bond with her and how close they'd become. He describes—tactfully—my relationship with Mac, how even though we divorced, we remained "good and loving friends." He talks about Mac's writing, his affinity for the outdoors, his love of music. He ends with a generic prayer, but when I look up I catch him sheepishly crossing himself.

Now people start getting up and telling their stories about Mac. The number of people who want to talk surprises me. Also some of the things they say. A journalist named Karla talks about his generosity, the way he'd helped her with a novel manuscript. Alan says he was a "gentle soul and a fine writer." Kristin calls him emotionally honest. I stare at her. Seriously? Gabe Cleveland gets all choked up, saying Mac "played life without a helmet."

Then Skye stands up. Everyone's attention is riveted on the young Amazon, her fair hair moving slightly in the breeze. She reads Section 52 of Whitman's "Song of Myself", and her voice is clear and strong until the last three lines...

> *Failing to fetch me at first keep encouraged,*
> *Missing me one place search another,*
> *I stop somewhere waiting for you.*

She falters then, but by that point everyone has fallen in love with her. And then it's my turn. CM nudges my foot gently with hers.

Even under the best of circumstances I'm not good at speaking to more than one person at a time about anything. Now here I am with thirty people looking at me expectantly, waiting for me to say something touching or meaningful. What do I say about Mac McLeod? My ex-husband. And other complicated job titles. Lover. Friend.

I bunch the wad of tissues in my hand and stand up.

"Mac was..." I begin, and then my brain goes suddenly dark. I'm sure they all think I'm going to cry, but it's not that. There simply are no words waiting in the queue. What do I say?

That there was a time when I hated him, with that special intensity reserved for people you love beyond all reason and who then disappoint or hurt you? That during his periodic wrangling with depression, I'd managed to not hate him, but just to temporarily forget that I loved him—or at least to not act on it.

"Mac was a huge part of my life, and I'll miss him every single day. Thank you all so much for coming. I'm sure it would…mean a lot to him."

My knees fold and I sit down.

Thank God, Big Jim Bozeman picks up his guitar and begins to play softly. CM, thank God for her too, invites everyone to the buffet. Conversation begins as a hiss that swells to a buzz, and I escape inside.

When I step out of the powder room, a man is standing by the front door, his back to me. Broad shoulders, dark, longish hair curling over his collar. Familiar. When he hears the door click shut, he turns around.

Alex.

He doesn't say anything, just comes over and holds me for a minute. He feels solid and warm, like a rock wall in the sun.

"Sorry, my flight was late," he says.

"Thanks so much for coming. It's great to see you."

He holds my shoulders. "It's great to see you too. I just wish it wasn't for this."

Death always seems to make people hungry and horny.

When Alex and I proceed to the dining room, the guests are stuffing themselves, tossing back champagne. Half the male contingent is hitting on Kristin and the other half is eyeing Liv, who immediately zeroes in on Alex.

In the kitchen, Skye huddles in a corner with her cell phone, eyes darting from one stranger's face to another.

"I can't talk now," I hear her say. "I'm at the bloody memorial service, for God's sake. I'll ring you later." She snaps the phone shut and slips past me without word, through the door to the hall.

My mother is talking with Tyler and CM...probably about me, judging from the sudden halt in the conversation.

"It was a beautiful service, honey," my mom says. "Mac would have loved it."

"The music maybe," I say. "The rest of it, not so much."

Tyler studiously avoids making eye contact.

"Nate's going to take Richard and your mom back to the condo." CM gives my arm an encouraging squeeze. "I'll stay here till we get everything cleaned up."

I circulate.

Thank you for coming. It means a lot. Mac would appreciate it...That was a lovely story you told about him...

The tiny sample bottle containing six Valium that Dr. Greer gave me is tucked into my top bureau drawer at home, waiting for me like a promise, and that's what keeps me going. Shaking hands. Hugging. Crying. Smiling.

Watching Kristin walk around this house, knowing that six months ago she was living here...it brings out this weird territorial thing in me, like I want to slap her hands and say *Mine! Don't touch.*

She and Skye are talking, heads together, by the bay window where Mac and I used to put the Christmas tree. They hug and then Kristin looks up and sees me. She comes over, still wearing her shades on top of her head. "Wyn, thanks for doing this. And for including me."

"I'm glad you could be here," I say. It's almost true.

"Well…take care of yourself." She touches my shoulder lightly and lets herself out.

"Classy lady." Alex is standing next to me. "Who's the other one? Liz?"

I come precipitously close to laughter, but I set my jaw against it, afraid if I start I won't be able to stop.

"*Liv.* She's harder to explain. Maybe we could have dinner one night. How long are you in town?"

He looks at his watch. "About three more hours. I already called a cab."

"Oh, no. Really?"

"That little shit Ferris is getting married tomorrow and going to Hawaii for a week, so I've got to be at the café."

I smile. "Haven't you told him chefs don't get to have normal lives?"

"I told him. He wasn't listening."

An awkward pause. Then I ask,

"How are the boys?"

"Good. Dustin's graduating next year. He's got early acceptance at Stanford and he's got a summer internship at JPL."

"In Pasadena? Wow. That's really great. And Jesse?"

"The skateboard king," he says. Then, "Any chance you'll be on the island this year?"

"Probably not. We're short staffed right now, and then November is—"

"Right. Your busy time." He thrusts his hands into his pockets. "We had a pretty good storm two weeks ago. Some trees came down on my road, so I went by to check on your place…"

The "place" he's talking about is the cottage on Orcas Island. Formerly Mac's and mine. Then mine via the divorce settlement. Funny, how badly I thought I wanted it. But after a year of finding reasons not to go up there, I decided it came with too much history and Mac obligingly bought me out. Now it's back to me, like some real estate fruitcake that keeps being re-gifted.

I ask, "Is it okay?"

"Yeah. Mostly."

"Erica hasn't mentioned anything about it."

"Erica won't mention anything till she can't rent it anymore. In that location with your view, she could probably rent a tool shed for a grand a week. It looks like it could use some work is all. If you want I could check it out."

"That's so nice of you, Alex, but I'm sure you have better things to do."

He gives me a small, rueful smile. "Right. You know, my life is pretty fucking exciting."

Now I do let myself laugh.

By two-thirty the buffet has been picked clean. Most people have said their goodbyes and drifted away. Father Paul, Jim Bozeman and the kitchen crew have taken their checks and left. Nathan has driven Richard and my mother back to their condo, but CM stays with me and Tyler and Skye. Everything's been tidied up and put away, but for whatever reason, I feel compelled to go over the kitchen again, collecting every stray crumb, mopping up every drop of water, scrubbing the sink, polishing the chrome faucets to blinding brilliance.

Tyler's getting antsy. She paces. She sighs.

"Wyn, for God's sake, give it a rest. Haven't you done enough today?"

She's right. I know. But…I wipe fingerprints off the refrigerator door.

CM says very gently, "Come on, let's lock up."

"Okay. Just a minute."

I bring the waste basket out of the powder room, empty it into the kitchen garbage, tie the bag closed and set it by the back door. Fine. But when I pull out a new bag and begin to fit it carefully into the garbage container, the volcano that is Mt. Tyler blows up.

"What the *fuck* are you doing?" On the shrillness scale her voice sits right between screech and whine. "He treats you like shit, you clean his house. And he's not even around to appreciate it. Not that he would anyway."

She rips the bag out of my hand.

"Tyler, that's enough." CM never raises her voice, but she always makes herself heard.

"Damn right it's enough." She wads up the bag and throws it on the floor. "It's way more than enough."

She grabs her shoulder bag and slams out the back door, leaving me speechless and staring.

"Excuse me." Skye's face has gone doughy white. She disappears into the bathroom, shutting the door behind her, and I hear the unmistakable sounds of vomiting.

CM looks at me. "Have we wandered into an alternate universe?"

A weird laughter bubbles up in my chest. In seconds, the two of us are laughing, crying, holding each other.

That evening Skye sits at my kitchen table in her white cotton nightshirt. Twenty-three years old, lovely and bereft. We're both too exhausted to sleep, but Charles, my seven-year-old Corgi, has no such problem. He's curled up in her lap, snoring intermittently. I keep picturing the Valium, tucked between my bras and underpants upstairs, but I can't do it. I can't leave her all alone and wide awake while I take the express lane to sweet oblivion.

I make tea and set out my good china cups, sugar and milk. There was so much food at the house today, but I had no appetite. Now I'm hungry, so I've put out half a loaf of raisin pumpernickel bread, salted butter, raw honey and a slab of cream cheese.

"I…um…heard you in the bathroom. Are you okay?"

"It was just all the junk I ate on the flight, and I drank too much wine because I couldn't sleep." She takes a sip of hot tea. "It's kind of you to have me stay," she says stiffly. "I could have booked a room."

"Skye, I'd hate it if you came to L.A. and didn't stay with me. I always wanted…"

My brain stumbles. What was it I always wanted? Some kind of closeness, I suppose. Some connection to make up for her being his child but not mine.

She cuts a piece of bread and spreads it thickly with butter and honey. "I was going to stay with Kristin, but she has to go to New York."

Well, okay. After all, Kristin was there for the past year and a half. Still, it stings, and I'm reasonably sure that was the intent.

I get up to open the French doors and the night air floods around us like cool water in the awkward silence.

"I loved the poem you read. The Whitman." When I touch her arm, I feel the muscle tense. As if she'd like to pull away without being rude. "I hope you know how important you were to him. I truly believe you saved his life."

"Bloody lot of good it did."

"You know, my father died of a heart attack, too. When I was seventeen."

"You told me before. At least you had time with him."

"Losing someone you love sucks, no matter how or when it happens."

She blots her eyes with a tissue. "I still can't believe it. I keep expecting he'll ring me or…something."

She takes a tiny bite of the bread and chews it for a ridiculous amount of time. Then tea.

"Were you there?" she asks dully. "When your father died?"

"He was at work. My mother came to school after lunch. They got me from biology class and walked me down to the office. The school secretary wouldn't say anything to me. Or even look at me. But the second I saw my mother's face, I knew."

"What did you do?"

The thought sends unexpected tears brimming in my eyes.

"I got down on the floor and started screaming. The bad thing was, I never thought about how my mother must have felt. I was just furious with her, coming to tell me that in school."

"Mum called me at the restaurant. It was so weird. I didn't know what to do. I just stayed on and worked my shift. Like if I just kept on and never went home, it wouldn't be true."

When she swallows more tea, I can tell by the little pucker of her mouth that it's cold. I pour our cups into the sink and set two wineglasses on the table, retrieve a bottle of Montepulciano from my wine cabinet and fish around in a drawer for the corkscrew.

"None for me, thanks," she says.

I refill her cup with tea and pour some wine for myself. "How's your mother doing?"

She looks at the ceiling. "We had a big row before I left. About the money and everything. She says I should put it in the farm. Upgrade our stock and equipment. Truth be told, I think what she really wants is for me to take it on. She keeps on about retiring. Her and Derek moving to Hastings."

"Why doesn't she just sell it?"

"She wants to keep it in the family," she says. "We're five generations on the land."

"Oh."

"The idea is for me to run the farm, marry Jack, raise sheep. And of course pop out a few sprogs to carry on the tradition."

I put my feet up on the chair and loop my arms over my knees. "Who's Jack?"

"A bloke I grew up with. His family owns a farm near ours. We were together in school, but not anymore. He just hasn't got it through his thick head yet that I've outgrown him. Of course Mum keeps encouraging him."

"Is he the one who called earlier?"

"No." A slow flush creeps up under her tan. "That was...um...Trevor. We're sort of...engaged." She turns the cup back and forth on its saucer. "Not officially. Yet. But we will be. He manages the restaurant where I work."

"Maybe you and he could take over the farm and you could—"

She grimaces. "I don't want to raise sheep. I'm sick to my back teeth of bloody sheep. And Mum'd sooner set the whole place ablaze than see Trevor on it anyway."

"Why is that?"

She scrapes more butter onto her bread. "He's...a wee bit older than me." Pause. "Actually, he's thirty-six."

"It can be difficult, the age difference. And if there's an ex-wife or kids..."

"Actually..." She runs the tip of her tongue delicately along her lower lip. "She's not exactly an ex-wife. Yet. I mean, he's been intending to leave, but then she got pregnant."

I bite the inside of my cheek.

"People can change, you know," she says.

"Yes, they can. The problem is, they so seldom do."

"No sermon, okay? Mum's about putting me up the wall with it."

"Don't worry. I believe that for better or worse, we all get to make our own mistakes."

"Was Mac one of yours?"

"Well...I...it depends how you look at it. Obviously we didn't have a... successful marriage. On the other hand, I don't regret loving him."

"You must have at one point," she says coolly, "else you wouldn't have divorced him."

"It's somewhat more complicated than that."

"Right." She strokes the dog's ears, and he twitches contentedly.

I say, "Tomorrow I thought we'd start sorting through things at the house. Get whatever you want packed up and shipped. I've got a couple of appointments set up with real estate agents, a meeting with the lawyer. There's going to be some paperwork…"

"What about the…ashes?"

"Did you see the tin box in the living room? With the turquoise concha?"

"The what?"

I go into the living room and retrieve the tin box that CM brought me from Santa Fe. "For now, they're in here. When I can get up to Orcas I'll take them and scatter them."

"I don't understand this whole thing. Couldn't we just bury the ashes? At least he'd have a proper grave and a stone…some place you could go and lay flowers or…whatever. If he's in the water, he's just…gone. Nowhere."

"I can put some of them in a separate container for you, if you want."

Her eyes can be disconcertingly like his. "Don't you find it a wee bit strange? Dividing him up into little packages?"

I breathe in deliberately, then a controlled exhale . "What you or I find strange is beside the point. This is what he wanted and I promised him I'd do it. I can put some of the ashes in a small container for you and you can bury them or keep them or whatever you—"

"Maybe I can get a T-shirt, too. One that says *I went to L.A. and all I got was this T-shirt and three grams of my father in a box.*"

"Skye…I'm doing the best I can."

There are a few quiet seconds before her face crumples like a piece of paper and she puts her head down on the table and cries. I want to touch her shoulder or hold her hand, but ever since she arrived, there seems to be some invisible boundary, like those electronic dog fences, something I can't cross.

"You must be tired. Maybe you should get some sleep?"

She raises her teary face. "I don't want to be alone."

"Why don't you go stretch out on the couch then. I'm going to have another glass of wine and by that time maybe we'll both be ready for bed."

She arranges herself on the couch with Charles and the comforter and before I've finished my second glass, they're both asleep.

I wake up in my clothes, on top of my un-slept-in bed with dog breath in my face, a pounding headache, and a purple tongue. I remember helping Skye into the guestroom bed, locking up and turning the lights off before I passed out.

I'm brewing espresso and cleaning up last night's dishes when the doorbell rings, sending Charles into a barking frenzy. Tyler is standing on my front porch, looking like she'd rather be shoveling dog poop with a teaspoon.

"Don't say it," she says before I can get out a word. "My bad. Out of line. I'm sorry."

"Well, that sounds heartfelt."

"Peace." She thrusts a white paper sack at me. "I'm not sorry I thought it, but I'm sorry I said it out loud. In front of…" She looks around. "Xena, Warrior Princess."

"Her name is Skye. And whatever problem you had with her father, it has nothing to do with her."

She puts her palms together and bows over them. "I know. It's just every time I think about all the shit he put you through, it makes me furious.

And now you're having to be her nanny and I bet he didn't leave you a buck ninety-five. Am I right?"

"Come on, Ty—"

"Come on, what? She's a big girl. If she has to have a babysitter, why can't *Krisss-tin* do it?" She flutters her eyelashes.

The dentist said not to grind my teeth, but sometimes I just can't help it. "First, Kristin's in New York—"

"Convenient."

"Second, I'm the executor of Mac's estate. It's my responsibility to—"

"Good morning."

Skye is standing in the kitchen doorway, looking daisy fresh because she was smart enough to drink tea last night.

Tyler jumps into the breach. "Skye, I came to apologize for my...outburst yesterday. I'm sorry if I—"

"You've a right to your opinion." She walks past us to pour herself a cup of coffee.

"Well...I'm heading back to work." Tyler sticks her hands into her jeans pockets and looks at me. "I don't guess we'll be seeing you today."

"I might stop by this afternoon. This morning we're going over to the house to start cleaning out everything. I was hoping you and János could come to dinner Friday night?"

"We'd like to," she says unconvincingly, "But I'll have to check my calendar. I'll call you later."

She heads for the door.

Little beast.

The assault of memory begins with the scent of eucalyptus and crushed peppercorns on a warm, dry breeze from the canyon. I open the car windows and drive slowly down the shade-dappled street. The neighborhood is quiet, grownups gone to work and kids at school.

Skye hasn't said a word on the drive over. She stares out the window, absently rolling the fringe of her woven belt between her fingers. We park in the garage and carry empty boxes into the kitchen. She goes back to the car for wrapping paper and tape while I stand still. Looking.

The air is heavy with memories.

Our old dog Brownie waiting patiently just inside the kitchen door. My garden, splashed with bright annuals. Mac sitting at the umbrella table drinking coffee and drying off after a morning swim.

I peer out the window over the sink.

The jacaranda tree is huge now. I recall the argument with our next door neighbors who wanted us to take it down because of the clouds of purple blossoms that blew onto their deck every spring. And the mourning doves who populated it. Mac said they were stupid birds who did nothing but breed and shit, but I found their cries melancholy and romantic.

Skye doesn't want anything from the kitchen, so we wrap it all in newsprint and pack it in boxes for the hospice store. Nor does she have any interest in the furniture. We originally discussed having an "estate sale" but neither of us liked the thought of watching strangers pick through all his stuff, so in the end we agreed to donate everything to Furniture Bank and Goodwill.

After a quick and mostly silent lunch of the ham and provolone sandwiches Tyler brought from the bakery, Skye begins the intimidating task of sorting through her father's books and papers while I stand in the master bedroom trying to overcome my reluctance to touch anything.

It just feels too weird.

I never understood how he could live in this house, sleep with another woman—or women—in this bed. And Kristin—why would she want to share a house with Mac's history? Maybe it's true that love makes fools of us all.

The racks on the left side of the closet are empty except for a few naked hangers. That's where my clothes used to hang, and then probably Kristin's. On the right are his clothes, slacks and jackets and shirts, wool and linen, cotton and cashmere, all bearing the Italian designer labels he'd developed a taste for. Floor to ceiling shelves full of pullovers and T-shirts, and along the bottom, shoe racks with loafers and expensive running shoes, tennis shoes and deck shoes and flip flops, hiking boots with dried mud in the Vibram soles, rock climbing shoes soft as ballet slippers, and the custom made Paul Bond cowboy boots that he loved.

On the end wall at the very back is a row of pegs where his collection of baseball caps resides, along with one knitted ski cap and a motorcycle helmet. How odd. I never knew him to ride a motorcycle.

At first I fold everything, arranging it all in careful stacks, fitting things snugly into boxes so they won't slide around.

But after an hour or so the air in the closet has turned warm, my forehead is damp, breathing is an effort. Finishing becomes a higher priority than neatness. Pretty soon I'm pulling slacks off hangers, rolling them up, tossing them on top of everything else, along with belts, hand-kerchiefs and a few ties. I stuff socks and undershirts and boxer shorts into the gaps and pack it all down.

I throw all the shoes into a box, then pull his ski parka off its hook and lay it flat on top. When I turn back to the rack there's only one thing left. Hanging against the wall at the end of the rod is an old Harris Tweed sport coat, well worn and sporting a few moth holes. I recognize it immediately and reach for it without thinking, gathering the scratchy fabric in my hands, inhaling the peaty scent.

When I met Mac, this was his only sport coat. He wore it whenever he needed to dress up his jeans. He wore it when he took me to dinner at the Queen City Grill in Seattle after Ellen and I sold the bakery. He wore it to New York after Alan sold his first book to Drummond. And he wore it against all my protests—it was out of season, out of style…he argued that it was a classic—the night we got married in my mother's backyard.

By the end of the week, the house is spotless and listed with Nancy Holland, real estate broker *non pareil*. She convinced me that leaving the furniture in place would make it more appealing, thus leading to a quicker sale, but even fully furnished, the rooms feel empty and strange.

Legal papers have been reviewed, taxes paid, life insurance claims filed, bank accounts closed, safe deposit box emptied. Skye has dutifully initialed and signed and dated till her eyes glazed over. Her green legal size file folder bulges with copies.

When I escape to the bakery a couple of afternoons I invite her to come with me, but she wants to nap, she says. Or read. Or go to the pool. I'm sure she also doesn't want to see Tyler. It's just as well. Work is my refuge and when I'm there, I don't have to deal with her mood swings. Or my own.

She seems content to spend the evenings watching TV or reading, plugged into her iPod, Charles glued to her side. It's incredibly affecting, the way he sits and watches her, his little dog eyebrows knit together in concern.

For her last night in L.A. I wanted to have a nice dinner with my mom and Richard, CM and Nathan, Tyler and János. But my mother and stepfather have gone back to Grass Valley, CM and Nathan are in New York, János is working and Tyler has unearthed a very important social engagement that precludes her joining us. Okay, fine. We can still have a nice dinner.

I grill chicken breasts and serve them with mustard sauce (Alex's recipe) a big green salad and some grilled country bread brushed with olive oil and garlic. Rafe's apple tart is dessert. I drag out the Italian Majolica plates and my French crystal, buy cut flowers for the table. She doesn't seem to notice any of it.

I ask her to choose the wine, and she finds a lovely un-oaked Chardonnay from New Zealand. After dinner we linger on the patio, wrapped in fleece throws, while she explains more than I ever wanted to know about malolactic fermentation of chardonnay.

"Sometimes only part of the blend goes through malolactic fermentation and then it's put back in with the rest," she concludes. "So the wine keeps its fruit, but holds the acidity down a bit."

"Where did you learn all that?"

"I've been working weekends at the Silks tasting room the last two summers. I help set up the wine flights and the wine and cheese pairings. I've learned a lot from Josh…even if he is an Ozzie."

I nibble on a piece of smoky crust, kick off my sandals and pull Charles up on my lap. One of my neighbors is having a party, but the noises seem dreamlike and far away.

I'm just about to ask another question about the winery when she blindsides me.

"What happened with you and him? Why didn't it work?"

Since that first awkward evening, our conversations have focused on relatively safe topics…school, politics, food, wine, films, travel, music, city vs. country life, dogs vs. cats. She's demonstrated sheep shearing technique on a patient Charles and I've showed her how to knead and shape bread dough. We've talked about Mac, but thus far our discussion has been confined to historical fact. Now I decide to keep it light.

"If I knew the answer to that I'd be getting rich on talk radio."

She says, "You must have thought about it."

"When we first split up I hardly thought about anything else. But it's kind of like trying to go somewhere with one foot nailed to the floor. Lots of motion, no progress."

"There have to be reasons for everything," she persists. "Did you just stop loving him? Was there someone else?"

I turn in my chair. "Why on earth would you think that?"

She stops with the glass halfway to her mouth. "Do you know why Kristin moved out?"

"You'd have to ask Kristin."

"I did. She said it was because he wouldn't get married."

"Well, there's your answer."

"He didn't love her," she says.

I want to tell her she sounds like a romance novel, but that would be unkind, not to mention pointless. After all, she's twenty-three.

"That's one of those things you'll probably never know for sure."

Her eyes are an angry green flash. "The truth is he couldn't marry Kristin because he loved you."

"This is not something we need to speculate about."

"You just don't want to think about what you did to him."

What I did to him.

I don't know how to defend myself and she appears to take my silence as an admission of guilt.

"I saw how he felt. The way he talked about you. He was devastated that you left."

"Skye, come on. I know you're upset, and I am, too. Mac was a really wonderful man and we'll miss him—"

"*Every single day,*" she parodies my words, tilting her head back and forth. "Oh, save the memorial speech, can you? *God damn it.*" She starts to cry.

"Life is messy. People love each other and hurt each other. The truth is, Mac and I had gotten past the divorce. We were close in a different way."

Her face is flushed and damp and she keeps rubbing her eyes with her dinner napkin. "Too right. He'd have done anything for you. Including pretend to be your friend. Pretend to be happy with Kristin. The truth is, he was lost without you. He didn't care whether he lived or…not."

I stare at her, tired beyond rational thought. "You're out of your mind."

And then I feel instantly ashamed, because of course she is. It's been thirty years since my father died, but I have total recall for the insanity of grief, the pain, the anger, the need to lash out at whoever was handy. Most often, my mother.

Since Gillian's not here, looks like I'm the body double.

She settles back in the chair, quiet for the moment, but I notice her hands trembling.

"Things change," I say gently. "No matter how much you love someone…sometimes it just doesn't work. Skye, I'm sorry. I wish—"

She covers her face with both hands, then looks out between the fingers, like a child. "I just want to scream sometimes. I go round doing normal things and then all of a sudden in the midst of it, I think *shit*…he's dead."

"I know—"

"Bloody hell you do." The words are sharp, but the voice is weary.

She watches me gather up the dishes and take them inside. I pour the wine down the drain, stash the plates and forks in the dishwasher, pull a towel off the rack to dry my hands.

24

The door slams and I turn around.

"I've dropped the goblet." She looks stricken. "Is there a broom?"

"Leave it. I'll get it in the morning. I think we both need some sleep."

"I feel badly."

I can't decide if she means about the crystal or about what she said to me.

"What will you do when you get home?"

"What I've been doing all along, I expect. Till I sort things out." She turns away. "Good night, Wyn."

As she disappears up the stairs with Charles at her heels, I hear her say, "I'll miss you, little Scruff."

We'll miss her, too, Charles and I. In spite of the bumpy road we've been on.

Tomorrow she'll get on a plane and I'll slip back into my life; no more awkward silences or pointed questions, no accusations or misunderstandings. It will be an immense relief.

Still, I don't want her to go. I'm afraid the connection, such as it is, will be broken. Afraid she'll be too busy, too angry, too enmeshed in her tragic romance.

I'm afraid of losing her, which is ridiculous, since I never had her to begin with.

The tin box that holds what the people at the crematory call "the cremains," which I can't help thinking sounds like dried cranberries, is still sitting on the counter. I pick it up and carry it out to the garage, reaching around the corner to flip the light switch.

There sits my other bequest from Mac—Elky 2, a cream and turquoise dream under the flickering fluorescent light. CM rode with me when I drove it over from the house—she called it the positioning cruise—and I haven't driven it since.

Now I open the door and slide in, settling Mac in the passenger seat. The truck smells good, like real car wax and a trace of cigarette smoke. None of those stupid air fresheners shaped like pine trees. I sit for a minute, holding the wheel, tapping my fingernails lightly in response to some old song, teasing my memory.

I look over at the box.

"I'm not doing so well with Skye."

No response. Not that I was expecting one.

I lean my head back against the head rest. "Damn, I'm glad I'm not young anymore. Remember that song? From *Gigi*? No, probably not. But, it's hard. You really need to believe things make sense. Or at least that they will, once you've figured out all the secrets. Too bad there aren't any secrets and nothing ever makes sense...does it?"

I reach down for the seat bar and push back, stretching out my legs.

"Tonight I was sitting there across the table from her at dinner, and I suddenly thought about that time in Seattle. On the ferry going over to Bainbridge. Or was it Vashon? We took so many ferry rides. They sort of run together. This was right after I came back from my mom's wedding and you were telling me about New Zealand. And Gillian and how you left...of course, you didn't know about Skye then, but...

"Did you ever imagine it would turn out like this? I didn't. Not in my wildest imaginings. I had a lot of plans for us, and none of them included talking to your ashes in a tin box.

"You know what? About a week ago I went through all the messages on my cell just to see if maybe there was an old one from you. Just to hear your voice...I must've deleted them all."

26

I close my eyes for a minute. The air is absolutely still.

"Well… I guess I should get some sleep. I'll talk to her in the morning."

I get out of the truck, leaving the box on the passenger seat.

In the morning when I knock on the guest room door, there's no response. Downstairs I find Charles disconsolate, lying on the foyer rug. Her sheets and towels are piled in the laundry room and a hastily scribbled note awaits me on the kitchen table.

Got an earlier flight. Thanks. Skye.

PART TWO

THEN

The mind is its own place, and in itself, can make a heaven of Hell
and a hell of Heaven.

—John Milton

Two

Los Angeles, Y2K

I could be at home right now. Curled up on the bed with my dog, a glass of good Shiraz, and a Turner Classic movie. Gigi was on tonight. We—by which I mean the Brown Dog and I—are fond of musicals, and anything with Maurice Chevalier. In *Gigi*, I love his duet with Hermione Gingold, "I Remember It Well." It's a song about two former lovers who each have different memories of the end of their affair.

I've seen the movie probably a half-dozen times, but I'd rather be watching it for the seventh time than teetering on these ridiculous heels, trying to appear thrilled to be at this party, when the truth is, I'm tired and my feet hurt. You'd think my husband might have noticed this. That he might have sidled up earlier in the evening, nibbled my ear and said,

Let's go get a pizza and have dinner in bed.

There was a time when he would have. But not tonight.

A white-jacketed waiter appears with a tray, and two of the women reach for little canapés of brown bread with smoked salmon and crème fraîche, dusted with chives. The waiter distributes cocktail napkins and lifts empty glasses from their hands, but their eyes never stray from Mac's face. I understand the attraction.

Of the four male writers here tonight, one is gay, one is a nineteen-year-old with acne and tongue piercings, and one is a sixty-five-year-old anthropologist, wide of ass and high of trousers. Mac, by contrast, is a rather fit specimen of forty-two, with nice eyes and fair hair going a bit gray at the temples.

Add to that, his novel *December Light* has just come out in trade paperback. It's the story of a woman in the 1950's who gives up love in favor of her career as a photographer and goes off to study and work in London. It's been selling briskly—at least in L.A.—and suddenly he's wearing the mantle of the "sensitive man" last seen on the shoulders of Alan Alda.

I watch the little group for a minute, imagining that I've just met him tonight, that I never knew the old Mac. Or, as I've started thinking of him, First Edition Mac—the guy whose idea of clothes shopping was a trip to REI. Who was happy driving a 1971 Chevy El Camino. Whose drink of choice was a decent pale ale.

Sometimes I still catch a glimpse of his ghost, wandering around the house in jeans and a flannel shirt, but for the most part, I live with New Mac, a man who has more Italian designer labels in his closet than a Miami pimp. Who drinks Macallan single malt scotch and tools around the Palisades in a self-absorbed, arrogantly sexy, black BMW 740, which my best friend has dubbed The Death Star.

I never imagined he'd sell the truck.

He and Elky were together long before I came on the scene, and I always felt like he and the truck were bonded somehow.

I imagined the three of us—Mac, Elky and me—growing old together, driving down Pacific Coast Highway on summer afternoons, Elky's silver paint flashing in the sun. Alright, so the paint was oxidized white with a few rust spots, the tires bald, the upholstery splitting. That could have all been fixed.

But then Mac comes into the kitchen one day and announces that somebody's coming over to look at Elky. I'm stunned. He never mentioned that he was thinking of selling it, much less that he's been running an ad in *Auto Trader Classic Trucks*. Of course, that's his M.O. He considers it, decides to do it, does it, and only then tells me.

Actually three somebodies show up to see the truck that afternoon, and the last one wants it. Bad. His name is Kyle, and he looks about seventeen. Tall, lanky, cute and a little shy. Sort of how I've imagined Mac at that age.

While I've always thought of the Elky as male—a buddy of sorts—Kyle's pale blue eyes caress the truck as if it were a girl. He goes to get his older brother and two hours later Elky's backing out of the driveway with my fantasy Mac at the wheel. I have a nearly overpowering urge to run out and jump in the passenger side and ride into the sunset with him.

I flag down the waiter and ask him for a glass of Pellegrino with lime. The pianist at the venerable black Steinway is serving up cocktail party jazz lite and elevator arrangements of Beatles songs. It's not his fault. Nobody wants anything they actually have to listen to. He's probably as bored as I am.

I lean against the instrument, stirring a dish of peanuts with a tiny silver spoon. Among all the writers, agents, editors, favored members of the press and one or two P.R. "specialists" at this party, I'm the baker. The one who does manual labor. Quite honestly I'd be happier in the kitchen swapping recipes with the caterer. There are a few trailing spouses besides me, but most of them seem to enjoy basking in the reflected limelight. Either that, or they're better at faking it than I am.

"Wynter, how are you?" It's Sylvia, our hostess, looking regal in lavender silk pants and a matching ribbon-knit sweater. Her husband Alan Lear is Mac's agent. She hugs me, then looks at my face. "I haven't seen you in...well, since the Stockwell's dinner. You look lovely for someone who's about to fall asleep."

I can't help laughing. "I'm fine. And I'm off tomorrow, so I can sleep in."

Sylvia reads people the way some people read books. Probably why she was such a good therapist. She's retired from private practice now, but she still speaks at conferences and conducts workshops for therapists.

Now her eyes flicker towards Mac and his groupies and she gives me a disconcertingly direct look. "Good. Let him take you out for breakfast."

Suddenly someone calls from across the room, "Sylvia, come tell Marion about that darling little hotel you and Alan found in Tuscany last year."

She looks over her shoulder. "One second, Joyce." Then back to me. "Alan says this project's been hard on him. That means it's been hard on you, too."

I'm not tracking too well, so it takes me a few seconds to figure out that she's talking about Mac. I love Sylvia, but this is not a conversation I want to have. Fortunately, someone else is calling her name from a different corner of the room.

She sighs and squeezes my hand. "Take care of yourself, Wynter. Let's try to get together soon. Have lunch or something." And then she's gone.

Out in the foyer, the first wave is preparing for take-off, holding their jackets, air kissing, conversation dwindling down to witty exit lines. Alan is a notorious night owl, though, so it could still be an hour or two before we get out of here. I look at my watch.

I've been up since 4 A. M. and I'm about to hit the wall.

The dark wood doors of the library click shut behind me, and I sink down on the leather couch, set my glass on the table, and kick off the offending sandals. They're really nothing more than a sole balanced on a chopstick with a couple of skinny straps over the foot…probably not a good choice for someone who wears clogs to work, but the salesman was very convincing. He said they made my legs look sexy.

A fire sputters fitfully in the broken-tile fireplace, taking the chill off the April night. I love this room. Actually I love the whole house. It's the kind of house my father used to call an OSD—Old Spanish Dog—built in the twenties, all white stucco, dark wood floors, and some of the most gorgeous Malibu tile I've ever seen. The brass doorknobs are burnished from seventy years' worth of hands. Backing shows through the worn spots on the Persian rugs. The wood floors dip slightly just over the threshold of every door where your first step naturally lands.

The furniture looks as though it's been well used by a family with children, which it has, and I find it endearing that the Lears have never felt the need to replace everything with new, expensive stuff. Most of the paintings hanging on the walls were done by Sylvia. Every room holds family photographs. It's the kind of house you don't so much walk into as pull up around you like a comforter.

For the last fifteen years, my work schedule as a baker has accustomed me to grabbing naps whenever possible. Now, stretched out full length on the couch, I have reason to be grateful for that skill.

"Wynter McLeod."

My eyelids snap open.

"Darlin', your husband is becomin' mighty careless. Leavin' a gorgeous hunk of woman like you just lyin' around." The voice is very Mississippi. Its owner is all Hollywood.

I smile drowsily. "Hi, Gabe." I start to sit up, but he puts his hand on my shoulder.

"Don't you move so much as an eyelash. I'll just sit right down here on the floor and gaze longingly at your supine form." He arranges his meticulously creased slacks and folds himself down to the rug. "You know you're the most interesting woman at this soirée."

I roll onto my stomach, pillowing my head on my arms. "And you're the best liar. It's one of my favorite things about you. What are you working on these days?"

"My tan." He smiles, showing dazzling white veneers. "What are you doing sneakin' off alone? Is Matthew misbehavin' himself?"

"He's talking shop," I say lightly. "And my feet were killing me. I'm not used to these tea party shoes."

"Lady, it's your good fortune that I happened along." Suddenly he's kneeling at the other end of the couch massaging the soles of my feet with his thumbs.

"Ohhh. Gabe, don't. That feels way too good. You better stop it right now."

He ignores me. "Gabriel K. Cleveland, at your service. I did tell you about my foot fetish?"

"What's the K stand for?"

"Kenmore. My momma always said it was a family name, but honestly…" His voice sinks to a stage whisper. "I've always believed my real daddy was the washing machine repair man."

I smile. "Maybe you should write a memoir."

"*Bury Me Not* was as close to a memoir as this boy's ever going to get. As it was, my momma sued me for libel…No, really, she did. Honey, you don't mess with Lydia Landis Cleveland of the Slocum, Mississippi Landises."

"What part of the book didn't she like?"

"The part where the protagonist's mother runs over her husband with his own Cadillac."

"Your mother didn't…"

"No, she didn't kill him, but when he dropped over from a heart attack the first thing she did was take his Patek Phillipe and his diamond ring. *Before* she called 911."

He digs a knuckle into my arch.

"Oh, God, yes. Right there."

"Honey, you better keep your voice down or we're gonna be startin' some big time rumors."

I'm laughing, so I don't hear the door…just Mac's voice.

"Thanks for handling the preliminaries, Gabe. I can take it from here."

"Uh-oh. It's your insanely jealous husband. I'd best be leavin' out the back door." He stands up with a last brush of fingertips on my toes that sends a shiver up my spine. "'Night, Darlin'." He gives Mac a cheery smile. "You too, Matthew."

I sit up, tucking my feet underneath me. "Bye, Gabe. Thanks for the foot rub."

Mac sits down next to me, waits for the door to close. "Having fun?"

"More fun than watching you get drunk and act like you're on Oprah."

His arm is resting on the couch behind me and I can hear the faint, impatient drumming of fingertips on leather. "I take it you're ready to leave."

"I was ready an hour ago." I stand up, wincing as I step into the shoes.

"All you had to do was say so."

"It's hard to get your attention when you've got a live audience."

He gets up, fishes in his pocket for the car keys, hands them to me.

I drive slowly. No sudden stops or fast starts, no unnecessary lane changes. On Friday nights CHP is out in force to intercept careless revelers. We got stopped at a DUI checkpoint about six months ago. Unfortunately Mac was driving. Fortunately the judge at the hearing was Alan's golf partner. I've been the designated driver ever since.

I turn onto Pacific Coast Highway and he lowers the window, letting in the full complement of night beach smells—the salty, rusty ocean, the chill, metallic fog, smoke from beach fires.

Whenever I pass this particular stretch of oceanfront, I'm swamped by successive waves of memory. My body relaxes a little, my grip loosens on the steering wheel and I see my seven-year-old self, wading cautiously at the waterline while my father treads water beyond the breakers. He calls me, telling me to run and dive into the swells while my mother sits on the blanket, biting her lip.

In my head I hear that Spencer Davis song—the one they used in the California Cooler commercials—the one played endlessly at high school beach parties…I picture CM in her bikini, dancing with abandon, driving all the boys over the edge. Mac and I came here a lot when we were renting the studio apartment in Santa Monica, taking long walks in the evenings because there was no money to do anything else.

The garage door rumbles up to admit us, then back down to enclose us. I turn the key off. There was a time, not so long ago, when we might have come together in a kiss, or sat talking for a minute, laughing about something that happened at the party, listening to the end of a song on the R & B station or just the ticking of the engine as it cooled down. Tonight we get out quickly, reluctant to be caught in the dim light of the silent garage with nothing to say. I lock the car and toss the keys to Mac.

He pauses on the way in, reaching down to give a scratch behind the ears to Brownie, who waits patiently just inside the door to the kitchen. Of unknown parentage but unquestionable heart, once she was sleek and shiny, fast as a weasel; now she's a bit lumpy and slow-moving. Her muzzle is gray and her eyes are beginning to cloud. She's almost 12 years old.

Mac disappears up the stairs, leaving me to take her out through the laundry room and into the back yard. I hug myself inside my pashmina and study the one or two visible stars while the dog snuffles her leisurely route around the perimeter till she finds a satisfactory spot to pee. Then we head back inside.

I fill her water dish and walk around, checking windows and doors. Brownie used to sleep in our bedroom, but these days she doesn't do stairs very well, so she usually prefers her egg-crate foam bed in a corner of the laundry room. I hear her pawing at the cover, fluffing it up, as I turn off the light.

"Sweet dreams, Brown Dog."

He's in his office across the hall from the bedroom, sitting in one of the wingback chairs, staring at the empty fireplace. There's about an inch of amber liquid in a glass on the desk. I don't remember if it was there earlier. I stand in the doorway for minute, then come in without invitation and settle myself on his lap. His breath smells of scotch and peanuts.

"What is it?" I say. "Tell me what's wrong."

He leans his head back. "Nothing."

"So you've just been in a bad mood for the past two years."

"You're the one who goes off and sulks in the library—"

"I was not sulking. I just needed to take off my shoes."

"So that twit Cleveland could suck on your toes."

I burst out laughing. "He wasn't sucking on my toes. He was giving me a foot rub. Come on, don't be grouchy. I've been up since 4 AM. I worked a full day. Then I have to come home and get dressed up and go make happy talk with a bunch of anorexic, surgically enhanced—"

"Wyn…you're a snob—"

"*I'm* a snob?"

37

"Correct. A reverse snob. You think that people who are attractive, successful and creative must also be phony and shallow—"

"Because they *are* phony and shallow."

"I thought you liked Alan and Sylvia."

"I do. It's the other ninety-eight percent—and none of them are interested in me because I'm a baker. I do—gasp!—manual labor."

"So. They're not paying attention to you. They're not interested in bread. Which makes them phony and shallow."

"I'm interested in other things besides bread. I like music and art and books and movies. All they talk about at those parties is industry gossip and their new plastic surgeon and the great deal they got on a previously owned Lamborghini and going to Japanese day spas where tiny little fishes nibble the dead skin off your feet."

"If you hate it that much, don't go."

"Doofus." I pull back to look at him. "I go to be with you."

Unspoken but implicit is *I go so people will know I'm with you*. When your husband starts going to parties by himself, it sends a bad message.

"Don't do me any favors."

"I'm sorry…I'm just tired and my back hurts…and my feet hurt…" I lay my head on his shoulder. "Why can't we be like we used to be?"

"You mean poor?"

"No. That's not what I mean."

I wait for him to say that he doesn't really like the parties either, that he just goes because Alan expects him to, that deep down underneath it all, everything still is the way it used to be.

Finally he moves a little. "My arm's asleep."

I kiss his forehead. "Let's go to bed."

"You go ahead. I'll be there in a minute."

This is the pattern lately, and it disturbs me. I go to bed alone, fall asleep alone, wake up alone.

I kiss the corner of his eye, move down to his mouth. "Come hold me."

"I'll be there in a minute."

When I stand up, he reaches for the Bose. Fiddles with the dial till he finds what he's looking for. It's one of those songs…a melody that's so aching, so haunting it makes me stop in the doorway and listen.

"What is that?"

He answers without looking at me. "Baker's Blues."

I smile. "Really?"

"Sam Baker," he says. "An old R & B guy."

"Oh."

Mac

In the dream he's climbing.

The rock opens up before him, crashes closed behind him, like some treacherous enchanted forest. Drops of water shimmer on the wall. He clings for a minute then his fingers crawl into a crack overhead. He shifts his weight, straightens his right knee, commits to the move, and his body rises. His left foot feels the next hold through the soft sole of his shoe.

When he reaches the overhang, he has to cut loose, pushing off the wall and swinging up and over. Just like a kid on the jungle gym, except he's much older, and this is much higher, and there's no soft pile of sand waiting below.

His fingers are wet…not damp, but actually dripping wet. They slip off the rock and he feels himself falling. Almost with a sense of relief.

It's 3:20 AM.

He knows it without having to look at the clock. For weeks he's been waking up almost every night at the same time. Wide awake, as if he hadn't slept at all. Knowing it's 3:20, knowing he won't sleep again for hours, and knowing that something is happening. Something like a barely noticeable change in the direction of the wind.

Three

I could make cornbread in my sleep…crack a couple of eggs into a glass measuring cup, beat in milk and melted butter, stir the mixture into the dry cornmeal and flour, baking powder, salt. I always throw in a little brown sugar—just a tablespoon to bring out the natural sweetness of the corn. Bake it in a preheated cast iron skillet, so it gets all brown and crusty on the bottom and sides.

I love it hot out of the oven or toasted the next morning with butter melting into it and a swipe of honey. And I love it stale and dry, crumbled into a glass of cold milk and eaten with a spoon about 11:30 at night. My father taught me that.

"When's lunch?" Mac stands just inside the back door in his swim trunks, rivulets of water trickling down his chest, towel slung over his shoulder, drinking a beer.

The dog has followed him in and is methodically licking the water off his legs.

I can't help smiling. "So what are you two—the opening act at SeaWorld?"

He takes a piece of tortilla chip out of the basket on the counter and flips it to Brownie, who catches it on the fly. "Actually, Flipper's opening for us. We're the main attraction, right BD?"

He sets the empty bottle on the counter and pulls another IPA out of the fridge. I want to suggest that it's too early to start drinking, but things have been pretty congenial so far this morning. So I just say,

"I made some iced tea…"

He gives me his slow grin. "Iced tea's for wimps, sissies and fools. Do I have time to take a shower?"

"You've got twenty minutes."

He brushes a cold, wet kiss on my neck as he heads for the stairs, leaving a trail of water.

The cornbread batter sizzles in the hot skillet and I slide it into the oven, stir the bubbling chili with my oma's old wooden spoon and wipe the sponge over the dark spatters on the stovetop. I set out placemats, flatware and napkins. Butter goes on the table, and a bottle of Tabasco, because the chili's never hot enough for him. I toss a few more ice cubes into my tea, wondering which category I fall into—wimp, sissy or fool.

In a few minutes the upstairs plumbing groans, signaling the end of his shower. I turn down the flame under the chili and I'm just retrieving an onion from the pantry when the doorbell chimes. The first time he heard it, Mac said it sounded like *Lay-la*.

Brownie starts barking like a maniac. She may be old but she can still intimidate the occasional delivery person.

"Brownie, no!" I point at her and she sinks obligingly to the floor, her duty completed.

A young girl is standing on our front porch—about 17, I'd guess. My first thought is she's canvassing the neighborhood for world peace…*We want to take money out of the black hole of the Pentagon budget and use it for libraries and daycare and the environment*, was how the last one put it. They want you to sign a petition, make a small donation…I always do, even though I'm pretty apolitical. They're all so idealistic, so earnest… so adorably, appallingly naïve.

I'm about to tell her I'll go get my wallet, when it comes to me that she looks somehow familiar. Like a friend's child that you haven't seen in years. I feel like I should know her. The other thing is, they always wear jeans. It's the world peace uniform. This girl's wearing a dress. A green and white sundress, and cute little ballerina flats. And no clipboard.

She smiles nervously, looking around for the dog, then back up at me. "Does Mr. McLeod live here?"

It's her voice—that funny, twisty, musical accent that I've only heard a few times in my life—that causes my brain to start firing on all cylinders, making all the connections. Suddenly I know exactly who she is, and the hair rises up on the back of my neck.

The bottom stair creaks as Mac appears, barefoot, wearing jeans and a sun-faded Shepard Surfboards T-shirt, his hair still wet. He starts toward the kitchen, then, sensing the open door, he turns around.

"Hello," the girl says. Her voice is nearly a whisper. "I'm Skye."

He looks like a guy who's just slammed his hand in the car door and is only belatedly becoming aware of it. It takes him a full ten seconds to say,

"What are you doing here?"

"My friend and I were just…I'm sorry…I just wanted to see you. I hope…" The words drift into silence as we all trade glances.

"Wyn, this is Skye Welburne," he says finally. "My daughter."

"Pleased to meet you." Her smile trembles.

I can't speak. I can hardly breathe. I hold tight to the doorknob because my knees feel like wet spaghetti. When you know what to look for, it's obvious. His mouth, his eyes, the thick, straight, pale hair— she's even got that little place at the hairline where the hair grows back instead of forward.

"Should we sit down?" I hear my voice, sounding like a computer generated recording. "Can I get you some tea?"

"Oh. That would be—"

Mac suddenly takes over. "We'll be in my office," he says. And then to make sure I understand that I'm not included, he adds, "I'll be down in a minute."

With an awkward glance back at me, she follows him up the stairs. In the kitchen, the timer is beeping.

I turn off the chili and move it to a back burner, take the cornbread out of the oven and set it on a cooling rack. And then I stand at the sink, afraid to move, afraid the slightest misstep would send me crashing to the floor in a thousand pieces. I just stand there, inhaling the comforting, familiar scent of cornbread as if it were pure oxygen.

Afternoon sun flashes on the surface of the pool and my eyes land on the bougainvillea tumbling over the back fence—San Diego Red is the cultivar. The graceful, drooping leaves of banana plant, the softer, silvery foliage and white blooms of rose campion. My spiky blue bachelor's buttons, South African daisies, fragrant pinks, chocolate cosmos—annuals, that in the benevolence of the Southern California climate return year after year.

I stand motionless for so long that Brownie comes over and lies down next to me, resting her head on my feet.

It wasn't sunny, but at least it wasn't raining—rare for Seattle in March. Mac and I were strolling aimlessly through Pike Market trying to decide whether to go over to Bainbridge for a local author's book signing or just go home and make love all afternoon. As we walked, he slipped his hand under my hair and stroked the back of my neck, putting me more in favor of the second option.

Then it happened. We passed a young couple walking the other way. The guy was wearing a baby backpack with a child in it. I'm not good at children's ages; this one was in that alert but pre-verbal stage. He was smiling—a fetching, toothless, drooly smile and looking all around, head bobbing like a dashboard hula dancer. And as we passed, that baby's big blue eyes locked on mine and held them. He and I turned towards each other and he held out his arms to me, his little pink starfish hands waving.

The whole motherhood concept that had always been so alien to me, suddenly crystallized. I looked at Mac out of the corner of my eye, but he was staring straight ahead. I knew he'd seen the baby. The whole atmosphere between us was different, everything suddenly unfocused.

I remembered him telling me how he left New Zealand and the woman he was with there—Gillian.

"She wanted to get married, have babies, raise sheep. I didn't. So I left."

But not so fast, Mr. McLeod.

He walks into the kitchen.

I stand still, watching the slight movements of flowers in the breeze, noticing for the first time a hole the size of my little finger in the window screen. He comes right behind me and puts his hands on my shoulders. I know this only because I see his reflection in the window glass. I can't feel anything.

"Where did she go?"

He removes his hands. "She had a plane to catch."

"How long have you known?" My voice sounds shakier than I want it to.

He steps away from me. I hear him turning on the burner under the chili.

45

"Mac…?"

"A few weeks. A month. I didn't think she'd actually—I didn't want you to be upset."

"When were you planning to tell me?"

"Wyn, turn around. I can't talk to your back."

"Apparently you can't talk to my front, either."

"You wanted—you used to talk about having a baby…and I never wanted to. I felt bad that I had one with somebody else."

"Yes, there is that."

"She said she was going to…Gillian was going to terminate the pregnancy. It was legal. There were clinics. It was no big deal."

I look at him over my shoulder. "No big deal?"

"You know what I mean. It wasn't a back room thing. It was safe. Lots of women did it. I left. I didn't know."

I turn now, resting the small of my back against the soapstone counter, watching him.

"It was over before I ever met you."

"Except it's not over. You've got a child, Mac. Present tense. She's a person. You're her father—".

"I've taken care of it."

"She's not a parking ticket."

He exhales but says nothing.

"What did you tell her?"

I watch that little muscle working in his jaw.

"I wrote her a check."

Four

The week slips past like a long dream, the kind where you wake up and think, oh, this is just a dream, and then settle back in where you left off. If I didn't know better, I'd say everything was fine.

He's working every morning when I leave...or at least he's in his office with the laptop open on his desk. He swims before lunch, takes a shower. He wants to know what's going on at the bakery. We talk about our investments, about his book tour next week to San Francisco, Portland and Seattle. We talk about going to Orcas in June. We do not talk about his daughter.

He's suddenly affectionate, always holding my hand, lifting my hair to kiss my neck. Still no sex. He reads me passages from his work on the screenplay and tries to look enthralled by my insightful comments, but I'm certain that if I forced the issue, he wouldn't recall a single one. Behind the phony smile, he's totally absent.

On the first Saturday of May, the normal Southern California weather forecast would call for a dense marine layer along the coast, burning off by midday. But today when I roll over at 7 am, the sun is already beating on the east window of our bedroom. Ugh. It's going to be one of those nasty, breath-sucking days.

Mac's not in bed. In fact, from the looks of the neatly turned back sheet, he never was. I walk across the hall to his office and he's not there either. I look out the office window, down into the back yard. Not in the pool.

I pull on a pair of shorts and a T-shirt, step into my flip-flops and go downstairs. His car is gone and the paper is still on the front walk. What time did he go out this morning? Slowly it comes to me as I'm standing there reading the comics, waiting for the Jura to heat up. He didn't go out this morning.

He went out last night.

I hit the brew button and wait impatiently while dark liquid fills the tiny cup and overflows into the drip tray. I turn off the machine and take my too full cup out on the patio. Brownie follows me out and settles herself on a shady patch of grass.

The morning air is balmy, no breeze at all, a preview of the deadening heat to come. In our entire neighborhood of older homes probably only two or three have A.C. We don't get enough really bad heat to justify the expense, but because the upstairs sometimes gets unbearable, Mac has a window unit in his office.

That's where we hole up during the bad spells, like last fall when the Santa Anas whipped up the temperatures to record highs. The memory of pasta salads and Popsicles, drinking gin & tonics, sleeping in sleeping bags on the floor makes me smile. Then I remember why I'm sitting here having coffee by myself on Saturday morning.

I review the possibilities. He could be at Alan's, I guess. But if he was at Alan's surely he'd have called by now. Sylvia would have insisted. I suppose he could be at some other friend's house, but who? Mac doesn't have a lot of friends. He could be sitting on a rock staring at the ocean. He could be in jail on a DUI. He could be in the hospital.

Should I call the police? I'd feel stupid. Besides, if there'd been an accident or something, wouldn't they call me? I stand up abruptly, slopping cold espresso on the flagstone patio. In the kitchen, I dial Alan's home number. No answer. Then I try Mac's cell phone.

Thank you for using Verizon. The party you are calling is currently unavailable. Please leave a message after the—

I hang up, grab my purse and keys and head for the garage.

Two hot, frustrating hours later, I sit at a stoplight on Sunset Boulevard, resting my head on the steering wheel of my old Volvo. I've driven by Alan and Sylvia's. No signs of life. I cruised the Palisades where he goes to run. I went to Sunny Side Up, the little breakfast place he likes. I even tried the Beverly Hills Library, where he sometimes goes to do research. Nothing left to do but head home. If he's not there, I'll think about calling the police.

His car is in the driveway.

I let myself in, breathless with a combination of relief and anger. Brownie's whining in the laundry room, her water dish dry as a stone. I fill the bowl and she slurps happily while I stroke the tufts of fur along her spine.

"Where's Daddy?" I ask, but she just keeps drinking.

I start up the stairs, about to call out his name, when a woman's sudden laughter rings in the stairwell.

Through the open bedroom door I see Liv Keppler, the publicist who works with Alan, sitting cross-legged on the corner of our unmade bed. Smiling, nodding, combing her fingers through her blonde hair, tilting her face appraisingly. Mac stands in front of the dresser holding up three different shirts for her approval.

"Hi, Wynter," Liv chirps when she sees me.

I barely look at her. "If I'd known we were going to play dress the author I'd have come home sooner."

Her smile wavers. "I was just helping Mac pick out some clothes for the—"

"He's been dressing himself for almost forty years now. Why does he suddenly need help?"

"It's for television," Mac says. The edge in his voice tells me he's pissed off, but I figure that's his bad luck. So am I.

Liv looks at her watch. "Oh my *God*, look at the time. I've got to dash. That's okay, I can let myself out."

She disappears down the stairs and we both listen till the door shuts.

"Thanks," he says.

"For what?"

"For barging in here, being rude to someone I have to work with."

"Since when does working involve her picking out your clothes? In our bedroom?"

"Wyn, it's for some TV thing she booked for me. In Seattle." Every word is measured for emphasis. "And the bedroom is where my clothes happen to be."

"It's not's the kind of problem that requires a house call. No plaids, no Tommy Bahamas, don't wear white." The heat in this room is suddenly overwhelming. My hair clings wetly to my face. "I don't like coming home to find other women in my bedroom. Just a quirk of mine. And by the way, where were you last night?"

He sighs. "Could we discuss one thing at a time?"

"Fine. Let's discuss where you were last night."

"I went over to Alan's."

"That's right. We had a drink, talked about some things—"

"Things…?"

"Like the screenplay and publicity for the book—"

"And I suppose since you were discussing publicity, the publicist had to be present."

"Liv was there, yes."

"I drove by Alan's house an hour and a half ago. You're car wasn't there."

"We went out to breakfast—"

"And then you suddenly remembered, hey, I have a wife! And she's probably wondering where I am—"

He walks over to stand in front of me. "I think you're confusing me with Husband Number One. Should I start wearing a name tag? *Not David Franklin...?*"

Just the sound of my ex-husband's name summons way too many memories that I always think I've relegated to landfill. Until they reappear without warning.

"Well, you're doing a great imitation."

"What's that supposed to mean?"

"What it means is this." I let my purse slip off my shoulder and onto the floor. "You used to be someone I not only loved, but liked and respected. You were independent. You were smart. Now all of a sudden, you're driving around in your Beemer talking on the cell phone. Having all night publicity meetings, which must feature martinis, by the way, because you smell like a distillery—acting like a typical L.A.—" I stop, suddenly hearing myself. I push my hair back and sink down on the bed, out of breath.

When I raise my eyes, my vision swims. "Couldn't you have at least called me?"

"I didn't want to call too early, and then we were at the Morningside and it was noisy. I didn't think it was going to be a major—"

"Mac, please. Talk to me."

"About what?"

I stare at his sweet, blank face. "About why you're suddenly out drinking all night with the Insomniac Social Club. Why you won't talk about Skye. Why Liv Keppler is parked on the corner of my bed—and maybe we should talk about why you don't want to make love anymore. What's that about?"

It's one of those silences that's more than the absence of sound. It's a huge physical presence, sucking the oxygen out of the room.

He reaches for my hand. "I'm sorry. I wasn't thinking. I haven't been sleeping and I'm just really tired."

I let out some of the tension in a long breath. He hasn't answered a single question, but I'm afraid to push. Instead I look for it in his eyes—some kind of answer, something…but he pulls me to my feet and puts his arms around me. In that moment I know he's doing it to avoid looking at me.

The bedroom is warm and dark except for the faint green glow of numerals on the clock. All the windows are open, but there's not much air moving.

He doesn't turn on any lights as he comes up the stairs, stands in the doorway, listening…trying to decide if I'm asleep, if it's safe to come in. I don't move while he undresses stealthily, eases into bed, carefully turning the sheet back, adjusting his pillow.

Then I say, "Mac…"

His exhalation sounds like disappointment. "I didn't want to wake you up."

"I wasn't asleep."

I turn on my side to face him. In the dark I can see his profile, looking straight up at the ceiling.

"I'm sorry for what I said this morning."

He turns slightly. This is clearly not what he was expecting.

"It's just…I'm worried about you. About us. I don't want to lose this…" My throat tightens around the words.

He reaches for me in the dark, tucking me against his body, and I can smell him, the clean smell of soap, the soft dampness of his undershirt.

"Where were you?"

"Driving," he says.

He could've driven to Monterey and back by this time. But at least he hasn't been drinking. I slip my hand under his.

"Remember when we drove the Elky down from Seattle? How beautiful it was, driving at night…all the stars…"

He relaxes slightly against me. "Remember sleeping on the beach that night in Oregon?"

The feel of him next to me, the sound of our voices in the dark, the almost imperceptible breeze that's starting to lift the curtains…this is how it's supposed to be. This is how it was.

"I can't wait to get up to the island. Did you book a rental car?"

"No," he says.

"We should do that now if we want to get any kind of decent rate."

He doesn't say anything.

I say, "That's okay. I know you've got a lot going on. I'll take care of it this week."

"Wyn…"

"What?"

"I don't know about this trip."

"What do you mean?"

"I just don't think it's a good idea to go up there right now."

I sit bolt upright. "We've been planning it for months—"

"I know that, but when we planned it I thought I'd be through with this goddamned screenplay in April. I'm not even close."

"We haven't been up there in two years. Why do we even have the place if we're not going to use it?"

"Just because we haven't been up there in a while doesn't mean we're never going to use it again." It's the exaggerated patience tone of voice.

"You can write up there, you know. In fact, I think Orcas would be the perfect place to work."

"That's great, except you're not writing. For me it's easier to work here."

"I guess that's why you've written so much lately."

"Wyn—"

"No, Mac, listen to me. We both need a break—"

"I can't leave till this project is finished."

I throw off the sheet and get out of bed.

"What are you doing?"

"Resisting the temptation to put a pillow over your face."

He sighs. "Come on. Let's get some sleep. We don't have to decide tonight."

"You expect me to sleep now?"

"Well, I'm going to."

He rolls onto his back, flings his arm above his head. I don't know if he's really falling asleep, and part of me doesn't want to know.

I slam the bedroom door on my way downstairs.

"Should I drive you to the airport?"

Sunday morning. I'm sitting on the edge of the pool. I know it's because of all the chemicals I detest, but the water feels so silky, draping like a scarf across my legs.

Mac is reading the paper and drinking coffee and polishing off his third scone in the shade of the market umbrella. He considers my offer for about five seconds. "That's okay, I'd rather have the car there when I get back."

"I could come pick you up and we could—"

"Traffic's always a bitch on Fridays. It's easier if I just have the car there."

I squint at the sunlight flashing off the water. "Is…um…Liv going?"

He doesn't say anything, so I turn, pulling my legs up out of the pool.

He says, "You never used to be insecure."

My face flushes hotly. "You never used to stay out all night, either."

"Of course she's not going." He tugs at the bill of his baseball cap. "Why would she?"

Because she's a hyena. One of those predatory women who lurks on the outskirts of wounded marriages, waiting for a shot at the carrion. That's why.

I don't say it out loud.

Five

When I was a little girl, my oma told me that three A.M. is the magic hour. When witches ride across the moon and animals converse. Years later I learned that it's also the time when most first shift bakers are dragging themselves out of bed. This is no coincidence. It has to do with the alchemy that happens in a bakery. These days the magic is assisted by the thermostat on our proofing cabinet which has (hopefully) kicked on two hours earlier, raising the temperature, bringing the dough to life.

Monday morning the bakery is dark and warm and the air is thick with yeast from the thousands of loaves of bread baked here over the past seven years. Brownie watches me punch in the code that turns off the security system, and walk around turning on the lights. Technically she's not supposed to be here, but I hate leaving her alone all day. So far I've been lucky; the health department has never showed up on the rare occasions when I've brought her in with me. Most people don't even know she's here. She dozes on a cushion in my office, rousing herself once in a while to accept an offering of crust or a bite of scone from one of her admirers.

The bakery was built mainly for bread making, and it began as a no-frills operation, a storeroom in back, a kitchen, a fournil or baking room with a Bongard four-deck oven for bread and a stack of convection ovens for most everything else. A few tables and mismatched chairs for customers, a staff room for breaks and meetings. And my little office that's just big enough for a computer desk, a book shelf, one file cabinet, and Brownie's bed.

The embellishments came later, starting with the antique display case I found at auction and had refitted with a marble counter, some art on the walls, a few plants, with a plant service to take care of them. I always hate walking into a shop or café where the plants are all brown and droopy.

Two years ago we took over the defunct card shop next door and turned it into a small café area to take advantage of our location in the middle of the village of Luna Blanca, and now it seems that the place is always busy, always noisy. Except for this magic time early in the morning, which is when I like it best.

I check the temperature of the proofing cabinets, turn on the espresso machine, run the grinder for the first pot of drip coffee, pop a Vivaldi violin concerto into the CD player. I've just started pulling trays of dough out of the retarder when Tyler shows up.

"Brownie! Hi, sweet girl. How are you?" She bends down for a big wet one.

"She's fine. And I am too, thanks for asking."

"I see somebody hasn't had their coffee yet. Leave that alone; you're going to hurt your shoulder." She unzips her windbreaker and hangs it on a hook.

"I'm not a cripple." I pull out another tray, ignoring the pinch in my left shoulder.

She grabs the brew basket and blasts it with steam from the frother. "Leave that alone, Wyn. I mean it." She fills the basket with ground coffee, tamps it expertly, inserts it in the brewing head and pushes the button. "You totally need to see somebody about that shoulder." She overrides the auto shot, making a longer pull for me.

"When it becomes more than an annoyance, I will."

She hands me the cup, bangs out the used grounds, rinses the basket and repeats the process. Tyler was the barista at the Queen Street Bakery in Seattle, and even after moving on to become cashier, cake decorator, bread baker and now manager, she's never lost her touch. When I was putting this place together I took her with me to buy our espresso machine. She still trains everyone who touches it. And I love having her make my first cup of the workday.

"You should get an MRI," she says. "So you know what it is."

"I don't need an MRI to know what it is. It's tendonitis."

Her first sip of espresso produces a beatific smile. "It's really great that you've got that X-ray vision. Maybe you should set up a little table over by the coffee station and, you know, diagnose everybody's hurties. We could re-do the sign. The Bread Maven Bakery, Café and Orthopedic Center."

"And comedy workshop," I say.

Mike and Danni will be in next, shaping baguettes and boules. Not much talking between those two. They know each other's rhythms and move by instinct. By 5 AM breads will be on the deck, and by 6 the first loaves will be coming out. I love the sweet toasty smell, the blasting heat of the oven room, the popping and crackling of hot crust cooling in the morning air.

Pretty soon someone will mutter "Can't take this anymore…" and replace the Vivaldi with Etta James.

In the kitchen, Raphael will be in high gear. I love to watch him work. Strong, but oddly delicate brown hands lifting the croissant dough out of the cooler, giving it a final turn, feeding it through the sheeter, cutting and rolling the layers of pastry, arranging them on sheet pans for their final rise. He calls them the plain croissants, but to me, there's nothing plain about those multi-layered, butter laminated, chewy, crisp crescents. Next he'll use the same dough to make the *pain au chocolat*, and *almondines* and the morning buns, our version of cinnamon rolls, only way better.

Once those are proofing, he'll start on desserts, assisted by one of our revolving door procession of young men and occasionally women who think they want to be a pastry chef. When they find out what the job entails and the level of craft necessary to be really good, most of them fall back to the comfort of a nine-to-five job. Rafe, as we call him, is really more sorcerer than pastry chef. He moves serenely through the morning, crafting tarts and Napoleons, friands and macarons, galettes and éclairs that could make the angels weep. But his specialty is something he calls a Guadeloupe Tart, which is sort of like a moist, dense macaroon in a flaky crust. Customers have been known to fight over the last piece in the case.

Pete, our work/study baker from the community college, will be cutting butter into the scone mix, scooping the bran muffins. He'll be singing—he has a great voice, not conventionally appealing, but kind of gravelly and poignant. A Tom Waits with flour. Danni has a bit of a crush on him I think.

Sally will be cleaning the cases, setting up the cash drawer, filling the cream pitchers and spice shakers, tidying the service counter and the coffee station, refilling the napkin dispensers. Sometimes it all makes me a little wistful, like I'm on the fringe of things, not quite part of it. Not one of them.

Because I'm The Boss.

In my office, I turn on the computer and prepare for the third time to install this new bakery software that does everything from inventory control and costing to formula keeping. When an ingredient price changes, the program automatically adjusts the cost of the formula and spits out a new retail price. At least in theory. The problem is I can't seem to get it loaded.

After thirty minutes, when I've tried every command, rebooted, uninstalled and re-installed the program, and still can't get it to perform, I call the software company's helpdesk. A pleasant voice informs me that the current wait time is six minutes. The music on hold is an old, very annoying song by the Jackson Five.

I hit the speaker phone button, and open my email program.

Tyler pops her head in. "Are you busy? Or just brushing up on your seventies music trivia?"

"What do you know about the seventies? You were still in diapers."

"You told me all about it once, how you did macramé by candlelight and walked to school in your bellbottoms through drifts of snow."

"You must be confusing me with some old person. Now, what can I do for you?"

"I wanted to talk to you about Cheryl. It's getting to the point where we need a dedicated person to take over wholesale, and I thought she might be good at it."

"Yeah, I've been thinking about that, too. Let me just pull the invoices for last month and—"

She deposits a bulging file folder on my desk. "Last two months."

Standing there with her sleeves pushed up, she looks serious and efficient—but somehow I still see the little blue-haired delinquent I met my first day at the Queen Street Bakery in Seattle.

"I'll take a look at these and then we can talk about it."

"*Si, jefe.*" She grins and starts out the door. "Oh, and there's one… other thing I need to—"

The speaker phone crackles. "Tech Support, this is Gail."

"Hey, this is Wyn at Bread Maven. I can't seem to get this inventory software to load…"

I give Tyler an apologetic shrug and she mouths, "Later."

At 4:30 in the afternoon Prince Charles is sitting on my front porch licking his boy parts while CM stands behind him, arms folded, admonishing him to behave. I should explain that Charles is a two-year-old tricolor Pembroke Welsh Corgi with a very unfortunate name.

Charles isn't actually CM's dog, much as she would like it to be so. Her apartment building doesn't allow pets, plus her life as a dancer and choreographer makes it impossible. Charles belongs to her friend Susan, who got sole custody of him in her divorce, but had to move into a small condo with no yard and go back to work full time, leaving Charles to fend for himself. He showed his displeasure by eating his bed and having to have stomach surgery to the tune of about two thousand dollars. Susan was on the verge of surrendering him to Pet Rescue when a bunch of her friends got together to take turns keeping him out of trouble and today is CM's lucky day.

We bundle him and Brownie into the back of my station wagon, and head for the Luna Blanca dog park. We've barely cleared the driveway before they've jumped into the back seat, jockeying for position and singing their funny songs.

CM tosses each of them a cookie. "When I retire I'm going to have a little house on a big piece of land somewhere and be one of those crazy ladies who has fifteen dogs."

"Ha. I can't wait to see you on a big piece of land covered with dog poop, twenty miles to the nearest coffee house and dry cleaners."

I park in the lot and the dogs scramble out barking deliriously. It's amazing how Brownie can slough off the years when she has an accomplice. We follow them down the dirt path towards the lake, leashes in hand. The sky is overcast and the air is thick and still.

"I hope we don't get rained out," I say.

"I've got so much to do, I can't stay too long anyway."

"Oh…I was hoping we could get some dinner after."

"Tonight's really not good; I leave for London on Thursday and I've got a jillion loose ends to deal with." She pulls an old tennis hat out of her pocket and jams it on her head. Anyone else would look ridiculous, but on her it's adorably scruffy. "Where's Mac tonight?"

"San Francisco. I think."

"How's the book doing?"

"Fine, I guess."

"Are you okay?" she says. "Has he said anything else about the girl?"

"Not a word. It's like it never happened. I'm starting to think I dreamed the whole thing."

She gives me a quick one-armed hug. "He'll come around. He just has to process the information." Then, "Oh, *damn*."

I follow her gaze to the water's edge, where the dogs have found something dead and are rolling in it with great enthusiasm.

I make a face. "Well, at least I know what I'll be doing tonight."

By the time I get Brownie bathed, dried and fed, get the back of my car cleaned out and all the towels washed and put in the drier, it's almost nine o'clock. I should go to bed, but I know I won't sleep. I'm hungry, but I don't know what I want, so I take a raspberry juice bar out of the freezer and wander out into the yard, only to discover it's finally raining, a gentle, soaking rain that reminds me of Seattle. I retreat back inside, into the living room, through the dining room, the hall, back to the kitchen, vague uneasiness growing until suddenly it's a huge knot in my gut.

I like to think of myself as a sensible woman, not given to panic or flights of fancy...but I just have this creepy, unfocused sense of wrongness. Maybe it's because Mac's not here to tell me I'm imagining things or that he's tired or any of his other standard issue excuses. I hate being cynical. I want to think that he really is simply exhausted and stressed. I want to trust him.

But the fact is, I don't.

His desk top is fairly clean. Where there were lots of small piles of papers, there's now one large pile. The bottle of Remy does double duty as a paperweight. The trash basket is empty; two crumpled rejects lie nearby where they landed after a bad bounce. The book shelves are crammed full of books in no discernable order. The ones that won't fit are stacked on the file cabinet and in the wingback chair. Even a few of mine have migrated in here, including one that lies inexplicably on the floor...*The Baker's Book of Days, A Memoir*. It was a present from Mac a long time ago when he was trying to convince me to give up the boring and pedestrian idea of happiness and throw my lot in with him.

I pick it up and hover uneasily between desk and chair, pausing to consider that what I'm about to do goes against everything I believe. But right now my need to know trumps everything else—self-loathing, fear of what I might find, and certainly any scruples about privacy. I sit down in his chair and slide open the center drawer.

Pens, pencils, paper clips, ruler, scissors, rubber bands, toothpicks, peppermints from various restaurants...all reassuringly mundane. *See? There's nothing wrong here*. I don't even know what I'm looking for. If there is anything incriminating, it's probably on his laptop or his cell phone, both of which he has with him.

In the bottom right-hand drawer is a bottle of scotch, three quarters empty. *God*. I've tried to overlook the Remy...telling myself that cognac is expensive and elegant and not what people drink when they have a problem. And the level in that pretty bottle with the fancy label seems to go down slowly. But scotch is just booze. Although this Macallan stuff probably costs more than the Remy.

I pull open the top left drawer. In the back, rubber-banded together, are his American Express, MasterCard and Verizon bills for the year to date. As I'm reaching for them something catches my attention. Something blue in a stack of pristine white envelopes. An edge of blue vellum.

It could be a fan letter or something. Except he doesn't save those. I've never understood how he could be so casual about them. If anyone ever wrote me a letter telling me how much they love my bread and what a genius baker I am, I could never throw it away.

I pull out the envelope and lay it on the desk, my heart thudding against my ribs. The pretty seashell stamp says New Zealand and the letter is addressed to Mac in care of Drummond Publishing. I draw out the pages, but before I can open them, a small photograph falls out.

It's a standard school photo of a young girl, her flawless skin and vacant smile retouched to artificial perfection. Actually, Skye was prettier in person.

In spite of the ugly little knot that the idea of her makes in my chest, I feel as if I know her. I lost my father, too, although under different circumstances, but I know all about the longing, about that empty place nobody else can fill.

The letter is written in dark blue ink with careful penmanship:

Dear Mr. McLeod,

You don't know me, so I will introduce myself. My name is Skye Welburne. I am your daughter. My mother is Gillian Welburne and she knows I am writing this letter even though she asked me not to. This is rather awkward, but apparently when you were in New Zealand seventeen years ago, you stayed at my family's farm and you and my mother were in love for awhile. She said you left before she discovered that she was pregnant.

I have always wondered and asked her about you, and one day last month she and I went in a bookstore in Napier and saw a book called <u>December Light</u>. When mum saw your photo on the dust jacket, she was acting a bit off, but then later she told me who you were, and I was thrilled to finally know.

I am sixteen (of course) and I have one more year of sixth form, and have not decided whether to do seventh and go on to university. I love horses and have my own gelding named Raleigh. I was excited to find that you are a writer, because I like to write also and I am learning how to juggle.

I want to know all about you. Can you come to see me? Or at least ring me? A letter would be fine, although it would be my last choice. Here is my phone number. 843-2564. I would like to hear from you soon, if you don't mind.

Yours truly,

Skye (McLeod) Welburne

P.S. I have enclosed a photograph of myself. Will you send me one of you?

The return address, *Napier, North Island, NZ* is just below the P.S. and under it is the date, nearly at the bottom of the page. I stare at it for a minute.

December 12, 1998.

Nearly a year and half ago.

Six

Friday night I'm kneading walnuts into hearth bread dough when the door to the garage opens.

"Hi." He gives me a tentative smile. Brownie is dancing around him.

When he leans close to kiss me, I flip the dough over, sending up a cloud of flour on his black Armani jacket.

"Oh, sorry." I try to sound contrite. "How was your trip?"

"About as good as a book tour can be, I guess." He brushes distractedly at the flour, but only succeeds in rubbing it in. He sets down his computer bag and takes off the jacket, draping it over the back of a kitchen chair. "Have we got anything to eat?"

"There's some deli stuff in the fridge."

He goes back out to the garage for his suitcase. "Could you make me a sandwich while I unpack?"

I look him straight in the eye. "I'm in the middle of something right now. Presumably you remember the basic sandwich process. Bread, ham, cheese, repeat bread."

He tries a laugh. "Sounds vaguely familiar. Can I fix you something?"

"I've eaten, thanks."

He makes his sandwich, puts everything back in the refrigerator, opens a beer, sets a glass of red wine on the counter for me and sits down to eat. The kitchen is silent except for the thump of dough on the marble counter.

I've had three days to think about this…how to act, what to say…now he's here and I'm drawing a blank. I take a sip of wine, holding the stem of the glass between floury fingers.

"So how were the signings?"

"Okay. Probably 30 people at all of them." He tips back his beer.

"And the interviews?"

"Had two good radio interviews, one asshole TV talk-show host." He pauses for effect, then adds, "I don't think he liked the shirt."

It's a throw-away line, so like his old self that I almost laugh. If I could laugh, then he'd laugh and he'd come behind me and put his arms around me and it would be like hitting the reset button. Everything would revert to normal. Except not really. Not now. Because now there's no way to un-know what I know.

I've been kneading the dough so long it's like rubber. I lay a damp towel over it and start cleaning the counter with my bench scraper.

He slips the dog a piece of ham.

"There's a new spa hotel in Bellingham," he says. "Right on the water."

"I thought you were going back to Seattle that night." I wipe the counter, squeezing water out of the sponge over the dried smears of dough.

"I did go back to Seattle. I ate at the hotel before the signing—"

Brownie makes a strange little whimper.

"You'd like the restaurant. We should go up there sometime."

"Like next month?"

He ignores me.

Brownie whines again, noses the door.

I absolutely believe that dogs can sense an earthquake about to happen. It supposedly has to do with electromagnetic fields or faint tremors in the ground that humans can't feel. Brownie doesn't really need to go out; she just knows that things are going to get bumpy in here and she doesn't want to be around for it. I don't blame her. I lift the towel and press gently on the dough.

He gets up slowly and takes his plate to the sink. "It's been a long day. I'll take her out and then I'm going to bed."

"Mac...I've been thinking. About Skye."

He turns on the water and rinses his plate, doesn't look at me. "What about her?"

"I was thinking..." I clasp my hands to stop them shaking. "I know that December is when they all take vacation down there, and I was thinking maybe we should invite her to come for Christmas. I mean, I'll be really busy for a few weeks, but you two could..."

He shuts off the faucet abruptly and turns to me. "Have you lost your fucking mind?"

I'm stunned into silence.

"I don't want her to come for Christmas. I don't want her to come for anything. Ever. And I don't want to talk about it anymore."

He opens the back door and Brownie escapes into the dark yard. But before he can disappear after her, I blurt out,

"Why did you lie to me?"

"*What?*"

"About Skye. She wrote you a year and a half ago."

He closes the door and leans against the wall and his face goes very still.

"How would you know that?"

"I found the letter in your desk."

"What were you doing in my desk?"

"Trying to figure out who you are these days."

"I thought we had a certain level of trust—"

I dust the residue of flour from my hands and face him. I'm still shaking, but now it's from anger. "Trust is not the default mode. Trust is something you build with openness and honesty. Both in short supply around here."

"You actually went through my desk—"

I was hoping for something a bit more like regret, remorse...or at least embarrassment.

"I'm your wife, Mac, not your roommate. Apparently you don't know the difference."

"Sure I do. A roommate would respect my privacy." He heads for the stairs.

I take the towel off the dough, divide it in half with the bench scraper. It's cool against my damp palms, and slack now, easy to shape. I do it automatically, rounding the dough, stretching its skin, moving scattered bits of walnut from the counter to my mouth, chewing them without tasting.

When the loaves are proofing on a baking sheet in the refrigerator and the counter is clean, I call Brownie inside and go upstairs.

His suitcase sits open on the floor of our bedroom. It takes me a few seconds to understand that the clothes inside it are clean, not dirty. Folded and stacked, not wadded up for the wash. He's packing, not unpacking. I hear his office door open across the hall and he walks in.

"Where are you going?"

"Alan's. That little apartment over the garage where Sylvia's mother used to live. He said I could stay there." He avoids my eyes. "I think we need a time out."

Before I can come up with anything to say, the suitcase is filled, shut, waiting by the door.

"I'll be back tomorrow," he says. "To get some books and files."

"Why are you doing this?"

"I can't stay here."

"Okay, look...I'm sorry—"

"You're not sorry."

"I was worried, that's all. I don't understand what's going on with you."

"What's going on with me is I need some time to myself. I need some quiet. I need to work. I don't need you following me around, going through my stuff, accusing me of—let me ask you something. Do you really think if I was screwing Liv I'd be bringing her up to our bedroom on Saturday afternoon?"

"Honestly? I have no idea what you would or wouldn't do anymore." I put my hand on his arm. "I know you need to work, but how can you work when you're wound so tight you're about to snap? I think we should go up to Orcas like we planned—"

He shrugs off my hand. "What you think we should do has nothing to do with reality. Believe it or not, this is not about you."

"Then tell me what it is about, because I'm damned sick and tired of trying to figure it out. I'm tired of walking on eggs. I'm tired of you staying out till all hours, drinking too much, acting like I don't exist. Just be honest for God's sake. Tell me what's wrong—"

"Wyn...I just did." He picks up the suitcase and walks out of the room.

I sit on the bed, holding my pillow, until a shadow of movement makes me look at the doorway. Brownie stands there, swinging her tail slowly back and forth.

"Hey, Brown Dog." I slide off onto the floor and pat the space beside me. She comes to lie down at my side. I can't believe she dragged herself up the stairs. I comb my fingers through the silky fur on her back while she twitches contentedly.

We sit there together for a long time.

My mother's house appears welcoming and familiar from the outside, but inside it's a mine-field of memories.

This is the house where I grew up, where my father died, where I had to move back home after David, my first husband, locked me out, where my mother and stepfather got married. And it was here, seven years ago on the patio (the patio they're getting ready to tear up, appropriately) that Mac and I were married.

If it were up to her, my mother would keep the place like a museum, but Richard has an architect's sensibilities and a compulsion to reno-vate, so over the years walls have been knocked out, ever more daring colors of paint applied, the kitchen totally made-over, a master suite added downstairs, three new sets of French doors installed. In spite of all that, the place feels haunted to me, and no amount of remodeling is going to change that.

At the moment, my mother is sleeping off the after-effects of cataract surgery. I took her this morning, waited for her at the surgical center, and drove her home afterwards because Richard is in Palo Alto for his class reunion. In spite of her protests that she's just fine, thank you, Brownie and I are spending the night, and I'm going to have to tell her about Mac. I've been dreading the moment.

It was bad enough when David and I split up, but she didn't love him the way she loves Mac. For the last seven years she's taken every opportunity to remind me that he's a "keeper." Like marriage was some kind of catch-and-release program.

I take my lunch and a bowl of ice for Brownie out to the patio and settle on a wicker loveseat under an arbor covered in bougainvillea. I nibble on a hunk of crumbly cheddar and try to read the book I brought with me, but it's an exercise in futility. Memories clamber over me like a fast-growing, thorny vine.

Our first two years in L.A. we lived in a tiny, crummy one-bedroom apartment over a garage in Santa Monica. Mac was working as a bartender and trying to write while I labored to get the bakery underway. I'd just invested most of my divorce settlement in it and we couldn't afford luxuries like movies or eating out. Our recreation consisted of reading, watching television, walking on the beach and marathon sex.

Working at the Queen Street Bakery, even as a partner, hadn't prepared me for the crushing responsibility of having my own business. The tax forms called it The Bread Maven LLC, but really it was just me. Fortunately I had Tyler, and she was a glutton for work. As was my one other employee, Doris, who wasn't a baker, but had a cheerful demeanor and a good memory and could fix the toilet and balance the register to the penny.

I was a nervous wreck the first few months after we opened, I reviewed the bake sheet and inventory compulsively, afraid I'd forget to bake something, or that I'd order too much or too little of our supplies. I obsessed about our used equipment—kind of funny, since nearly everything at Queen Street was ancient. I worried about quality, testing and re-testing and tasting things till I couldn't fasten the top button on my jeans.

But the hardest thing of all was to watch all those beautiful loaves of bread come out of the oven in the morning, sit on the shelves all day to be bagged as day-old and then finally thrown away. The second week we were open, I came to my senses and called the food bank, and they picked it up for distribution to the missions and hospice and Meals on Wheels. That helped, but not enough.

Some days after Tyler and Doris had left in the afternoon, I would lock myself in my office and pour over the finances and cry, then wash my face and redo my makeup and go home. I never wanted Mac to know. He was working hard, too, and there was nothing he could do about it anyway.

Most nights I stayed at the bakery long enough so that he would have left for his job and I'd have time to collect myself before I had to face him. But one night I walked in to find him lying on the couch reading a book. I couldn't manage more than a terse,

"Why aren't you at work?"

"Jason wanted to trade for Thursday night," he said.

I headed into the kitchen without further comment and started pulling cheese out of the fridge and slicing the bread I'd brought home and pouring a huge glass of wine for myself. Before I could take a swallow he came into the kitchen, took the glass out of my hand and led me back out to the living room. He sat me down on the sagging couch, unlaced my Doc Martens and took them off, peeled off my socks and swiveled me around so my feet were in his lap.

"Oh, ick. Don't."

"Quiet," he said. He started to massage my feet. Gently at first, then stronger and deeper. I could feel my whole body melting into the couch. When he started on the aching muscles in my calves I began to cry.

I pulled a Kleenex out of my pocket.

"You could've just told me," he said.

"Told you what?"

"That you were sitting there crying in the bakery every night."

"I didn't want you to worry."

He laughed. "I don't have to. You're worrying enough for both of us. Besides, I know it's going to work."

I blew my nose. "How do you know?"

"I just do. Make a note on the calendar. Six months from today. You'll be scrambling to hire more people."

He stood up and tugged me to my feet, led me into the bedroom, parked me on the bed. Instead of sitting down next to me, he opened the closet and started flipping through my extremely limited wardrobe. I kept dripping tears, like a leaking faucet. A couple of times, he took things out, considered them, put them back. Then he got to the last thing. The gold panne velvet dress from my mother's wedding, slumbering in its plastic cocoon. He pulled the cleaners' bag off.

"You should wear this one," he said.

"Now?"

"Two weeks from Saturday."

I looked at him. "Are we going somewhere?"

He hung the dress on the closet door. "To your mother's house."

"What's happening at my mother's house?"

"A wedding…?" There was just enough of a question at the end.

"But—" I hiccupped. "I thought you didn't want to—" Hiccupped again. He sat down beside me and I hiccupped again.

"Hold your breath," he said. "Count to thirty."

While I counted he picked up my hand and kissed my floury cuticles. "I didn't. But now I do. Do you?"

I gulped air. "Is this a proposal or are you taking…a survey?"

"Both, I guess."

"Yes, but…you don't just get married. There's paper work and blood tests and witnesses and—" I took a long, slow breath. The hiccups seemed to have stopped.

"You think you're the only one who knows how to make things happen?"

"No, but…"

"It's mostly taken care of. You just have to get a blood test."

"There's a minister?"

"A judge."

"What about CM?"

"Trust me, it's all done."

I hiccupped again.

Eventually, my mother shuffles out, wearing one of her pastel warm-up suits.

"Nice eye patch," I say, smiling. "Too bad it's not Halloween; you could be the queen of the pirates."

She sits down next to me and pulls a grape off the bunch on my plate. "Mmm. Now I remember. I'm hungry." She tosses a cube of cheddar to Brownie, who rolls it around on the brick patio for about five minutes to make sure it's dead before eating it.

I go in the kitchen, fix her a sandwich and a glass of tea and bring them out. She's put on the giant sunglasses the doctor gave her. As soon as I sit down, she turns to me.

"How's everything going at work?"

"Oh, you know. Fine. Busy."

She takes a bite of the sandwich, chews it slowly. "And Mac. How's Mac?"

I bite my lip.

"That's what I thought," she says. "You're walking around like you're held together with piano wire."

"No, I'm not."

"Can you tell me about it?"

"He's…um…staying over at Alan's for a while."

She frowns. "Why?"

"He's angry at me."

"He must be pretty darned angry to be staying over at Alan's."

I let out a long breath. "He's pissed off because I went through his desk."

"That's not like you, Wynter." She gives me a raised eyebrow. "What were you looking for?"

"Some clues about what's going on with him."

Ever one to cut to the chase, she asks, "Do you think he's having an affair?"

"No," I say immediately. Then, "I'm not sure. He's just acting…weird."

"Weird?"

"He seems unhappy all the time. Angry."

"He's a very private person, Wyn. The surest way to run him off is to interrogate him, snoop through his desk, check up on him—"

"For God's sake, Mom, it's not like I'm stalking him."

"I'm trying to be objective—"

"I don't want objective. You're my mother. You're supposed to be on my side."

She reaches for my hand. "I am on your side, Wynter. Always. But I have to tell you the truth as I see it."

"He has a daughter."

It's like a cold, silent splash of water. I can see her recoil from it.

"A daughter?" she repeats. "Really? Well...that's...I mean..." She gathers herself. "When did this happen?"

"The girl is seventeen."

She relaxes a little. "So, long before he met you."

"Yes, before he met me. But he knew about her over a year ago."

"And when did he tell you?"

"He didn't. She turned up on our doorstep two weeks ago."

She takes a thoughtful sip of tea. "Well, did you ever stop to consider that he was probably just concerned about your feelings?"

"It makes me wonder what else is going on."

"I wish you wouldn't be so quick to think the worst. That whole experience with David made you very distrustful."

"I like to think it made me smarter."

"Obviously, you'll need to talk to him—"

I set down my glass too hard. "Don't you think I've tried? It's like doing a monologue. He never says anything back. Except he's tired. Or he's stressed."

"Well, maybe he is." She sighs. "Wyn, you probably don't want to hear this, but every marriage has peaks and valleys. The valleys are a very vulnerable time. But you can work through it. Maybe you should consider seeing someone."

"Seeing someone" is her euphemism for getting a professional involved. The very thought puts my teeth on edge.

"Are you still planning to go to Orcas in June?" she asks.

"I'm planning to go. I can't speak for him."

"Do you think that's a good idea—going up there alone? Leaving him here by himself?"

"I think he's by himself whether I'm here or not. It's been like that for months. Maybe longer."

She looks doubtful. "Are things really that bad?"

Four feet away, just where the willow love seat is now, that's where we stood. I don't recall being that happy at any other time in my life before or since. It wasn't as if I was a 19-year-old virgin bride. When I met Mac I was 32 years old and in the throes of getting a divorce from David. I'd learned a lot about love and its aftermath. Learned the hard way.

Now his desertion feels like even more of a betrayal because it calls into question all those hard lessons I thought I'd learned.

Finally I say, "Yes. Things are that bad."

"I'm sorry," she says. She feeds Brownie another chunk of cheese. "I hope…"

"Me too." I turn to look past the patio to the beds where Icelandic poppies nod in the breeze and I make myself smile. "Why don't you show me what you and Richard are planning to do back here?"

Seven

The lights are already on inside when I arrive at the bakery, and both Tyler's and Cheryl's cars are in the lot. My head is humming with plans, a product of several sleepless nights.

I pull the list out of my pocket. *Run the monthly financials on new software, more training for counter employees on new terminals, complete revision of employee handbook...try a new bread recipe from Kathleen, talk to Rafe about changing fruit tarts, ask Tyler for price check on Hemmings unsweetened baking chocolate...*

I start to call out, but something about the voices coming from the staff break room makes me walk quietly to the half-open door.

Tyler says, "She was probably just having a bad day."

"Yeah. The longest bad day in history. She's all of a sudden hanging around all the time, looking over our shoulders, second-guessing everything we do, nit-picking, bitching. It's like she all of sudden doesn't trust us. She yelled at Hannah for making sandwiches too fast, for Chrissakes. Tiffani made a simple suggestion and was cordially invited to put in an application for employment at Great Grains. It used to be fun to work here, but—"

When Cheryl sees me in the doorway her face goes chalky. She flounders for a minute, then plunges ahead.

"The others got together and asked me to talk to Tyler. Wyn, I'm sure there's a reason, and we all feel bad about—whatever it is—but you're driving us nuts. I'm sorry."

I pull out a chair and sit down. "The truth is, I think we've all gotten a little sloppy. Myself included. So possibly I've over-reacted...in the last week or so."

She takes off her black geek glasses and regards me with concern. "You know, I have a friend who's a therapist—she's totally compassionate and—you might feel better if you talk to someone about whatever it is..."

Tyler gives her a filthy look.

"Cheryl, I understand your concerns. We'll talk about it later. Okay?"

She nods and slips out of the room, closing the door gently.

I swivel in the chair to face Tyler. "Are the peasants revolting?"

She offers a weak smile. "Well...they do smell a bit, but they can't help it."

"Ha. Ha."

"Actually, you *have* been a little...snappish lately. Tiffani thought you'd fired her."

"I want things done a certain way. As the owner, I believe that's my prerogative."

"Well, you sort of suggested she should go fill out an application at Great Grains."

"All I said was—oh, crap, I don't even remember what I said." I slump in the chair.

"What's going on?"

"Sorry. I guess I should have told you. Mac and I are...sort of separated." It's almost a relief to say it out loud.

"*What*? When? Why didn't you tell me?"

81

"I thought I could muddle through. Obviously that is not the case. But I really didn't think I was—"

"I knew this was going to happen."

"You did?"

"Of course. That's what they always do when they get successful. Dump the one person who made them a success."

"I didn't make Mac a success. He worked hard for it."

She snorts. "If it wasn't for you he'd still be writing bad poetry on legal pads. What the hell happened?"

"I don't know...exactly. We just haven't been getting along. Stress, maybe. He's having a hard time with this screenplay thing. I wish he'd... Anyway, he—we decided...mutually...that it would be best if he moved over to Alan's for a while."

"Right. Mutually. So what will you do? Get a lawyer? Or just put out a *fatwa* on him?"

I smile at her, my ever cynical, ever practical Tyler. "I have no earthly idea what I'm going to do. At the moment I'm just trying to put my shoes on the appropriate feet."

"That son of a *bitch*." She kicks an empty waste can, which lands with a crash across the room. She goes to retrieve it and I stand up, pushing the chair back to the table.

"I guess we should have a staff meeting this morning. Better alert the troops."

That afternoon in a desperate attempt to distract myself and clear my head, I go to Beverly Center with a vague notion of buying towels I don't really need. Instead I end up aimlessly riding the escalators, staring at the window displays.

It's been a long time since I let myself think about having a child, but when Mac and I first got married, I thought about it a lot. The idea was never very compelling when I was married to David, but with Mac I felt differently. Everything about us seemed so right, so rock solid. For the first time in my life I was willing to make the commitment.

I knew it would be a tough sell with him, but I was unprepared for his reaction to my (I thought) fairly low-key *What would you think about maybe having a baby?*

"Why don't we just get divorced now and save ourselves a lot of trouble."

He proceeded to lay it all out for me. It was an unnecessary and dangerous complication. It would destroy everything we had together. He couldn't believe I would even consider it. It was too much to ask of him. He'd never even expected to get married.

I was stung by his words. Especially that last part. He made it sound like I'd tricked him into getting married. Ironic, since I would have gone on the way we were; getting married had been his idea.

We had a rough patch after that. I was heartbroken...not so much because he didn't want a child, but because of the way he framed it...as if by suggesting it, I'd betrayed him somehow. I went off the rails for a time, doing research on adoptions. I considered "forgetting" to take the pill and not telling him, but deep down I knew he'd leave me if I took that route. And even if he didn't, it would fundamentally change everything that was important to me about the relationship. I had to choose.

Now, riding the escalators, it seems everywhere I look, I see young mothers pushing strollers. Of course I wouldn't have been a "young" mother. I was already thirty-two when Mac and I got together.

I wander through Gap Kids, studying displays of little pink hoodies and smocked peasant blouses and miniature jeans. Wondering what Skye was like as a child. And what she's like now.

I go to the Hard Rock Café for a late lunch and let my grilled chicken sandwich languish on the plate till it's cold. I leave my credit card on the table and the cute little server runs after me, hollering "Ma'm! You forgot your card."

I think about stopping at Whole Foods, but by this time the aisles will be clogged with skinny women in workout ensembles that cost more than my car, heading home from Pilates class. That, together with my guilt at having left Brownie alone all day, prods me towards Luna Blanca.

What would I do without the Brown Dog? She's always at the back door, always glad to see me, whether I've been gone fifteen minutes or six hours. We take our long, pokey walks to the corner and back. After dinner she sits at my feet out on the patio, and every night since Mac left, she pulls herself up the stairs to sleep on the floor by the bed. Sometimes I wake up during the night and reach down to see if she's still there and she always is.

It's not a sound that wakes me; it's pain. But as I'm sitting, groggy, on the edge of the bed, rubbing Ben-Gay into my shoulder, Brownie growls, deep in her throat. I stop rubbing and listen, imagining vandals, burglars, ax murderers.

Brownie gets up and goes to the bedroom door, whining.

Twice last summer we had some kids come through the alley and climb the back fence to go swimming in our pool. I pad barefoot across the hall into Mac's office without turning on the light, and pull the drapes to one side just enough to see out.

The underwater lights are on, and yes, someone's in the pool. But even from up here, I can see that it's Mac. I recognize the lazy rhythm of his strokes, the way he knifes effortlessly through the water. The dog knows him, too, and she stands on her hind legs with her front paws on the window sill, whimpering softly. I hold her head against my leg and rub her ears and tell her to hush.

Three in the morning and he's swimming laps.

I want to call him, I want to go down and hold him, make him talk to me, but in a few seconds I know I'm not going to do any of that. He doesn't want to see me or hold me or talk to me. That's why he's here now, not three in the afternoon.

Two years ago in the spring, right after finishing the first draft of **December Light,** *he got it in his head to go to Baja. We talked very little as he drove my Volvo station wagon down through Tijuana, past the lobster restaurants of El Rosario and the perpetual parties of Ensenada to a little fishing camp someone had told him about where you could stay in a palapa for fifteen bucks a night including dinner. Meals were served in an open air pavilion, always fish that had just been pulled from the water.*

The place had a solar shower—meaning black plastic bags of water that were heated by the sun—a couple of outhouses and view of the Pacific to kill for. We took our sleeping bags, bathing suits and a change of clothes, some books, a few bottles of wine, a bunch of granola bars, apples and oranges and not much else. There were only three or four other people around at any given time, and they all seemed more interested in contemplation than conversation.

We stayed for five days, sleeping a lot, hiking a little. It was beautiful in a stark, unearthly way. The piercing blue sky devoid of clouds, the *turquoise Pacific tufted with white foam, the sand, golden and shadowed. The wind blew constantly—off the ocean at night, off the desert during the day. There was a strange respite of an hour or so at dawn and again at sunset while one wind died and the other revived. I read Steinbeck's **Log from the Sea of Cortez** and a few neglected issues of **Artisan Baker** and watched somewhat uneasily while Mac sat staring at the water or walked down the beach till he disappeared from my sight.*

The camp owner's two daughters made awesome margaritas, squeezing the limes by hand and adding secret ingredients out of battered plastic bottles. The last night we sat on the beach after dinner, drinking them and watching the sun inch its way towards the sea. For the first time in weeks he was talky; we joked about seeing the Green Flash. But as it grew darker, he grew quieter.

I was glad we were leaving in the morning. I was worried about Brownie. My mom had always kept her for us, but she and Richard were out of town, so Brownie was stuck in some posh kennel. I was anxious to get out of here, to get home and find that everything was fine.

When I couldn't keep my eyes open any longer, I left him sitting there and went to our palapa. I hung my jeans on a peg and lay down on top of my sleeping bag, intending to go back to the beach and get him if he didn't come soon. Instead, I fell into one of my hard sleeps.

Some time later I was startled awake, in silence and near total darkness by a breath of air, the sense of invisible motion. Only partly conscious, I whispered, "Mac...?"

He laughed softly. "Were you expecting somebody else?"

I mumbled some sleepy nonsense and closed my eyes again, but he nudged me towards the wall and lay down half beside me, half on top of me on the single bunk bed. His skin was chilled and damp and rimed with a thin layer of grit. When he kissed me he tasted of salt and his hair was wet. Something began to coalesce in my stomach, circling. The way a storm begins.

"Did you go in the water?"

"Just for a while," he said. "Not too far out." His mouth was on my throat and one cool hand trailed down my leg. My heart began to race, whether from desire or the thought of him out in the black Pacific with Jaws and jellyfish and riptides, I couldn't say. I turned, putting my arm across his shoulders and realized he was completely naked. I was still a little bit drunk, and now I was scared as well as incredibly aroused.

"One of the people in this bed has too many clothes on." He tugged my T-shirt off over my head and without further conversation we began to make love with an urgency I barely remembered.

By the time he pulled me on top of him, I was nearly frantic with love and lust and mingled fear, the thought of losing him in the vast dark ocean. But it was good then, better than it had been in a long time. We were going home in the morning and it would be good again…the three of us together, Mac somehow shrugging off his strangeness, reclaiming the life I wanted to believe we'd had.

It's mid-afternoon when I get to the bakery on Friday, having spent most of the morning waiting to see the doctor. The lunch crowd has thinned out. Only a few diehards remain, sipping espressos and reading the *New York Times* and *Variety*. I carefully avoid commenting on anyone's work, disappearing instead into my cubbyhole and turning on the computer. For an hour or so, I answer emails and enter evaluations into employee files. I can't do much else because I promised the doctor I'd wear this stupid nylon sling at work to remind me not to do any heavy lifting, pushing or pulling.

Eventually I wander out to the ovens. The lingering smell of sweet roasted grain always lifts my spirits, which are currently in dire need of lifting. Lydia and Alise are bagging the day-old scones and muffins; Tyler is making up the production sheet for tomorrow while Benny and Hola clean the work tables. I look around at my employees, who are studiously not watching me, and say,

"Anybody mind if I put some bread out?"

A few faint chuckles.

"Wyn, you don't have to do that," Cheryl says. "Let one of us—"

"Cheryl, there's not a loaf on this rack that weighs more than a pound and a half. I can handle it."

Ignoring her whipped puppy look, I wheel the cooling rack out front and begin arranging loaves on the big brass-trimmed baker's rack I ordered from France last year. Walnut whole wheat *levain*, kalamata olive, raisin pecan rye, and sourdough *boules*.

Tyler appears and parks her butt on the corner of a table. "What did the doctor say?"

"He said, if it hurts, don't do it. That's going to be my new mantra."

"What else did he say?"

"It's most likely tendonitis. There's a chance that there might be a small tear in the rotator cuff…"

"So what do you have to do?"

"The usual. Ice. Anti-inflammatories. I'm not supposed to do anything too strenuous for the next six weeks. Then if it's not any better, I have to get an MRI."

"I'm not even going to say I told you so. Because that's the kind of girl I am."

I fluff her bangs. "Which is why I pay you the big bucks."

"I think you should take some time off."

"I am. I'll be on Orcas for two weeks."

"I know you. It'll take you two weeks to realize you're on vacation. Then you'll have to turn around and come back."

"And your point is…?"

"My point is, when was the last time you took any time off?"

I pause to consider. "Last fall I went with Mac to that writers' conference in San Francisco."

"Three whole days. And two years ago you went up to the island for ten days."

"Is your life so boring that you have to resort to reading my personnel file for entertainment?"

"Believe me, it's a very short read. Also not terribly entertaining. I think you need a serious vacation. Minimum six weeks."

I laugh. "Are you tired of defending my honor?"

"No." She says it straight-faced.

"I can't be gone for six weeks."

"Why not?"

"Well…because—"

"You think I can't run this place without you?"

"Of course not. In fact, you usually do, but—"

"Then what's the problem?"

"I'd be bored silly up there for six weeks."

"Okay, then, four weeks. Minimum."

"I'd go crazy—"

"Wyn, I want to tell you something. Not as your manager, not as your little foundling. Just as your friend. You need to be away for a while. Somewhere where you won't be trying to do too much—"

"I'm not using my arm. Hardly at all." Lifting the sling to make my point, I wince slightly.

"I'm not talking about your arm."

When the bell over the door jingles, she looks past me and her expression changes instantly.

"What do you want?"

"Fine, thanks. How are you, Tyler? I'd like to talk to Wyn for minute, if it's okay with you."

She glares at him, then starts towards the break room. Halfway there, she turns back. "Oh, by the way, Mac…"

When he looks at her, she flips him off, and I have to bite the inside of my cheek.

"I got your message," he says to me.

"The one from three days ago?"

He follows me past the kitchen and into my office, pulling the door shut behind him.

He nods at my arm, cradled like a baby in the sling. "How's that doing?"

"You didn't come all the way over here from 90210 to inquire about my shoulder."

"I was over at the house getting some files, so I thought I'd stop by."

"When are you coming home?"

Instead of answering, he picks up the piece of argillite that I use for a paperweight and rubs the quartz vein aimlessly with his thumb, then sets it down. He probably doesn't remember that it came from Orcas. That he found it on North Beach the first weekend we spent at the cottage.

"You said you wanted me to do something."

I sit down in my chair and make myself look directly at him. His hair is too long and he looks thin. "You need to get the mail and pay the bills while I'm gone. Water the inside plants. And the window screen over the kitchen sink needs to be fixed."

He frowns. "Where are you going?"

"I guess it slipped your mind that we were supposed to be going to Orcas."

"When are you coming back?"

"Two weeks."

"What about Brownie?"

"I'm taking her with me."

"I thought we decided she's too old to fly."

"I'm not flying."

"You're driving? In the Volvo?"

"That's the plan. Unless you want to loan me the Death Star, of course."

He gives me an exasperated look, but says nothing.

"Oh, I forgot. Your coolness quotient might be seriously compromised if you were seen driving a '76 Volvo wagon."

"That car isn't up to a long road trip."

"I'll have James check it out." I look away and try to keep my voice steady. "You could still come with me. We could—"

"No. I couldn't."

My right hand grips the edge of my chair. "Do you hate me? Are you— is there someone—?"

"Don't say stupid shit."

"Then what's wrong? *Tell* me. Make me understand."

"How can you not understand? I'm pissed off. I'm sick of you questioning everything I do. I don't like being cross-examined. I'm tired of you checking up on me and going through my mail and my desk and—"

"If you ever told me anything, I wouldn't have to."

"I told you everything you needed to know—"

"I had a right to know that you have a child—"

"Yeah. Knowing about it really made everything great, didn't it? Are you happy now?"

I lean towards him. "Mac, it's not just about being happy. I love you. People who love each other talk to each other. I've always had to find out the most the most important things about you from other people. What does that say about us? About our relationship?"

"It says our relationship never depended on your knowing things about me that are none of your business," he says calmly.

"Does it matter to you that we might split up?"

"Of course it matters. That doesn't mean I can fix it. Or that you can."

"But you won't even try. You're willing to just watch it all go away. I don't understand you."

"For the record," he says, "I don't understand you either."

My throat aches from the effort of control. "The difference is, you never wanted me to."

His hand is on the doorknob. I can't stop him and I'm not even sure I want to. It's like the Mac I know is already gone, leaving this cold-eyed stranger as a placeholder.

Eight

CM is slumped next to me, snoring softly in the throes of jet-lag. She was only home from London for forty-eight hours when I shanghaied her into coming to the island.

So far she hasn't been much company, losing consciousness almost before the flight to Seattle left the ground. She rallied when we landed at SEATAC, but as soon as I turned the rental car onto the I-5 she zoned out again and didn't budge till we were parked on the ferry's auto deck and I dragged her up to the passenger cabin. Where she promptly dozed off again, her jeans jacket serving as a pillow against the window.

Mac was right, of course. About the Volvo. James, my ace mechanic in North Hollywood, said the car might make it up and back. Or it might not. And if anything untoward happened anywhere north of San Francisco it could be a problem getting it fixed. I love my car but I trust James.

So, after a brief custody skirmish, Brownie went with Mac. He promised to carry her up and down the stairs to the apartment, to walk her twice a day, and to feed her on time, mixing her vitamins and a little chicken broth into her kibble.

Still, it nearly killed me to leave her. She didn't understand why we three weren't together and why she was in a strange place. Or maybe that's just my anthropomorphic projection. After all, it was me who cried when I drove away, not her.

At last, about fifteen minutes from Eastsound, CM opens her eyes, smiles and stretches. Her first words are,

"I'm starving."

"The café's back there." I point over my shoulder. "Don't expect anything gourmet."

"Just a little snack to tide me over." She slings her purse over one shoulder. "What do you want?"

"See if they have a strychnine latte."

She waves away my ten dollar bill. "I'll get us a surprise."

"Nothing you eat would surprise me."

"I hope you're not going to be this crabby all week."

"Sorry, I'm just—"

"Hush, child. Mama's gonna get you something good."

In a few minutes she returns with two cups and a huge piece of shrink-wrapped coffee cake. She disposes of the shrink wrap and sets the cake between us.

I swallow some of the gritty mocha and pinch off a piece of streusel topping. "So how was London?"

"Cold. Rainy. I don't know how they ever got so many people to live there. But the workshops went great. And...the weirdest thing happened..." She takes a huge forkful of cake into her mouth, chases it with the mocha and licks the sticky glaze off her lips. "I saw Nathan. At least I thought it was him."

"Really? Where?"

"I was coming from a class and he was just getting in a taxi in front of my hotel."

"Did he see you?"

"I don't think so."

"You didn't say hi?"

"It probably wasn't even him." Another large piece of cake disappears into her mouth. "Anyway, I didn't have time to think of anything clever to say."

"How about *Hello, Nathan, Do you still want to get married?*"

She shrugs. "I heard a few years ago that he'd gotten married."

"People get divorced every day. You could've at least gotten on the waiting list."

She ignores me and looks longingly at the last bit of cake. "Don't you want that?"

"You go ahead."

She pops it into her mouth and finishes her drink just as the PA system crackles to life and a cheery voice announces our imminent landing on Orcas Island.

There are still at least four hours of daylight, when the rental car clatters off the ferry ramp, heading north on Horseshoe Highway, but the shadows cast by the tall conifers make a dark tunnel over the road, giving the impression of twilight.

We cruise through the village of Eastsound, skirt the oyster beds at Ship Bay, and head south on Olga Road. At the rustic former strawberry packing plant that houses Café Olga and the Orcas Island Artworks, we turn left onto Pt. Lawrence Road and wind our way another two and a half miles to a battered, rusty mailbox. We don't actually get mail delivered here, but we leave the box up to mark the turn. At the end of a long, rutted driveway the house is waiting to welcome us. At least that's how I always feel.

I usually sit in the car for a minute, windows down, listening to the wind, breathing in the smells of the earthen-damp forest and the ocean just beyond the trees. But CM's already scrambling out.

"Ooooh, yes." She sucks in a deep breath. "I'm never going back. I'm going to stay here forever, communing with nature. Hello, little birdies and beasties, Auntie CM is here."

Leaving suitcases by the stairs, we take the boombox, an Ella Fitzgerald CD, and a couple of gin & tonics out the French doors to the deck. After traveling all day it feels good to stand at the rail and peer between the Douglas fir and blue spruce at the bright waters of Rosario Strait and Doe Island, floating like a dream just out of reach.

She flings one leg up on the railing and stretches out over it, sighing.

"Look..." She points to a couple of sailboats skimming the water. "Wouldn't that be fun?"

I zip up my hoody against the fresh breeze. "I wish you could stay longer. We could probably get Alex to take us out on his boat."

"Who's Alex?"

"This guy Mac sails with. He also owns the best café on the island."

She says, "He sounds very close to being my Platonic ideal of a man. Do you think he's read the Kama Sutra?"

"There's a rumor that he wrote the Kama Sutra." I smile. "Wanna go out for dinner?"

At eight-thirty Rafferty's is packed with spillover from the Memorial Day weekend. People are milling around on the front deck, sipping drinks and squeezing in next to each other on the wooden benches. Even though the dining room is small, Alex could probably fit in another three or four tables if he wanted to. But he doesn't. And nobody seems to mind waiting. Another new hostess from his seemingly endless supply of beautiful young women greets us with,

"Do you ladies have a reservation?" When I tell her we don't, she says cheerfully, "It's probably going to be about an hour before I can seat you. Inside, outside, or first available?"

"First available—wait…you have outside seating?"

"Brand new last year." She smiles and nods towards the back of the café. "Go take a look."

After a stop at the bar for two glasses of champagne, we maneuver between tables to the open French doors and when I step across the threshold I catch my breath.

The small gravel parking lot formerly relegated to garbage out/deliveries in has been replaced by a flagstone terrace shaded by a rustic ramada. Set among planters bursting with sunflowers and poppies, zinnias and geraniums, are ten French steel café tables with bistro chairs. The far wall is topped with sections of glass window to shield diners from the wind while showcasing the view. But the real focal point—at least for me—is on the left side of the dining area—a stone fireplace and magnificent wood burning oven.

CM looks over at me and laughs. "You're drooling."

"Oh my God, I want that oven."

"Hey, Wyn. When did you guys get here?" CM and I turn towards the voice behind us.

His face is damp from the heat of the kitchen, but even at the height of the dinner rush, Alex's white jacket is relatively clean and you can still see the creases pressed in by the laundry.

"Welcome back." He barely kisses my cheek. "You like it?"

"It's amazing."

"Where's Mac?" He's looking at me, but I can tell that CM has registered in his consciousness.

"At home chasing a deadline. This is my best friend, Christine Mayle. Alex Rafferty."

He holds her hand a few seconds longer than necessary, then drags his gaze back to me. "So who the hell's going to crew for me?"

"All I can tell you is, it probably won't be Mac."

"Well, damn." Then, "You guys have a reservation?"

"No," I say wistfully. "We just got in and I wanted to bring CM here for her first dinner on the island, but…"

"The hostess said it would be an hour…" Right on cue, CM produces an impressive look of distress. "And we haven't eaten since breakfast."

I look at my watch. "What we should probably do is just have an appetizer at the bar and make a reservation for later in the week."

"No way. It's your first dinner on Orcas." He grins. "Besides, I'm pretty sure you called earlier and I just forgot to write it in the book. Let me check with Celia." He heads for the reception area, stopping to schmooze at several tables along the way.

CM holds out her glass and I touch it with mine.

"Two words," she says. "Ooh. Wee."

Twenty minutes later we're seated on the patio, sharing ahi tartare and shrimp-scallion potstickers. I slather salted butter on my sourdough bread while CM daintily dips hers in olive oil.

At some point I set down my fork.

"Okay. I want you to be brutally honest. Have I gotten sloppy? Have I been too focused on the bakery—?"

For a second she looks blank, then she glares at me. "You know, some-times I could just smack you. I don't understand why you insist on taking responsibility for everything. No, actually I do understand. In that twisted little psyche of yours, you believe that if you can just figure out how you caused the problem, you'll be able to fix it."

I twirl my glass and watch the light shimmer in the golden liquid. There's a certain amount of truth in what she says.

"I thought I sort of had things figured out. I mean, after all that shit with David I thought I'd learned something about relationships."

"Not to sound too much like your mother, but you know, this could just be a phase. I mean, he's not bonking some literary chicklet—"

"So he says."

"At this point why bother to lie?"

"Who knows why men do anything."

She picks up a small demi-lune of cucumber and nibbles it thoughtfully. "What do you think is really going on?"

"To put it succinctly, you can't get married and I can't stay married."

"Let's leave me out of the discussion," she says testily. "It seems to me that you and writer-boy both have some issues to deal with—"

"ME? Like what?"

"Like his daughter, of course. And it's got to be upsetting for him, too—"

"Right. Here's a check, kid. Have a nice flight home—"

"Plus didn't you say he's having problems with the manuscript? Maybe a little breather is all you need."

A bus boy whisks away our empty plates and seconds later our server is setting down the featured attraction. Green garlic gnocchi with fava beans for her, Dungeness crab and avocado salad for me.

She looks at mine. "That looks fabulous."

"So does yours. God, I love carbohydrates."

We switch plates.

She folds her arms across her boobs. "I know you, baby. You crave resolution. But don't do anything crazy. You need to learn to live with a little ambiguity."

"Is that the secret to your sensational love life?"

We laugh in tandem, a laugh drawn from deep in our long history.

"Why can't I be like you?" I say around a mouthful of the rich pasta.

"Why on earth would you want to?"

"Because you're self-reliant. You like men, but you don't need one underfoot everyday. Why can't I be like that? I'm so damned needy."

"You think I'm not needy?" She smiles and reaches over to spear one of my gnocchi. "If having to perform for the approval of strangers in hopes that they'll like me enough to clap politely isn't needy, I don't know what is. Everybody's needy. We just all need different things."

"That and the fact that you eat like a longshoreman and never get fat."

She gives my hand a BFF squeeze. "Please don't die before me."

We cram summer into the following five days—lazy mornings of coffee and toast, walks in the woods and along the north shore, foggy evenings by the wood stove. We do the pedal boats in Cascade Lake and try a swim, but it's too early. The water's freezing. Afterwards we lie on a big warm rock in the sun like two lizards. One morning we get up early and take the water taxi over to Friday Harbor, spend the day shopping and visiting galleries. In the evenings we cook and drink wine. Out on the deck we sing along with Motown's Greatest Hits on the boombox. We talk about all the men we've loved and hated and the one or two we've liked.

For five blissful days I don't think about the bakery or obsess about Mac—well, not too much. And I especially don't think about what it's going to be like after CM leaves. Which she does, on Saturday, despite my reminder that she said she was going to stay here forever, communing with the birdies and beasties.

Official start time for the Eastsound Farmers' Market is 9 AM, but like everything else on the island, "start time" is a fluid concept. Because I'm out early I have no trouble getting a parking spot in front of the green where the growers are drinking coffee and exchanging news and gossip while arranging their wares into artful displays.

The market is small but primo, and in high season it becomes an exercise in competitive shopping not unlike Filene's basement. Not only do you have to contend with year-round residents, vacation renters and the boat crowd, but most of the cafés brag that they buy local as well, so that burly guy who swipes the last carton of sugar snap peas out from under your hand could end up cooking them for you tonight.

By-passing the tables of handmade jewelry and scarves, I head for the Waterman Farm table for a bag of their beautiful salad mix. I can't resist the slender white-tipped French breakfast radishes and the sweet baby carrots. I don't like beets but I love beet greens, so Mrs. Waterman gives me the ones that other customers don't want.

I add goat cheese to my bag, raw honey, a half-dozen brown eggs in a cardboard carton, then stash my purchases in the trunk of the car. It's still early, and I'm loath to give up my parking space, but undecided what to do next. While I'm debating between the bookstore and the resale shop, my feet are carrying me down to Main Street. To the quiet, shady patio at Rafferty's.

Alex's oven reminds me of the old *fours banaux* or communal ovens I saw in France, some of them built during the Middle Ages. Every week the women of the village would bring their loaves for baking, each with its maker's mark cut into the dough for identification. I touch the oven's mossy slate roof and find to my surprise that it's warm.

"I found a guy used to work for Alan Scott in Petaluma." Alex's disembodied voice is coming from behind the kitchen screen door. "He came up from Seattle to build the oven, and a couple of local stonemasons did the rest."

"So you're making your own bread now?"

He steps outside and comes over to stand beside me. "Pizza. Actually it's Ferris' baby. Wednesday to Saturday night."

"Seems like a waste to have this beautiful oven sitting here and not be making bread. How big is the baking chamber?"

"About six by eight."

I'm doing the math. "Probably about fifty pan loaves...maybe thirty-five or forty hearth loaves."

"You could always try it and see."

I laugh. "What would I do with forty loaves of bread?"

"Sell them to me."

"Besides, I don't know anything about baking in a wood fired oven."

"I heard somewhere that illiterate peasants with no internet access learned how to bake in them. I think you could probably figure it out." He looks around. "Where's your buddy?"

"She had to leave this morning. I just took her to the ferry."

"Too bad. So when's Mac coming up? I was hoping he'd be here for the two-hand race."

"Hard to say."

The open space in the conversation is filled by a pre-pubescent whine.

"Da-ad, Dustin won't let me turn the handle."

I remember being vaguely aware that Alex had kids...two boys from one of his marriages.

"He's doing it wrong," comes another voice, pitched somewhat lower. "He ripped a hole in this one."

Alex turns to yell over his shoulder. "It's okay. Let him try. We can fix the hole." He turns back to me, laughing. "We're making pasta."

"Sounds like fun."

"Come in and meet the guys."

"I don't want to interrupt."

"You're kidding, right?"

In the café's kitchen two small flour covered humans are struggling for control of a piece of metal. The tussle stops long enough for them to give me the once-over.

"Dustin. Jesse." He points at them in turn. "This is Mrs. McLeod."

"Hi, guys."

"It's nice to meet you," says Dustin. He looks twelve, maybe thirteen, slight and fair, dark eyes. While he's busy being polite, the younger one, an eight-year-old Alex clone with spiky hair, seizes the opportunity to jerk the handle away from his brother. Then he turns to me.

"Are you the new girlfriend?"

"Uh…no. Actually, I—"

"Jesse, chill, okay? I want you to apologize to Mrs. McLeod." Alex shoots him a look that has been known to paralyze grown men who work in his kitchen.

Jesse remains unfazed. "For what?"

"For being rude."

"I was just asking."

"*Now.*"

"Sorry."

"No problem. A simple case of mistaken identity."

Alex pulls a stool up for me and hands me a cup of coffee and for a few minutes I watch him demonstrate how to fold the portions of dough in thirds and feed it into the machine while the kids argue about who gets to turn the crank and who has to catch it when it comes out the bottom. Dustin is charge of turning the dial to gradually close down the space between rollers, making the dough thinner with each pass.

When the café phone rings. Alex says, "Excuse me just a minute," and disappears into his office, shutting the door behind him.

"*That's* probably the new girlfriend," Jesse says. The way he rolls his eyes to the ceiling makes me laugh.

His brother sighs. "Jesse, shut up."

"Shut up yourself, propeller butt."

"Propeller butt?" I set down my coffee. "There's an interesting image."

Dustin laughs, a dry little chuckle that would seem more appropriate to a middle-aged college professor in a short-sleeved shirt with a pocket protector.

"Are you going to be a chef like your dad?"

They both explode with laughter and various unintelligible expressions of disgust.

Dustin informs me that he's interested in astrophysics.

Jesse says, "I'm gonna skate like Tony Hawk."

Since it's obvious I have no idea who Tony Hawk is, he condescends to explain that Tony Hawk is the best and most famous skateboarder of all time.

"But you don't call him that. You say he's a skater."

"I'll try to remember," I say.

"Ever heard of a 900? Tony Hawk's the only one who ever landed a 900—"

Dustin says, "Technically he was past regulation time and his hand touched—"

"Did. NOT!"

"Here's an idea, guys. Why don't we get some pasta underway here before your dad comes back. We can surprise him."

"What do you know from pasta?" Jesse demands.

"Well, I don't do it a lot, but it's dough, right? And I'm baker, so I should be able to handle it."

"Really?" A glimmer of interest.

"Yeah."

"You bake cakes and cookies and shit?"

"You're not supposed to say shit."

"You just said it."

"I didn't say it to be saying it. I was saying what you said."

"I bake mostly bread."

I've just lost whatever traction I was gaining.

"And cupcakes," I add lamely.

Dustin is working a piece of dough, flattening it, stretching it, folding it.

"Is that one ready?" I ask.

"I'm not sure. It seems very extensible."

"Let's give it a try. By the way, what kind of pasta are we making here?"

"Lasagne," they say in unison.

Good. One thing we can all agree on.

We set up an assembly line, me feeding the dough into the machine, Jesse proudly turning the handle, and Dustin lifting the thin, eggy-gold sheets up from the other end with a surprisingly deft touch for a 12-year-old boy. We drape them onto the parchment-lined trays and I dust them lightly with flour.

By the time Alex emerges from his office, we have produced almost a half pound of perfect lasagna sheets.

"Wow," he says. "Good job, dudes."

Jesse ignores his father's offer of a high five. "Who were you talking to?"

"None of your business, Sport."

He cuts his eyes to me. "See? Tolja it was the girlfriend."

I smile. "It was great meeting you guys. I've got to run before they ticket my car."

Jesse wants to know what kind of car I have and when I tell him it's a rental sedan, he totally loses interest in me.

Alex moves to hold the door open and as I pass, he mutters,

"Nice exit strategy."

Nine

"What's this?"

Alex is standing on my porch holding a white bakery box. He follows me to the kitchen, sets it on the counter and tips up the lid.

"Just to say thanks for putting up with the gang of two."

"Lasagne? Alex, this looks fabulous. But you didn't have to do that. It was actually fun. I can't remember the last time I made pasta." I lean over the box and sniff appreciatively. "Mmm. Sit down. You want something to drink? A beer? Or would you rather have espresso?"

"A double would be great. Get ready for work."

I look at him sideways. "Since when did you need to get jacked up for work?"

"Since last week. When the guys are here it's like having two jobs. I'm whipped. Then I had to get them ready to leave this morning and drive them down to the ferry. I don't usually get up at 5 AM."

"Will they be back?"

"They were supposed to come for the Fourth, but Alison's parents are renting a house in Bend for the month and she wants to take them down there…"

I heat the cups with a burst of steam, pull two doubles and set them on the table.

"Thanks." He picks up the espresso, holds it under his nose for a few seconds before taking a small sip.

I pull out a chair and sit down across from him. "Anyway, they seem like really nice kids."

He laughs. "They're a lot to deal with. It's usually a long stretch between visits and they change so much I can't keep up with them. What they're into, who their friends are, what music is cool, the slang they use…Sometimes I look at them and it's like I picked up the wrong kids at the ferry."

"Well, there's no mistaking Jesse for anyone else's offspring."

"True. Not only does he look like me, he acts like me. And it's only going to get worse."

"I think he's adorable." I smile. "And Dustin seems very bright."

"Scary bright. God knows he didn't get it from me. Alison's no brain surgeon either. He's just our teenage mutant ninja scientist. He wants to be an astrophysicist. Or so he says. Like Neil deGrasse Tyson."

"Good. We could use a few more like him."

"You know who he is?"

"Of course. He's practically a rock star."

"I never heard of him until three months ago." He drinks some more espresso, sets down the cup and leans forward. "Okay. The lasagna was actually a bribe. The official reason for this visit. I need a favor."

"From me?"

"I'm doing some classes. Six weeks. Mondays when the café is dark."

"Classes?"

"Yeah. Cooking classes. Evie Campbell—she owns that little bakery on A street—she was going to teach a pastry class next Monday, but her mom's sick and…long story short, I was hoping I could talk you into filling in as a guest instructor."

"Oh, Alex, I don't think so. First of all, pastry's not really my—"

"Of course. I mean, I thought you could do bread."

"Second, I don't like talking to a bunch of people."

"Not a bunch. Fifteen."

"That's about fourteen over my comfort level." I shake my head. "I'm really not good at things like that."

"How can you say that? I've heard you talk about bread," he says. "You've got the knowledge, you've got the passion. You'd be great. Why don't you just try it? It's one afternoon. Three hours. How bad can it be?"

I look past him out the French doors to the deck. "Anyway, you can't teach anything about bread in three hours."

"We can go longer. Come on, do it. It'll be fun. I did the second one today and it's a good group. I was hoping you'd do it a week from Monday, but I can re-arrange the schedule. I'll give you a class fee plus a percentage of the tuition. Not to mention my undying gratitude."

"I'm supposed to be on vacation…"

He leans to the side, placing himself directly in my line of vision. "If you want me to grovel, I will. But with my knees, you might have to help me get back up."

I laugh. "Okay. I guess it won't kill me. It gives me a week to build up my starter and get some recipes together."

"Awesome. I owe you."

"Yeah, you do. Big Time. I'll have to think about some appropriate pay back."

"You should talk to Ferris about the oven if you want. He'll be there Wednesday morning." At the door, he turns back. "Why don't you come down for dinner some night?" And then he's gone.

Right. I'm just dying to have dinner at Rafferty's again so I can sit at a table by myself and watch all the couples on holiday whispering and laughing with their heads together and eating off each other's plates.

Can't wait.

Wednesday morning as soon as it's light I'm downstairs in my underwear and a T-shirt rummaging in the fridge.

My starter begins with pumpernickel flour, and the final dough contains some stone ground whole wheat as well as white flour, so the finished bread is more substantial than most country French loaves. It's our best seller at the bakery—a rustic, wheaty tasting bread with a rugged crust. Inside it's a creamy gold color, flecked with wheat bran and full of the irregular air holes that are the hallmark of breads made with a starter. It makes great sandwiches and fabulous toast, but I like it best simply sliced and slathered with a good salted butter.

Finally, behind the orange juice I locate the small white plastic tub I brought with me in my carry-on bag. The lid pops when I open it, and the pleasantly musty tang assaults my nose. This is the *chef* I started at the Queen Street Bakery in Seattle and took with me to L.A., where it became the starter for the Bread Maven.

I pinch off a tiny piece and put it on my tongue. The sharp acidity gives way in seconds to an earthy, nutty aftertaste, bringing a memory with it.

I was nineteen years old. My crush on Jean-Marc passed for love and my father's death was all I knew about pain.

I'm standing at the work table in Jean-Marc's boulangerie. He watches me critically, frowning at my awkward movements, admonishing, "Wynter (except he pronounced it *Weentaire*), the bread will tell you what to do. You know from the way it looks, the way it feels. How warm, how cold. How wet, how dry. *Vous comprenez?*"

110

I scoop out half the creamy mixture and deposit it in the garbage. To the rest, I add water, squeezing it between my fingers till it's a slimy liquid, then stirring in flour till the long strands of gluten pull at the spoon. I scrape it into a bowl, cover it loosely with plastic wrap and set it on the table to ferment.

Even after all my years as a baker, I still feel a pang when I throw out part of a starter, but that's how you build it and how you maintain it—by keeping just enough of the old culture to jumpstart a new one. And it still seems like some kind of magic the way a starter goes native. No matter where it comes from, the local yeasts and bacillus will take over the culture and make it their own. So the L.A. critters took over the Seattle starter and now by the end of the week this piece of the Bread Maven will become an island culture, producing bread that can only be made here.

It's cold on the café patio and my Southern California blood is thin. I'm inspecting the stonework oven surround and shivering in spite of my turtleneck and fleece jacket when a muddy jeep grinds to a halt and a young man climbs out wearing shorts, Teva sandals and a T-shirt. Ferris Darling grew up on the island, which explains his immunity to the damp chill. He's worked for Alex since he was fifteen and embarrassed about his name. I remember him as a busboy, waiter, kitchen gopher, bartender…I think he was even host for a while, but Alex seems to prefer having pretty young females out front. Now he's in his twenties, tall, but no longer skinny, with a trendy scrub of beard and a Celtic knot tattoo on his forearm. He's never shown any interest in higher education or in leaving the island, and Alex has brought him into the kitchen.

"God, aren't you freezing?"

He pulls his dark shoulder-length hair into a ponytail and grins. "Nope."

"Do you remember me?" I ask.

"Sure. It's Wyn, right? Alex said you might be coming down."

"He did?"

"Yep. You get bored already?"

"I can only take so much peace and quiet."

He laughs. "I hear ya. So what is it you're looking to do?"

"Well…I've been thinking I'd like to try some wood fired baking one of these days, but I have no idea how to go about it. I was hoping you might give me a crash course."

"I'm no baker, myself. But I can give you Fire Management 101." He pulls the wood slab out of the oven door. "This one's a beauty. You're going to love it. Just a few things you need to know. And you're going to want to get some heavy duty gloves."

"Well, I wasn't planning to…I mean, I thought I'd just watch you."

"Only so much you can learn by watching."

He grabs a long-handled wire brush and pushes the cold ash and lumps of charred wood into a pile, then scoops them out with a banjo peel and deposits them into a battered metal bucket.

"We're starting cold," he says, "'cause the last time we used it was Saturday night. So we need to build a little warm-up fire first. Just raise the temperature gradually so the bricks don't crack when we crank up the pizza fire."

He pulls kindling and wood from a space under the oven where it's stored according to size, and builds a small base just inside the oven door. He lights it with a weed torch and it comes up fast; then he adds a few medium sized split logs. When it's burning steadily he tops it off with a few larger pieces and uses the peel to push it all about a third of the way back. We both stand, staring into the oven as a wall of flame fills the space.

"How long does it take?"

"A few hours. For tonight I need it to be about 800 degrees." He grins, obviously enjoying my surprised look. "A thin-crust pizza like I do cooks in about 90 seconds."

I feel myself smiling like a little kid. "How totally cool."

"I start throwing pizza about five, so I'll be making the fire about two o'clock. Come back if you want…"

"Thanks, I will. I have to check on my levain, then I'll swing by the hardware store and get some gloves."

"You sticking around the island for a while?"

I'm still peering into the oven.

"It's beginning to look that way," I say.

The phone's ringing when I walk in the door. I set down my purse and pick up the receiver.

"Wyn…" He doesn't even wait for me to say hello.

It's annoying the way his voice throws me off balance as if the tectonic plates were shifting under my feet.

"What's wrong?"

"It's Brownie—"

"Is she alright?"

There's a few seconds of empty airspace.

Then, "She's…she died."

I sink to a crouch on the floor, breathless, hugging my knees.

Finally I manage, "When?"

He says, "It was…she just went to sleep and didn't wake up."

"But…what happened? She was okay when I left—she was—"

"Wyn," he says almost gently, "She was old."

"Lots of dogs are old. Lots of dogs live longer than thirteen years." I ask again. "When?"

"Monday night—but I—"

"Wait a minute. Monday night? She died *Monday night*? Why didn't you call me yesterday?"

"I just found out."

"What the hell do you mean you just found out? Where were you?"

"I was here. She was—I took her over to your mom's for a few days—"

"Why? Was she interfering with your love life?"

"Wyn, stop it."

"You said you'd take care of her. You wanted to keep her, then you just couldn't wait to dump her on my mother—"

"I didn't dump her—your mom—"

"No wonder she died. She thought we'd both left her—"

"She died because she was old. Listen, I know you're upset...but I need to know whether you want to bury her or have her cre—"

"Did you ask Chuck to do an autopsy?" The tears that have been collecting in my eyes reach critical mass and begin to stream down my face.

He sighs audibly. "She's a dog. You don't autopsy a dog. She was old—"

"What did Chuck say?"

"Actually, Richard took her to the clinic—"

"I don't believe you." Anger shrinks my voice to a hard whisper. "How could you not even go get her yourself?"

"Look," he says after a few seconds. "I feel just as bad—"

"*You do not.*" I swipe my face with my arm. "You don't feel bad. You don't feel anything. Which is the whole goddamn problem with you and with us and with—"

"We're going to have to talk about this after you calm down. I'll call you tomorrow."

"I hate you," I say. But he's already gone.

Friday morning at 9:15 I'm sitting in my rented Kia in the parking lot of the Orcas Post Office with a small padded Express Mail envelope in my lap. I slit the tape with my key.

Brownie's tooled leather collar is cradled in bubble wrap along with a card bearing a sketch of a flop-eared mutt and a scrap of that shamelessly poignant poem by Isla Paschal Richardson.

Inside Chuck has written, *"We miss her, too."* and it's signed by all the clinic staff.

I sit for a few minutes absently fingering the rabies tag and Luna Blanca dog license while tears take turns rolling down my face. I knew she'd die eventually. Of course. I just never expected it to happen like this. Shouldn't there have been some kind of warning? Maybe there was, and I missed it.

Why did I leave her in L.A.?

I had to rent a car anyway; why am I so stupid that it never occurred to me to rent one there and drive up? Then I could have brought her with me. Then I would have known if something was wrong. Then, even if she'd died here, and even if it was true that there was nothing I could do, at least I'd have been with her.

One of the few things I've retained from 8th grade California history class:

According to the Kato Indians, the god Nagaicho created the world. First he erected four great pillars at the corners of the sky to hold it up and to expose the earth. Then he strolled around his new world and began creating things to fill it. Man and woman were made of earth; the rivers and lakes were made by Nagaicho's footsteps; each animal was formed and placed in its proper setting—each animal except the dog. Nowhere in the story is there any mention of Nagaicho creating the dog. Instead, the myth begins:

Nagaicho, the creator, set out to create the world, and he took along his dog.

Brownie was originally supposed to be a present for Mac. He'd told me once how he wanted a dog when he was a kid, but Suzanne refused to allow any animals in the house. So on his first birthday after we moved to L.A. I went to the nearest shelter to check out the candidates. I was only going to look, of course. I thought I'd make a short list and then talk to Mac, see what kind of dog he might like.

By the time the volunteer had walked me back through the kennels I was wrecked. Behind every gate was a face, a story, a dog who'd come there by some human carelessness or stupidity or cruelty. I wanted to take them all home.

The volunteer was about my mother's age. She had scraggly gray hair and a kind face with no makeup and she took the measure of me right away. When I hesitated at one pen which held a litter of squirming black puppies, she said gently,

"They're a lot of work at that age, so be sure you're up for that kind of demand on your time and energy. It's really sad when you have to bring them back."

She left me in a tiny room while she disappeared around the corner. In a few minutes she was back, leading a chocolate brown dog with a fine pointy nose like a collie and little floppy ears.

"This is Brownie," she said. "She's probably about three years old."
She unclipped the leash from the dog's nylon collar. "I'll leave you two to
get acquainted." Then as an afterthought: "She's very smart."

Brownie immediately demonstrated her smarts by coming over to
my chair and standing on her hind legs, front paws on my knees and
looking directly into my eyes. It was very like falling in love. I had no
time to think about it.

She sat primly in the passenger seat of my Volvo, looking around
at the scenery with great interest, but every time I stopped at a light,
she turned to fix me with that lover's gaze, just to be certain I hadn't
developed buyer's remorse.

People say that rescue dogs are the best because they're so grateful.
I'm not sure whether Brownie was grateful or just clever. Whatever her
take on the situation, she seemed aware that she had scored big-time,
and she blended seamlessly into our lives as if filling a space that had
been reserved just for her.

I don't know how long I've been sitting here. People stroll in and out of the
post office or the office supply shop next door. A guy in a classic T-Bird
convertible appears to be waiting patiently for my parking space.

I start the car and head out of the village.

At the Obstruction Pass Trailhead parking lot, I fetch my walking
shoes from the trunk and sit sideways with my feet out the door while
I lace them up. Only a few faint bird songs are audible as I slog down
through the dripping woods past shadowy stumps and fallen logs
upholstered in moss.

Just short of a mile the trail ends at a small campground. Beyond the
tents and fire pits and picnic tables, down a low bank is a beautiful crescent beach thickly carpeted with marble-sized, multicolored pebbles and

littered with huge driftwood logs like dinosaur bones. The view from here is one of my favorites, south to Lopez, Blakely and Obstruction Islands, but this morning it's barely visible. A marine layer hovers just above the water, infusing everything with its clean, wet smell, blurring the horizon.

Brownie hated the ocean. Water of any kind, really. Mac was convinced it was just conditioning and that he could teach her to swim.

Wet and shivering, legs rigid, she'd stand at the water's edge, barking at him, while he stood waist deep and tried to coax her to come. I remember Chuck Reese laughing when I asked why she wanted nothing to do with it.

"She's a collie mix, Wyn. A land dog. She's a herder, not a retriever."

Of course. She was a herder. That was why she got nervous when we went to the park and one of us walked away. That was why she barked at us and nipped at our heels to keep us together when we walked.

It's low tide. On a pile of boulders tumbling down to the water, I find a perch and watch tiny scuttling crabs and orange starfish draped and wedged into impossible cracks where the last few drops of retreating tide remain. I pull my knees up and rest my forehead on them.

Once the gardener left the gate unlatched and Brownie got out. She was gone for three days, and each night I had the same dream—Brownie scratching at the kitchen door crying to come in, and me—for whatever dream reason—unable to open the door. It's probably not true that I cried nonstop for three days, but that's my memory of it...until the man who owned the little village grocery found her in the alley behind his store and called us.

A breeze rustles my shirt. No, not a breeze. Something is touching the back of my arm. I whip around to stare into a pair of dark eyes peering out of a ball of brown fuzz. A dog.

He trots around on stubby little legs, checking me out from every angle. He smells terrible…like dead fish, which he's probably been rolling in or eating. His nondescript fur looks as if he's bathed in mud and then been blow-dried—sort of a primitive styling mousse. After completing his inspection, he lies down about an arm's length away and eyes me warily. Maybe he belongs to one of the campers.

I say, "You come here often?"

No response.

"You have a human?" He's not wearing a collar.

"I'm in mourning."

From the corner of my eye I can see him relax a bit. He rests his head on his paws and we sit for a while.

Pretty soon I'm wondering if he would follow me back to the parking lot. I'm thinking about getting him into the car—thank God it's a rental. I could clean him up and feed him and take him to the vet and maybe if he doesn't belong to someone, we could have a relationship. I turn slightly and he sits up.

"I'm a baker," I tell him. "Some people think I'm pretty nice. We could go for walks, but you'd have to stop rolling on dead fish. I'd make sure you always have food and water and a warm place to sleep."

He licks his chops.

"In fact, you could sleep with me if you want. Nobody's occupying the other side of the bed at the moment. You like movies?"

I move my hand towards him very slowly. He watches like it's a snake. When my arm is fully extended he gives my fingers a tentative sniff. Then a lick with his small pink tongue. I lean just slightly to touch his muzzle. End of story.

He's up, headed for the water, running full throttle along the wide arc of the beach. He scrambles up a steep bank and disappears into the trees.

His relationship history must be even worse than mine.

Mac

Above the sea air on PCH he smells it.

Charcoal lighter fluid. Not a good smell, full of petroleum and smoke, but it ignites a memory of hamburgers with crunchy bitter edges and the salty whiff of a newly opened bag of potato chips, a sweating can of Coke. And the inevitable plate of carrot sticks, radishes and curling celery that was Suzanne's attempt to add vegetables to their diet. He remembers the canned black olives stuck on the ends of his fingers, Kevin stuffing handfuls of mixed nuts into his mouth till he couldn't chew, the two of them collapsing on the grass in helpless laughter.

"Better slow down," Liv says. "And get in the left lane. The turn's just ahead."

In the bar a female voice wails wordlessly over a thrumming rhythm guitar. He looks past his drink, through his own face reflected in the glass out to where the ocean heaves restlessly, crashing on the rocks just below the deck. He remembers the winter storm a couple of years ago where the waves actually punched through the windows of this place and so many others along the coast, flooding them. They watched it on TV in their bed, Wyn curled up against him. She loved storms.

The wait is interminable. Which doesn't seem to bother Liv. She carefully monitors all the comings and goings. He orders another drink and tries to drink it slowly when what he really wants is to slam it down just for the burn and order another.

"Mr. McLeod?" The hostess is wearing black tights with a see-through black dress and a pink satin jacket, pink fingerless gloves. Her make up is thick and she smiles carefully to avoid disturbing it. "Your table is ready."

They follow her to a table by the window where the view of the sunset behind a bluff would have been unobstructed, had the sun not set an hour ago. It's also situated so that everyone who comes in from the bar has an unobstructed view of them.

"Great table," Liv whispers. "She must have recognized you."

He laughs.

"No, really. They pay attention to who's eating here. These days they can't afford not to." Her white gauzy blouse dips slightly off one tanned shoulder. Blonde hair gleams under a pendant lamp.

They haven't even opened their menus when the waiter appears to tell them his name is Sean and he'll be taking care of them tonight and did they want another cocktail.

"We'd like a bottle of Veuve Cliquot," Liv says, then turns to him. "I hope you don't mind."

"Look…" He clears his throat. "I don't know what your expectations are—"

"I went off expectations cold turkey about ten years year ago."

He watches the people entering the dining room. An older couple, the woman carrying an armful of flowers. Three twenty-somethings in denim mini-skirts.

At the precise moment that Sean returns to pour champagne, he hears a familiar laugh and looks up to see Gabe Cleveland in a Hawaiian shirt and Maui Jim reflectors walking towards the outdoor bar with two other men.

Mac turns abruptly towards the window and the breath sticks in his throat. Against the night sky, two gulls swoop and soar. Caught in the beams of light from the deck, they glow a pure, eerie white, two souls against the black ocean. A fine mist of sweat erupts on his forehead and he has a moment of irrational panic. He should leave. Now. Just get up and walk out. Leave her the car. He could call a cab. Shit, he could hitchhike.

Then Liv says, "What are you looking at?"

He breathes quietly, swallows some of the champagne. "Seagulls."

"Why do you care what people think?"

"I don't."

"Then why did you look away so fast when you saw Gabe?"

"Cleveland gossips more than ten old ladies."

She pushes the lettuce around on her salad plate. "Are you embarrassed to be seen with me?"

He sets down the flute, picks up the scotch, and takes a long drink, actually tasting it for the first time. "I don't like being talked about."

She laughs. "Then you're living in the wrong town, my dear. L.A. is all about people recognizing you, knowing about you, talking about you." She leans forward and looks into his face. "That's how I make my living, remember?"

Sean brings their entrees, setting them down theatrically, clasping his hands, asking if there will be anything else. She wants Pellegrino; he orders another scotch and ignores her almost imperceptible frown. Liv talks while they both poke at the food.

He keeps looking back at the window, but the birds are gone.

She sets down her fork, exasperated. "Like you've never seen a seagull before?"

"I can look and listen at the same time," he says, although he's completely lost the thread of conversation.

"I was just saying, I've been meaning to ask if you'd consider doing a few events this summer. Not book events," she adds quickly.

He frowns. "What kind of events?"

"Oh, parties, dinners, previews, openings. I have other clients, you know."

"I didn't think you were paying the mortgage off me."

"So, I have to go to these things, and it's always nicer if I have someone to go with. I think it would be good to be seen together. You're getting a lot of good press right now and I know a lot of people who could help you."

"Help me what?"

Her sigh is so deep it seems almost to alter the air currents in the room. "Don't be obtuse. Mac, everything depends on who you know and who knows you. Once this film is in the can, there could be a world of opportunities opening up for you. Provided you're in the right place at the right time and with the right people putting you forward."

"First of all, the chances of this film ever being 'in the can' are about the same as those of the proverbial ice cube in Hell. Plus, I can't imagine how being seen with me would be much of a career booster for you."

"You underestimate yourself." She opens her purse, pulls out a compact and touches up her lipstick. "But..." She snaps the silver disc shut and drops it back into her purse. "If you don't want to, that's fine, too. I just thought it would be good cross-promotion..."

"Is there some school you go to where they teach you this shit?"

"No. Is there some school you go to where they teach you to be an asshole?"

"No. It's hereditary."

"Look..." She sits back in her chair and favors him with a conciliatory smile. "Let's not snipe. Okay, I admit It's hard for me to understand why you apparently don't see the potential in our relationship, and you

123

probably can't understand how I'm always coming up with ideas to promote your work—ideas that could benefit both of us—"

"It's not that I can't understand how you do it, it's more that I can't think why you do it. It doesn't interest me in the least."

"If you don't mind my saying so, nothing seems to interest you."

"I don't mind. It's true."

"You have to fight it." She leans forward earnestly. "You have to find something to care about. If you don't, it'll chew you up and spit you out. I speak from experience."

"So I should care about events. About 'cross promotion.' About the right people putting me forward."

He signals Sean by rattling the ice in his empty glass, and in a few minutes another scotch arrives.

She frowns. "You're drinking too much. It's a depressant, you know. Not to mention you shouldn't be driving."

"Liv—"

"I'm concerned about you, that's all."

He checks for the birds once more. "Thanks, I already have a wife."

She pulls the flimsy looking wrap around her shoulders. "I'm going to the ladies," she says. "Meet me out front."

When she's gone, he leans back in the banquette and drinks half the scotch at once. The problem is, he's not quite drunk. He doesn't seem able to get there anymore. When he sets the glass down, the server materializes instantly. "Would you like some coffee, sir?"

"No, but another scotch would be good."

The guy smiles obsequiously. "I'm sorry, sir. Your companion has asked us not to serve you any more alcohol. She asked me to let you know that she's waiting in the car."

He decides against creating a scene, interesting though it might be. He digs in his wallet for the MasterCard and hands it over.

Liv is sitting in the driver's seat of his car, the engine running. He slides in on the right.

"So you're my companion."

She checks the side mirror before pulling out into the sparse traffic on PCH. "Your companion?"

"The waiter said my 'companion' asked him not to serve me another drink. That my 'companion' was waiting in the car."

"I could have left you there, I suppose."

He buckles his seat belt to quiet the warning chime and leans his head against the neck brace. "So why didn't you?"

She looks thoughtful. "Because I'm too nice?"

"Is this going to be multiple choice?"

She laughs. "God, Matthew, what will become of you?"

Suddenly it does seem, if not actually funny, at least amusing.

Ten

I'm standing at the sink eating strawberries out of a damp brown paper bag. A guy was selling them out of his pickup truck at the farmer's market, and the smell from ten feet away was intoxicating. They must be some old fashioned variety. Every bite makes a sweet explosion in my mouth, a memory of the berries CM and I used to pick and eat at her grandmother's house down in Orange County when we were kids. Before the whole neighborhood got bought up and bulldozed to make room for a few more desperately needed strip malls.

When the phone rings I savor the last one, trying to decide whether or not to answer.

It's my mother.

"Wynter, I'm so sorry about Brownie. I feel terrible."

My throat starts closing up. "It wasn't your fault."

"I offered to keep her. Mac just seemed so—"

"Mom, it's okay. Really."

"Have you talked to him?"

"No." I try to think of a way to soften that one-word answer, but nothing comes to mind. He's never called me back and I haven't called him.

As recently as six months ago it would have been unthinkable. No matter where we both were or what we were doing, how angry, how busy, how difficult things had become, we never got though a day without talking. It was a kind of reassurance that we were both still present, still trying.

"What are you doing with yourself up there? Aren't you bored? Or lonely?"

"Not yet." I try to sound cheerful. "In fact I'm going to a chamber music recital tomorrow night."

"That's nice." She pauses. "Honey...I know he's behaving strangely... and I hope you won't get angry at me for what I'm going to say, but do you think there's even the slightest chance that he's being punished for David's crimes? Maybe if you just came home and sat down with him..."

I crunch the tiny grit of strawberry seeds between my teeth.

"*Strangely* doesn't begin to cover it. And every time I—"

"When I saw him—"

"Where?"

"At Gelson's. Wyn, he doesn't look good. I'm worried about him. He could be depressed. That's why I offered to take Brownie. I thought—"

"Mom, let me ask you one question. When you talked to him, what did he say?"

She knows what I'm really asking.

"Well...He said he's working a lot." She hesitates. "I just thought it was so strange. That he didn't say a word about you."

My mother is a classically trained pianist. She played in an amateur chamber ensemble for years and she drummed it into my head that one did not attend a performance wearing jeans, no matter how many rhinestones they had on the pockets. So I rummage in the closet for the one dress I keep here, a generic packable knit thing that's so bland it never goes out of style—black, V-neck, sleeveless—and I wipe the dust off my old black flats, add the silver necklace CM gave me for my thirtieth birthday, French braid my hair, and head for The Orcas Center.

It's a pretty little venue of some 200 seats arranged in semi-circular rows around the stage. Come August when the annual Chamber Music Festival gets going, people will be arm wrestling for tickets. But right now I just walk into the lobby box office and buy one. Acoustically speaking, the front row is probably not optimal, but it makes me feel like a little girl again, feet not touching the floor, leaning against my father, watching my mother in her black dress, making beautiful music.

There's only one woman in the ensemble—the violinist—and the group is totally casual, wearing jeans and T-shirts, laughing while they tune their instruments, waving at people in the audience. My mother would not approve.

Finally everyone is seated, the whispering and rustling subside; the house lights go down. The music starts abruptly, with no introduction, and it surprises me with a rush of memory.

In a vain attempt to awaken the musical gene she was certain must be slumbering in my DNA, my mother was always instructing me on the fine points of the pieces she was working on. The Trout Quintet was one of her favorites. I remember her telling me the title came about because the fourth movement is a set of variations on Schubert's earlier song "Die Forelle" (The Trout.) She explained that the work was written for an unusual lineup of piano, violin, viola, cello and string bass, and has five movements instead of the usual four.

As a teenager, my reaction to this kind of information was a barely concealed yawn. But tonight, here on the island, by myself, and thirty years older…the music feels friendly and familiar. I find myself nodding in time with the Scherzo. By the fourth movement I'm happier than

I've been in months. I decide not to accidentally grind my heel into the foot of the jerk next to me who keeps looking at his watch.

When the Allegro giusto—the finale—ends, I float out to the vestibule. . I pick up a flier for the chamber music festival, even though I know I won't be here, and a glass of champagne at the bar to drink by the window watching a small yellow plane on approach to the airstrip.

"I like your hair that way."

I turn quickly, sloshing a little champagne on my shoe. "Alex. I didn't know you were a Schubert fan."

He laughs. "I'm not. Although that wasn't too painful." He drinks red wine from one of the two glasses he's holding. "Where've you been? Ferris thought you were going to come build fires with him."

"I was. I am...it's just...my dog..." Suddenly my eyes fill and my voice cracks and I feel incredibly stupid. "She died."

He hands me a cocktail napkin and waits for me to recover. "I'm sorry."

"I just haven't felt much like—"

"Hi, I'm Paulette Riley." A tan and graceful hand with French manicured nails relieves Alex of the other glass. Paulette Riley is thirty-something, a vision in hot pink knit. She tucks a strand of chin length blonde hair behind one ear before extending her hand. "So, are we ready to sleep our way through Part Two?"

I look at her. "I'm sorry?"

A tiny frown troubles her smooth forehead. "I found it a bit tiresome, didn't you? Not the performance, of course. The music. I mean, The Trout is sort of a dead fish. It's been overdone, don't you think?"

My toes curl inside the black flats. "Actually I enjoyed it."

She takes a sip from her glass but doesn't swallow.

"Paulette's a wine rep," Alex explains, while she swishes the wine around in her mouth.

For a minute I think she's going to gargle and spit, but she chokes it down and then asks me what I do.

"I'm a baker."

"Wyn owns a great artisan *boulangerie* in L.A.," Alex says.

"Oh, I *love* bread. Of course, I try to stay away from empty carbs these days."

"Me too. I've cut way back on the wine."

I think Alex wants to laugh. Probably the only thing stopping him is the fact that if he so much as smiles, his chances of getting laid tonight will be greatly diminished.

Fortunately, the lights blink, signaling the end of intermission.

"Nice to meet you, Lyn." She links her arm through his and they head for the auditorium.

I turn back to the window. The yellow plane is gone, leaving the sky empty. I drink the rest of my champagne, throw the plastic cup in the trash, and leave by the side door.

Alex looks at his watch. "High Noon," he says. "Let's get started."

A trickle of sweat rolls down between my breasts and I give him a look, indicating that I hate him for talking me into this.

He ignores me and favors his audience with a smile.

"I think some of you know Wyn McLeod—but for those of you who don't, I'll just say that she's about the best bread baker I know. Her boulangerie has been featured in the *L.A. Times* and she's written articles for *Food & Wine*, *Los Angeles Magazine* and most importantly, *The Orcas Sounder*. So I'll just stand over here and make like Vanna White while Wyn talks to us about artisan bread."

I swallow air. "Um...Thanks, Alex. Okay how many of you have made bread before?"

All but two raise their hands. "Then you probably already know that there are a lot of different techniques. In the next few hours we're going to talk about three that I think give particularly good results, depending on how much time you want to invest. Just keep in mind that there are others out there for you to discover if you're interested. The three methods are on the hand-outs Alex gave you. I just put four loaves of the *pain au levain* into the oven, so you'll start to smell it pretty soon and in a couple of hours we get to eat it."

Loud cheers. My neck and shoulder muscles start to relax.

"I could have printed out more recipes and just demonstrated them for you, but I'm fairly sure you can all read, so I've convinced Alex—against his better judgment—that we need to actually get our hands in some dough. I bet most of you have been dying to get back there in his kitchen anyway—yes?"

A petite woman with a precision haircut and a turquoise colored jogging outfit is waving her hand. "I didn't really dress for cooking," she says. "I thought this was going to be a demonstration class like the first two."

I smile and try not to sound annoyed. "Bread is a full contact sport. That's why God created aprons. But feel free to abstain if you're not comfortable."

Another woman—older, attractive, with lively blue eyes and long silver hair gathered at the nape of her neck—waves at me.

"My name is Sarah and I was just wondering," she says. "How does someone end up being a baker? I mean, is it something you were always interested in? Did you have other jobs? When did you first decide you wanted to have your own bakery?"

She's probably in her early sixties, dressed in retro hippie garb. I can imagine CM looking very much like her in another twenty years.

"Well…"

I can practically hear the pebbles knocking around in that hollow spot where my brain's supposed to be. I glance distractedly down into my cardboard box of supplies, and sitting on top of everything is my ragged old paperback copy of the *Tassajara Bread Book*. I don't even know why I brought it; I hadn't planned on using it today.

"That's sort of a big question with a long answer, but there is one thing I can share with you…" I open it and read to them,

"Bread makes itself, by your kindness, with your help, with imagination running through you, with dough under hand. You are bread-making itself…"

An old emotion wells up in my chest, surprising me, and I find myself wondering how it is that I've managed to get so far from this feeling. How did the bakery become a desk job? I'm not a real baker anymore; I'm a business owner.

"I baked a lot of bread before I ever read that. But I think it's fair to say that the first time I read it is when I became a baker."

The room feels different now. Quieter. The women are looking at me expectantly. A few of them are actually writing down the *Tassajara* quote. I smile at Alex.

"Vanna, I think that's your cue."

He laughs and circles the tables, doling out fresh white aprons. "Any other questions for Wyn before we head back to the kitchen?"

The woman who's afraid of flour waves her hand. "I just got a bread machine. Are you going to talk about making bread with a machine?"

I set down the book. "In my admittedly biased opinion, bread machines are a tool of Satan. They defeat the whole purpose of making bread. If all you want is good bread to eat, you should be supporting your local artisan baker. If you want to make your own bread, then you have to be invested in the process, not just the product. A bread machine short-circuits the process and takes it out of your hands, which is where I think it belongs."

"But it makes the house smell so good," she says.

"If that's all you want, you could get yourself some bread-scented room freshener."

A couple of people snicker.

A woman with orange hair waggles her fingers at me. "But Wyn, you must use machines at your bakery?"

"True. For certain things, machines are great. However, I assume none of you will be working with forty-five pounds of dough. At the bakery, the mixing and kneading are done in Hobart mixers that look like the mother of all KitchenAids. But for things that require finesse, these are your main tools." I hold up my hands "Human hands are amazing pieces of equipment. They're so sensitive and flexible and they can do things and tell you things about your dough that no machine ever could. Even at the bakery, we do all the scaling and shaping and docking by hand."

"You do all the what?"

"Scaling is weighing out the dough for each loaf and docking is making those slashes in the loaves of bread."

Someone pipes up, "Those slashes—why do you do that? Are they just for decoration?"

"Have you ever had a piece of bread with a big hole under the top crust?"

"Every time I bake bread," someone else says, and they all nod and laugh.

"That's what happens when the crust sets before the steam can escape. The steam that comes from the moisture in the bread gets trapped under the top crust. Slashing prevents that. It also affects the bread's shape and crumb. It tells the bread where to expand. And over time it's become sort of an art form."

"I got one of those *lame* things that you do that with and all it did was mutilate my pretty loaf."

"Me too."

I hold up one hand to quiet them down. "There are a few tricks to docking. And I'll show you how to do it when we get to that point. But we won't get to that point if we don't get back in the kitchen and get started."

In five minutes everyone is aproned and standing around the big prep island. I give them a few minutes to examine the huge black stove, the grill, the ovens, the prep sinks, the gleaming stainless pots and fire-blackened pans hanging overhead. I know how it feels. I remember the first time I stepped into the inner sanctum of the *boulangerie* in Toulouse. It was like a trip to fantasyland.

"Hey, Alex, do you clean this place yourself?" someone calls out. "And if so, will you marry me?"

They all erupt in raucous laughter.

We divide them up into three teams and Alex gives each team their *mise en place*—pre-measured flour, water, salt and yeast. We walk through the first recipe, Professor Calvel's white bread, and they dive in.

The class winds up in just under five hours, every crumb of *pain au levain* has been devoured, and still no one wants to leave. I feel buzzed, like I've been on an espresso binge.

I stand just inside the kitchen and watch Alex escort the last holdouts to the door, clutching their plastic containers of dough to proof and bake off at home and smaller tubs filled with Orcas Island levain. These women clearly adore him. I always thought he simply accepted the attention as his due, but watching him now, it seems to me that he genuinely likes them as well.

In a few minutes he's back, holding two sweating glasses of a beautiful pink-gold wine.

"Rosé?"

"It's a Côte du Rhone. Dry. Very refreshing." He hands me a glass.

"Did Paulette turn you on to this one?" I ask innocently.

He laughs. "She's not a fan of rosé."

The wine is cold and crisp with a stony undertone. I'm so thirsty I drink half of it before I set the glass down. I should probably not get drunk before we finish cleaning up. He fills a mixer bowl with hot soapy water while I gather up spoons, bench scrapers, measuring cups.

"Here's an idea. Maybe while you're on island you could bake some bread for the café?"

"I'm on vacation. Plus, you can't afford me."

"You could work in the kitchen here. There's not much going on in the mornings except deliveries."

"Sounds like fun, but I'll pass."

"Did I mention free dinners?"

"Alex…"

"I could probably find a bread machine you could use…"

I look up quickly and we both start to laugh.

He says, "Tool of Satan, huh? I'll have to remember that one. I wish I could be there when she goes home and tells her husband to junk the bread machine."

I study him for a minute as a completely different person than the one I've known all these years we've been coming up here. "Alex, you close down after Christmas, don't you?"

He nods. "Till April. I hibernate. Read. Sail when I can. Go to Seattle or Vancouver. Take the kids to Hawaii."

I set down my cleaning cloth. "I think you should do a culinary tour. In Europe. France, Italy, Spain…"

He looks mildly amused. "Culinary tour."

"I was watching you with those women. You're a natural."

"I can't picture myself herding a bunch of women around to different restaurants—"

"It's not like you're just taking them out to dinner. You're teaching them about food. You'd take them to meet a lot of great chefs, bakers, chocolatiers, winemakers, cheesemakers, butchers—people they'd never have a chance to meet, places they'd never get to see on their own."

"Why would those people want me there?"

"Because you'd be bringing wealthy people to their establishments to spend money, *bien sûr*. Winter can be slow for them, too. They'd be happy to see you."

He looks dubious. "It can't be that easy or everybody and their brother would be doing it."

"Everybody and their brother *is* doing it. But people here know you. They'd go with you because they like you and they love your food. You could have some cool fliers printed up…'Join Chef Alex Rafferty as part of a small, select group to experience gastronomic highlights of Europe.' "

Now he's laughing.

"I could set you up with Jean-Marc—"

"Who?"

"The baker I worked for in Toulouse. You guys would like each other, I think. He knows lots of food people in Gascony. And he knows bakers in other *départments* who'd know other food professionals in Burgundy, and the Loire Valley, Bordeaux, and—"

"Whoa, whoa. And I want to do all this because…?"

I give him an impatient look. "Because you get to travel and eat and drink for free as the group leader. Plus you get paid for your services— not *those* services—your group leader services. And then you could come back and promote your new seasonal menus 'after a winter spent collaborating with great chefs of Europe.' Fabulous idea, right?"

"Where do you come up with this stuff?" He's still laughing.

"I was married to a marketing guy for 7 years."

He stops smiling and gives me an inquisitive look. "I didn't know you were married before."

"Yes, believe it or not, there was life before Mac." When I realize how that sounds, I pick up the dish cloth and start wiping down the Hobart.

"Well, it's something to think about," he says.

With the two of us working quickly, the kitchen is spotless in less than thirty minutes. He sweeps a few remaining crumbs into a dustpan and empties it into a garbage can, then leans against the work island watching me load my supplies and notes into the grocery store carton.

"Thanks. For making me do the class. It was good for me."

"You did a great job. I don't know why you were so nervous about it."

"It's not just that. I mean, it helped me remember some things… I think the last few years I've been so caught up in running the business that I'd about forgotten why I wanted a bakery in the first place."

"Yeah…It's a fine line," he says. "I go through the same thing with the café."

"You do?" When I pick up my Tassajara Bread Book and turn to toss it into the box, one of my tortoiseshell hair combs slips out and lands on the floor.

"Sure." He stoops to retrieve it, wipes it on his towel.

"Thanks. Just throw it in the box."

Instead, he reaches over to brush a loose strand of hair off my cheek, securing it with the comb. He does it with a sort of casual competence, as if fixing a woman's hair is something he does every day. The way it slips gently against my scalp makes the hair rise on the back of my neck and I scramble for something to look at other than him.

I reach for my empty wine glass and turn it upside down in a washer tray, take off the apron and toss it in the laundry basket by the door.

"Why don't you let me cook dinner for you," he says.

"Thanks for the offer, but I'm not very hungry. I just want to go home and put my feet up."

"Okay." He puts his hands behind him on the edge of the table. "Don't forget to make a reading list for me to hand out. If I don't give them something next week, it could get ugly."

"I'll do it tomorrow so I don't forget to give it to you before I leave." I blot the perspiration off my face with the towel.

"When are you leaving?" he says after a few seconds.

I move things around aimlessly in the box. "Friday. I need to go home and check on things. The bakery."

"Are you coming back?"

"I don't know. It depends."

I pick up the box before he can reach for it. "Can you just get the door for me? Good night, Alex."

Eleven

Four weeks. How is that possible? I'm supposed to be lonely. To miss Mac. To be worried about him. But the truth is, I missed him more and worried more and felt lonelier when I was at home.

How strange that I barely registered the tension in our house, when it was there, day after day, wearing me down. It's like not realizing you've been walking around with your teeth clenched until you finally relax your jaw. Suddenly I dread going back, re-submerging in that toxic fog.

Thursday afternoon I get as far as dragging the suitcase out from under the bed and zipping it open. Then I stand there looking down into the empty compartment, thinking about packing my clothes, shoes, books, papers. Closing up the house and putting all my personal stuff back in the locked storage room. Getting up in the middle of the night to make the early ferry, traveling all day to get home, where there's a train wreck waiting for me.

I lie back across the bed and study the angled ceiling, the wooden beams, remembering what this place looked like when we first saw it. There was a hole in the ceiling right above where I'm lying, and a nest full of baby birds tucked up over one of the beams. The mother bird kept dive bombing us while we inspected the closet. Trying to put a good spin on it, the real estate agent said a bird's nest in a new house was good luck. I remember Mac laughed. "Yeah," he said. "Good luck for the roofers."

I sit up and reach for the phone, punch in the number of the direct line to my desk

"This is Tyler."

"Hey, Ty. It's me."

"Hi, me. How are you?"

"Okay. Listen, I was wondering…what would you say if I didn't come home?"

"Ever?"

"No, doofus, not 'ever.' Tomorrow. I just don't think I'm ready—"

"Yay!"

"I can come home now if you need me, it's just—"

"Perhaps you didn't hear me? I said 'Yay!'"

"I'm trying to have a serious discussion here. How's everything going?"

"Fine. In fact I'm thinking of pulling the fire alarm just to liven things up a little."

"How's traffic?"

"We're busy. You want the numbers?"

"Can you email them to me?"

"I can do that. I'll send you the month to date."

"What else is going on?"

"Not too much. I hired a new dishwasher."

"What happened to Juan?"

"He said he had to go get his teeth fixed. In Guadalajara. And what's her face… from the bookstore…"

"Lorna?"

"Right. They want to do a book signing over here for some cookbook author. They want us to make some of her recipes. It's in September. I told her okay."

"That's good." A short pause while I chew on my lower lip. "I don't know…maybe I should just come home."

"Why?"

"I feel sort of guilty. Like I shouldn't be here having a good time while other people are doing my work."

"Right. You should be here, having a miserable time, while other people are doing your work."

"Ty…"

"Oh, come on. It's not like we're doing you a favor. We work here. You pay us, remember? Not nearly enough, of course…I'm worried about you," she says. "You don't usually feel the need to ask my permission to do things."

"It's just that I feel like I've dumped a lot of responsibility on you. I need to be sure you're okay with that."

"After all this time, don't you think I'd tell you if I wasn't? I hope you're not going to start calling me every week to ask if you can stay another week. Stay as long as you want. The only permission you need to get is your own."

"Okay, thanks for the input."

"Please stop worrying about the Maven. Why don't you worry about famine in Africa. Or the economy. Or space junk falling out of the sky."

I hear another voice in the background, then she says, "Gotta go check in the Marigold delivery. I'll email you that stuff tonight."

Most people on the island use the tennis courts at Buck Park, but there's one behind Smuggler's Cove, a low-key resort on the north shore. Technically you have to be staying in one of the villas to use the pool or court, but the manager is a friend of Alex's and Mac met him a few years ago and played tennis with him. He said we could just come use it if none of the guests were playing.

I find my way over there early on the morning of July 5th, before anyone else can claim the court.

My old wooden racquet needs re-stringing and the grip is slick from long hours in my sweaty hand. The can of balls, however, is brand new, left over from the last time Richard and my mother visited us here.

It takes a while to get into the rhythm, to adjust to the backboard's return and the ball's unpredictable bounces off cracks in the cement. Somewhere just outside my peripheral vision, my father leans against the fence, tan and smiling in his tennis whites. *Watch the ball, Wyn. Don't look where you want it to go; look where it is.*

Mac and I used to hit without keeping score, just long, intense rallies that I found simultaneously energizing and calming. Today it's a mere twenty minutes till I'm out of breath and dripping with sweat, knees creaking in protest, but I feel better. My mind is a complete and lovely blank.

I'm putting the balls back in the can when a voice that is definitely not my father's says,

"You giving up baking to go out for the women's tour?"

I use my racquet to flip out some old balls trapped in the net. "I was just working out some…negativity."

Alex bursts out laughing. "You can take the girl out of L.A.…"

The balls are dead, so I toss them into a rusted trash can and give him an annoyed look, which he ignores.

"I thought you were going home Friday."

"Changed my mind." I blot my face with an old blue bandana.

"You look like a woman who could use a beer."

I look at my watch. It's 11:15 AM.

"You're on vacation, remember?"

"Thanks, but I can't. I've got things to do."

"Like what? Clean out the lint trap? Come on, let's put this stuff in your car and go sit on the *Dancer.*"

Actually a cold beer sounds pretty good.

Private Dancer is a thirty-foot sloop. Which means it has a single mast. That's about all I know or care to know about it. He keeps it at Brandt's Landing, a long, narrow cut between the villas and the airport runway with just enough room for three docks and a launch ramp. It's not a particularly picturesque setting like Rosario or Deer Harbor, but it's a coveted spot for locals because it's a safe shelter against the winter storms that blow down from the North...or so I remember him saying once. People wave from other boats or call out greetings as we walk along the wooden dock, and it makes me feel weird. I duck my head, pretending to look for something in my shoulder bag.

"What are you looking for?" he says.

"Nothing. My sunglasses..."

"They're on your head." He climbs aboard first and then holds out his hand to me. "Tide's in," he says. "Want to take her out for a while?"

"Oh...no, I don't think so. I'm..."

His eyes crinkle just slightly. "That's okay. If I thought you trusted me implicitly, I'd feel like I was losing my edge."

I sit on the deck, my back against the wheel housing. The breeze helps the late morning sun dry the sweat on my face. Snatches of conversation, laughter, the hum of motors as boats leave their slips, chug out into open water. I watch one just beyond the marina; sails opening to catch the wind like huge wings. For a minute, I'm tempted to change my mind about going out.

He disappears below and comes back with two beers. The bottle is icy and I take a long swallow.

"Did you see the fireworks?" he asks.

"No. I didn't feel like fighting the crowd."

He laughs. "Compared to what you're used to, it wasn't much of a crowd. Shit, if I'd known you were here, you could've come to the party at the café."

"That's okay. I had a relaxing evening on my own little deck." And then I hear my voice saying, "I was actually going to call you this afternoon...I was wondering if maybe you still wanted me to make some bread for the café."

He's almost as surprised as I am. "Absolutely. What made you change your mind? Free dinners? My company? I hope it wasn't the 401K and health insurance."

"None of the above. It's just that ever since I taught that class, I've been waking up at 3 AM wanting to work."

"Does that mean you're staying for a while?"

"To be honest, I don't know what the hell it means."

He looks at me and for a few seconds, it feels questioning, like he's walking around, looking at different angles, scouting vulnerable places, pushing buttons, seeing what happens.

I take another swallow of beer. "Do you play tennis?"

"I play Neanderthal tennis. Every ball goes over the fence. No finesse."

"Don't be silly. You're a chef. That's all about finesse."

"I figure you can only do a couple of things really well. I cook and I sail. That's it for me."

"How did you end up getting into food?"

"Well...both my parents worked. My grandmother took care of us, but then she died. Since I was the oldest I was in charge of my brothers.

By the time I was ten or eleven, I was sick of frozen pizza and peanut butter sandwiches."

"So you just walked into the kitchen one day and whipped up a soufflé."

"No. I walked into the kitchen one day and started reading my mother's *Joy of Cooking*. I figured I couldn't do any worse than she did."

"I thought maybe you learned from her."

"Shit, no. She was a bookkeeper. Good with numbers, but no food sense. No imagination. No passion for it. Anyway, I got interested in all the different ways you could cook the same stuff. Like chicken. Pretty soon I was making up my own recipes. By the time I was fourteen I was working after school in a restaurant. After that I never thought about doing anything else."

"Did you go to cooking school?"

"No. I never went anywhere after high school. Just straight to the kitchen. My dad was okay with it." He gives me a funny little grin. "To my mother, it was the same as if I said I wanted to be a hairdresser. Took her a while to get over it."

"And your brothers? Where are they now?"

"Tommy—the middle one—he's in New York. Making shitloads of money as a financial analyst. He was always the brainy one. Frank—the baby—he was a cop in Seattle. Killed in the line of duty, as they say."

"Oh, God, I'm sorry."

"It was a long time ago."

"Some things you never—"

"What about you? What did your parents think about having a baker in the family?"

"My father died when I was 15, so I don't know what he would have thought. But people in my family went to college. They worked in offices. They didn't get their hands dirty. My mother..." I smile, remembering.

"Of course, this was all before bread baking became sort of an artisan thing. Back then it was just manual labor. She couldn't understand why I wanted to do something like that.'"

"And why did you?"

"I did this work/study gig in a bakery in France my junior year in college. It was mainly supposed to pay my room and board with the baker and his family while I studied French. But then, the baking, the bread…it was like…I don't know…like someone turned on the lights. I came home at the end of the semester and went back to UCLA, but nothing was ever the same after that."

"So you started working in a bakery?"

"No. I wasn't brave enough. That came later."

He leans against the gunwale and clears his throat. "Can I ask what…'negativity' you were smashing tennis balls about? Or is it none of my business?"

"Nothing interesting. I was just in a bad mood." I close my eyes against the sun. With only a piece of toast in my stomach the beer's going straight to my head.

"My guess would be Mac. My next guess would be that's why you're here and he's not."

At the sound of his name, all that negativity comes rushing back on stage for an encore.

"You feel like talking about it? Sometimes it helps. Even without all the gory details."

I don't know why he's interested. Or even *if* he's interested. Maybe he feels sorry for me. Maybe he thinks I'll sleep with him. At the moment I really don't know or care and my defenses are so far down they're around my ankles.

"It's hard to talk about."

"That's okay. I just thought if you wanted to—"

"No, I mean, I can't explain it when I don't understand it myself. All I can tell you is things were good for a long time. And then they weren't. Now...he's this other person." I bite the inside of my cheek. "And I don't know what to do about it."

"Sometimes there's nothing you can do."

"Thanks for the encouraging words."

He shrugs. "It's true, though. Isn't it? Something I finally learned between marriage number two and three."

"So what do you do—just give up?"

"The first thing you do is quit blaming yourself."

I smile involuntarily. "CM says I think I can fix everything because I always believe I'm the one who screwed it up."

He turns the amber bottle around, wipes the condensation on his faded T-shirt. "Mac's been a good friend. I always felt like I could count on him, you know? When you sail with somebody, that's important. But nothing you could tell me about him would surprise me."

I look at him over the tops of my sunglasses. "What do you mean?"

"I mean there's some parts of Mac that I bet nobody knows. Not even him."

I draw my knees up and rest my forehead on them. Alex doesn't move. Or speak. Or sigh. None of the little tics people seem to use...small sounds or movements to fill up a break in conversation. He just sits.

Finally he says, "About three years ago...you remember that time he and I sailed up to Vancouver for the boat show? We were just coming around the buoy at the entrance to the harbor. It was a great day, wind was up and we were heeled over pretty good, and he looks over at me and says, 'So, Rafferty, are you fucking my wife?'"

The neck of the bottle slips between my fingers.

I never would have imagined Mac saying anything remotely like that, and yet I don't doubt the truth of it. Not anymore.

"What did you say?"

"I said, 'Not yet.' We both laughed and that was the end of it."

"Why did you tell me that?"

"Maybe I shouldn't have," he says after a minute. "I think it's always sort of bothered me...like your friend says...the way you take responsibility for everything."

"Am I that bad?"

"I should talk." He drinks the last of his beer and lays the empty bottle in a cardboard box. "You're a lot like me, Wyn—a borderline control freak. I think it's a requirement for the kind of work we do. You pretty much have to know what's going on with everything 24/7. That's good in a business, but it doesn't always work in a relationship. Sometimes we can get people in a corner..."

"Okay." I hand him my empty and he lays it next to his. "What do you do when you notice you're getting somebody in a corner?"

"Depends. Sometimes I take a deep breath, step back and look at what I'm doing." He smiles. "Other times I just blunder on through and fuck everything up."

We both laugh then, and it's full of recognition, one of those times when something's understood, and so true that no words are required.

"I should go. Thanks for the beer."

When I get to my feet I feel the movement and see it at the same time. The tide is changing and the *Dancer* is tugging gently at the ropes that hold her in the slip.

Twelve

Alex has arranged a work station for me in the kitchen at Rafferty's. A marble pastry slab tucked into a corner with flour bins, scale, utensils, sheet pans, loaf pans, parchment, misters, a peel—all within easy reach. His mixers—two bench Hobarts—12 and 20 quarts— look like doll furniture compared to our floor models at the bakery.

I unload my bag. A file folder of recipes and notes, one of my own aprons. A cup of my chef to use as a seed for levain. I open the file and scan the recipes I know by heart.

Oblivious to the screen door's click, I only look up when a woman's voice says, "Oh, hi, Wynter."

She's gray-haired, tall and slim, wearing a khaki shirt, jeans and work boots, carrying a colorful market basket. I know her. I just can't think from where.

"Sarah," she reminds me. "From the baking class. What are you doing here? Are you working for Alex?"

"Just for a week or two." I lay down my pen. "What are you doing out so early?"

"Delivering eggs." She lifts a pink Styrofoam egg carton out of the basket, sets it on the worktable and lays back the top to reveal a mosaic of white, ivory, brown, and a delicate shade of blue-green.

I pick up a blue-green one and cradle it in my palm. "These are gorgeous. What chickens lay these?"

"Araucana." She smiles. "Great little birds. They're like dogs. They follow me around, jump up in my lap when I sit down...and their eggs always remind me of that Dr. Seuss book."

The egg is warm and smooth and it rocks gently in my palm. "It feels alive."

"That's because it is." She smiles. "Remember this?

"In the garden there was nothing which did not understand the wonderfulness of what was happening, the immense, tender, terrible, heart-breaking beauty and solemnity of Eggs."

"The Secret Garden! I loved that book. I haven't thought about it in forever."

"I re-read it every spring. It makes me happy."

I replace the egg gently in the carton. "Do you sell at the farmer's market?"

"Oh, yes. I've got enough regulars that I don't really need to, but I love being there." She eases herself up on a stool. "What are you making?"

"Pain de campagne..." I nod at the covered bowl. "That's for tomorrow—and for tonight, some buttermilk dinner rolls. My grand-mother's recipe. Ferris can bake them off this afternoon."

"Mind if I watch for awhile?"

"Feel free. It's not very exciting."

"Not to you, maybe. I was totally fascinated with that class you gave. There were so many things I wanted to know that I didn't get to ask."

"Like what?"

"For one thing, I really like whole grain bread, but I can't get it to rise as well as the white flour stuff. Plus it seems drier. Is there any way to fix that, or is it just the nature of the beast?"

"Yes and yes." I rip off a corner of a paper, scribble VWG on it and hand it to her. "The main reason whole wheat doesn't rise as well as white flour is because the bran and natural oil in the flour make it impossible to get really good gluten development. One thing you can do is use half whole grain and half white bread flour. If you want to use all whole grain flour, you can add some vital wheat gluten…about a half tablespoon for each cup of flour. The dryness can be fixed with a little more water. Also you need to remember that any dough with more than half whole grains is going to absorb water more slowly, so after you mix the dough, let it rest for about thirty minutes before you knead it. That lets the moisture content even out."

"How come none of my damn books say that?"

"I think there's so much to know about bread, no one book can cram it all in."

"Can you stay here and be my personal bread guru?"

"Unfortunately, no. Although it's tempting. But I'll be around another couple of weeks and I'm always ready to talk bread."

She laughs. "You may live to regret saying that."

I look over into her basket. "Have you got any extras you could sell me?"

"No. But it happens that I have a six-pack I can give you." She pulls a cardboard half carton out and sets it on the table. "Here on the island we barter everything."

"That's not a fair exchange. I got product and all you got was a few words. Please let me pay you for the eggs."

"It's not like big bucks, you know."

"I know, but—"

"Okay, here's a better idea. I need a favor, and I think you're just the woman for the job."

"Okay…."

"Would you be available to go with me tomorrow afternoon to get a tattoo?"

For a second I think she's kidding.

She smiles and points to her left shoulder. "I want a chicken. Right here."

I laugh. "Why do you want me to go?"

"I need someone who's not going to faint. Plus I need someone to drive. Just in case."

"Where do we have to go?"

"Friday Harbor. The Mama Said No House of Tattoos. Is that a great name? What do you think?"

"I...are you sure you want to do this?"

She picks up the container that holds my bubbling starter and sniffs appreciatively, eyes closed.

"Hell, yes. I've been wanting to do it for a long time. We can have an early dinner afterwards at that little Mexican joint by the ferry landing—Pequeño. They have very tasty margs."

The tattoo artist is named Jonathan and he's from Calgary. He's tall with a mane of shiny brown hair halfway down his back, nice blue eyes, and a thing that looks like a #3 cake decorating tip sticking out of his face just under his lower lip. I try not to stare at it, but he says,

"You like my labret?"

"It's very...shiny," I say.

"Titanium," he says proudly. He looks from me to Sarah. "What I can I do for you ladies? Ear piercing?"

Sarah leans her elbows on the counter. "I want to get inked."

Jonathan has superb control of his facial muscles.

"D'you have something special in mind?"

"What have you got in the way of chickens?"

"Chickens."

"Yes. I sell eggs over on Orcas. I thought it would be kind of cool."

"It would indeed." He smiles and reaches behind him for a red binder and lays it on the counter. "Not sure what I've got in the way of chickens. Not a lot of demand for that. See if there's anything in here you like. If not, I can design something for you. Of course, an original design costs extra."

Sarah leans on the counter and starts flipping pages. Jonathan raises his eyebrows at me.

I say, "I'm just here to share the experience."

He laughs. "Californian, eh?"

"Check this out, Wyn."

The picture Sarah's looking at is a woman's back, the entire upper right quadrant of which is a fantastical bird with multi-hued feathers draping gracefully around the shoulder blade.

"Not for me, of course," she says. "But isn't it amazing?"

I nod. "Amazing."

"Here's one I like." She flips a few pages backwards. "It's sort of big, though."

Jonathan comes to look over her shoulder. "I can leave off the sunflower and the fence. Just give you the sweet little chicken."

"Could you put ear tufts on her? Then she'll look like an Araucana. And no comb." She takes the pen from him and draws on the photo.

"Oh, like mutton chops," he says. "And lose the Mohawk. Sure, I can do that. Of course, that sort of makes it a custom design."

"Do you like it?" Sarah asks me.

"Sure, but do *you* like it?"

"Well, I know you have to add a couple items," she says to him, "but you also don't have to do the sunflower, which seems like a lot more work than a couple of little ear tufts..."

Jonathan laughs. "That's true, okay...you can have it at standard price. So, when would you like to have it done?"

She hands him the notebook. "Right now."

He shakes his head. "That's not how I work. You need to be certain you want a tattoo; it's not really one hundred per cent removable and the removal process is expensive and painful, so we ask that you take a few days to think it over and then come back—"

"Jonathan, honey..." She's leaning over the counter now, right in his face. "I'm fifty-seven years old. I'm divorced. I'm a cancer survivor. I've had lots of time to think it over—'it' meaning 'everything.' I know what I want. I want this tattoo. I want it today. I'd really like you to do it because I like to shop local, and plus I want to go to Pequeño's with my friend here and have a marg afterwards, but if you don't want to do it, I'll get on the ferry and go to Anacortes or Seattle and get it done."

He looks at her. She looks at him. He opens the three-ring binder and removes the page with the chicken design. They exchange a smile.

"I do admire a woman who knows what she wants," he says. "Would you step into the next room?"

Two hours later Sarah has a bloody chicken on her shoulder and a margarita in her hand. Our server, a tall skinny kid with spiked black hair and several tattoos of his own, is impressed when she tells him she's celebrating getting inked.

"Hey, that's really cool. Who did it?"

"Jonathan at Mama Said No."

He nods approvingly. "He's the best. Be sure and take care of it like he says. My girlfriend's got infected and it was, like, literally a pain in the ass. That's so cool. Hey, your first drink's on me."

He takes our food order and bops off to the kitchen.

"I notice he was careful to specify that he was only buying my *first* drink." Sarah removes a small plastic bottle from her purse, unscrews the top and tips it into her glass. "Want some?" She tilts the bottle in my direction. "Tequila. These things taste great, but they never have enough kick."

"No, thanks. I'm the designated driver. Does it hurt?"

She touches the gauze patch gingerly. "No. Well, yes. But I've been poked and prodded and had so many needles stuck in me in the last few years, this was a piece of cake."

I lean back in my chair and watch her stir the extra booze into her drink. She dunks a blue corn chip into the dish of salsa and crunches it between her teeth with satisfaction. Then she notices me watching her.

"You think I'm crazy," she says.

"Why would I think that?"

"Getting a tattoo." She laughs with her eyes closed. "I'm just so damned happy. I can do anything I want."

"Don't you think that was always true?"

"Of course. But I didn't know it. Too bad I had to go through breast cancer to figure it out."

"I didn't realize you'd had cancer," I say. "Till you said that to Jonathan."

She sighs. "It was four years ago. I went to Houston that summer— which was bad enough in itself. Bill and I stayed with an old friend and I went through surgery and chemo and radiation at M.D. Anderson."

"Are you okay now?"

"Yep. Just a little lopsided. Had a partial. Only one boob and one lymph node 'involved,' as they say. They have all these euphemisms for the various degrees of stark horror. I had a three month chemo 'protocol,' which sounds like some goddamn diplomatic tea party, then radiation. The worst part of the whole deal is, you forget what it's like to feel good. As opposed to excruciatingly awful…or on a good day, not so bad. You forget what life was like before lab results and needles and puking your brains out and losing your hair." She flips her ponytail. "I was a blonde before. Grew back in completely gray."

"Bill is your husband?"

"Was. He pulled a Newt Gingrich. By the time I got to radiation he was history. Oh, yeah," she says noticing my look of dismay. "I was pissed. But you know, I figured out that some people just don't handle that kind of stuff very well."

At that moment our server reappears. "Don't touch these plates, they're super hot. How about another margarita, Ladies?"

Sarah accepts; I order iced tea.

"It's interesting, people's reactions." She pokes at her enchiladas. "Sometimes the most unlikely people step up to the plate. My best friend on the island…Jody…it was like she disappeared off the face of the earth. I think she came over twice. But this woman I barely knew from the farmers' market came by every afternoon to check on me, see if I needed anything. And Alex…he brought me dinner two or three times a week." She takes a forkful of beans and blows on it. "That was almost worth getting sick for. Damn, I love Alex." She grins. "In a strictly platonic way, of course."

I make designs with my fork in the dark mole sauce. "We've known him for years, but I never really knew him that well. He was mostly Mac's friend."

"Damn, these enchiladas are good. How's yours?"

I nod, my mouth full.

She sighs. "Poor Alex."

I raise my eyebrows. "*Poor Alex?*"

"He's looking for Ms. Right," she says. "But he keeps going for the starlets. They're usually much too young for him. What he needs is somebody who's closer to his own age, more experienced. Somebody who knows how to handle him."

"Like you," I say.

"Lord, no. First, I'm too old for him."

"Oh, come on. Five years? Six? That's nothing. My God, you just got a tattoo. You're a cougar, Sarah."

She whoops with laughter. "Thanks for the compliment, but it's more like ten years. Anyway, it wouldn't work," she says flatly. "I like Alex, but there's no spark there. For marriage to take, there has to be that chemistry. I never felt it with anyone but Bill."

I shake my head. "I think chemistry is overrated. It seems to me that a good solid friendship would be a lot better basis for a relationship."

"I can be friends with a lot of men I could never live with. There's got to be something more compelling to make you put up with their bullshit."

Sarah orders dessert—fried ice cream with hot fudge sauce. While I'm sipping my decaf, she suddenly says,

"What would your husband do if you said you were getting a tattoo?"

I set down my cup on the damp cocktail napkin. "At the moment he probably wouldn't care if I had my entire body tattooed with a map of the world."

She looks thoughtful. "That's either really good or really bad."

"The latter. Mac and I are separated."

"I figured. You never say boo about him."

"It's not official. We haven't really talked about what might happen next. He just...moved out."

"Leaving you in limbo."

I shrug. "People keep suggesting that he's depressed, but even if it's true, I can't help him. He refuses to admit there's anything wrong. With him. He can find plenty wrong with me."

"That's pretty common," she says. "I know a thing or two about it. My mom had depression her whole life. It was really hard growing up with it. I'm sorry you have to go through that."

"Me too. Why couldn't he just drive off a cliff or something?"

She scrunches her face. "Oh, God, don't say things like that. It's really bad karma."

"I don't mean it. It's just...I love him." I finish the last of my coffee and set down the empty cup. "And I just want to kick his butt."

Since the ferry to Orcas doesn't leave till 10 PM, Sarah has made arrangements with her friend Jimmy to take us back on his water taxi, a retired salmon fishing boat. I help her ease into her jacket and we sit in the stern for the short, breezy ride. It's almost seven o'clock, still full daylight.

"How much longer will you be up here?" she asks.

"Another couple of weeks. The house is rented out the first two weeks of August, so I'll leave around the end of the month."

"I'll be leaving about then, too. Time for my yearly checkup."

"In Houston?"

"Yes. God-awful time to be in Texas. It's like living in a sauna."

"How long do you have to stay?"

She rummages in her purse and pulls out two peppermints, hands me one. "Depends on what they find. This is my fifth year since the surgery. If I'm clean, I can quit holding my breath."

"Will you let me know how it goes?"

"Sure. Just give me your email. What are you going to do when you get home?"

I bite down on the peppermint and it shatters in my mouth.

"Depends on what I find."

Thirteen

Mac

Whatever doesn't kill you makes you stronger. Sometimes you wish it would just go ahead and kill you. Like now.

Tonight it's more than being tired. It's like all systems shutting down, your whole body folding neatly in on itself like a lady's fan. But you're afraid to sleep. Afraid of the dreams that are really memories.

You dream about getting lost. You dream about falling. About drowning. About trying to call for help and not being able to make a sound. You dream about the floor of your house rotting away under your feet. About a long hall, the sound of someone sobbing behind a closed door. Maybe yourself. You dream about seagulls with human faces. And you dream, mostly, about a tiny silver ball, rolling off the edge of the world.

So you do the pills to work. And pot to relax. And drink to sleep. And It doesn't matter that none of it works anymore. You keep doing it because you don't know how to do anything else.

Then in the morning you crawl through the sparkling, over-chlorinated water of Alan's pool like a child learning to move. You must swim. You cannot *not* swim. Because swimming makes your mind move forward… haltingly but definitely…and it's the only thing that does.

Then you shower. And then you get in the car and turn on the music and drive.

The sunny morning has given way to an afternoon of lowering gray clouds and damp, heavy air, and he finds himself on the 405 heading south. Traffic crawls. He slides a CD into the changer without seeing what it is. Eric Clapton singing an old Tampa Red song, "It Hurts Me Too." He tries to concentrate on the music and forget the fact that he's probably number 4,892 in a line of 4,896 cars. It'll open up once they get past the South Bay Curve, start moving again. He has some vague idea of having dinner at a restaurant in Seal Beach where he and Wyn stopped years ago on their way home from San Diego, a funky kind of road house place with a biplane for a sign. The Glide 'er Inn. They had sand dabs. And that old fashioned salad...a wedge of iceberg lettuce with blue cheese dressing and crumbled bacon.

Funny he should remember that when he can't recall what he had for dinner last night—or even *if* he had dinner last night.

He inches around a curve and up ahead is the silent light show—police cruisers, emergency medical, a couple of fire trucks. He weaves slowly across the lanes, exits at Century and gets back on the freeway, heading north.

Suddenly he's driving home in the early dusk. To what used to be his home. His house...their house...looks deserted, windows shut, blinds drawn, dark except for the fixture on the front porch, which is on a timer. He parks at the curb. He opens the door with his key, stepping over the pile of mail on the hall floor.

Inside it's quiet, stale smelling. The security system begins to beep. He goes into the kitchen and stares at the control panel, realizing he's forgotten the code. Sixty seconds and the alarm starts screeching. Then the phone rings.

"This is ETA Protection Services calling. We just had an alarm come through from this address. Can I ask your name, please?"

Fortunately he does remember that. Also that the password is *Brownie*.

Memories inhabit the walls. The time when they were painting the living room after they first moved in and he stepped off the ladder into a bucket of paint. She fell on the drop cloth-covered couch, laughing till tears ran down her face. The time they came back from a ski trip to Mammoth and she said she was too tired to walk up the stairs. She lay down in front of the fireplace and refused to budge. He brought the comforter and pillows off their bed and they slept in their clothes, curled up together on the living room floor. The next morning, she made hot chocolate.

In the dining room, he puts his hand to the light switch, and the motion trips a different kind of switch. His fortieth birthday.

Always before they would go out to dinner for his birthday or cook something at home. He didn't mind being the sous-chef, doing all the chopping and cleaning up as they worked, while she moved like a dervish through the kitchen, throwing herbs into things, stirring, tasting, poking the chicken to see how it felt, thwacking the bread crust. It was soothing, distracting. Then when they were seated in the dining room, candles lit, rheostat turned down so low he could hardly see the food, she would give him his presents. She would open the champagne herself and pour his first, then hers and she'd raise her glass and wish him Happy Birthday. Completely without irony, he thought. Sometimes he would study her and wonder what the hell she was thinking.

As if happy and birthday belonged in the same sentence. As if he didn't dread the approach of that week all year, looming in mid November when the days were short and dark. The accident, then his birthday. Inextricably linked. He turned off for those days. Detached. Unplugged. Dinner was something to be gotten through, and his reward for enduring was later. After the dishes were done and the kitchen cleaned to her satisfaction, they'd take the rest of the cham-

pagne upstairs and drink it in bed and read or watch a movie until he could no longer stand not touching her.

Then she would press against him and wind her legs through his and he could forget everything except the feel of her skin, and the scent of bread in her hair and the sound of her breath in his ear.

But that year, his fortieth, there was a party. The house was dark when he came in and he thought she might still be at the bakery. They hadn't made any definite plans for the evening and he was hoping to keep it simple. Maybe go to the Asian noodle place in the village.

When he pushed through the swinging door to the dining room, fumbling for the switch, lights flashed in his eyes and people started shouting. He froze. He looked around the room. There was her mother and Richard. CM and some guy he didn't know. Tyler. Alan and Sylvia. Jean and Wyatt, their neighbors…he just stared. Suddenly Wyn was beside him, laughing, putting her arms around his waist.

"Happy birthday, old dude."

He tried very hard to produce an appropriate response.

"Wow," he said.

It was stupid, but he couldn't think of anything else. And he did not hug her back.

He stumbled through the evening in a slow, cold burn of fury. The edges of his vision seemed bordered with a white glare. He tried to be polite, to talk to everyone, laugh at the gag gifts, the cane, the vitamin organizer, the support socks. He thought he was doing okay until he looked up at one point into Sylvia's gaze.

There was something about Sylvia. Maybe the melancholy that seemed as natural to her as the thick, iron gray hair, the expression that haunted her face, even when she smiled. It could be a physical thing, the way her dark, almond shaped eyes turned down slightly at the outer corners, but he preferred to believe that it was wisdom, born of intelligence and honed by years of hearing people's worst impulses, their most hopeless tragedies.

They'd never actually exchanged much more than casual conversation, but he had the feeling that nothing would offend or even surprise her. That she could somehow absorb the shock waves, neutralize the poison the way a tree takes in carbon dioxide and gives back oxygen.

She would understand that he felt utterly betrayed. How could Wyn have done this to him? He didn't want a party. All he wanted was to just get to the other side, to get past this day. In all fairness, he never actually said that to her, but why did he have to? Why didn't she know? How could she possibly not know?

The cake, shaped like a book. She'd had Tyler or Rafael or somebody decorate it to look like his collection of short stories that had come out that spring and promptly tanked. Not only was it a reminder of the day, it was a symbol of all those boxes of books in the guest room closet. The ones he'd gotten from the publisher when they remaindered the book. The cake was his favorite—caramel with burnt sugar frosting, but it tasted like sawdust.

He'd never been that angry at her before. The intensity of it terrified him. If he loosened his grip, let the slightest edge of it show, it would surely overwhelm him, spew out of him like venom. He would do and say unspeakable things. And so he said nothing.

When she came upstairs later, carrying the remains of the champagne and two glasses, he pretended to be asleep and in the morning she poured out the flat and lifeless wine.

He turns off the light and pulls the door to the kitchen closed behind him, waiting. Leaning against it, shaking slightly, arms crossed over his chest.

He's made too many mistakes. Mistakes so huge that they dwarf everything else he does. So wide, so deep, so wrong, that everything that follows becomes wrong. Like a song that starts off in the wrong key.

He leaves abruptly, out through the garage where her old beast of a station wagon crouches. He doesn't reset the security system or lock the front door. He drives away too fast. West on Sunset, then north on PCH. Dark waves melt soundlessly against the beach. East on Topanga Canyon. Headlights burrow into the blackness and he rolls down the window to smell the night, the eucalyptus, the Pacific. He inhales deeply, pushing back against the seat. He loves this road, loves the rhythmic winding back and forth. Loves the darkness. The speed. The wind.

Without another thought, his left hand gropes towards the instrument panel and switches off the headlights.

Fourteen

It's four-thirty and about ninety-five in the shade. The air looks like the brown scum that floats on top of the rinse water at the carwash. SuperShuttle deposits me and my bag in front of the house and disappears while I'm digging for the key.

Eventually I find it in the bottom of my bag, and then stand there for a minute, bracing myself for whatever's waiting inside. Or not. No Brown Dog. Just all her food and bedding and toys. No husband. Just a marriage unraveling faster than an old sweater.

When I fit my key in the lock, it turns easily. Too easily. The door isn't locked.

I turn the knob and push. Nothing happens. I push harder and it gives just a little—not like the frame is swollen or the mechanism is jammed, but more like someone is blocking it from the other side. I put my back against it, pushing with my legs, and it gives way, sending me ass over teakettle into the front hall. I'm sitting in the middle of a huge pile of mail that's accumulated under the door slot. It looks like Mac hasn't been here since the day I left.

I push it all to one side, take my suitcase upstairs. The air is stale and breathtakingly overheated. I go room to room, opening windows. Dust covers everything like a fine snow. Obviously Carmen hasn't come to clean recently. In the kitchen, ants are having a fiesta on a dirty spoon in the sink. The plants are brown and crispy. The screen that I asked him to fix has been removed and left leaning against the fence. The pool is filthy, the water cloudy. The garden is choked with weeds.

Because it's summer and the house has been closed up for weeks, those little pantry moths are everywhere. For some reason this enrages me more than all the rest of it. I begin to take great satisfaction, not just in swatting them, but in smearing the brown dust of their wings on the white walls.

Two hours later, I've changed into shorts and a T-shirt, rinsed the ant party down the drain, put a load of clothes in the washer, sorted out all the mail, called the pool service, the gardener, and Carmen.

"Mrs. Wyn. I am happy to hear you," she says.

"Carmen, when was the last time you cleaned?"

"In June. Mr., he does not leave money, so my husband say I cannot go no more."

"I'm really sorry. Can you come next week? Any day? I'll pay you what we owe you plus a month in advance." She agrees to come on Tuesday.

The refrigerator is empty except for a container of yogurt with a green crust growing on it. I throw it out, hang a charcoal deodorant packet inside and make a grocery list. When I go out to the garage, I realize there is no way in hell that my Volvo is going to start after sitting idle for almost two months. A turn of the key produces only a hollow ticking noise. I decide to deal with that in the morning. I'm not hungry anyway.

I'm even less hungry when I start opening the mail and realize that Mac hasn't paid any bills since I left. We've got overdue notices from everyone, threats that our phone service, water and power will soon be history, warnings from American Express that a good credit rating is a terrible thing to lose, and a polite letter from the mortgage company offering free credit counseling.

I think about my mom and Richard, rolling through the Canadian Rockies on a train bound for Nova Scotia, and I wish I could talk to them. For comfort's sake more than anything else. In another way, though, I'm sort of glad they're not here. My mother would worry needlessly and Richard would be full of good advice.

He's a great guy, Richard. He treats my mother like a queen, and he's always been more than generous to me, but in some hidden corner of my heart, there's still a pissed off girl who wants her real father, not this reasonable facsimile.

Just before bed I call CM and I'm not surprised when her machine picks up. "Hi. This is the right number but you called at the wrong time. Leave a message and I'll get back to you." I smile. She's had the same message for twenty years.

"It's me. Well, I'm home and I wish I weren't. I can't remember if you're in town or out, so call me when you can."

Friday morning I call Triple A and in twenty minutes there's a guy in the garage putting a new battery in my car. I roll down to the closest station for gas, air in the tires and a run through the wash. I get a double espresso, stock up on groceries and head back to the house. When I get there, the pool service is hard at work.

"Hi, Mrs. McLeod. Pool's in pretty bad shape. We'll have to shock it, so don't try to use it till Sunday. You need some chemicals?"

"Wyn! Hi!" My next door neighbor, Beth Halloran, peers over the fence. She has to be standing on a step ladder. "Gosh, where have you been? I've seen Mac a few times…"

I grit my teeth and smile. "Hi, Beth. I've been up on the island." I hurry into the house before she can ask any more questions.

While I'm putting the groceries away the gardener comes.

"Sorry things got so out of shape, Mrs. McLeod. Your husband said you wouldn't be needing us to do anything but the front lawn this summer. I thought you was upset. Maybe we done something wrong?"

"No, Toby, not at all. We've been gone for awhile, so you can start coming again."

"Uh, yes ma'm....." He looks uncomfortable. "I was wondering if we could get something on the account." He fishes in his pocket for an invoice covered with dirty fingerprints.

"Of course. I'll write you a check right now.."

"Uh, Mrs. McLeod. Would it be possible for you to pay us cash?"

"Well, it would, except I don't have the cash right now. If you want to stop by tomorrow…"

His face is now very red and he can hardly look at me. "Mr. Monroe, he says we can't do the work unless I get cash up front."

"Why not?"

He shifts his weight from one foot to the other. "Well, the last two checks Mr. McLeod give me, they got returned by the bank."

"Oh."

"I'm real sorry, ma'm.."

"Toby, it's not your fault. Look, if you want to go ahead and get started, I'll go to the bank now and get some cash and I'll be right back."

He escapes to the garden, plainly relieved, and I run for my car. At the ATM, I insert my card and punch in five hundred dollars. A cheery sign blinks on the screen to say our balance is not sufficient. At this time we only have two hundred and seventy one dollars plus change in our joint checking account. Where the hell is our money?

People are lined up behind me waiting to use the teller, so I get a hundred dollars and transfer a thousand from savings and go back to my car. I sit there sweating in the heat, too stunned to put down the windows. Where is our money?

Back at the house I give Toby the hundred dollars, swearing on my oma's grave to pay him the rest in cash next Friday. Then I go to my business bank and open a checking account for myself with money from the bakery's account.

At home I sit down in the kitchen with a large wine spritzer and an even larger pile of bills. I call all the creditors and assure them the checks are in the mail, then I write checks from our brokerage account to cover everything. It's scary—the thought of what might have happened if we hadn't had the island house rented for the next two weeks. What if I hadn't come home yesterday?

I skim the items on the credit card bills. Nothing totally outrageous. Nothing that would explain the sudden drop in our balance. I turn on my laptop and sign into our on-line checking, sucking on an ice cube and scrolling down through the transactions, suddenly I see it and I nearly swallow the ice cube. On July 12th a withdrawal of seven thousand dollars was made from the account. For a few minutes I sit, reading that line over and over, trying to imagine what he'd do with seven thousand dollars in cash.

It's a mistake. A bank error. Or else somebody's hacked our account.

I sit back in the chair, take a long drink, and let my eyes go out of focus on the soothing blue of the bank website.

Saturday morning at 9:30 the bakery is packed and noisy, but the line is moving well and people seem happy. Under the voices and laughter I can just hear BB King. Tyler spots me before I can sneak into my office.

"Wyn!" She comes running out from behind the counter to give me a brief hug.

After we've reviewed the financials for the last two months and I've gone around and talked to everyone, she suggests lunch at The Shire in Topanga Canyon, an old unreconstructed hippie hangout where all the menu items have names from *The Lord of the Rings*.

We sit on the deck in the shade of huge Eucalyptus trees and order fat sandwiches with sprouts on their nine-grain Middle Earth rolls.

"The Maven looks great," I say. "I notice you've got a \new coffeecake."

She grins. "It's like that one Diane used to make at Queen Street. Remember?"

I nod absently, sipping my iced hibiscus tea. "The cardamom. Yeah, that was the best. How's it selling?"

"We only make it on weekends, but it's been selling out. I always loved how that cake smelled when it was baking. "Hey, remember that little old broad who always came in asking for doughnuts?"

I smile. "How could I forget Mrs. Gunnerson?"

The server sets down our orders with a flourish. "One Galadriel, one Frodo—my tuna salad, her grilled veggie sandwich with goat cheese.

Her eyes follow him as he walks away. "Nice buns."

"Sandwich looks good, too."

She laughs and I pour some roasted garlic vinaigrette on the greens piled on my plate. We eat quietly for a few minutes, enjoying the aromatic breeze. Then she sets down her sandwich and fiddles with the carrot curl garnish on the plate.

"How are you?" she says. "Really."

I stir my iced tea with the brown bio-degradable straw. "Pretty good."

"What's that mean?"

"It means better than two months ago, with room for improvement."

"What do you do all day up there?"

"I walk a lot. Ride my bike. Bake. I went to a chamber music recital. And I've actually been making bread for a café in Eastsound."

"So you're not, like, sitting around listening to sad music and crying or anything."

"I think I'm beyond that."

"Okay. Just checking. You think you'll go back for a while?"

"I don't know yet."

She picks up the second half of her sandwich, takes one bite, and puts it down again. "Have you talked to Mac?"

I decide not to tell her about my five unreturned voicemails. "I'm working up to it—but let's talk soap opera later. First of all, I want to say thanks for everything you've done…"

She looks embarrassed. "It's just my job—"

"It's a lot more than that—"

"Wyn, I need to talk to you."

"I'm pulling rank here, kid. Me first, then you can say whatever you want. I'm sure the last two months haven't been easy; it's a stressful job, and you've done it superbly and never complained or—"

"I've been happy. Don't you know that?" Her voice quivers.

I impale a piece of lettuce and twirl it around with the fork. "What I'm trying to say is, I appreciate you so much, and I don't want you to think I'm just going to pat you on the head and say, Good job, thanks. I've been debating for a while about what I could do that would be meaningful for both of us, and here's what I've come up with…I want to make you my partner. I'm going to call my lawyer on Monday and—"

It starts quietly, just a trickle or two, but then the flood gates open. For a minute I sit there like a dim bulb, telling myself she's crying because she's so happy, but some part of me knows it's not true.

"Ty…" I say it gently but loud enough so she can hear me over the Donovan soundtrack. "What's wrong?"

She just shakes her head and cries.

"Now you're scaring me. Tell me what it is. I'm sure it's nothing we can't work out."

"I wanted to tell you before you left…but I was worried because of Mac…and everything…" She stops and holds the napkin up over her face. I can hear her forcing herself to breathe slowly. She lowers the napkin. "And stuff kept happening and we kept getting interrupted. Wyn, I'm leaving. I didn't want to talk about it today, but…" She takes a deep gulp of air. "I applied to pastry school. And I'm accepted. And my loan was approved."

"Oh…" Now it's my turn. Tears pool in my eyes and start splashing on the table.

Then she starts crying again. "I'm sorry. I'm…just sorry." Her voice squeaks on the last word, making us both laugh. Naturally the server chooses this moment to see if we've saved room for Bilbo Baggins' chocolate cake.

"Excuse me," he says, "I'll come back."

"It's okay," I tell him between blowing my nose and drying my eyes. I hand him my plate. "Bring us one piece and two forks." I turn back to her. "So tell me. Where are you going?"

"Greystone."

I can't prevent a small gasp. "*Greystone*? Oh, my God, Ty. That's incredible. Really. I'm so proud of you."

She sniffles and tries to smile. "Better save it till we see if I wash out."

On some level I must have known this was coming, because while I'm feeling like I've been carpet bombed, I can't honestly say I'm shocked. She's an artist, after all. She should be creating beautiful pastries, not mucking around with production sheets and inventory print-outs.

But where is it written that everything must happen at once? Why hasn't the concept of queuing up been tried? If I were God I would have it set up like a deli. Things would not be allowed to just happen. They'd have to take a number. You'd stand behind the counter and call out the numbers and then take the shit and deal with it. It would still be the same shit, but you could take care of your dog dying and your husband's meltdown before you had to handle your manager bailing to the CIA.

"I've been working some with Raphael and he says I've got the touch."

"Well, he should know."

The server sets down a slab of chocolate cake the size of a brick, topped with a thick layer of fudgy ganâche and an avalanche of whipped cream.

"The good news is that I don't go till January."

I put my hands together. "That is definitely the good news."

"So I want you to go back up to Orcas—"

I shake my head. "I can't do that."

"Yes, you can." She cocks her head slightly so she's looking up into my eyes. "This is my going away present to you. I'm going to take care of the Maven till January. Then I still have two weeks to get up to Napa—"

"That's not enough time to do all the things you need to do. You're going to have to get packed, find a place to live—"

"Got one," she says around a mouthful of cake. "I didn't want to live in the dorm with a bunch of kids, so they matched me up with a lady who rents out rooms to students." She gives me a stern look that I swear she's copied from CM. "I'm not going to argue about this. I'm just telling you. I'm staying till January and I don't want you hanging around breathing down my neck."

I sigh. "Alright. But only on one condition. I'm paying for your first semester."

"Wyn, no. You can't. It's over ten thousand dollars."

"I can and I will. Or I won't leave you in charge till January."

"I'll pay you back."

"No you won't. We'll consider it a well-deserved bonus."

"Thanks, Wyn. So much." She cries some more. Another woman would probably say I love you. Tyler and I have never said that to each other. We've never had to.

I ask, "Who knows about this?"

"No one," she says, wiping her eyes. "I didn't even tell Raphael."

I sit back in my chair and study her. "You're pretty amazing, you know. And you're going to be a kick-ass pastry chef."

Sunday morning traffic is light, and just after nine A.M. I pull up in front of Alan's house. At first I hardly notice the silver Mercedes parked in front of the walkway—the Hills of Beverly are full of them—but when I get out I see the vanity plate LIV 4 PR. I hesitate. Am I up to a confrontation? Finally I decide that I didn't drive all the way over here just to slink away without seeing him. Let the chips fall.

The door opens almost before I knock, and it takes me a few minutes to understand that the man in wrinkly jeans, pulling a T-shirt over his head is Mac. He's sporting the George Hamilton tan, shaggy, sunbleached hair, a cut on his forehead and a scrape along his right jaw.

"You're back." He gives me a stiff smile. "I thought you were going to stay another week."

"I did. Several other weeks, actually."

I walk past him. The apartment looks like one of the sets for *Animal House*.

175

Empty bottles and full ashtrays. Plastic cups with the last undrink-able swallows of something. A basket with a few soggy tortilla chips sits next to a dish of congealed salsa with a cigar butt leaning on the rim like a beached walrus. There's a reek of smoke and alcohol that I suspect is coming from him as well as the surroundings.

"I love what you've done with the place."

"So, you just dropped by to critique my housekeeping skills?" He closes the door. "I had some people over last night. *December Light* made the *LA Times* bestseller list."

"Congratulations. What happened to your face?"

"I fell on the stairs. And just in case you were wondering, I wasn't drunk."

I hang my purse on the back of a chair. "We need to talk."

"This isn't a good time," he says. "You should've called first."

"I left you five voicemails that I was home and I asked you to call or come by the house."

He looks surprised. "I didn't get them. And I couldn't come anyway. I don't have a car."

"Where's the Death Star?"

"In the shop."

"Well, I'm sorry if my visit is inconvenient for you, but this is important."

I sit down and lay the manila envelope full of his mail on the table. "I guess you haven't been by the house lately."

He peers into it, then dumps it out on the table and starts sliding enve-lopes around into different piles. I have this sudden, weird flash forward of him as an old man, frail and querulous, pushing things aimlessly around on a hospital tray.

Finally he looks up. "So what do we need to talk about?"

"Money."

He picks up a pack of Marlboro Golds, taps one out and lights it. In the twelve years I've known him I've never seen him smoke anything. He takes a long drag and blows the smoke straight up.

"What money?"

"Let's start with the seven thousand dollars you withdrew from our checking account on July 12th."

"I have expenses, you know."

"Yes, I know. And they include a mortgage."

"I made some investments."

"In what? Cocaine futures?"

"It's really none of your business."

Frustration burns the back of my throat like cheap wine. "It is my business. Part of that money is mine. And I don't intend to help finance your self-destruction."

"Not unless you can be in charge of it."

At that moment there's a metallic screech from behind the closed door that I assume leads to the bedroom, then silence. That's when I realize that the steady hum I've been hearing since I walked in is the shower.

It's pathetic, the way I look automatically at him for some kind of explanation.

He says, "Exactly what is it you want from me?"

"Some answers that make sense. Why are you acting like this? And what did you do with our money?"

"You're the detective. You should probably go back to the house and see what you can find in my desk."

Some other approach is obviously called for here. Perhaps a bit less confrontational. I rest my arms on the table and sit forward. "Why can't you talk to me? Why won't you let me help you?"

He takes another drag off the cigarette and flicks ashes carelessly at an already full ashtray. "I don't need your help. And by the way, that's your biggest problem...thinking you can fix everything—"

"I know I can't fix it. But that doesn't mean I can't help. Can't you just tell me?"

He sits, seemingly mesmerized by the thin trail of smoke rising from the glowing tip of the cigarette. Finally he says, "You wanted to know about the money..."

"Yes."

"I spent it."

"On what?"

"I rented a limo and went up to Big Sur. Stayed a few days at the Post Ranch Inn."

For a few seconds I can't breathe. "The Post Ranch Inn...costs... over a thousand dollars a night."

"One thousand, four hundred and fourteen, to be exact. Plus tax. And then the room service and...but you probably don't want the details."

I'm so close to laughing. That hysterical kind of laughter I've always associated with hanging upside down on the roller coaster at Magic Mountain.

"Relax, I'll pay you back."

I start to say that it's not the money; but actually, it is. It isn't just money; it's tangible evidence of our combined hard work, of the life we made together. The idea that he could throw it away is shocking and infuriating.

"Mac..." I look straight at him. "I don't know what to do."

"I hope you're not expecting any helpful hints from me."

By now I'm beginning to get that nothing I say will be right or make sense to him because this is not Mac, my husband. This is somebody I don't know and don't really want to know. This is somebody scary.

It's probably a mistake, but I still have to ask. "Have you thought about seeing a doctor?"

"For what?"

"Well, for...because something's obviously wrong—" I stop just short of *with you*. "It could be physical—"

His laugh is sardonic and ugly. "You're the one who thinks you know everything, and you can control everything. I believe it's called delusional disorder, and you seem to be exhibiting several of the symptoms. So maybe you're the one who should see a doctor."

The cigarette hisses out in a half empty glass.

"I don't understand."

"It's not necessary that you do." He stands up and pushes the chair back against the table. "Not that it hasn't been great seeing you, but I've got things to do this morning."

Three blocks away, I have to pull over.

It's like being drunk. I'm so disconnected from myself I don't realize my hands are shaking till I look at them. What just happened back there? Who is this person calling himself Mac McLeod? In a sort of stupor I notice drops of water making dark splats on my cargo pants but it takes a few more seconds to realize they're coming from my eyes.

I sit there for twenty minutes, crying in the dappled shade of a jacaranda tree, until one of Beverly Hills' finest comes over to check me out. He puts his right hand on the roof of the car and bends down to the open window.

"Everything okay, Miss?"

I nod, trying to get myself together, to get control of my breathing.

He watches me for a minute, probably checking for signs of imminent psychosis.

"I can drive you to urgent care and my partner can follow us in your car."

"No, that's okay. But thank-you," I croak.

"Or I'd be happy to take you home." His voice is soothing. He's probably the one they get to talk people down from the ledge.

Finally I look up at him through my swollen eyes. He's younger than me, but not a kid. I force my mouth into a tight smile.

"Thanks, but I'll be fine in a minute. It's just a…really…bad day."

"Yes, I can see that." He nods gravely. "Can you sit right here for just a moment, please?"

I watch him turn and walk back to his cruiser. What the hell? Is he going to run my plates?

When he comes back, he hands me a bottle of water. "You need to be careful not to get dehydrated."

In the face of everything, I want to laugh. How very California. How Beverly Hills. But in a way, how sweet.

He taps gently on the roof. "I hope things get better for you, Miss."

"Thank you," I say.

They can hardly get any worse.

Monday is a total loss, wiped from the calendar. If I were accused of a crime and had to come up with an alibi for Monday, I'd be headed to jail. The phone rings twice but I don't answer and I don't pick up voice mail. I only get out of bed to pee and, much later, to eat a popsicle for dinner.

Tuesday morning I still feel like crap, but I make myself get out of bed, shower and dress. After a piece of toast, I wander through the house gathering up Brownie's bedding and grooming stuff and food. There's a lot of it. And of course the toys.

When we first brought her home I bought her every new dog toy that looked like fun to me. She didn't appear to know what to do with them. She didn't chew, she didn't fetch, and all my offerings ended up languishing in the corners of the living room or under the bed. It made me sad to think she could have grown up without learning how to play. Brownie waited patiently for me to understand that I couldn't compensate for her deprived puppyhood and it was okay.

She lived in the present.

I pack everything into plastic lawn bags and drive to the shelter in Santa Monica where I got her. The pigtailed young woman behind the desk accepts it graciously.

"You have a lot of nice stuff here," she shouts over the rising cacophony of barking, squealing, howling and yipping coming from the kennels. "Wouldn't you like to see who else might need a forever home?"

I guess no one's told her yet. Nothing's forever.

"I can't," I say. "Not today."

"Okay, then. When you're ready." Pause. "Would you like to make a small donation this morning?"

I think that's exactly what I've just done, but it seems ungenerous to say so. Instead I write a big fat check to assuage my guilt and make a quick escape. It occurs to me that this could be their fund-raising strategy. *Give us some money and we won't make you look at them.*

I peel out of the shelter's parking lot in a spray of gravel and get back on the coast highway, heading north. I must be feeling better because I'm finally hungry.

It's a gorgeous day, sunny with a brisk off-shore breeze, one of those days when you understand and forgive those last eight million people for moving here. It's only 10:45, but cars are already turning into Gladstone's 4 Fish, and half the population of the L.A. basin is moving relentlessly west towards the beach like so many cooler-toting lemmings.

About a mile past Pepperdine University, I turn into Malibu Seafood and spot CM sitting in her yellow Miata, top down, her face turned up to the sun. We leap out of our cars and run to hug each other.

We order steamed mussels to split and ahi tuna burgers at the counter and go out to wait for our food at one of the weathered picnic tables on the deck. From her huge tote bag she produces a split of Gloria Ferrer champagne, chilled and sweating, and pops the cork to the amused smiles of our fellow diners.

"You ladies must be celebrating," says a guy at the table next to us.

CM gives him her man-killer smile. "Yeah, my friend here just made parole. Maybe you read about it in the paper…?"

He smiles back, somewhat uncertainly, and returns to his clam chowder.

By the time they call our order number, I'm ravenous. We dunk our bread into the buttery broth and touch our plastic cups together.

"A day without champagne is like a day without—"

"Sex," she finishes my toast. "And God know there's been too many of those lately."

We eat and talk, dawdling over the champagne, enjoying the sun. She brings me up to date on work—a series of shows back east in November, love life—nonexistent, family—Shayne, her niece, is getting married.

"About time, don't you think? The kid starts kindergarten next year." She rolls her eyes. "Can you imagine doing that when we were in our twenties?"

I shrug. "I guess some people did it."

"Yeah. We called them trailer trash."

"No, we called them hippies. In fact, I think I missed my calling. Maybe I'd have been happier in one of those enclaves over in Topanga Canyon, three or four kids, some chickens. Swimming nude in the hot springs. Smoking dope with my biker boyfriend. Baking nine-grain bread for the whole encampment."

"Sounds ideal. Hold that thought for retirement. Meanwhile, what's the status with Mac?"

I set down my glass abruptly.

"You've seen him?"

I nod. "Sunday. And I wish I hadn't. He looks awful. But he acts like such a shit it's really hard to work up any sympathy for him. He cleaned out our checking account for a long weekend at Big Sur, which of course meant there was no money to pay the bills and the checks he did write were bouncing all over town, so I had to deal with that. When I went over to his bachelor pad to talk to him about it, there was—someone there. In the shower."

"The publicist?"

"Probably. At this point, who cares. And you wouldn't believe the apartment. It looked like something out of Hieronymus Bosch." I take a long drink of ice water. "I don't understand how someone could change that much. He hates me—"

"Wyn, you've got to know by now this is not about you."

"Well, what is it about? I have no clue."

She crumples up her napkin and tosses it on her empty plate. "He's depressed, honey. Like Boone. Remember?"

"That was different. Boone was…sick. Mentally."

"Well…depression is a mental illness."

The last bit of champagne in the bottom of my cup has gone warm and flat. I stir a French fry around in the little plastic cup of ketchup till it disintegrates.

She presses on. "I think you're right about him being angry. But it's not at you. I think he's angry at everything. Especially himself."

We dump our trash and she follows me down to the cars. "I'll call you tomorrow," she says, and hugs me. "We've got some serious shopping and lunching to do. And movies—I haven't seen a decent movie in months."

I climb in my Volvo and roll down the window.

She leans on the door frame and squeezes my arm. "Are you going to be okay?"

I squint up at her, shading my eyes.

"The problem is, I have trouble with the idea of Mac having a mental illness. I guess on some level I prefer to think of him as a bastard. I know how to deal with bastards."

It feels like fall—even though it's only August, even though in Southern California, the hottest, nastiest weather often shows up after Labor Day. There's an oblique quality in the light, a thickening of the air, a slowing of motion. The scorched brown hills sit waiting for the relief of the first winter rains.

I'm floating on an air mattress in the pool, dangling my arms and legs in the cool water. My flight is at 10:30 tomorrow morning. I need to get the house ready and wash some clothes and pack my suitcase. In spite of Tyler's insistence that everything will be fine at the Bread Maven, in spite of the fact that Mac apparently wants nothing to do with me, I'm uneasy about leaving.

The cordless phone on the table rings and I pull myself up the metal ladder to answer it.

"Wynter? Alan. Lear. How are you?"

"Hi, Alan. I'm okay. If you're looking for Mac, he's not here."

"I was looking for you. I was hoping to speak with you for a minute. About Mac."

"Yes?"

"Wynter, I want you to know I'm as sorry as I can be about...this situation. It's just, I saw you going up the stairs last Sunday and I thought to myself, well, maybe they're getting together. Maybe this is the initial, you know, rapproachment to...but then I haven't seen you again and I just wondered...that is, I hoped..."

"I was just there to talk to him about some financial stuff and he couldn't come here because his car was in the shop—"

"HA!" It's more an expletive than a laugh. "That's rich. His car is in the shop. Is that what he told you? His car is in the junkyard. His car is totaled. His car is a metal pancake. It's only by the grace of God he wasn't impaled on the steering column."

My heart stops. "He had an accident?"

"I'm sorry, Wynter, I thought—I got a call. Two in the morning. Right after I got back from New York. The highway patrol. Mac rolled the Beemer somewhere over in Topanga Canyon. I had to go to the emergency room at North County. My God, I'm thinking all the way over there, my God. What if he's dead? Or, God forbid, a vegetable? He wasn't even wearing his goddamn seatbelt—excuse me, Wynter. And he walks away with a couple scratches and a stiff neck."

"Was he drinking?"

"No, thank God. For a change. He's drinking way too much. It's just a miracle he wasn't—they tested him for every controlled substance known to man. He says he was tired. That he dozed off...I don't know..."

The breeze cools my wet body and goosebumps break out on my arms. With the total recall of guilt, I hear myself blithely saying to Sarah, *Why can't he just drive off a cliff?* Never imagining that's exactly what he was doing.

"I'm at my wit's end with him, Wynter. I don't want to lose Mac as a client. He's got a lot of talent, but he's gotten so—careless or distracted or something. He seems to not care about deadlines or meetings or— he's been saying some very strange things. I think he needs help. I was thinking maybe you could—"

I say, "Alan, I appreciate your trying to help, but there's really nothing I can do. I'm going back to Orcas tomorrow. Give Sylvia my love."

I wrap a towel around my shoulders and sit down at the table, shaking now, still holding the phone. For the longest time I think about calling him. I want to scream at him. I want to tell him I'm furious and hurt that he won't talk to me, that I'm worried sick about him...*Why did you, how did you drive off the road?* I want to tell him I love him, I want to help him.

I rub my thumb aimlessly over the number keys. Sure, I could call him and say all those things. But I just did that last week.

It didn't turn out well.

Fifteen

Mac

The party is at some new club off La Brea and the evening has begun with a disagreement about valet parking. In the end he drops her off and drives around for half an hour trying to find a parking place. By the time he walks back to the club she's gone inside, presumably to find her client du jour, a singer who's just released her first CD.

Outside, the place swarms with guys who look like body builders, dressed in black T-shirts and black jeans, milling around with clipboards and walkie-talkies, checking imaginary names off blank pieces of paper. There are radio and TV crews, glaring lights, stoned musicians, a guy in a Hawaiian shirt and blue fake fur top hat. There are people in khakis and polo shirts, evening clothes, sport coats, jeans and Doc Martens, sundresses and spike heels, shorts and flipflops. They're all kissing, hugging, talking on cell phones, sometimes all three at once.

No one says anything to him as he pushes past the black shirts, through the doorway, which resembles the entrance to a cave.

The interior looks like something out of Arabian Nights—a series of cavernous rooms that seem to go on for miles, huge overstuffed furniture, lots of cushions and draperies. Somewhere an invisible band is playing loudly—unrecognizable noise, so heavy on base that his bones vibrate.

The lamps are small and their light limited, leaving plenty of dark corners for sex or drugs or naps.

He lifts a drink off a passing tray and takes sip. Ugh. Sweet, slightly warm. He leaves it in a corner and locates the bar, but before he reaches it, Liv is clutching his arm.

She kisses his cheek and smiles warmly, as if she hadn't just called him a shit-head thirty minutes earlier.

"Before you start drinking, I want you to meet Denise. She loved *December Light* and she's dying to meet you."

Resistance is futile. She leads him to a couch where a vacuous looking young woman with long scarlet hair is surrounded by equally vacuous looking admirers.

"Denise, this is my friend, Mac McLeod. The writer? And a very big fan of your music."

She extends a pale hand. "Which of my songs do you like best?"

"The last one," he says.

"*Locked up in Your Heart*," Liv says quickly. "We both love that one."

Denise seems disappointed. "That's actually a cover …You're a writer…What magazine are you with?"

Liv laughs delightedly. "He's not a journalist, darling, he's a novelist. He's the one who wrote *December Light*."

"Oh. Is that that book you gave me?"

"Looks like you're about as impressed with my work as I am with yours."

Liv laughs again. "Honestly! You two…Frick and Frack… What a pair!"

Bodies are stacked three deep at the bar but he manages to insert himself at the very end. Eventually the lone bartender makes his way down.

"Red wine, white wine, beer or campari & soda?"

"Scotch. On the rocks."

"Sorry. It's a host bar. You got some vouchers when you—"

Mac takes out his wallet, lays a hundred-dollar bill on the zinc bar top.

The guys smiles and pockets the bill. "J & B okay?"

"If that's all you've got."

The first swallow burns going down.

He sits on the stool, oblivious to the noise and motion, the flickering lights. When he finishes his drink, he reaches over the bar and takes the scotch from under the counter, pours his glass full to the brim. Each time the level of scotch falls below an inch from the top, he refills it. The alcohol begins to work its peculiar magic.

Suddenly Liv is there, clutching his arm again. "We need to leave soon." She smiles and pulls the hair back from her face. "We're meeting Denise and her manager at Fail Safe in about thirty minutes." She leans close to kiss his cheek and see how much he's had to drink. "I'll drive," she says. "Where did you park?"

"Around the corner," he lies.

"I'm going to just say goodbye to some people. I'll be right back."

Right back means at least fifteen minutes. A meeting in thirty minutes means an hour. Fail Safe means lots of noise, table hopping, air kissing and bullshit.

The man standing next to him leans over and shouts, "How do you know George?"

Mac stares at him, his leathery tan, his too white teeth. He pretends not to hear, picks up his glass and the bottle and heads into the next room where he finishes the scotch. Then to the men's room, where two guys are snorting coke off a drink coaster. They offer him a line. He locks himself in a stall and stands with his forehead pressed against the cool metal door, wondering briefly who George is, if he knows him, and why.

When he leaves the men's room, he's weaving a little. Some fresh air is called for. He pushes through the crowd out to the sidewalk where people clump together, chatting and laughing. Laughing nonstop. What can they possibly find so funny?

And where did he leave the fucking car?

While he's standing there trying to remember, a Metro bus pulls up and he boards it without thinking, without caring, and is instantly enveloped in scents of sweat, tobacco, garlic, hairspray, men's cologne—always stronger than the women's counterpart—the familiar smells of public transit. He stuffs money into the fare box and makes his way down the aisle past a young black girl with ear buds in, eyes closed, swaying to her own private music. All the way to the last row of seats.

For a long time he didn't drive.

One of the terms of his probation was no driver's license till he turned twenty-one. As if he wanted to get behind the wheel of a car. At times he thought he never would again. Learning to drive, getting his permit, his license, his own car had changed overnight from an obsession to a sweaty, shaky dreaded thing, finally fading over the years into disinterest.

He walked, hitchhiked, bummed rides, rode buses and trains—easy when he lived in Manhattan, less easy the farther west he traveled. Finally in Colorado when he was working construction he fell in with a group of rock climbers. Fanatics who lived to climb and worked jobs that were measured in days or weeks only to finance their habit. Three or four vehicles circulated among the group of eight. Sold by the current owner for whatever he could get, bought by whoever had money, each knowing he could sell it back to the original owner or to one of the others when their monetary positions were reversed.

It was there that he acquired the Elky.

He has no idea which bus this is, where it goes, and it doesn't make any difference. He sits by the window, watching the lights. Flashing neon, changing traffic lights, blinking turn signals, streaks of headlights and tail-lights. Someone on a street corner smoking, the glowing circle of fire. And what's left of the day, a razor thin band of pink on the horizon.

He used to love the night. Huddled under the blanket, his old transistor radio pressed to his ear, listening to the music beamed out from stations in New York and New Jersey, playing Bo Diddley and Jerry Lee Lewis, Garnett Mimms and LaVerne Baker, Jackie Wilson, Elvis, Buddy Holly, Little Richard, Chuck Berry. He would close his eyes, finally turning off the radio, or sometimes falling asleep with it still playing, sending the music deep into his unconscious until the batteries died and the music stilled.

He leans his face against the cool glass and lets himself shut down.

The memories release their power slowly, like glowing coals. They are the story. The story that is the accident; it's what his life is about, a book he's read too many times.

He thought he'd died, too. Even though they told him he'd survived, that it was a miracle, something to be grateful for. That's when writing became a way—for a long time, the only way—to prove he was alive even though he felt dead.

The sensation was like floating. Skimming over the surface of hours and days. He must have talked to someone, but the memory is blank. There was no talking at home. There seemed to be a tacit agreement that he and Suzanne would not speak to each other unless absolutely neces-sary. In case of fire or flood. At some point he realized that she'd stopped fixing dinner. He ate hotdogs punctured with a fork so they wouldn't explode in the microwave, dry buns slathered with yellow mustard, burnt popcorn, frozen pizza, lots of apples.

Some days she got up and went to work. At home she stayed in her room and when they met by accident in the hall, he could read the expressions that chased each other across her face…surprise. Then disbelief. Then disappointment. That he was still there and Kevin was gone.

These things are coming out now, out through his skin, his joints, his mouth, the palms of his hands. The way, it was said, that shrapnel could come out of a body years after the wound had supposedly healed.

"Hey, Buddy. End of the line. You gotta get off."

He half-walks, half-stumbles to the front. "Where are we?"

The driver eyes him curiously. "Santa Monica Pier. Ocean and Colorado."

Through the bus windshield the huge Pacific Wheel arcs slowly over the beach, its five thousand red, white and blue lights flashing nine stories high above the pier.

"You okay?"

"Sure." He raises one hand as he steps down onto the crowded sidewalk. A lighted beer sign draws him into a liquor store where he wanders the aisles aimlessly till the nervous-looking clerk asks what he's looking for.

"Scotch."

"Right behind you."

He takes a fifth without looking at the brand, pays for it, and stuffs the change into a charity box on the counter. He clutches the paper bag against his side and tries to concentrate on picking up each foot, setting it down. Careful. Careful.

He remembers the action comics Kevin loved. The heroes were always gritting their teeth and saying things like *must not let go. Must. Not. Fall.* Now it strikes him as hilarious and he grits his teeth. *Must not laugh.* Little bursts of laughter explode from his mouth anyway and he has a sense of people turning to look at him.

He veers off the sidewalk, crosses the street to the accompaniment of car horns, and heads towards the pier. When his steps sink into the sand he loses balance, drops to a crouch, then rocks back into a sit. Behind him is a flower bed with a few large boulders. He scoots back to lean against one of them and fumbles with the bottle till he gets the cap off.

Hmm. No glass, no ice, no twist. What to do…The first long drink from the bottle goes down his throat like a comet. God, yes. Let the evening begin.

He's not sure how long he sits there, drinking. He finds a couple of pills in his shirt pocket. No idea what they are. Dex? Aspirin? Vitamin C? What the hell. He swallows them anyway. People walk by. He can see them, but they can't see him. The beauty of darkness. The bottle is becoming emptier, but heavier. A couple of times it slips from his mouth, dribbles down his chin, the front of his shirt.

A guy walks by, pulled by a golden retriever on a leash, and he suddenly remembers Brownie. He remembers running here with her. Maybe this exact place. The sound of her panting beside him, the way the wind rippled through her fur, how her ears flopped as she ran. How she smiled, showing her pink and black gums and sharp white teeth.

He feels like a runaway truck on a mountain road…where was the ramp packed with sand where you could bury your wheels up to the axle and it would slow you down till you could catch your breath?

An odd, whirring noise draws his attention to small black disks like mushrooms rising from the ground and it begins to rain. By the time he understands that the watering system has come on, he's wet. No point in moving now, even if he could. He turns his face up to the sky and sits, watching the slow unchanging arc of the Pacific Wheel through a spray of water. The ground softens under him, the mud soaking through his Stefano Ricci slacks. The cycle only lasts a few minutes and then shuts off abruptly. The black mushrooms disappear as if sucked into some underground bunker.

The wind off the ocean is cold now, and he begins to shiver.

The bottle falls from his hand and he pulls his knees up like shield, rests his forehead there. His grief has now passed beyond the loss of Kevin, Amanda, of Dennis, of Suzanne. Beyond the fact that his career is in the crapper. Beyond the knowledge that Wyn is surely gone by now and Brownie has died, and that he's going to die, too. Just not soon enough.

Water drips out of his hair, down his face, and he begins to weep, thin cold tears.

Vaguely aware of voices, movement, he raises his head just enough to see a group of men coming towards him, now several yards away. Talking, laughing, abruptly going silent as they notice him. Their voices drop to whispers. Then,

"Hey…are you okay?"

Why does everyone keep asking him that? Stupid fucking question. He's drunk, wet, muddy, just on the verge of getting sick. Sure, he's great.

"Yeah."

"Can we call anyone for you? A cab?"

"I'm fine."

"Matthew?"

He squints at the group of unfamiliar faces till one comes into focus. Gabe Cleveland. *Shit.*

"I'm fine."

"The hell you say." He steps closer. "Come on, I'll give you a ride back to Alan's."

"No. I just…"

Just what? Lost his car? Ran out of pills? Drank too much? Forgot how to write? Killed two people? Fucked up his life? All of the above?

"Damnation, you're soaked, Matthew. Are you sick?"

As if in answer, he turns his head just in time to keep from vomiting on himself.

"I'm not leaving you here." Gabe hands something to one of the others. "Rick, could you go get my car please?"

At some point he's lifted from behind by several pairs of hands. He tries to fight, swinging one arm loosely, but his limbs seem to be rubberized and don't respond to directions from his brain. He can't talk. His tongue has grown too big for his mouth.

He can't see the Ferris wheel any more.

He slept folded in thirds. He's on a couch covered in something slick. Plastic. He pushes himself into a sit. Both shoes, caked in mud, sit on a pile of newspapers on the floral patterned rug. He's wearing one sock, still a little damp. His mouth feels like a beach at low tide.

"Mornin', Matthew."

He stares at the blindingly white smile. He sighs. "Gabe."

"Don't worry I still respect you."

He looks up sharply and Cleveland laughs. "Reckon I shouldn't joke before caffeine."

The coffee is hot and strong, cut with steaming milk. It's about the best thing in his short-term memory. Gabe sits in a delicate looking chair across the coffee table.

"Where's your vehicle?"

"Somewhere off La Brea."

Raised eyebrows. "La Brea?" How'd you get over to the pier?"

"La Metro."

"Sounds like an interesting evening."

"Any chance of getting some more coffee?"

In a few minutes Gabe returns with the pot and refills both their cups.

"Thanks." He takes a slow, breathy sip. "And thanks for last night. Although I've slept in bathtubs that were more comfortable."

Gabe looks smug. "It's a Queen Anne chesterfield. Horsehair cushions. Not really designed for passing out."

"Why didn't you just leave me at Alan's?"

"You were dead weight, son. I didn't think I could get you up the stairs. And I didn't want to wake everyone up at 2 AM. They frown on that sort of thing in his neighborhood. You should really speak to Alan about installing an elevator." Cleveland sips his coffee. "How about some breakfast?"

"You don't have to do that."

"Let me put it this way. I'm going to eat breakfast. It's no trouble to throw a couple more eggs in the pan."

"Okay. Thanks."

"While I'm doing that you might want to clean yourself up a bit. I don't much care to breakfast with someone who reeks of booze, mud and vomit. There's a clean pair of jeans and a T-shirt in the bathroom. Down the hall on the left. And Matthew? Stay out of the medicine cabinet."

He sits at Gabe's elaborately carved kitchen table with sun filtering in through plantation shutters. They eat bacon and eggs and biscuits. And grits loaded with butter and salt and pepper. The salt, especially. He can't get enough of it. Gabe makes orange juice with one of those fancy presses with the big handle and serves it over ice in crystal goblets along with more of that strong, dark coffee.

He natters on as usual, gossiping about people Mac doesn't know. But finally there's a silence. The kind that follows a lot of food and not enough sleep.

Cleveland gets up and starts clearing the dishes. At the sink, he turns. "What now?"

Mac stifles a yawn. "Go find the car. Take a nap."

"I mean, what about your life?"

"What about it?"

"It's a mess."

"Depends on your perspective."

"Matthew, don't try shittin' me. I'm just like you. Except with nicer furnishings, of course." He smiles briefly. "I've been where you are and I know what it's like. Big. Bad. Relentless. Ignore it at your peril. It doesn't go away; it gets worse. And then you die. I pretty nearly did. "

He can get a bus back up to La Brea, walk around till he finds the car. Unless he parked it illegally, in which case he'll have to start calling the police garages and find out where it is.

"All you can do is start, Matthew. Take one step. Fix one thing. Go on to the next one and work on that. And you don't have to do it alone. That was the hardest thing for me. Asking for help. Asking the right person."

"Strictly out of curiosity, who's the right person?"

"Willow Maidenhair."

He laughs. "Let me guess. Eagle feather and sweat lodge.

Cleveland folds his arms and returns the stare. "She's not about any of that. But even if she was, have you got just a whole bunch of alternatives tucked away someplace?"

Mac drinks the last of his coffee and sets the cup back in its saucer.

"She's down in Laguna," Gabe says. "I know, I know. It's a schlep. But she is so worth it, Matthew."

Even with the map she insisted on sending him, the house isn't easy to find. After thirty minutes of winding around up in the hills above Laguna Beach he spots it, a nondescript bungalow surrounded by tall grass and eucalyptus trees. A brushfire waiting to happen.

If she has clients willing to drive up here every week, she must be good. The thought reassures him, helps quell the uneasiness that kicks in at the mere thought of seeing a therapist named Willow Maidenhair. And a three-hour first session. What the hell do you do for three hours?

He parks the rented Mustang in a dusty patch of gravel and climbs out into the dry heat of the canyon. Tiny grasshoppers startle away and dry weeds crunch under his feet as he walks up the path. The porch is shaded by a huge eucalyptus, gray leaves drooping like an old man's beard.

He shifts his weight on the creaking boards, imagining how this is going to change things…everything. That's what he wants, it's why he's here. So where is the dread coming from? Why the faint dampness on his forehead and the taste of ash in his mouth? Why does he want more than anything to get back in the car and drive down to the beach, to sit on the deck at the Laguna Hotel bar, a cold beer in his hand, warm salty wind on his face?

He raises the knocker on the faded green door and lets it fall.

Willow Maidenhair is elfin, barely up to his shoulder, and her face, with its pointy chin and nose, reinforces the impression. Her long hair is light brown and woven into numerous little braids, some with brightly painted beads plaited in. She turns huge gray eyes up to his and holds out her hand.

"Hello, Mac. I'm Willow. Please come in."

Great. My therapist is a 25-year-old hippie.

He follows her to a pale green room with a bare pine floor. The polished black rectangle of her desk is clear except for one file folder. The room feels empty and he decides it's the absence of a computer.

She motions him to a chair.

"There's water if you'd like some." She nods at a green anodized metal carafe on the corner of her desk.

He turns over a glass and fills it, just for something to do.

She settles into her own chair, which is big enough for two of her, opens the file, takes out several sheets of paper, uncaps a pen and says, "How old are you, Mac?"

"Forty-two. How old are you?"

She looks slightly surprised. "Thirty-eight. Why?"

"Because you don't look old enough—you don't look like a therapist."

She smiles. "I have a Sigmund Freud mask. Would you feel better if I wore it?"

He has the sense that she's only half joking.

"Are you married?"

His left hand is tan enough now that even the telltale white ghost of his ring doesn't show.

"No. Yes…separated."

"Any children?"

"No. Well…one."

"What do you do for a living?"

"I'm a writer." He notices that the top piece of paper on her desk is actually some kind of form with columns and boxes.

"Before we get started talking, I have some questions for you," she says. "Boring stuff. But information I need to form a clearer picture of your situation. Have you had a physical exam recently?"

"January."

"Any blood pressure issues, high cholesterol or blood sugar levels, digestive problems, prostate, allergies…anything like that?"

"No." He looks at the painting hanging on the wall behind her, his mind already starting to wander. It's one of those feel-good watercolors, all pastel flowers and sunlight on a glass bowl.

"Any complaints you didn't mention to the doctor?"

"Can't think of any."

"Try again," she says.

His eyes shift back to her face.

"You're paying for my time, Mac. Don't waste it. I'm trying to eliminate any possible physical causes of your troubles."

He nods, takes a drink of water and a long breath. "It's been about two years since I slept through the night. And I was having trouble getting an erection."

"Any particular reason why you didn't mention the insomnia or the impotence to your doctor?"

"I guess I thought it was...temporary. That it would all go away and I'd get back to normal."

She twists one of the silver chains looped around her neck. "Two years seems rather a long time for a temporary condition. Are you taking any drugs?"

"Like prescriptions?"

"Prescription. Over the counter. Street. Homeopathic. Vitamins. Anything."

"I had to finish a project and I couldn't concentrate—"

"So you took some...?"

"Dexedrine."

"Are you still taking it?"

"No."

"When did you stop?"

"Two weeks ago."

"And how was that?"

"Not pretty."

"Anything else?"

"I've started smoking. Cigarettes. Some marijuana. Mostly when I was taking the dex. To help me come down."

"Alcohol?"

"Some."

"How many drinks a day?"

"Depends on the day. Sometimes I'll have a beer in the afternoon. Sometimes I start drinking scotch before dinner and keep going till I pass out."

She wants to know about his eating habits, she makes him describe his last three meals. She asks if he's getting any exercise. He watches her write down his answers.

She says, "If we're going to work together, there are a few things I need you to do. If you're unwilling or unable to do them, I'll try to help you find another therapist. First of all, no more self-prescribed drugs. And no alcohol of any kind. At least not right now. Alcohol is a depressant, and it's also one of the things that keeps you from getting any significant sleep. Cigarettes are nasty, too, but if you feel you can't give up all your bad habits at once, go ahead and smoke. Just no marijuana. Are we agreed?"

He hesitates, then nods.

She slips the form into the file folder and tucks her feet up under her skirt.

"It's always hard getting started with someone new. It's hard to over-come the inertia that makes you want to just slide right back down into your hole and stay there." Her voice is so quiet that he leans towards her slightly. "Have you been seeing a therapist?"

"No." He presses his fingertips together hard. It seems to relieve some tension in his chest.

"Let's talk about what you're feeling. Why you came to me."

"I'm not really feeling anything. I just can't seem to do anything. It's like a fog. I can't even describe what it's like. It's like I'm not all there."

"What about physical pain?"

"Sometimes. For no reason it just hurts."

"Where?"

He looks at her. "I don't know. I mean, it hurts everywhere, but I can't tell where it starts. And I forget things."

"What kinds of things?" she asks. "People's names? Where you left your sunglasses?"

"Things like what I did yesterday. Starting a sentence and then forgetting what I meant to say."

"That must make writing difficult. When did that start?"

"Last fall, I think. Maybe longer. I…can't actually remember."

She lays the pen on the desk. "Have you ever wanted to die?"

The question seems melodramatic, but her straightforward delivery makes it less fraught, more like *Have you ever wanted to visit Morocco?*

He considers it briefly. "I think there have been times when I wished I wasn't alive…but I don't recall ever wanting to go through the process of dying."

"Good. So you probably aren't going to kill yourself before we get things resolved. Tell me what else is going on in your life."

He looks at her blankly.

"Your work. Your relationships."

"Do you think—" He feels heat rising up the back of his neck. "Can you help me?"

"Do you want me to?"

"Why else would I drive down here from Beverly Hills?"

"I know you want to feel better, Mac. That's not what I'm asking. Tell me, have you ever heard the term *codega*?"

"Not that I remember."

"In Venice, during the Middle Ages there were men called *codegas*, whose job it was to walk in front of people at night with a lantern, showing them the way and protecting them from thieves, giving them the confidence to walk through the dark streets at night. That's essentially my role in this. But you're the one who has to take that walk through the dark."

"Great. Just one question. Wouldn't the light also alert thieves to your whereabouts?"

Her laugh is unexpectedly hearty. "I think we're going to work well together."

She stands up and he checks his watch.

"No, we're not through. We're just getting started. Come with me."

At the far end of the hall, she stops in front of a closed door. "Have you had massage therapy?"

"Massage therapy?"

"I guess that's a 'no.'" She taps gently on the door.

"Is this...standard operating procedure?"

She smiles. "Of course not."

The door swings open.

"Hi, Mac. I'm Mary." Tall and slender with very short black hair and dark eyes.

"I'll see you in a while," Willow says, and she pads down the hall. He notices for the first time that she's barefoot.

Mary shows him into the dimly lit room, where some weird, African sounding music is playing. The padded massage table takes up most of the space, leaving only a narrow corridor around it.

"Everything off but your shorts, please, Mac. Then face down on the table." She goes out, shutting the door behind her. He strips quickly, hangs his faded jeans and T-shirt on the back of the door, kicks off his loafers and crawls under the sheet. It smells like it was dried outside in the sun. He lies on his stomach, face cushioned on what looks like a small padded toilet seat.

A discreet knock announces Mary's return.

He can't see her with his face down, but he can sense her efficient, unhurried movements. She slips a pillow under his ankles, turns the music volume down. Now she's standing at his head and a penetrating scent opens his nose, relaxes him.

She folds down the top sheet, tucking it into the waistband of his boxers, and then her cool hands are sliding on his back, sticking on bone and cartilage. She presses harder, pushing around things that feel like marbles under the skin.

When his eyes have adapted to the dark he can see her feet, directly under him at the table's edge, long toes gripping the rug as she rocks back and forth, kneading his neck, his shoulders, his back.

Shit. He tries to shift inconspicuously.

"What's wrong?" she says.

"Nothing. I'm just...I've got..."

"Don't worry about it, Mac. It's very common to get an erection during massage. Especially if you're not accustomed. It's the sensory stimulation and the increased activity of the parasympathetic nervous system. You must be right handed. You've got quite a knot here. How's this pressure?"

"Fine." He winces.

"Have you ever had massage before?"

"Once. At a—ow—resort."

She sniffs disdainfully. "A Dr. Feelgood massage." Her thumbs excavate his shoulder blades. "Don't tense up. Let go. Let your mind drift. Breathe with me. Long inhale through the nose. Long exhale through the mouth."

As if cued to his breathing, the music settles into a hypnotic rhythm. The words are unintelligible so he focuses on the melody line, which seems to have a mind of its own, spooling out like a highway. Every time you expect the phrase to resolve in typical western music fashion, it begins a new pattern in a different direction.

"What is that? The music."

"Ethiopian," she says. "Isn't it wonderful?"

"I'm sort of a rock and roll guy."

"Too much stimulation," she says. "We want to relax. No more talking now. Listen to the music. Fall into it. Float on it. Let it carry you like a river. Come on, now. Breathe. Long. Slow."

Her voice soothes him, overcomes his stubborn reluctance, lulls him into a dream zone where he's borne up by the strange melody and lost in his own breath.

"We're going to do some energy work now." The words seem to come to him from a distance. "I want you to try and make your mind totally blank. Think of a white wall. An empty canvas. A blank page."

Now instead of kneading, she places her fingertips in certain spots and applies pressure, first gentle, then firmer, then deep, with only a slight circular motion. Suddenly it's as if she's plugged into his central nervous system.

Every place she touches calls up a different image. Memories of such cold clarity that they burn. His father standing in the hall with a suitcase. Creasing the brim of his hat. Leaving or coming home?

Playing baseball in the street. Long, golden evenings in late June. Kids would get called to dinner, and they'd come back out and it would still be light. And then all of sudden it's so dark you can't see the ball. Walking home with Kevin, up the hill and Suzanne sitting on the front porch smoking a cigarette...

Running. Dry pine needles crunching under his feet, releasing their summer smell. Kevin right behind him, their feet pounding on the dirt path in unison, then in counterpoint, the vibrations making his legs sting, a stitch in his side, Kevin's feet right behind, trying to catch up, branches slapping and then he's falling and rolling and the rhythm has changed and his stomach contracting with laughter, and then just breathing and then trying to yell, and not stopping, and that noise coming from the back of Suzanne's throat, like a scream.

The noise is coming from his own throat now and his face is wet. His whole body is open and cold and shaking. Mary is rubbing his neck, his shoulders, with her cool hands and crooning—there's no other word for it, that universal mother noise.

"Good job, Mac. Let it all out."

Minutes later he's dressed and sitting in the chair in Willow's office, wrapped in a light blanket because, in spite of the afternoon heat, he still feels chilled. He can hear their voices but not their words, talking about him out in the hallway. In a minute Willow comes in with a steaming mug, which she sets on the desk in front of him.

"Chamomile." She waits patiently for him to drink some of the tea and then she says, "What are you feeling?"

"I don't know." His voice is tight and hoarse. "Like everything's a mistake. Like I could have fixed it but I never did and now...I can't. Like every wrong thing comes from the one before and makes the next thing wrong. Like dominoes. Like I don't know how it started and I can't make it stop."

He sets the cup down because his hands are shaking and he looks at her, waiting for the answer. Waiting for her to say, *nothing's really wrong. All you have to do is...*But she doesn't say that.

"Okay, what is it? What's wrong with me?"

"That's what I need you to tell me, Mac."

She sits back in the big chair and folds her arms and looks at him some more. "What happened?" she asks in her soft voice. "Mary said you brought up some very disturbing memories."

He wipes his hands on the thighs of his jeans.

"There was something devastating. What was it? How old were you? What did you lose?"

"My...brother." His voice cracks and heat races up into his face.

"That's a terrible loss. Tell me what happened."

"It was an accident. A car accident. Kevin died. And Amanda. His girlfriend."

"And you were there? In the car?"

He swallows. "I was driving."

Sixteen

I miss the last ferry out of Anacortes.

Because of the summer tourist hordes the only place I can find a room is an old motor court. In a different mood, I might find it quaint and amusing, but the walls are almost as thin as the curtains, so the noise and lights keep me awake most of the night. That and the sudden urgency I feel about getting back to the island.

I finally sleep and then I oversleep and miss the early ferry, so it's almost noon when I finally arrive on Orcas.

The house appears slowly out of the fog. I'm up the steps before I see the metal bucket full of zinnias and sunflowers sitting next to the door. A gift from our renter, no doubt. Most people who stay here fall in love with it. A lot of them leave us things—flowers, a nice bottle of wine, or just a little note saying how much they enjoyed it. Several years ago a couple from San Francisco offered to buy it, furnished.

I'm ambivalent about renting it, although the money comes in handy. There's so much of Mac and me in this place and it bothers me to think of strangers sleeping in my bed, using my dishes, reading my books. Even though the cleaning service is pretty thorough, there's always a lingering trace of the unfamiliar. Once it took almost a week to get rid of the penetrating lime scent of a man's cologne.

Unpacking takes all of ten minutes, then I pull out my kitchen file to find the recipe I wrote years ago on a piece of yellow legal pad. It may be the best chocolate cake I've ever had...we use it at the bakery. It's the one people invariably ask for when they want a birthday cake. It's called Ellie's Deep South Chocolate Cake after the young woman from Alabama who worked for me four years ago and gave me the recipe, but our customers never ask for it by name; they always just say, "I want that chocolate cake."

There are a few tricks to it...one is a small amount of mayonnaise, which keeps it moist; another is using brown sugar; the last is substituting black cocoa for part of the natural cocoa. That's really what gives it the deep, dark and incredibly chocolate edge.

I start pulling ingredients out of the pantry.

By two-thirty the fog is lifting, but behind it are banks of gray clouds and the temperature hovers in the low sixties. Out on the deck, the air is still, the only sound a steady dripping of water off the trees.

The cake layers are cooling on racks, the ganâche is ready to spread and I'm suddenly exhausted. The bedroom seems cold and remote, so I pull a sleeping bag out of the cedar closet, unroll it in front of the woodstove. Getting kindling from the basket, I think of my father showing me how to build a fire in the fireplace at Lake Tahoe when I was fourteen. I practiced all that summer. We didn't go back the next summer, and that fall, he died.

I never had occasion to build fires again till I moved to Seattle more than fifteen years later. Then it was Mac who taught me the art of heating by woodstove, how to damp the blaze down so it would last, radiating a slow, delicious warmth all through the night.

I arrange the kindling in the shape of a teepee, scrape the wooden match along the rough hearth, releasing a burst of sulfur, and touch it to the shavings at the bottom. It catches instantly. As the flames grow, I add larger pieces of kindling, and finally a small log and close the glass doors. In minutes the blaze begins to take the edge off the damp chill. I pull down a pillow from the couch, take off my shoes and my jeans, and crawl into the sleeping bag.

I'm swimming upwards through a thick black ocean. Somewhere over my head a telephone is ringing. I should answer it, but I can't make myself move. It's dark and cold. The stove has gone out. By the time I extricate myself from the sleeping bag, the call has gone to voicemail. I stretch for the lamp switch, shivering and squinting into its glare as I pick up the message. Dead air. Whoever it was hung up without saying anything.

I roll up the sleeping bag and put it away. The ganâche has hardened, so I beat it for a few minutes with my hand held mixer and forgo the crumb coat, slathering the cake with every bit of frosting I can scrape out of the bowl. I set it in the fridge to firm up.

Upstairs the shower's steam fills the bathroom. When I'm clean and dry, reality is somewhat closer, but not quite within my grasp. I watch myself in the mirror, wanting to ask that woman what she's doing, where she thinks she's going. I twist my hair and tuck it up under my baseball cap, slip into my jacket, grab a flashlight, the cake.

And my toothbrush.

Fifteen minutes later I'm standing in the kitchen at Rafferty's, surrounded by four hungry guys in the process of de-constructing my chocolate cake.

"Sour cream," Ferris says. "It's got the moistness and that little tang."

I shake my head.

"Buttermilk, then."

"Espresso," says Will. "That's the edge."

I love restaurant kitchens—the smells, the whoosh of flame from the burners when something spills over the pans, the clink of plates, the talk, the laughter.

"There better be some left for me," Alex says from the stove.

"Then you better hurry up," Will says, jamming a huge bite into his mouth.

"I don't hurry," Alex says straight-faced. "I like to take my time."

This sets off a round of hoots. I cut a large piece of the cake and put it on a plate. Fredo hands me a fork.

"No, this is for Alex. I'm going to put it away so it doesn't disappear in the feeding frenzy."

I cover the plate with plastic wrap and take it into his tiny office off the storeroom, setting it on the desk, tucking the plastic around the edges. When I turn around, Alex is shutting the door behind him. We look at each other for a minute.

"Did you call earlier?"

He nods. "How was L.A.?"

"Hot. Smoggy."

"That's not what I meant."

"I know. I just really don't want to talk about it. I came back, didn't I?"

"Yeah," he says. "And thank you, God, for that."

It's only a couple of steps and we move in unison, as if it's been choreographed—where to step, which way to lean, how we would fit together, and he kisses me deliberately. With intent. Producing a sensation I vaguely recall but haven't felt in a while. I love the scent of him—olive oil and grill smoke and toasted bread. When I move my arms up around his shoulders he bends his head to kiss my neck and his fingers brush the side of my breast almost imperceptibly, but it's enough to buckle my knees.

"I want you to stay with me tonight," he says.

I smile against his shoulder. "You thought I came down here to bring you chocolate cake?"

He's in the process of kissing me again when Fredo hollers, "Alex."

"What?"

"We're out of orzo for the chicken special."

"Use rice."

"I don't think there's enough."

"Then use potatoes. I don't give a flying fuck." We try again, but there's a knock at the door.

"Hey, Alex, where's those artichokes?" Will's voice.

"Check the prep sink." He looks at the ceiling. "I'll kill them all. It'll only take a minute."

This is so not me.

I've always been the sensible one, the dependable one, the one who does the right thing. I pay the bills and balance the budget; I do the employee evaluations—the good as well as the shitty; I insist on confronting my husband's mother even though he wants nothing to do with her; I invite his daughter by another woman to come for Christmas.

This time around, I'm doing what I want. Even though I know I shouldn't. Even though I know things will get messy; people will get hurt, undoubtedly including myself. I don't care if he likes me in the morning. I don't even care if I like myself in the morning. In fact, I'm pretty sure I won't. But I've decide not to care. Not right now. I can always care later.

I've been to parties at Alex's house a couple of times, but Mac was driving and I wasn't paying any attention; I'd forgotten how middle-of-nowhere it is, down several dark, narrow, twisty roads. It's good that I can follow him there because I never would have found it on my own.

It's raining now. I can hear it tapping on the windows as he walks around with me, turning on all the lights. When he starts laying a fire, I intervene.

"Alex, I can build a fire. Probably better than you. Go back to work."

"I'll be back by eleven-thirty." He picks up a strand of my hair, rubbing it between his thumb and fingers. "Please don't go anywhere."

"I can't. I'd never find my way back to the road."

He leaves me alone in his house.

I finish making the fire in the massive rock fireplace and settle myself on the couch. The couch, I remember very well. Milk chocolate colored leather, soft as cream. I remember wondering how it would be to take all my clothes off and roll around on it. I could give it a go now, but I'm not feeling quite that brazen. Instead, I check out the reading matter on the coffee table. Restaurant trade journals and sailing magazines. Paperbacks by Tom Clancy, Scott Turow, Len Deighton. Not my thing.

A dim light draws me down the hall. It's coming from a desk lamp in his office. I flip on the overhead switch. The man is into leather. Loveseat, desk chair, ottoman. There's an antique roll-top desk, two oak file cabinets. Gorgeous Persian rug. Pretty tidy for a guy. Must have a cleaning service.

One wall is covered with photographs, mostly of sailboats. There are some pictures of him with different women, usually blonde and skinny with big boobs. A portrait of the boys, they look about two and seven, all dressed up, jackets and ties.

One older picture is a family grouping—a sturdy, square-jawed father with an unruly shock of fair hair, his wife is small and dark-eyed, holding a baby. Two boys, the older one would be politely called chunky, dark like the mother. The other is fair and slight. I stare at them. Is that fat little kid Alex?

In a stack of books on his desk, I spot a copy of *Treasure Island*. The inscription on the title page says, *To Alex. Happy Thirteenth Birthday. Your friend, Robert Louis Stevenson.* I carry it back out to the living room and curl up on the couch to read. At eleven-fifteen I hear the Porsche, quick steps outside, and he bursts into the room, arms full of take-out containers and brown paper bags.

I look at my watch. "You're early."

"I would've been even earlier, but we had eight covers show up at nine-fifteen."

I laugh. "And they wanted to eat? How inconsiderate."

"Really. What are you drinking?"

"Nothing yet." I wander into the kitchen.

"Sorry, I meant to show you—"

"I could have found something if I really wanted it. I've just been reading. I...um...found a copy of *Treasure Island* in your office. Signed by the author."

He smiles shaking his head. "My old man was a joker. You want red or white?"

"Red. I'm having a hard time picturing you at thirteen."

He pulls a bottle out of his under-counter wine cooler and opens it quickly and perfectly, like he was born with a corkscrew in one hand. Chateau Margaux.

"Alex, for God's sake, that stuff's expensive."

He grins. "You're worth it."

We take the wine and two glasses to the couch and he throws another log on the dwindling fire. He pours the wine and touches his glass to mine.

"What do you think?" he says.

"It's wonderful. But I think it'll be even better when it warms up and breathes a little."

"I wasn't talking about the wine," he says.

"Neither was I."

We laugh and it diffuses some of the tension.

"I'm sorry, but I just have to ask about the picture in—"

"Yeah. The fat kid is me." He sets his glass on the coffee table and leans back, stretching his legs out in front of him. "The neighborhood where I grew up was considered rough—although by current standards, it seems like Disneyland. There was this one particular bunch of kids that used to follow me home at least once a week and pound on me... I was a perfect target. A fat kid who liked to cook. I couldn't even run away fast enough."

"So what happened?"

"I got pissed off. When I was fourteen and I was working at this diner, there was a gym across the street. I started hanging out there, lifting weights. There was this black guy named George Canady." He laughs. "I used to think he was so old. He was probably about thirty-five, a retired heavy-weight fighter, strictly small time. A good guy. He taught me how to hold up my hands."

"How to what?"

"Fight. He thought I had the makings of a boxer. I really wasn't that interested in it, but I did learn how to take care of myself."

"Nice picture of the boys."

"I keep thinking I should get a new one, but I don't know if I could get them both cleaned up at the same time." He clasps his hands behind his head. "Dustin asked about you by the way. Not by name, of course. He said 'How's the pasta lady?'"

"I'll answer to that. When are they coming back?"

"Who knows. When they were little they used to love coming up here. We'd go sailing, fishing, hiking. Now Jesse wants to spend every daylight hour skateboarding and Dustin sits in his bedroom reading about some kind of particles."

"That's pretty typical. They're growing up, finding their own lives."

He shakes his head. "I feel like it's my fault for not trying harder, not being around when they needed me."

I think of Mac giving Skye a check and sending her on her way.

"Kids always need you. Not being around is something you can still change."

He looks at the fire for a minute, then turns his face to me. "No more boring shit," he says. "I just want to hold you."

It's a hazard of monogamy—the way sleeping with one man for ten years leaves a kind of imprint on you—a physical memory. The shape of his body against yours, the way his arm rests in the crook of your waist, how your head fits perfectly under his chin. When you try it with someone else, it's like trying to dance in the wrong size shoes.

All I can think of is Mac—how Alex is not him. His hands are wider, shorter, strong like Mac's, but not as graceful. His mouth is fuller. His body is compact, muscular, covered with wiry black hair, where Mac is long and lean and smooth as river rock. Mac smells like mountains and pine trees. Alex smells warm, earthy, spicy. Like food.

Finally I roll away, sit up, button my shirt, pull on my jeans.

"I'm sorry. I just…" I get up and stir the fire, sit cross legged in front of it. I hear him behind me pulling on his clothes and then he sits down next to me on the floor.

He pushes a long strand of my hair back and tucks it behind my ear. "I've always had sort of a crush on you."

"I think I need to go home." I move to stand up, but he takes my arm.

"Wait a second. Wait."

"It's not going to happen, Alex. I'm sorry."

"Stop worrying about what is or isn't going to happen. Just relax. Are you hungry?"

I suddenly realize I'm starving. "Um…sort of."

"Good. I brought us some stuff. It'll just take a few minutes."

"Can I help?"

"Nah."

I smile at the situation, new to me, of not being the one in charge of feeding us. He pours more wine in our glasses and takes his into the kitchen. I drink mine greedily. It's wide open now and the perfume of it fills my head.

I'm only vaguely aware of his movements, the sound of the refrigerator door. He has the hood fan on, so I don't have to worry about making conversation. Something smells fabulous.

Plates appear on the coffee table, carelessly artful. Sliced cold roast chicken with a mustard sauce. Bread and cheese. Spicy glazed carrots, barely warm. Field greens dressed in a lemony vinaigrette. And in a basket, cradled by a white linen napkin, a tumble of beautiful, gold-brown curls. Still hot from the oil. The aroma is devastating.

"Oh, *Alex…*"

"I've been waiting all summer to hear you say my name like that. If I'd known all it took was potato chips, I would've made them a lot sooner."

I take a chip from the basket and bite into it carefully. No grease. Just warm crunch and the perfect amount of salt.

He brings a bottle of white wine and two glasses.

"I'll stay with the red," I say, but he takes my glass from me.

"Just try this. Vouvray goes really good with the chicken and tarragon."

I eat everything with my fingers, including the salad. He's right about the wine, of course. It's so good that I have another glass and stare at the fire some more.

By now it must be after 2 A.M. When he takes my hand and pulls me to my feet, there's no resistance left in me. I'm sleepy, sated with good food and wine, charmed by my host. In his bedroom we undress and move together under the covers.

"I don't know if I can do this—"

"Hush," he says. "All I want to do is make you feel good. All you have to do is let me."

It's like being in a play. It feels like reality sometimes—a lot of the time, in fact. But no matter how well I know my character, how closely I identify with her, I know at some point I'll cease being this woman. I'll scrub my face, take off the costume and go back to real life.

Meanwhile, Alex wants me to come to the café for dinner, or to be at his place, waiting for him to come home so he can cook dinner for us. He likes to listen to music and talk, make love and then sleep until ten or eleven in the morning.

Sounds lovely, except my body doesn't work that way. Too many years of baker's hours. Eating at 11 pm might be chic, but it gives me indigestion. And hanging around the café smacks of being the flavor of the month. The chef's girlfriend, just like in Seattle I was the bartender's girlfriend. He doesn't really get that.

Every afternoon when he goes to the café he says, "See you tonight?"

Every day I remind myself that I have options. What if just once I said no. I could stay home and read. Watch a movie. Do my nails.

Go to bed early. Hmmm. Not quite as compelling as watching Alex cook, eating the amazing dinner he makes for us and polishing off the *vin du jour* while we do the dishes...and then...well, then comes the part I've been waiting for all day while pretending to think about other stuff. The part where he looks at me and holds me and does interesting things with his hands and his mouth, things that make me feel like a lamp that's been unplugged all day, waiting for a jolt of electric current.

One night when I'm lying in his bed, completely spent, watching the moonlight through the blinds that we forgot to close, I suddenly remember the risqué parody two women performed at a party a few years ago—a riff on an old Arlo Guthrie song—*You Can Get Anything You Want at Alex's Restaurant*. Something about it is vaguely disturbing, but before I can decide what it is, I'm asleep.

"Let's go out for breakfast," he says in the morning.

This is a departure from the norm, because he enjoys cooking breakfast. It's the one thing he never gets to do at the café.

Groggy and vaguely grouchy, I roll out of bed, slip on my jeans and a cotton turtleneck. He takes me to Evelene's, a strange choice, I think, as we scoot into the Naugahyde booth. The coffee is okay, nothing to write home about, and the case is full of Danish drizzled with sticky white icing, shrink wrapped muffins, and scones that appear to be huge globs of overworked dough.

The only thing that looks appealing are the sticky buns, which we both order. They're surprisingly good, and the caramel has that true burnt sugar edge, not like those sugary blocks a lot of places melt in the microwave.

"Alex, hi there." A pretty woman in a denim jumper wanders out of the kitchen and heads for our table, pulling a scarf off her dark hair. "How's it going?"

He pulls up a chair for her. "Evie, this is my friend, Wyn Morrison." She takes my hand in her warm, damp one. The hand of somebody who cooks for a living. She looks at the half eaten roll on my plate. "Evie Campbell. Everything okay?"

"Great." I smile. "It's just so huge. I'm trying to pace myself."

"How's Bea?" Alex asks.

"Oh, you know…" She sighs. "Good days and bad days." She looks at me. "My mom. She's kind of losing the plot, if you know what I mean. I keep trying to get her to go to the doctor, but she's stalling. I think she's afraid of what they're going to tell her. She lives on Lopez. All by herself, and I worry about her. When I try to talk to her, she makes a joke out of it. Says things like, *well I guess you'll be locking me in the attic here pretty soon.*"

"Bea used to own this place," Alex says.

"So it's been handed down from mother to daughter," Evie says. "I hate to give it up, but she isn't about to leave her place, so one of these days I'm probably going to have to move over there."

Alex says, "Wyn's a baker, too. She owns a great boulangerie in L.A.. They do the artisan type breads. I've been using her bread at the café."

"Oh, you're the Bread Maven! Gosh, it's great to finally meet you. I used to think that might be good here—the rustic type breads," Evie says. "There's only two places on the island you could call bakeries—us and Village House. They don't do any kind of yeasted stuff. And we just do your basic French bread. And a whole wheat sandwich loaf. Seems like if somebody started doing really good bread it might go over. I just never got ambitious about it."

"I'm not sure there's enough of a market here for bread that costs five bucks," I say. "You'd have to be doing wholesale."

She shrugs. "Well, I don't know. It does sound pricey, but you get a lot of traffic here from Seattle and Portland and California—at least in the summer. They probably wouldn't think twice about it."

"Evie," the girl at the cash register calls. "I tried to do a merchant's discount and this thing's locked up on me."

"Something to think about." She stands up and smiles at both of us. "Nice to meet you, Wyn. Come back and see me."

When I'm not with Alex, I'm with Ferris.

At first I just watched him fire the oven, then I helped him, then he watched me. Now on Friday mornings I come to the patio alone to build the warm-up fire.

I love firing the oven in the early morning. It's sort of like working the first shift at the bakery, but completely stripped of embellishments. No hissing espresso machine, no Vivaldi on the sound system, no sweet scent of pastry. Just the damp chill of fog, the crackling fire and the wood smoke.

Ferris' obsession with the fire, which at first struck me as a possible latent tendency to arson, is now totally comprehensible to me. He reminds me that sitting in front of a fireplace or around a campfire, you notice that after a while, everybody is just sort of watching the flames, mesmerized. With a wood burning oven, the effect is magnified because the fire is so much more intense, more contained.

During the initial firing, the oven walls turn black with soot, but as the fire gets hotter, the soot burns off and the walls turn white. At about this point, the gasses sitting just below the oven's dome become hot enough to ignite, creating a river of rolling flame that's incredibly, hypnotically beautiful. Alex calls it the Plasma Beast, and it does seem to be alive.

Ferris shows me how to check the oven temperature with the infrared thermometer and I graph the rise, and then the fall when the fire's burned down. I learn how long it takes the oven to equilibrate once the coals and ash are swept out. I also learn—very quickly—not to grab the handle of the metal bucket that contains the coals and ash I've just swept out. And then I begin to work out how to coordinate the readiness of dough and oven.

I sort of assumed that once I learned to build the fire and manage the oven, I'd be ready to start baking wonderful bread, but this is not the case. In fact, my first baking attempt produces six one-pound charcoal briquettes, an object lesson in the physics of brick oven baking.

In an electric or gas oven, bread is essentially baked by heated air circulating around it. In a wood fired oven bread is baked by heated air and by radiant heat from hearth, walls and dome, all of which are upwards of fifty degrees hotter than the heated air. This means a loaf of bread that would take fifty minutes to an hour to bake in a conventional oven, is done after about twenty minutes in a properly fired wood oven. Done at twenty, overdone at thirty, napalmed at anything longer.

Alex studies them, folds his arms and says, "So much for illiterate peasants with no internet access."

The next batch looks better, but the loaves are doughy inside. The third try yields something almost edible. By the following week, baking every morning, I bring forth some *ciabatta* that Alex is willing to use in the café. It's not my finest effort, but people go nuts over it, ripping off chewy hunks and dipping them in the golden green olive oil and sea salt Alex has started putting on all the tables.

On the menu he calls it *pain d'autrefois* or bread made the old way. I prefer the literal translation, *bread of another time*. It evokes the smell of the fire and the mark of the oven and the rustic taste of real bread—just flour, water, yeast and salt—baked in the most primitive, elemental way.

Seventeen

"I talked to Sarah yesterday," Alex says.

It's a lazy Monday morning, and we're lying on his couch drinking coffee and reading the remains of the Sunday papers.

"When did she get back from Houston?"

He folds the paper and sets it on the coffee table. "She's not."

I look up. "What do you mean—she's still there?"

"They found cancer in her other breast."

"Oh, no." I sit up. "What did she say? How did she sound?"

"She didn't actually say too much. Just that she'd be going through chemo again. The worst part is her insurance company dumped her."

"How can they do that?"

He shrugs. "I guess she reached their limits of coverage. She wanted to know if I could find a real estate broker and have them get in touch with her. Looks like she's going to have to sell her place."

"*Shit*. Those assholes." I stand up, then sit down again. "Surely there's some way to do this without selling her house."

"Probably not."

"How can that happen? How can they just cut you off? What the hell is wrong with our goddamn health care system? Why can't we do it like every other civilized country? This is insane."

"All true," he says. "But it doesn't change anything for Sarah."

"That's why she didn't answer my email."

We sit there for a while, not talking.

Then I ask, "Did you know Bill? Her husband?"

"Yeah."

"What's he like?"

"He's an engineer. Kind of quiet. Seems like a good guy."

Then he notices I'm still watching him.

"What do you want me to say? That he's an asshole because he left?"

"I don't want you say anything in particular. I was just wondering—"

"It's nobody's business but theirs," he says abruptly.

I pick up the Style section of the paper and stare at it till the words blur.

He takes his cup to the kitchen. "You want some coffee?" he calls back.

"No. Thank you."

When he comes back he doesn't sit down. He stands beside the couch for a minute, then he takes the paper out of my hands and pulls me to my feet. He leads me through the kitchen, out the French doors to the small deck and stands behind me at the rail, arms around my shoulders.

By island standards the term "view" implies water, or at least mountains, so technically Alex has no view—just a sunny slope where meadow grass ripples hypnotically in the wind and redwing blackbirds stand sentinel on fence posts. In the distance, a line of dark clouds spills over the top of the cool, green forest.

"Maybe we'll get some rain tonight," I say.

"Listen…Bill did the wrong thing, in my opinion. But he did some other things right. He's been paying her insurance. He gave her the title to the house, free and clear."

"Good for him. But what about emotional—I mean, didn't he care? Didn't he want to hold her hand when she was sad or scared? Didn't he—"

"No. The answer to that is he didn't." He moves to stand beside me and brushes some hair away from my eyes. "I think everybody knows on some level what they can handle. I think Bill loved Sarah, and he just couldn't deal with what was happening. And with what he was afraid was going to happen. Does that make him a bastard? I don't know."

We sail out to one of the tiny, uninhabited islands just offshore with the picnic he's packed—grilled chicken sandwiches on my focaccia with pesto aioli, provolone, and roasted red peppers. My favorite Kettle blue corn chips and a wonderful Oregon dry Riesling.

Afterwards, when he opens the thermos of coffee, I reach in my day pack and pull out a small plastic bag.

"What's that?"

"Just a couple of butter tarts."

His eyes light up. "When did you have time to do that?"

"The fact is I've got nothing but time." I look past him, out to the blue open water and tiny dots of islands beyond. "I guess the free ride's about over."

He frowns. "Which means what?"

"It means I need to go home. Get back to work. Somebody else is running my business, and that's not good for me or fair to her. Beside, she's leaving in January."

"I've got a better idea." He finishes the butter tart, wipes his hands on a napkin and takes a swig of coffee. "Stay here."

"Alex, I have to go back to work."

"Stay here and work."

"Doing what?"

"Making bread. At the café. I'll buy from you and you can sell at Evie's."

"Why would she want to sell my bread?"

"So you could see if there's a market for it here, and if there is, you could buy her shop."

"I can't buy her shop. I don't have that kind of money."

"You could if you sold your place in L.A."

I don't know if the goosebumps springing up on my arms are from the sudden breeze or from the fact that he's just articulated something that's probably been lurking unformed in the back of my mind. It's a few minutes before I can trust my voice.

"Alex, how would you feel about selling Rafferty's and moving down to L.A. and opening up a new place?"

He smiles a rueful half smile. "I really wanted it to be a good idea."

"It is a good idea, it's just…"

"Don't say no yet." His voice is as quiet as I've ever heard it. "Think about it a little bit first. Anyway, you don't have to leave yet."

This is the closest we've ever come to talking about the "situation."

I say, "The week before Thanksgiving is the start of our busiest—"

"You'll be back by then. Look, I'm closing the café November 1. We could go up to Vancouver for a few days. We could see a play. I'll take you to a couple of my favorite restaurants. There's a great little B & B there, right near Stanley Park. We can do some Christmas shopping—"

"It sounds perfect, but—"

"I know you have to go home. You say you might not come back. I don't believe that, but just in case…Let's do this one thing. Then we'll just deal with whatever happens after that. Okay?"

He looks straight into my eyes and runs his index finger down the length of my arm, producing another set of goosebumps for a whole different reason.

By the time we get back into the berth at Brandt's Landing, the wind is gusting and dark clouds are gathering to the west. I run between the dock and the car carrying gear, jackets, trash and the picnic leftovers while he takes in the sails and secures the boat. It's sprinkling as we come into the village. Only a few businesses are open and he drives slowly through the empty streets.

I'm lost in a memory of Seattle, rainy afternoons spent at Mac's apartment listening to music, reading, making love. Is this just the way things go? You walk and laugh and touch and argue and go to movies and drink coffee and you stare at each other and wonder how you ever existed without this other person…and this is how it ends up?

"You want to get a movie?" Alex's voice draws me back through that tunnel into the present.

"Okay."

He pulls into the Island Market parking lot and turns off the car. We sit there for a minute, listening to the rain, watching the windows fog up.

"Any preferences?"

"No, get whatever you want."

"So…*RoboCop*?"

I attempt a laugh. "Maybe something more culturally enriching."

He's looking straight ahead. "Wyn, I'm sorry."

"For what?"

"Remember a long time ago when I told you sometimes I see what I'm doing, but I just blunder on through and fuck everything up?"

"You didn't fuck anything up." I smile. "And it wasn't a long time ago. Fifth of July, if my memory serves me."

"Just seems like a long time, I guess. In a good way."

"In the best possible way," I say.

He gets out of the car.

In a few minutes he's back, tossing a DVD of *The Big Chill* in my lap. "How's that?"

"You did good."

"Hey, I had an idea. About Sarah." He shuts the car door. "I was standing there looking at the movies and I just thought, shit…why not do a fund raiser. At the café."

"That's a really great idea."

"I usually have a Halloween party, so this year, it'll just be a really big one, and all the proceeds go to Sarah." He looks over at me. "We'll have to push our Vancouver trip back a day."

"That's okay."

Gears I don't even recall having are creaking to rusty life in my head.

We sit in his kitchen drinking wine, making notes and lists for the party, *The Big Chill* at least temporarily forgotten.

"Six weeks isn't much time to make this happen," I say.

He looks surprised. "Why not? What do we need to do besides plan the menu, order the food, hire some extra help and send out invitations?"

I can't help laughing. "Oh, Alex…you're obviously an event virgin."

"I do stuff like this all the time."

"Fund raisers? Benefits?"

"No…but, you know…parties."

"Big difference. Hand me that ruler." I start marking off columns and lines on my piece of paper. "In my former career as an executive wife,

I was on all kinds of committees to raise money for various good causes. Most people have no idea what goes into planning one of these things."

"Wyn, this is Orcas, not L.A...."

"Are you saying you want to give Sarah a check for two hundred dollars? Two-fifty? Because if you just throw a nice party and ask people to kick in a few bucks, that's about what you're going to get."

He looks blank for a minute, so I press on.

"The first thing we have to decide is what the evening's going to be. Then we figure out what we can get donated. Then we need a committee—"

"Wait a second—"

"We can't do it all by ourselves. You've got a café to run, so your time is limited. I have more time, but I don't know the people here. We need a few worker bees that we can count on to take the ball and run with it. Just stay with me here..."

"Okay...So what's the evening going to be? Besides dinner and drinking and maybe some music?"

"It's Halloween. Let's have a costume contest with prizes. And how about a silent auction?"

"Auction of what?"

"This island is crawling with artists and craftspeople. Surely we can get some of them to donate some work."

"Yeah. Of course." The light has begun to dawn on him. "And Sarah knows most of the business owners—"

"And the restaurant owners. We can ask for gift certificates for meals, tickets to movies, events at the Orcas Center."

Then he sobers up. "There aren't that many people on the island come Halloween. Who's going to buy all this shit?"

"People who live here. People who live on the other islands. And I assume you have a mailing list…?"

"Sure. But a lot of them live out of the area, out of state. People aren't going to come up here at the end of October for a party."

"No, but they can make donations. And they can participate in the auction on line. We just need to make sure all the right people know what's happening and why."

"So I'll donate all the food…"

"Maybe we can find some nice rich person to buy the booze."

He looks at the ceiling. "Good luck with that."

"We'll just have to ask. All they can say is no. Now, who do you know that we can get to work with us? Preferably people who know Sarah and love her."

"That's pretty much everybody," he says.

"Well, out of everybody, if you were hiring people for a job, people with talking skills and organizational talent…"

"Ivy Jacobsen. She's been here so long she's practically a native. She's got money and connections and she had her own tour company in Seattle."

"Excellent. Who else?"

"Rocky Whalen. Former mayor of Eastsound. He knows everybody. He'll be a good arm twister."

"Perfect. Let's start with those two and they can probably bring other people on board."

He refills our wine glasses and laughs. "I'm trying to imagine you in your executive wife days. I bet you were unstoppable."

"I suppose you could say that." I smile and touch my glass to his. "To Sarah."

Eighteen

Mac

This trip could hardly be more different from the first one.

He'd sold everything except his clothes, books and music to buy a ticket on a charter flight to Fiji. After only a few days of snorkeling, learning to windsurf, and drinking Fiji Bitters he was feeling desperate and claustrophobic. Island Fever the locals called it, but he knew it was more than that. His somewhat vague plan to work on a boat or find a cheap flight to Australia wasn't coming together and he needed to get off this island. A chance encounter with some New Zealand foot-ballers at the Royal Suva Yacht Club Bar led to the offer of an empty seat on their charter flight back to Christchurch.

That night was all about the butt-numbing bench seat of the flight from Nadi to Christchurch, drunken snores around the cabin, the cold air blowing in his face the whole trip. Tonight he settles into his sheep-skin covered, fully reclinable seat in Air New Zealand's first class cabin while a pretty flight attendant comes by to hang up his jacket, offer a drink, a menu, headphones and magazines.

He moves over to the vacant window seat and opens the ARC Alan asked him to write a blurb for. He reads the first page three times, before closing the book and dropping it into the seat pocket in front of him. The same flight attendant appears to collect the drink, which he's barely touched, and the plane begins to taxi out to the runway. He closes his eyes, dozing lightly until the engines rumble. The plane rolls, picking up speed, lifts with a grace that belies its mass, and banks in a wide arc out over the Pacific. The lights of Los Angeles recede into the autumn night.

The 6:30 AM traffic is light on the motorway south from the Auckland Airport. This is a good thing. Between remembering to drive on the left, trying not to hit the windshield wipers instead of the turn signal, dealing with the treachery of roundabouts…he doesn't have much attention to spare for other vehicles. Soon enough the road dwindles to two lanes.

Why the hell didn't he just book a connecting flight into Napier and save himself an eight hour drive? He'd had some vague notion that he would be glad of this time alone on the road. To get himself together. To get ready for what's ahead.

As if that were possible.

The sun inches higher, his hands begin to ache, and he realizes he's been clutching the steering wheel in a death grip. He pulls off the road and walks around the car a few times, shaking his hands, tilting his head from side to side, stretching out the ache in his back.

He returns to the car, buckles the seat belt, takes a deep breath and nearly pulls out in front of an SUV because he's looking the wrong way. The other driver swerves and honks as Mac slams on the brakes, heart pounding. *God.* He survives everything else, finally gets here to see Skye and ends up just another stupid Yank getting scraped off the highway.

He looks both ways twice before pulling out again.

Just north of Taupo is Huka Falls. That's where Gillian's father had picked him up hitchhiking, his first question not "Where you headed?" but "Have you worked construction?"

In those days there was nothing but an amazing channel of roaring, churning turquoise water where the whole of Lake Taupo seemed determined to push through a narrow granite chute into the Waikato River. Today he sees signs for a retreat and conference center, jet boat rides on the river.

In Taupo he stops to buy a sandwich and eats it on a bench overlooking the gray-blue, choppy lake. At a shop, he buys flowers—some kind of brightly colored daisies Wyn always liked and which he can never remember the name of—and lays them carefully on the passenger seat. A gentle rain begins.

Back on the road, he falls in behind a silage truck and for a while he relaxes into the monotonous, slow pace, smiles at the sign on the truck's back end…

Please do not overtake when I indicate.

He's forgotten how polite Kiwis are—at least officially.

His memory of the drive over the mountains into Hawke's Bay that day is hazy. Graham wasn't much of a talker and beyond explaining that he was looking for some help at rebuilding a shearing shed that had burned, there wasn't a lot of conversation. He remembers the smell of wet dog from the grizzled huntaway snoozing in back, the dirt and hay on the floor of the old Land Rover. The sun darting in and out of the clouds, the limestone cliffs and green hills dotted with sheep.

At the farm, Graham showed him around, and left him at the bunk house, where he'd discovered that he was not the only recruit. Besides himself there were a couple of Samoans, one South African and an Aussie, none of whom had any experience in construction. That made him the de facto foreman.

Then, as now, it was spring and the weather was unpredictable, changing moods the way some women change clothes, several times a day. When it was raining too hard to work on the shed, the hands would drink and play cards. Everyone was friendly enough, but he couldn't keep up with them in either drinking or cards and sometimes he couldn't even understand what they were saying, although everyone presumably was speaking English. Then, too, his lungs rebelled at breathing the smoky air in the small, dark room off the bunkhouse, so he got in the habit of wandering around the farm, watching Graham and his son Rory and their dogs work the sheep. When the shearing crew came, he watched them, too, fascinated by the strength, skill and speed of the men, most of whom were Maoris— large, tattooed, chain smoking, unflappable except when drunk.

Gillian had gone off on a trip with her cousins, and by the time she came home, the shed was finished. Pay had been distributed; the others had left. Mac had stayed a few days longer to go rock climbing with Rory and when they came back he made plans to head to Tongariro for some hiking and then over to Raglan to try the surfing.

Graham had said if he wanted a lift out to State Highway 5 to be in the driveway at 10 AM when he would leave on an errand.

How do you ever know when some seemingly unimportant event is going to change your life? A thing as trivial as showing up fifteen minutes early. At 9:45 he walked up the hill and set his pack on the ground. He was knocking the dried, caked mud off his boots when a dirty yellow car pulled in from the road. A girl stepped out holding a battered leather duffle, said something to the driver, then laughed and shut the door. She stood waving as the car retreated down the gravel drive, trailing dust.

It was her hair that caught his attention first, a rich brown the color of walnuts, highlighted with gold in the sun, bound into a thick braid that hung halfway down her back. He had a sudden flash—something a woman or a different sort of man might have called intuition—an image of her with the braid undone, hair loose, tumbling over her shoulders. That image stopped his breath for the length of a heartbeat.

When she turned to go up to the house, she seemed to notice him for the first time.

"Oh," she said. "Hello."

He'd seen her before, he realized. She'd helped her mother serve them all dinner for a couple of nights before she left for her holiday. The men had been exhausted and ravenous. He remembered her mainly as a pair of hands that set down plates of food and then cleared them off the table when they were empty.

Now he looked at her for several seconds before responding to her greeting. She returned his gaze the whole time, no blinking or blushing or turning away. She wore jeans and jandals and a sleeveless white shirt that showed tan, well-muscled arms.

She looked at his pack and her eyebrows lifted just slightly.

"You're leaving us, then?"

Without consideration or hesitation, he said, "Not just yet."

Her face opened into a smile. "Good," she said. And she turned and walked into the house.

He's getting close now. Skye had said to watch for a white sign for a boarding kennel. He sees it as he comes over the rise and his stomach feels suddenly hollow. Two kilometers later he turns into the gravel road with several black mailboxes and a row of poplars just leafing out. He doesn't remember the trees.

But he does recognize the white farmhouse with black shutters set back at the end of the drive, the huge Norfolk Island Pine at the corner of the garage. He stops the car, turns off the engine and sits very still, aware of the sound of his own breath. The carefully rehearsed speech is useless now. He gets out of the car and then leans back inside, grabbing the flowers off the front seat. Their heads nod lazily on limp stems. He should have waited to buy them. Stupid.

Lifting his hand to the door knocker, he sees Gillian through the window. She's looking out across the lawn, not at him, but she's obviously seen him. Her profile is clean and sharp against the glass; hair pulled into a loose knot—to her, there's no such thing as a hair style; it's just hair—the memory of her smell, that mix of grass and sweat and soap suddenly returns with perfect clarity.

Now she's opening the door, motioning him inside, and he's close enough to see the silver threads shot through her hair.

"Hi, Gilly."

She says nothing till they reach the kitchen. Then, "So they let you in. Immigration must be slacking off."

"You haven't changed." He can't prevent the slight smile, which she doesn't return.

"Mac, I want this one thing to be perfectly clear. You're not an honored guest. The only reason you're here is because Skye wants you to be, and I feel I owe her that. She can get to know you and decide if you're worth the trouble. And by the way, in case you haven't noticed, she never cashed your check. She said it was the only thing she had from you and she wasn't parting with it. Pathetic, eh?"

"So you haven't told her what a shit I am."

"No need. She'll find out soon enough."

He sighs and sets the flowers down on the table. "I had no way of knowing."

"Of course you didn't. You made damned sure of it. How you could just walk away, never call or write to see if I was okay...or the child...or even just to say hello..."

"When we talked about it, I thought you—"

She turns on him angrily. "You *thought*. What did you think? That I could flush a child out of my body like brushing a burr off my sleeve? And never look back. And never think about who she might have been. You are a total ass. Do you have other children?"

"No."

"Good then. For them."

"I can't excuse what I did. I can't make it right. I don't blame you for hating me."

"And I don't need your permission to hate you."

"Maybe this was a bad idea. I should go to a hotel."

Gillian laughs, but it's not a happy sound. "Believe me, I thought of it. We don't have any hotels around here that are up to your standards, I'm sure."

"I'll find a farmstay. I can drive out in the mornings. I don't want to make things uncomfortable."

She shakes her head, somewhat mollified. "Just the fact you're in the country makes it uncomfortable, there's no changing that. But no. She and I have worked this out, and I'm asking that you just not tip the boat."

"Whatever you want," he says.

Her stare is level. "When was it ever about that?" She wipes her hands on a towel and tosses it on the counter. "Perhaps you remember where the bunkhouse is."

He hesitates. "Where is she?"

"At a friend's house. She said she couldn't bear hanging around here, waiting for you to not appear. I've already called her. She'll be here soon."

It's an ironic bit of symmetry, him walking down the steps with his bag when a dusty green Subaru pulls up and a girl gets out and walks towards him. Nineteen years ago it was Gillian. Today it's Gillian's daughter. Gillian's and his.

The car horn beeps and Skye waves carelessly at the driver without taking her eyes from Mac.

She looks different now in jeans and a T-shirt, jogging shoes with no laces. Tall. Amazingly tall. And beautiful. Older somehow, although it's been barely six months since she stood in the doorway of his house. He stops and sets down his bag. Is he supposed to shake her hand? Hug her? Is she angry? Happy? Wary? Nervous?

She stops a few feet away. How is it possible that someone whose existence was unknown to him for sixteen years should have his eyes, Suzanne's mouth?

"I didn't think you'd come."

"I said I would."

"I thought you'd change your mind. Shall I call you Matthew? Or Matt?"

"Mac."

"Mac." She holds the compact syllable in her mouth like a hard candy.

He picks up his bag, unsure what to do or say next. "Maybe you should go tell your mother—"

"She knows I'm here. She can see everything from the castle tower."

"Well...I guess I should..." He gestures vaguely and begins to walk slowly down a dirt path that leads around the house. She falls in beside him. In the bunkhouse she sits on one of the stripped metal beds while he unpacks the few clothes he brought and she tries to study him without seeming to.

"Why did you decide to come?" she asks.

It's annoying, disorienting, all the things he planned to say falling away, useless, forgotten. What to say? Excuse me a minute while I find my notes.

He takes a breath. "I felt bad...the way I acted when you came."

239

She shrugs. "Rather a surprise, I imagine."

"And…I sort of wrecked my car."

"Sort of?"

"I went off the road. It scared me."

She frowns slightly. "I expect so. Were you hurt?"

"No. What scared me was I realized I might die without …before I got to talk to you."

"Derek went to Rotorua," she says abruptly, twirling a strand of pale hair around her little finger.

"I guess that's understandable."

"He's a great bloke," she adds hastily. "He's been a…he's been great to me." She looks away, flustered, then back quickly, seeking his eyes. "I didn't mean to start off about Derek straightaway—"

"That's okay," he says.

"I'm just nervous. I've been waiting so long. Now you're here, I don't quite know what to do. How long can you stay?"

He smiles. "Long enough, I guess. A week."

"Alright then. Come on." She gets to her feet, links her arm through his, pulling him towards the door. "Shall I show you the farm?"

Soon they're winding up a rutted road that tops a series of green, sheep dotted hills.

He says, "I wanted to tell you that I think you were very brave. To come to L.A. after I didn't answer your letter."

She seems surprised. "Not really so brave. First off, I had no way of knowing if you actually got the letter, since I had to send it to your publishing company. I was hurt when I didn't hear from you, but…" she shrugs. "I was going to be in Los Angeles anyway. What did I have to lose? Maybe you didn't want to meet me, but at least then I would know and not waste any more time on it."

The road narrows, becoming a rock strewn path, and begins to switchback down a steep slope. She moves ahead of him, sure-footed as the sheep that appear to cling to the hills by magnetized hooves, while he slips on small rocks, wishing he'd worn something more substantial than Gucci loafers, tries not to appear totally inept and prays to reach the bottom in one piece.

"I've read all your books," she says. "I loved them. Except the first one."

"*Accident of Birth*? You didn't like that one?"

"No. I mean, I haven't read it. It's out of print."

"I brought you a copy."

"Oh, brilliant. Thank you."

It's embarrassing the way her face lights up. As if he'd done something exceedingly generous.

"I wanted you to read that one."

"It's about you?"

He's about to respond with an interview-formulated observation regarding the tendency of first novels to be somewhat autobiographical, but when he looks at her, he just swallows and says, "Yes."

"When did you start writing?"

"About twelve or thirteen. At first it was just a way of making sense of things. Then I discovered that if I was afraid of things and I wrote about them, they didn't seem quite so horrible."

"What were you afraid of?"

He considers the question. What has he been afraid of all these years? "I don't know...getting lost. Not knowing what to do."

She raises one pale eyebrow. "Getting lost?"

"That's one reason I never really made plans. If you were never supposed to be anywhere, you couldn't be lost."

"You're not talking about a real place, like a city."

"Sorry. I'm not being very clear, am I?"

She shakes her head, smiling. "That's okay. I don't know anyone else who says things like you do. I quite like it."

To his relief, the path finally bottoms out in a lush little valley by a rushing stream. He wonders briefly if the way back involves retracing their steps. She sits down on a jutting rock and pulls something out of her vest pocket…a foil-wrapped chocolate bar. She pats the space next to her.

"Let's sit for a minute. Then I have to go help Mum with tea."

She breaks off a piece of dark, aromatic chocolate and offers it to him. He doesn't really want it, but it melts on his tongue like a bittersweet song. Quite suddenly he finds a memory of Wyn, the way she always carries chocolate in her purse…*for emergencies*, she said. He was never clear on what sort of emergency would require chocolate.

"There's the old orchard." He follows her gaze across the stream to the foot of the next ridge of hills. "We don't really work it anymore, but a few of the trees still bear the most wonderful apples."

Yes. The apple orchard where he had tea with Gillian once. Where they lay down afterwards in the tall grass and watched squadrons of dragonflies cruise the meadow and fat honeybees lose themselves in the fragrant white blossoms.

Just as he's taking the last bite of chocolate, she says proudly, "Mum said that's where I was conceived."

A piece of hazelnut sticks in his throat and he begins to choke. Skye thumps him on the back. "Are you all right?"

He coughs again and tries to talk before he can breathe and it comes out all squeaky. "Swallowed wrong."

"Right." She laughs. "So you didn't know."

Dinner—or tea, as they call it—is excruciating. The discomfort index is equaled only by that awful night when he took Wyn to meet Suzanne. One of them—probably Skye—has stashed his drooping flowers in a jar of water and placed it in the center of the old wooden table. They stand just tall enough to interfere with everyone's line of sight, but no one seems willing to remove them.

When they first sit down, the only sound is the soft ticking of the grandfather clock in the hall. Much of the house seems to have hardly changed in nineteen years, but he doesn't remember the clock. He asks about it.

Gillian's reply is carefully civil. It was her grandmother's and had been at an aunt's house for years. When the aunt moved into a small flat in Hastings, it came back to the farm. She makes no attempt at conversation after that, as if the effort of the explanation has exhausted her. Skye does her best, chatting about her friend Angela and how they're planning to share a flat in Auckland next year, wondering aloud if she'll have to sell her horse, describing for his benefit the class party at the end of term.

"What kind of job are you looking for?" he asks.

"I don't know. Something interesting. Something in the media. Maybe a presenter."

"Have you had any interviews?"

"No, but something will turn up," she assures him. "It isn't a problem."

"It might become a problem when your first rent comes due," Gillian says drily.

This is obviously an on-going issue that he's stepped in the middle of, so he steps out again, addressing Gillian.

"How are your parents?"

"My da is gone. Influenza about five years ago. My mother lives in Napier in a home."

"She's not my gran anymore," Skye says. "She's just a sweet old lady who doesn't know who we are."

"We won't bore you with details," Gillian says firmly.

When he tries to help clear the table, she takes the plate from his hands and asserts that he must be tired in a tone of voice that brooks no discussion. So by nine o'clock he's stretched out, fully dressed on top of his bunk, reading *The Manticore*, by Robertson Davies.

Just as he's about to get up and undress for sleep, there's a tapping at the door. Skye says, "I brought you a torch. In case you need to find the loo."

"Thanks." He takes the heavy flashlight from her.

"I'm not sure if it has batteries." She giggles irresistibly. "It was just an excuse to come see if she'd scared you off."

"Not yet," he says.

She walks past him and takes up her earlier station on the bunk next to his, tilts her head to inspect the book.

"What's a manticore?"

"It's a mythical creature with the head of a man and the body of a lion."

She wrinkles her nose. "Why are you reading a book about that?"

He hands her the book. "Actually, it's about a man undergoing Jungian analysis. The manticore represents him, the point being that he's a man who's partly a beast." He adds casually, "My shrink thought I should read it."

"Does everybody in Hollywood have a shrink?"

"I'm not exactly in Hollywood. But I think in general Southern Californians tend to believe that the unexamined life is not worth living." He sits down on the bed and stuffs the pillow behind his back.

"So that's why you're going? To examine your life?"

"I'm going because…"

"I'm sorry." She seems abashed. "You don't have to tell me."

"No, I don't mind telling you. I just don't want to tell you more than you really want to know."

"I want to know everything. Of course."

"Well…I suppose I should say that the reason I've been seeing a therapist is that I wasn't functioning very successfully."

"Could you be a bit more specific?"

"Clinical depression." He smiles to soften the impact. "I believe the politically correct term is 'affective disorder.'"

"That sounds much more dignified."

"I can assure you there's nothing dignified about it."

"Does it mean you're sad all the time?"

He looks at her. "Not just sad. And not all the time."

"Had you rather not discuss it?"

"Not right now. We'll talk about it later, but not tonight."

"Okay," she says. "Anyway, I wanted to tell you something about Mum." She holds a pause. "I know she's been rather rude since you got here, and I don't want you to think it's just about you."

"What else is going on?"

"She's under a lot of pressure. Financially, I mean. Derek is a lovely bloke and all, but he's no farmer. Mum pretty much runs the place herself. I help her now, but I'll be moving away next year."

"What about her brother?"

"That's the other thing, you see. Uncle Rory was killed two years ago next month. Rock climbing down in the Remarkables. It was terrible. None of us could believe it. Mum stayed in her room for weeks."

"I'm sorry to hear that. We did some climbing together when I was here. He was a good man. A good climber. I liked him."

She gives him an odd little smile. "He didn't like you."

"What do you know about it?"

She shrugs. "Nothing, really. I just heard him say once that he'd never hated anybody till he met you. Then Mum told him to never to say another word like that in front of me."

"You can't really blame him."

She frowns. "It wasn't your fault, after all. You didn't know she was sprogged."

His stomach drops. She doesn't know. Of course she doesn't know. Gillian wouldn't have told her that.

"What's on the agenda for tomorrow?"

"I thought we might go to Napier." She grins. "I'll show you what passes for culture hereabouts."

He smiles. "Don't get cynical just yet. You've got your whole life to develop an attitude."

He walks her to the door, still awkward about touching her, but she turns quickly and puts her arms around his waist, her face against his chest. "Sleep well, Mac. I'll see you at breakfast."

Suddenly he's exhausted. He wasn't able to sleep on the flight, and his internal clock is in turmoil…driving all day, eating at wrong times…

Tossing on the thin mattress in the dark, waiting for sleep, but barely able to lie still, it occurs to him that he might be headed for another episode.

He shakes off the thought, gets up and pulls on his clothes, briefly considers going for a walk, but that would be stupid. It's pitch black out and he'd probably trip over a boulder or step in a hole or the entire pack of dogs would take after him. He finally settles for lying on his back in the grass, hoping there's no sheep shit or dog shit or the leavings of any other animal, and watching the unfamiliar constellations wheel around. He finds the Southern Cross and squints at it. Fixing his location by its sight. Proving that he's really here.

A spring rain moves in Tuesday and Skye hauls out the family photo album. He groans inwardly but soon finds himself riveted by the pictures, only intermittently hearing her breezy commentary.

One of the first shots is of a dozen or so people at a wide, sandy beach. There's a table laden with food, bottles of wine, beer and soda. Everyone is smiling into the camera except Gillian, heavily pregnant, looking off to the side. Skye has obviously taken charge of the scrapbook, drawing an arrow to her mother's belly and writing in childish script "ME!"

There's photo in front of a church—one of the little wood frame Anglican churches that dot the New Zealand countryside.

"That's my christening," Skye says. "This too."

She points to a close-up of Gillian and her parents, smiles plastered on pinched faces. Baby Skye rests in the brawny arms of someone— Rory? Derek?—whose head is cut off in the shot. She's gazing straight up, eyes wide, looking stunned by the strangeness of her new circumstances.

"I don't even know your whole name," he says. "What is it?"

"Skye Marie Wellburne."

"Where did Marie come from?"

"My great grandmother."

There are more photos than he would have expected from a family that worked so hard all the time. He wouldn't have thought they'd find time to be constantly grabbing the camera for shots of Skye, squatting over a mud puddle, studying a birthday cake with four candles, first day of school, perched on a small sturdy pony, a smiling man in gumboots and a sweater standing next to her, one arm looped protectively around her back. Derek.

One shot of Skye, alone at the water's edge, except for the shadow of the photographer, is particularly arresting.

"How old were you there?"

"Seven," she says without pause. "That's when I thought you were a Selkie."

He laughs. "A what?"

She runs her finger along the bottom edge of the page. "You don't know the story then?"

"No."

"My gran told me. Her Irish gran told it to her. The Selkies are an old race, living in the sea. Once a male Selkie shed his seal skin to be a man for one night so he could father a child by a mortal woman. The legend says a Selkie who was with a mortal had to go back to the sea for seven years before being human again. I thought it was time for you to come back. Whenever we went to the beach, I used to watch for you."

The afternoon is darkening on the steady rain, and noises of meal preparation are coming from the kitchen.

"Do you have pictures?" she says when he closes the album.

"No," he says. He hadn't even thought about the fact that she would want to know about his family.

"What about your mum and dad?"

"I don't remember my father too well. He wasn't home much."

"He travelled for work?"

"I think that was his excuse. He did some kind of technical writing. He changed jobs a lot."

"What about your mum?"

"She was beautiful. You look a bit like her. You have her smile. The same color eyes. Like mine."

"Has she passed on, then?"

"No."

"You said she was beautiful."

"I haven't seen her in about …twelve years."

"You weren't close."

He shakes his head. "I recently found out that she had depression, too. But when I was a kid, I just thought she was always sad. I thought it was my fault. I tried to stay out of her way."

She listens, digesting this.

"It runs in our family," he says. "Depression. You need to be aware. If you start being sad or scared or angry for long stretches of time—"

"You mean like the entire holiday when Joe Dealy dumped me?"

"No, not like that. It's a sadness that has no name, no reason. It seems never ending. It makes you lose interest in everything. It can make you angry. At the wrong people. For the wrong reasons."

"But you don't have it now?"

"No…"

"How do you get rid of it?"

"I don't know. I think it's like a cycle."

She studies him, frowning. "Does that mean it might come back?"

The room is quite dark now, and he reaches behind her to turn on a lamp.

"Probably," he says.

"What about drugs? One of the teachers at school had a breakdown but she's on pills now."

He settles into the couch. "I don't want to take meds. But I guess it could come to that."

"Why don't you want to?"

"Oh…lots of reasons."

"Like what?"

"For one thing, most of them have side effects. So you have to take more drugs to deal with the side effects. And sometimes they stop working...and I guess I just don't like the whole idea of drugs changing your brain."

She looks at him. "What if it needs to be changed?"

The rain tapers off during the night and after breakfast Skye proposes taking a lunch and driving up Te Mata Peak.

When he walks up to the house Gillian is at the kitchen table with a ledger, which she closes abruptly when she sees him.

"She's getting dressed. She'll be down soon. You'll probably be more comfortable in the parlor."

"Gilly...Skye told me about Rory. I'm sorry to hear it."

"You're lucky he's gone. He said if you ever showed your face here he'd kill you. And I think he might have done."

"She said things were difficult now...with the farm."

"A couple of lean years is all. It happens." She folds her arms. "We had a bad drought in '98. When we got the sheep to market, nobody wanted them. Couldn't afford to feed them. We had to sell at a big loss."

"I could—"

"We'll be fine."

"Jesus, don't be so stubborn. Let me help."

"We'll be fine."

He pushes on doggedly. "What about Skye's school fees? I could help with that."

She gives him a measured look. "Are you in some sort of program?"

"What?"

"You know, where they make you search out everyone you've wronged and make amends."

"No, nothing like that. Not that it's a bad idea." He sighs involuntarily. "I wish it was that simple. I wish I could make amends. To you especially. And her."

There's a reluctant smile that he remembers. "Well, it's good you owned up to it...even if it did take you eighteen years. Oh, don't look so grim. I've a good life and so does she."

"No thanks to me."

"We didn't need you." She says it quietly, without anger. "I just had to be practical."

"You were always practical."

"Not always..." She shakes her head. "I had my moments of fancy. For awhile I kept thinking you'd suddenly re-appear. Like in the movies."

"I'm sorry. I know I can't—"

"Never mind. I didn't say it to make you apologize again. I just want you to know how it's been. Finally I fell in love with Derek. Really in love. He always jokes about how he wore me down, but yes, I love him. He loves Skye like she was his own. It hurt him that she didn't want to be adopted. So it was just sad, you see. Sad for him because she was always holding out for you. Sad for you because another man raised your daughter." She looks at him suddenly. "Oh, Mac, for God's sake, don't get all weepy."

"Sorry." He swipes at his eyes, embarrassed. "Gilly ...do you think someday you could forgive me?"

She spreads both hands, palms down on the table and studies them. Then she looks up at him. "I never expected the question to come up," she says. "So I haven't thought much about it. Quite honestly, I don't know."

At that moment Skye comes through the door, seeming about to speak, but she stops, looks from Mac to her mother.

They both smile.

Gillian says quickly. "You'd better go while the weather holds. And take a tarp to sit on. It's going to be wet."

He points the rental car towards State Highway 2 and the coast while Skye brushes her hair.

"When did Derek and Gillian get married?" he asks.

"About ten years ago. But he was mooning over her forever. In fact…" She pauses thoughtfully. "I don't remember a time when he wasn't around."

"Did you ever think he was—"

"Heavens, no. He's always been Derek to me." She looks over. "He wanted to adopt me, you know. When they married. He asked me if I wanted it. I said no."

"He must be a very good man."

"He is—Mac, are you nervous?"

"No, why?"

"Because you're driving on the wrong side of the road."

He veers to the left quickly, stopping the car on a pullout, resting his head against the steering wheel with a sigh.

"Maybe I should drive."

He walks around to the left side of the car while she scrambles agilely over the gearshift into the driver's seat.

They stop to buy bread, honey, cheese, olives, chocolate. Outside of Havelock North, she turns the car onto an impossibly narrow twist of blacktop, switchbacking up four hundred meters sans guardrail. He feels vaguely nauseous as she nonchalantly twirls the steering wheel, chatting the whole time about the Maori chief Te Mata O Rongokako who legend says died there from trying to eat a passage through the hills to court a beautiful princess.

"You probably heard that one before," she says.

"I don't remember. It seems like a strange way to impress a woman."

She wrinkles her nose. "Too right. Who'd want to kiss someone who'd been eating his way through a hill? Not to mention sheep shit."

He looks at her sideways and laughs.

At the top she parks on a level patch of gravel; they gather their groceries and she leads the way to a nook in the lee of the hill that offers some protection from the gusting wind. He spreads the tarp on the damp ground and she adds a lovely wool blanket, tossing it down like an old rag. They sit down, backs to the hill.

"I want to know everything about you."

His heart stops momentarily, then lurches into a faster rhythm.

"What do you want to know?"

She laughs. "Whatever you want to tell me."

What does he want to tell her? That he loved her mother, but not enough?

Or should he tell her about the rest of his life? The accident, of course. Followed by a series of escapes from things that became too familiar, too close. The depression. The way he screwed up his marriage. Maybe she'd like to know about his work. How it began with promise and sank into drivel.

"Tell me about your wife. Her name's Wyn?"

He nods. "Wynter. She's a baker. We're not actually together…at the moment."

"Oh. Why not?"

"Mostly my fault. And the depression. I haven't been very good to be around for a long time."

"Come on, Mac." There's a touch of impatience now. "Don't make me drag it all out. Talk to me. Don't you want to?"

Her hair flies wildly in the wind around her solemn face and the tenderness he feels is like pain.

"Of course I want to. But parts of it are…there are things I've done that—"

"I need to know the truth. It's the way I am."

"It's just…now that I've found you, I don't want to lose you."

"I found you," she corrects him. "And you're not going to lose me."

She opens the white paper sack, tears off a chunk of bread and holds it in her front teeth while cutting a healthy slab of cheddar. He opens a can of soda and hands it to her, but she declines.

"A whole can of that stuff is too much," she says. "I'll just have a wee bit of yours."

Why had it seemed so unbearably complicated when she first appeared? So overwhelming. Now it feels entirely natural to sit with her and watch the gulls and gannets riding the thermals over a wrinkled green ocean of hills. Below them two cyclists struggle up the steep road and beyond the hills Hawke Bay is a distant crescent of turquoise water. She tugs the soda can from his hand and steals a drink.

"When it's clear you can see Mt. Ruapehu," she says, pointing over her shoulder. "Too hazy today."

"I think New Zealand is about the most beautiful place I've ever seen."

She nails him with a look. "Then why did you go?"

No more fill in the blank and multiple choice, it's time for the essay question. He picks up a handful of pebbles and tosses them one at a time over the cliff into oblivion.

While he's still searching for the right words, she says,

"I don't want Mum to hate you."

"I hope that might change someday, but you have to understand... how hard it was on her—"

"I know it was hard, but it wasn't like you did it on purpose. I mean, you didn't know."

Now the hills are changing color under the fast-moving clouds. He says nothing.

"Did you?" Her voice is fainter now, more hopeful than certain.

When he turns back to her, she's chewing her lower lip. He wants desperately to lie. No. He wants to say he didn't know and have it be the truth. But it wasn't and it isn't and he has to tell her.

"I did," he says. "I did know."

One tear slides down her cheek so quickly that it seems it must have been there all along, waiting. He wants to brush it away, but he can't touch her. Not now. Not before he tells her the rest. She doesn't say anything, but her silence isn't a weakness, a lack of knowing what to say. It's a demand. She's waiting for him to speak.

"I knew and I couldn't stay. I didn't want a family. I told Gilly I thought she should…"

What? Have the problem taken care of? How do you say that when the problem is sitting there looking at you with tears on her face?

"I gave her money. To go to Auckland. To a clinic. To get an abortion. She said she would, but I'm sure she never intended—"

"Why would she say it if she never meant to?" The tiny liquid tremor in her voice is like something sharp between his ribs.

"Because she only wanted me to stay if I wanted to, not because she asked me to. Not because I felt like I should."

She begins to cry freely now, like a child. He makes himself watch her. He grits his teeth against the meaningless words of explanation and comfort that might spill out. When he leans towards her, she says, "And why did she never tell me that later on?"

"Because she didn't want you to grow up hating your father. Skye, I'm so sorry."

She scrambles to her feet and walks back down the path. He watches her climb in the driver's side and, after only a second's hesitation, start the car and pull out onto the empty road.

He's hitchhiked this road before. One short ride, then a long one returns him to the State Road near Hawke's Bay and it's beginning to rain again. He walks back to the farm. It's late and he's soaked to the skin when Gillian answers his knock. He sets down his sopping bundle.

"Can I talk to her? Just for a minute."

"You just had to tell her." She says it calmly, without obvious emotion, but he can feel the cold eddies beneath the surface.

"She wanted the truth. I couldn't lie to her."

"Ah well, now we're suddenly noble. You lie about everything else, all your whole, goddamned life. Selfish lies. What's one more if it would spare her the pain of knowing you wanted her dead?"

"I didn't want her dead, for God's sake—"

"*Shut up!* Haven't you done enough?"

"Gillian—"

"Derek was the one who loved her, changed her dirty diapers, played in the mud, took her to school. Then you come riding in like the white knight and sweep her off her feet and break her heart. Just go away and leave us alone. Just go."

That night, with his bag packed and sitting on the table, he falls asleep and dreams.

Wyn and Gillian sitting at a kitchen table, heads together, two cups of tea before them. Wyn's reddish porcupine to Gilly's sleek dark ferret. They're laughing in that way that women do—and smoking cigarettes, which is weird, because neither of them smokes. Suddenly he wakes to the smell of smoke. He's on his feet with the lamp on before he realizes that Skye is sitting on the couch, tin ashtray balanced on her knee, puffing awkwardly but vigorously.

He rubs his eyes. "I didn't know you smoked."

"I thought I'd try it," she says. "It's not very tasty, is it?"

"No. Not really." He pulls on jeans and a flannel shirt and sits down on the bed.

She stubs out the cigarette and looks at his duffle bag, open on the table. "Are you going?"

"I think it's time."

"I read the book," she says.

He notices then that she's holding the copy of *Accident of Birth*, hugging it against her stomach.

"It made me cry."

"It was a long time ago."

"It's all true?"

"More orderly than real life, but essentially…" He runs a hand through his hair. "You think writing's going to help you understand. You hope it'll be cathartic. So you can stop thinking about it, stop dreaming about it. But it doesn't do any of that."

"So why write it?"

He shrugs. "I'm not sure. Maybe you have to. Maybe it's like the cork in the bottle. You have to get it out before you can pour anything else."

"Will you sign it for me?" She holds up a pen.

He moves over to sit beside her, takes the book and opens it to the title page.

For Skye Marie

He rolls the pen back and forth between his fingers. There's a thickness behind his eyes and his throat is tight.

My lovely daughter

Tears are sliding down her cheeks, wetting the front of her shirt. She says, "I don't care what you did. I don't care who said what and I don't care whether you knew. I love you. Do you love me?"

"Yes—" he nearly chokes. "I don't even know how to say it or what to do."

"You don't have to do anything. Just be there when I call you on the phone. Let me come visit you. Talk to me. I need to know who you are."

She sits beside him on the dusty, sprung couch with its ugly blue plaid slipcover, resting her head against his shoulder. He holds her, strokes the silky hair so much like his own. He holds her while the jerky sobs become slower, the gulps become shallow breaths and the darkness outside the window turns to silver.

He feels the hard place in his chest go slack.

His heart is breaking and for once he's going to let it.

Nineteen

The island is beautiful now, the leaves underfoot, the bits of blue sky overhead, the cool mornings, the damp afternoon chill. Living in Southern California, you sometimes don't notice fall until it's almost over. Here, it's obvious and intense, lovely and sad.

It's also been mostly a blur because of frantic preparations for Halloween. The thing has taken on a life of its own, which is what you always hope for. It's been so long since I've been involved in anything like this that I'd forgotten how mighty a small but motivated group of volunteers can be. Sarah is clearly well loved by everyone who knows her, which includes many of the full time Orcas residents, as well as summer people, who know her from the farmers' market.

Ivy Jacobsen has turned out to be the irresistible force, and any immovable objects have been swept aside. She has recruited two other women to the cause and between them they've brought in a tidy little trove of arts and crafts, gift certificates, tickets and passes for various events. Through her tour company, she's friends with the GM at Rosario, and she persuaded him to offer a weekend stay in one of the resort condos.

Because the café is so small, we've branched out into tenting the patio and she got that donated, too, as well as some friend of hers picking up the liquor tab, which is truly amazing. Tickets to the party itself sold out mid-month, and rather than turn locals away, Ivy and her buddies have set up two auxiliary parties in private homes.

Three other restaurants are providing food, which is good, because, formidable as he is, I don't think Alex could have done it all.

Rocky Whalen, the former mayor, is like the character in the movie that the hero calls on to get seemingly impossible tasks accomplished. He's our go-to guy for permits and contracts and insurance. He also convinced the movie theatre to donate the proceeds from a special screening of *The Rocky Horror Picture Show* by promising to attend dressed as Dr. Frank N Furter. His son, Rocky Jr., who's in graduate school, has volunteered to handle the on-line bids for the auction, and his wife Ava is coordinating all the decorations.

By the third week in October, my work is pretty much done. The volunteers have taken over and I'm reduced to maintaining the Excel spreadsheet that tracks all activities, expenses and income.

The morning of the party, Alex is making breakfast for us while I sit on the counter by the stove, reading aloud from his new copy of *Kitchen Confidential* by Anthony Bourdain. Alex alternates between shaking his head and roaring with laughter at some of the more outrageous parts.

"Is all that stuff true?' I ask after a particularly raunchy passage.

"In some kitchens, sure. I worked at one place like that in my wild and crazy days. Boniface. It's not there anymore. I always wonder what happened to those guys."

"They're probably either dead or in rehab."

He turns on the flame under a sauté pan and tosses in a knob of butter, tilting the pan from side to side.

The stove is so hot that the butter's foaming as soon as it melts. He tosses chopped garlic into the pan and the air is instantly full of one of my favorite smells.

He throws a few handfuls of spinach in with the garlic. After a very few seconds, it's slightly wilted and he pushes it to the outer edges of the pan leaving space for four eggs. "Can you drop a couple pieces of bread in the toaster?"

In five minutes we're sitting at the table. In front of us are two plates of jewel green spinach topped by two perfect sunny-side-up eggs with deep golden yolks. A few crumbles of goat cheese softening on top and a piece of warm whole wheat toast on the side.

The combination of warm egg yolk and spinach is like swallowing silk. I stop eating for a minute just to enjoy the sensation.

"I love this goat cheese."

"It's from Windward Farms over on Lopez. I'm going over there when we get back from Vancouver. You should come with me."

I press a piece of the cheese with my fork and deposit it on my tongue. It has an elusive quality to it, mildly tangy and sweet at the same time, and super creamy.

"Are you dressing up for the party?" I ask him.

"Ivy thinks I should. She wants me to go as Arlo Guthrie. You know that old song…"

"Alice's Restaurant."

"Yeah, that's it. This woman wrote a riff on it a couple years ago. Alex's Restaurant."

"I heard it once."

"What are you going to wear?"

"I'm not going." Sometimes you say things that you don't realize are true until you hear your own voice. That's when I realize it was always true. I never intended to go.

It's quiet for a minute, then he says, "Why?"

I look up into his dark eyes. "Because I can't. It just feels wrong. This is not the time for me to be going to parties."

"But it was your idea—"

"No, it was your idea."

"Well, just the beginning. You came up with all the cool stuff, you planned the whole thing—"

"It was for Sarah. Everything's under control now. I don't need to be there."

"I want you to be there. I want to introduce you to—"

"Alex, that's exactly why I can't do it. Don't you understand?"

"In a word, no."

My eyes are welling up, and I have to wait before I can say, "It's the end."

"We're still going to Vancouver. Right?"

"Yes, but that's just you and me. And as soon as we get back I have to leave."

"You said the week before Thanksgiving—"

"I said the week before Thanksgiving is the *beginning* of our busiest time. I can't wait till then to go back. I've got…things to do. To get ready."

"Okay." He gets up and pulls on his jacket.

"Alex, I'm just—"

"We'll talk about it later." He picks up his keys off the counter. "I've gotta go meet Ivy."

He doesn't quite slam the door.

I sit still for a minute, my appetite gone. Isn't this what always happens? No matter how careful you are, how honest you try to be, somebody ends up getting hurt or pissed off. Usually both.

As penance I clean up the kitchen before I get in the car and head back to my place.

Just as I'm unlocking my front door, my cell phone beeps that I have a message. I call voice mail and hear Tyler's voice, slightly breathless.

"Hey, *jefe*. Just wanted to let you know we're all okay, so don't worry. I'll call you later."

I stand there, staring at the phone, feeling a slow chill steal up the back of my neck. *We're all okay?*

I plug in my computer and dial up the internet. After an interminable wait, it opens to CNN and I see the headline.

5.8 Temblor Rattles L.A.

I'm first car in line for the early ferry. I spent all day yesterday cleaning the house and packing and at 4 this morning I locked the door, tossed my suitcase in the trunk and headed for the landing. A light rain is falling and the road gleams wet and black as I wind down the hill. The streets of the village are empty and I avoid looking at the café. I considered calling Alex, but I didn't want to wake him. I didn't call him last night because I knew things would be crazy. And he didn't call me. Still angry, I guess. I'll call him when I get to Seattle.

When I finally reached Tyler yesterday she was nonchalant.

"Is everyone okay? No one's hurt?"

She sighed. "Didn't you listen to my message? We're fine. It was right after six and Cheryl and I were the only ones in the bakery. We got under the big table and just rode it out. Have you talked to your mom?"

"They had a couple of pictures come down, but nothing else."

"The front window's broken, but it's in place. Some things came off the shelves…Power's back on now. The EMA guys came and yellow tagged the building, which means there's damage but it's safe—"

"Tyler, I grew up in L.A. I know what a yellow tag means."

Silence.

"I'm sorry, Ty. I'm just upset."

"Well, you should be. The earthquake never would've happened if you'd been here."

In the space of time that I'm in the Village Market buying a latte, the wind picks up and the rain goes from steady to deluge. I get soaked on my run back to the car and when I grab the door handle I inadvertently squeeze the cup, squirting a geyser of coffee all over my coat sleeve.

At the instant I jump in, pulling door behind me, I realize that Alex is sitting in the passenger seat. I stare at him.

"What are you doing?"

He gives me back a steady look. "Saying goodbye, looks like."

I set the coffee cup on the dashboard and push the wet hair off my face, blot my sleeve with a rain-soggy napkin. "I was going to call you from Seattle. I didn't think you'd be up yet."

"I saw it on the news last night when I got home. So I figured this is where I'd find you."

I lean my head back against the seat. "Tyler says the damage isn't bad. A broken window. Stuff fell off shelves."

"That's good."

"How was the party?" I take a sip of coffee and offer him the cup.

He shakes his head. "Incredible. It was so...I wished you were there. I'm going to call Sarah today."

"Give her my love."

"There were a lot of things I wanted to talk about," he says. "Any chance you'll be back?"

My eyes begin to sting. "Probably not any time soon. Getting the place put back together before the holiday is going to be a push...and Ty's leaving in January."

"Maybe in the spring," he says.

"Maybe. It all depends…"

The ferry has docked and trucks are rolling up the ramp. We watch them in silence and then the guy is waving his flashlight at me.

"Alex—" It's all I have time to say. He leans over to kiss me and gets out of the car.

"Be safe," he says before he shuts the door.

I know I should be thrilled that the tag on the door is yellow and not red, but the sight of the boarded up front window is distressing, like seeing someone you love in a full body cast. Before I can get my key out, Tyler opens the door.

She stands stiff-legged while I hug her, looking over her shoulder at the pile of debris in the middle of the floor.

She says, "There was supposedly an aftershock about noon, but we didn't even feel it. Did we?"

"Nope." Cheryl has come out front, wiping her hands on a towel and smiling determinedly. "We're getting things put back together."

"I know you are and you're both doing a great job and I really appreciate it." I set my purse down on a table and pull out my camera. "Let's have a look."

I walk around taking pictures of the damage, and they follow, not talking. The only sound is our steps crunching on plaster crumbs and broken glass. The Bread Maven may be considered habitable from a building safety standpoint, but all that really means is we can get in and do the clean-up. It's probably going to be several days before we can open for business.

The coffee station has fallen over, contents flying off the open shelves—napkins and flatware, sweeteners and empty carafes, boxes of tea and condiments, and what looks like about half of our china cups. In the work area, one of the huge mixers has wandered to a different location, ripping its plug out of the wall socket and taking the GFI plate with it. Pans and utensils are stacked on the tables waiting a turn in the dishwasher.

One of the break room cupboards came open, disgorged its contents, mainly plastic glasses and packages of paper towels. All the others stayed shut.

Everything that was on my desk is now on the floor, except, thank God, for the computer. My bookcase lies on its side, the books piled haphazardly around it.

I'm kind of surprised by the extent of the damage because the only casualty at the house was a picture off the wall that gouged a chunk out of the hall floor. And of course some of the pool water got sloshed around the yard, so there will be chlorine damage. But it beats having the china cabinet fall over.

Tyler and Cheryl are watching me, trying to gauge my reaction. Finally I say,

"Well…it could be worse. Cheryl, why don't you call Benny and Hola and Ottmar and see if they can come in and work tomorrow. We're going to need some muscle."

For four days we sift through the debris, salvaging what's usable, junking what's not. We mop and scrub everything with bleach solution, set up the cabinets, attach the coffee station to the wall with L brackets, call the electrician and the plumber and the glass company. We use the opportunity to re-paint the wood trim a soft sage green. We throw out the spoiled bread dough, send everything still edible to Santa Monica Red Cross for the volunteers, repair equipment and restock supplies and on day five we re-open.

I spend the morning in my office filling out forms and arguing on the phone with our insurance agent who wanted us to wait until everything was approved by the claims department to do anything. I point out to him that waiting another week would have increased the amount of our losses. He tells me that it's going to be "really difficult" to get approval now that no one can look at the actual damage. I offer to bring him the photos I took. After a lot of back and forth we say goodbye politely. Having worked five twelve-hour days in a row, I'm too tired to care.

I open Outlook to find—along with a half dozen offers of earthquake insurance and information on low-cost SBA loans, the only catch being we have to be declared a disaster area—an email from Alex.

Hey—hope things are back to normal. Talked to Sarah…finally. She sounds like a train wreck. Her farm will go up for sale after the holidays. When I told her about the party she cried for ten minutes. Grand total take was $4730 and some change. I guess it's not much in the overall scheme of things, but I think everyone was happy. Let me know when you have time for a phone call. I miss you. A

I create a new file named Orcas and drop the message in.

After lunch Tyler takes me around, pointing out new products, introducing me to a few new staff. It's as if she's the proud owner and I'm a tourist. Bread Maven employees are a bit tentative at first. Understandable. The witch who owns the place has returned, and it will be awhile before they know if they're getting the benevolent Glinda or the green skinned Elphaba.

Tyler has tactfully removed her things from my office and later when we're sitting there with the door closed, she says,

"I know you think we didn't need you…"

I shake my head. "No, I feel like you did need me. And I wasn't here."

"You're crazy. You know that, right?"

"Are you excited about Greystone?" I ask.

"Scared brainless."

"You're going to do great."

She's looking a little sad. "Cheryl's doing really good, but there's bound to be a few hiccups."

"We've still got almost two months. That's a good transition period. I'm glad I came back."

She nods. Then, "What about Mac?"

"I don't know. Just have to figure it out."

"He was in here a few weeks ago."

"Really?"

"Having coffee with some guy."

I laugh. "Well, as long as he pays the bill, there's no need to terrorize him."

"You better change the damn locks on your house."

"The place is still half his."

"Hmph." She frowns and I reach over to take her hand.

"Don't worry. It'll work out, one way or the other. You just keep your eyes on the prize."

Saturday the Maven is crazy busy. On Sunday morning CM calls me.

"I hate to ask you, but I need some help. I've been in Chicago all week and my apartment looks like Tornado Alley. Can you come?"

We spend the day cleaning up, throwing out broken dishes, putting bookshelves back together and art back on the walls. When we finish shampooing the living room carpet, it's after 8 PM, and she insists on taking me out to dinner. At Farm Girl in Sherman Oaks we chow down on their rare roast beef salad with sweet yellow peppers and crunchy snow peas. To wash it down we split a bottle of Zinfandel. By the time we finish a shared piece of Shaker lemon tart, I know I'm not driving back to Luna Blanca.

I fall asleep on her couch without so much as washing my face, and sleep straight through till 8:30 Monday morning. She's already gone when I wake up.

After a long, hot shower and a leisurely breakfast I hit Gelson's to stock up on food. It's past noon when I get home and I realize I forgot the garage door opener, so I park in front and schlep two bags of groceries into the kitchen, then go out for the other two. When I come back in and kick the door closed behind me, I notice a stack of books on the living room couch.

While my brain is still processing this information, the squeak of the stair makes me gasp. And there he is.

Standing at the bottom of the stairs, wearing sweatpants, a T-shirt, tube socks, and carrying his running shoes. It's incredibly weird. Like seeing someone on the street who you know is dead.

"Hi," he says.

Finally I manage, "What are you doing here?"

"Well...I...moved back in," he says.

I feel sick. If thinks he's moving the bimbo into my house, I swear I'll shoot both of them and go to the gas chamber with a smile on my face.

I lower the grocery bags to the floor.

"What's going on?"

He sits down on the bottom step and pulls on the shoes, tying the laces double. I start mentally ticking things off. Like...his hair is neatly trimmed and he's clean shaven. And I don't smell cigarettes.

"I guess you didn't get my message."

"I guess not."

"When I got back from New Zealand I left a message at the Orcas house. The land line—"

"You went to New Zealand?"

"When was the last time you checked messages?"

"I…don't remember."

"When I got back, I had to go to New York and I called to ask if it would be okay to move my stuff back over here. When I didn't hear from you, I just…"

My brain is racing like a gerbil on an exercise wheel. "But…when…?"

"I got back last night," he says. "Late. I was just going out to run, but I can put those away first." He looks at the groceries.

"No, that's okay. Go ahead."

"I won't be long." And he's out the door.

I'm totally lost. Alice down the rabbit hole. The Mad Hatter has moved into my house.

In the kitchen I boil water for raspberry iced tea. I put the food in the refrigerator and the pantry and the cabinets. Small things, mindless tasks. Just let me stay busy and stop my brain from racing ahead, anticipating what he's going to say, what I need to say. I scrub the sink even though it's not dirty. The hole in the screen has been mended.

A while later I hear the front door. He comes into the kitchen shirtless, mopping his face with the T-shirt. I avoid looking at him, the familiar long curve of his back, the shape of his shoulders. I suddenly recall the feel of his skin, the scent of him. He fills a glass with ice and pours warm tea over it, then looks at me.

"Did you want some?"

I hold out my glass and he fills it.

We sit, silent for a few minutes, like two strangers forced to share a table in a crowded café. We shake the ice in our glasses, make finger marks in the condensation. He pulls the shirt on over his head and looks at me.

"This is so hard," he says. "I feel like I've been living in a foreign country. Wyn, I'm sorry. For the way things have been. The way I acted. I'm sorry for the way I treated you."

He talks slowly, choosing his words carefully, watching my face. "I know being sorry doesn't change what happened, but…I was sick. I am sick, I guess. It took me a long time to accept that. To get some help."

So this is what I've been waiting for all this time, for him to say *I'm sorry. I didn't mean to hurt you. You didn't do anything wrong. It was me. Here's what happened…*

Now it's been said. Why doesn't it make any difference? What do I say? *Glad you're feeling better, but while you were in your foreign country I did some traveling of my own.*

I want my anger back. I hate the sadness that's mushrooming in my chest.

"I can't do this right now." I stand up. "The bakery. We've been putting things back together. CM. Her apartment was trashed…"

He looks disappointed. "Okay. I know you're tired. We can talk later."

I leave the kitchen and start up the stairs.

"I'll put my stuff in the guest room," he calls after me.

Twenty

It's after 6:30 when I come into the kitchen Tuesday evening. His car isn't in the garage and the house is silent. My clogs are covered with flour so I leave them on the mat. There's an open bottle of Malbec in the pantry. I pour some in a wineglass and sit down at the table, but I'm too tired to lift the glass. Instead I lean forward, pillowing my head on my arms.

The rumble of the garage door makes me sit up. For a second I think about taking my wine upstairs, but I can't muster the energy for a quick escape.

And then he's standing in front of me, holding a brown, grease spotted sack that can only have come from one place. When he sets it on the table, the smell confirms it. McMurdo's fried chicken is the poultry equivalent of heroin. We look at each other and, as if by unspoken agreement, we fall immediately into a familiar routine.

"Rough day?"

"Not really bad. It's just…losing Tyler is such a body blow. She's been more than my right hand for so long."

"She's leaving?"

I'd forgotten he didn't know. "CIA Napa. She's been accepted into the pastry arts curriculum."

"That's a pretty big deal, isn't it? You think she'll come back?"

I shrug. "She says she wants to, but it's almost two years. A lot can happen. I feel like maybe I pushed her too hard."

He takes a wineglass out of the cupboard and fills it.

"I think she liked it that you depended on her. It gave her a way to repay what she felt she owed you."

I take a sip of wine and rub the back of my neck.

He asks, "How's the Maven? Did you have much damage?"

"Enough. But it could have been a lot worse. What did you do today?"

"I worked this morning, then went for a run along the Palisades. Ran into Gabe. We went to the Daily Grind. He said to say hi."

"Gabe…Cleveland?" I look up quickly. "Six months ago he was an obnoxious twit, now you're having coffee with him?"

He says, "We're starting a male bonding encounter group. Sensitivity training."

The laugh I'm trying to stifle makes me choke.

He smiles, obviously pleased with himself. I look at him leaning against the counter in his faded green NYU sweatshirt and jeans, his hair a little messed up in front, flopping down on his forehead. Those beautiful gray-green eyes that crinkle around the edges when he smiles. Telling me about his day, asking me what I did. It all looks so normal. As if the last six months were simply a bad acid trip.

I get plates and silverware and napkins. He parcels out the chicken, tops off our glasses, and we begin to eat. Silently. After two bites, I stop and watch him. He cuts up his chicken, carefully herding the crisp crumbs into a neat little pile on the plate. I remember now. He has incredible dexterity with knife and fork. I generally eat with my fingers, except in restaurants.

"What are you thinking about?" His voice cuts through my brain fog.

"I was thinking…how strange it feels to be sitting here with you having dinner and a quasi normal conversation after six months of—"

"It feels strange to me too. But it feels so good." He looks down at his hands, then back up into my eyes. "I wish I could make everything like it never happened. But I can't. We just have to deal with it."

"And how do we do that?"

"I think we have to start by talking about it."

Anger runs straight up my spine like a steel rod. "You know…I come home expecting that the next time I see you will be in divorce court, and surprise! My husband's back. And he's moved into the house. And he suddenly wants to talk. Sorry, but I'm confused."

He tilts the chair back on two legs.

"I was hoping that ten good years would at least be worth a—"

"Not ten, eight. See, I finally figured it out. You were leaving for the last two years and I didn't know it. I didn't want to know it. I kept trying to understand, I kept asking what was wrong and you totally shut me out. It was like talking to a brick wall. I thought it was me. And you let me think that."

I drink some wine. I pick up a drumstick and set it down. I'm so twitchy I can hardly sit still.

"But now I'm trying to explain myself. To tell you how I feel. All those things you always said you wanted from me—and you won't listen."

"Did it ever occur to you that I might get tired of trying?"

He sighs. "Goddamn it, I'm sorry. Can we just talk about it?"

"So what happened? Things didn't work out with Liv?"

"Please believe me, this whole thing with Liv was a symptom, not the problem. It didn't even—"

"Were you sleeping with her or not?"

Instead of answering, he rocks the chair forward. "Were you sleeping with Alex?"

It's like riding a bicycle off a cliff. Pedals spinning, suspended in air for a few seconds. My breath catches, making a little gasping noise.

"He's always had a thing for you. Didn't you ever notice?"

I find my voice again. "No. Actually I didn't notice. I was too busy trying to be with you."

His hand on my arm feels like some inanimate object. "I'm not trying to make you feel bad. I don't blame you. Or him. I just want to talk about everything. About us."

"I'm not sure there's still an 'us'."

"We won't know till we talk about it."

Suddenly I'm exhausted. The energy of fury has drained out of me and I feel like an empty balloon.

"I can't right now. I've been running on adrenaline for the past week and I'm totally strung out. I can't even think about it."

He hesitates. "Do you want me to move out?"

I can't help laughing. "Oh, that's good. All those months I wanted you to come home and you wouldn't—"

"Couldn't."

"Whatever. Now you're back and I don't know if I want you here."

"Just tell me. I'll do whatever you want."

The problem is, I don't know what I want.

Am I angry at him for something he says he couldn't help? Am I angry at myself for still caring? Or am I simply angry because I thought I had everything figured out and now he's thrown me another curve ball? Is it just, as Alex said, about not being in control of things 24/7?

"I suppose…if we're going to get things sorted out…you should stay. In the guest room."

"Of course."

"And don't expect anything from me for a while."

"I wouldn't dare."

"And don't try to be funny."

"Okay."

I get up from the table and pick up my keys.

"Wyn…"

"What?"

"Thank you."

"You're welcome."

Everyone should be gone by now but Cheryl's car is still in the lot. She's carrying a sheet pan with three cake layers from the kitchen to the baking room and when the alley door slams shut behind me she drops the whole thing in an eruption of batter and clanging of pans. Both hands clutch at the neck of her T-shirt.

"Oh my God, Wyn! You scared me. I'm—What are you—?" She looks around. "Oh shit, what a mess. I'm so sorry. I'll pay for the ingredients—"

"That probably works out to about a buck seventy-eight." I look at my watch. "Why are you still here?"

Her face is red and splotchy. "I was…um…sort of experimenting. With a recipe. I'm sorry, I know that's not my job, but I just wanted to try this technique I read about…I'm really sorry."

I pull an apron off the shelf and loop it over my head. "I hope this doesn't mean you're applying to pastry school."

"Not me." She takes a bench scraper and starts scooping batter back into the pans while I fill a bucket with hot soapy water and grab some towels.

In fifteen minutes there's no trace of mishap except a damp spot on the floor.

"What have we got in the day-olds?"

"Peanut butter cookies. Brownies. Some blueberry muffins and a few cream scones," she says.

I'm impressed that she actually knows. I open the reach-in and immediately spot what's left of a Guadeloupe Tart.

"This is more like what I had in mind. You want a piece?"

"Oh…well…I think that's the last one."

"Then it's our duty to eat it so Rafe can make fresh ones for the customers."

She watches me cut the remaining tart in half, slide the pieces onto two plates and hand her one. We take them to the break room table.

"You know, I think this stuff is even better cold." I suck on my fork.

"I still can't believe Tyler's leaving." Her voice sounds like she might start crying. "Not just because she does so many things, but also because she knows so much stuff that she doesn't even know what all she knows."

"Come again?" I give her a sideways look and nibble at a piece of coconut.

"She has so much…knowledge is what I mean. She takes it for granted, and she probably hasn't even thought to tell anyone else. We won't realize everything she has in her head till she's gone."

"It's going to be hard for a while."

"Wyn, can I ask you a personal question?"

"How personal?"

"I was just wondering if you're planning to go back to Orcas. I mean… not immediately, but…"

I get up and fill two glasses with ice and cold coffee. I pour an unconscionable amount of half and half in mine and take a drink.

"No. I'm not." With my little finger, I press the last flake of Raphael's perfect crust and deposit it on my tongue. "I'm sure everyone will be thrilled to know that I'll be here breathing down your necks till I keel over at age 98, clutching a loaf of walnut *levain*."

Her laugh is a nervous little whinny. "You know we all think you're the best boss—"

"Come on, Cheryl. If you're going to be my manager, you're going to have to stop being polite. The job of the manager—whoever it is—is to tell me the truth, not to make me feel good."

When the silence has gone on for several seconds, I say, "Are you having second thoughts?"

"No…it's just…I don't see how anyone can do as good a job as Tyler."

I resist the temptation to agree with her. "She'll be a tough act to follow, that's true. But if I didn't think you could do it, I wouldn't have offered you the job."

"I'll do my best."

"If it's not good enough I'll just fire you."

She looks stricken.

"Cheryl…I'm kidding."

On Sunday before Christmas, I meet CM for lunch at Le Dome on Sunset. We have a glass of champagne in the bar under the soft ochre rotunda. Her first toast is our oldest one.

"Forever Amazons," she solemnly pronounces. "And Happy Birthday, Baby."

"How can I be forty-four? In my head I'm still twenty-four. No, make that thirty-four. It was a better year."

We follow the maitre d' to a table, lugging our shopping bags full of presents for each other and our families.

"So when does Tyler leave?" she asks after we sit down.

"January third."

"It's hard to imagine the Maven without her."

"No one could ever replace Tyler, but Cheryl's coming along. I think she's going to be okay."

She sips her champagne. "What about Mac?"

I survey the menu, but I can't seem to focus. "That's the sixty-four thousand dollar question."

"And what's the sixty-four thousand dollar answer?"

"I don't know. When I first got back I wanted to kill him and divorce him. In that order. Right now…we're roommates. Civil. Sometimes even…friendly. But…you know, I always thought that when—or if—we got back together, it would be pretty much like it was before. Like he would go back to being his true self. But it's different. He's different."

"People change," she says gently. "Especially after something like he's been through. Don't you think it would be weird if he hadn't?"

I turn over my knife a couple of times and arrange the napkin on my lap. "It's just…he's just so not Mac. I keep looking at him and wondering… if I were meeting him now, would I love him? Would I even like him?"

"Ah. There's your sixty-four-thousand-dollar question."

"You ladies ready to make some choices?"

"Give a us a few minutes." CM favors the waiter with a smile, then turns back to me. "For one thing, it's all so unexpected. You come home thinking it's game over and suddenly he's acting like he wants to be with you. I'm sure it was disorienting. But there's no rush to make a decision, is there? Even if it's over, nothing's going to happen till after the holidays. Right? So why don't you just sit with it. See how things shake out."

"I hate ambiguity." I smile involuntarily. "But you knew that."

I'm weighing the merits of lemon roasted chicken with garlic mashed potatoes vs spinach salad, when she says,

"And before you let him back in your bed, you need to take a look at your Christmas present."

I peer down into the shopping bag by her chair.

"Not that one. I left your big present in the car. They wouldn't let me bring him in."

"You know, the Chippendales are so last century."

She smiles mysteriously and asks me what I'm ordering for lunch.

I rip a piece off my roll and dip it in olive oil. "Spinach salad. And dessert."

She beckons the waiter and he hurries over to take our order. Without consulting me, she orders two more glasses of champagne.

I study her. "What's up?"

She purses her lips thoughtfully. "Remember that dress I bought for you to wear when I was supposed to marry Nathan?"

"One doesn't easily forget an orange dress with a purple sash."

"Can you still get into it?"

"I suppose with the right underwear anything's possible. Why?"

"I'm having a party New Year's Day."

"Really? A costume party?"

"A wedding."

"*What?!*" I shriek, causing everyone in the restaurant to turn and stare. She smiles slyly. I lower my voice. "Do not mess with me, woman. Tell me immediately."

"She leans back in her chair, folding her arms, like she always does. "Remember when you called me in New York and I said I was going to a play?"

"Nathan! You saw his play—What's the name of it?"

"*The Hunters.* I read a review of it about two weeks ago, and I wanted to see it, but it was sold out, so I called him. I told him I was in town for a few days and I really wanted to see his play and I asked him if he could get me a ticket."

"Was it him you saw in London?"

"No." She smiles. "That was the first thing I asked him. But he seemed really glad to hear from me and he asked me if I would go with him to the play and then have supper."

"This is starting to sound like something on the Lifetime Channel."

"So he came to pick me up at the hotel, and he looks wonderful— getting a little gray, but still so...I don't know...whatever it was that he had, he's still got it." She flutters her fingers over her heart. "I felt like I was twenty six again."

"Only smarter."

"Anyway, the play was great and we went to supper at one of those New York places that you never heard of but it's wonderful. He ordered champagne and sent everyone away who came over to schmooze and we just sat there talking. It was like no time had passed at all. Finally they threw us out at three A.M."

"And then...?"

"And then we went to his place on Central Park West..."

"*Central Park West?*"

"Well...it's very small. But we made love and slept and made love and O M G.. I was in love. I am in love. And while we were having breakfast he said, 'Let's do it right this time.'"

I jump up and throw my arms around her. "You're the only woman I know who can go in looking for a theatre ticket and come out with a husband. Has he been pining for you all these years?"

"Hardly. He's been married twice, but he's been divorced for the last five years."

I have a sudden, sobering thought. "You did tell him that moving to New York is a deal breaker."

She smiles. "We'll be bi-coastal—it's very hip."

The valet brings my car up first.

"Thanks for lunch. Let's get together the day after Christmas and talk wedding."

"Wait a minute, wait. I wasn't kidding about your present. You stay right here till they bring my car."

Even as she says it, her yellow Miata comes roaring up to the valet stand and I can see my present, his little fox face peering out the window at me. I stare at CM.

"*Charles?*"

"Susan's moving to Hawaii and she can't take him. He'd have to be in quarantine for six months or some awful thing. Since I can't have him, I decided the next best thing is for you to be his new mom. Then I can see him whenever I want."

She opens the passenger door of her car and I open my door and Charles jumps into my arms, sniffs me and hops into the Volvo. He settles himself on the passenger seat and waits patiently for me to get my other packages in the back, tip the valet, hug CM once more and take off down Sunset Boulevard.

Twenty-one

After the endurance run to Encino in the rain and gridlock, I pull into my mother's driveway to find a For Sale sign stuck in the front lawn. I'm stunned.

She answers the bell and draws me inside to hug me, ignoring my wet coat. Then she spots Charles, sitting politely on the door mat, waiting for the all clear.

"Oh, you adorable thing! Where did you come from?" She sits down in the foyer and pulls him into her lap. When he goes off to explore the house I help her up.

"My Christmas present from CM," I explain. "What's up? Where are you guys going?"

She laughs and brushes at the dog hair on her sweater. "We've bought a place up in Grass Valley. I can't wait for you to see it. It's an old Victorian, almost completely restored."

I smile. "Almost?"

"Richard wouldn't be happy if there weren't a few projects to work on."

We go into the den where the man in question is pouring mulled wine. "Hey, Gorgeous. It's good to have you home." He takes my wet shopping bag and arranges the packages under their huge Christmas tree where Charles is investigating the ornaments.

"Just in time for you two to take off," I say.

"Oh, it'll be awhile." He grins. "We have to sell this place first. And there are one or two small things I need to do to get it ready…"

My mother laughs again and goes to hang my coat on the hall rack. The room looks like a window at Macy's, decorated with silver and gold ornaments and candles, flocked greenery. Perry Como is singing "O Holy Night" and suddenly I'm ten years old, looking for the optimal place to hang my stocking. The ghost of Christmas Past is my father, leaning against the mantle in his Fair Isle ski sweater. And he's smiling.

When I announce CM's impending nuptials, my mother presses her hands together as if in prayer. "I knew he'd materialize one of these days. Took him long enough, didn't it? Are you going to be the matron of honor?"

"I don't respond well to anything involving the word 'matron.' I'm going to be the Best Babe."

Richard sets a pile of birthday presents in front of me on the coffee table.

"Happy Birthday, Best Babe."

"Go ahead and open them," my mother says. "The roast still needs a few minutes."

I've never been able to rip into beautiful packages. I have to deconstruct everything carefully, folding the paper and rewinding the ribbons. Richard watches me, trying not to laugh. "She is her mother's daughter."

There are books—a couple of novels and a baking book—a beautiful pale orange sweater and some Blue Grass bath powder, my perennial favorite.

"So what's happening with you and Mac? I nearly fainted when he answered the phone."

I knew this was coming, but it still somehow trips me up. Saved by the kitchen timer.

I stand up. "Let me help you get things on the table."

She looks like she's about to protest, but Richard says, "I'll get a fire going in the dining room."

I follow my mother out to the kitchen.

"What smells so wonderful?"

She pulls on oven mitts and retrieves a beef tenderloin from the oven, sets it on the stove and drapes foil over it. Then she turns. "We've got fifteen minutes. Can you tell me what's going on and mash potatoes at the same time?"

"I could if I knew what was going on." I pull my oma's big wooden potato masher out of the utensil crock. "He seems to have moved back in."

"Oh, honey, I'm so glad."

"Don't get too excited. We're only sharing the house. He's in the guestroom."

She lifts the lid off the stock pot and I start smashing the steaming hot chunks of potato. She throws in half a stick of butter and pours in some scalded cream.

She says, "I tried making mashed potatoes with chicken broth, but it just wasn't the same. So have you two talked about... your situation?"

"Sort of."

"I take it he wants to get back together."

"I suppose."

"And what about you? How do you feel about it?"

I keep working the potatoes, watching the cakey white lumps crumble, absorb the cream and butter, and transform into a voluptuous, golden mass.

"I don't know." I turn and look at her. "For the first time in my life that I can recall, I don't know how I feel."

The drive back to Luna Blanca is a rerun of the drive there. Southern Californians don't know jack about driving in the rain. On one hand you've got the macho assholes in their fifty thousand dollar SUV's who need to prove that a little rain isn't going to slow them down, and on the other hand you've got the wimps who creep along at forty-five.

By the time I pull up to the house, my eyes hurt from squinting into the night and my hands are molded into the steering wheel's contours. So when I first see it, I think that in my stupor, I've turned into the wrong driveway.

A Christmas tree occupies the bay window of the living room, ablaze with tiny white lights. When I open the front door, the unmistakable scent of balsam greets me. Mac hovers in the foyer, arms full of light strings. Charles trots in and starts sniffing his shoes.

"Hey. Who's this?"

"This is my dog. And what's this supposed to be, Santa's Workshop?"

He gives me a sheepish grin. "It's Christmas."

"You're crazy."

"That was last month. But I've decided that just because you want to leave me doesn't mean I have to make it easy for you."

"So you thought it would be a good idea to act like nothing happened?"

"No. But I can't stand all this tiptoeing around being polite to each other. Let it out, for God's sake. Cry. Yell at me."

"You know what? I've already done all that. I'm through. It's over."

"Hit me. Come on. I know you want to."

"I don't want to hit you."

"Yes you do." He plants himself in front of me. "Right here." He points to his stomach. I remember you told me once you wanted to kick the shit out of David. I can't believe you're not at least that angry at me."

I'm seriously considering it when the doorbell rings.

Standing in the amber circle of the porch light is a very young girl. About sixteen, I'd say.

"My name's Kendra," she says, "and I'm walking the neighborhood for World Peace."

The damp night air is making her curly hair stand like a halo around her face. She smiles, flashing her braces. "We want to take money out of the black hole of the Pentagon budget and use it for libraries and daycare and the environment." She shows me a petition that looks like a familiar blur. "Does this agenda sound like something you could support?"

"I hate to tell you this, but none of that stuff is ever going to happen."

She gives me a look of pity. "Just because we can't change everything doesn't mean we can't change anything."

"Who told you that pretty lie?"

"My father." Her smile closes over her braces. "Well...sorry to bother you. Merry Christmas."

I watch her walk down to the man—presumably her lying father— who's waiting for her at the end of our driveway. He puts his arm around her shoulders and bends his head to hear about her encounter with the heartless witch who lives in this house.

"I guess that clarified things for her," Mac says behind me.

I shut the door, my chin trembling foolishly. "Wait till she finds out it's all bullshit. No matter what you do, things never turn out the way they're supposed to."

I snatch up a startled Charles and head up the stairs. Mac divests himself of the Christmas lights and starts up right behind me, but I slam the bedroom door in his face and lock it.

"Wyn—"

"Leave. Me. Alone."

I shed my clothes in a pile on the floor, brush my teeth and take two pain pills leftover from my visit with the friendly orthopedist. *If it hurts don't do it.*

I get into bed, settle Charles next to me, turn off the light and wait for that fuzzy, spacey little buzz behind my eyes that tells me the drugs are kicking in. Now I understand how you could get addicted to these things. It's so lovely to just turn everything off and float away.

I know it's morning but I don't want to get up. I turn over, fully intending to let myself slide back into the comfort of darkness, but… I hear someone breathing. Someone other than me. Too loud for Charles. I force my eyes open in the pale light, raise up on one elbow and peer over the edge of the mattress.

Mac's lying on the floor curled up under an old quilt, a pillow wedged awkwardly under his neck, sound asleep.

My throat tightens at the familiar contours of his face. The lines at the corners of his eyes, sprinkled gray in his hair, perpetual little sunburned patch on his nose. Part of me wants to reach down and touch him, but I don't. Instead I curl my fingers into fists, shut my eyes and let the warm tears leak onto the pillow.

Wait a minute.

"How the *hell* did you get in here?"

"Credit card." His voice is thick with sleep.

I look over the edge again just as he opens his eyes.

He blinks a couple of times. "Why are you crying?"

"Because I don't know who you are. And I don't even know who I am anymore."

"I'm just a guy, Wyn. A crazy, fucked-up guy who's so in love with you that I can't make myself believe it's over."

The Kleenex box is empty so I blot my eyes with the sheet. I turn on my back and stare at the ceiling. Charles lifts his head, looks around, yawns.

Mac groans softly, gets to his feet, stretching. He stands there a minute, then the bed sinks as he sits down cautiously. Charles crawls across the quilt on his belly to rest his chin on Mac's thigh.

Growl, damn it. Bite him.

"Remember that night down in Baja at the fishing camp?" Mac says quietly. "You don't know how many times I wished I'd just kept swimming. I think the only thing that stopped me was the thought of you waiting for me. How cruel it would be to just disappear. How it would hurt you. So I came back and I disappeared in a different way and hurt you anyway. But I swear I never meant to."

I'm crying and glaring at the light fixture. "I could just kill you. I hate you. Why are you telling me this now? Why not six months ago? Why did we have to go through this? I could have helped—"

"Wyn, listen to me. The one thing I was right about from the start was that there was nothing you could do. I have this thing, this…sickness. Depression. Call it whatever you want. I'll never not have it. I have to figure out how to live with it."

Now he's lying on his side, facing me, Charles sprawled between us like a small rug.

"I missed you," he says. "Even when I didn't want you. Even when I was crazy."

"That doesn't make any sense."

"I know."

A few tears leak out of my closed eyes. He brushes them away so lightly that I'm not even sure it's real. Damn. There it is. That pesky little surge of hope. We can get it all back if we try really hard.

"Don't," he says. "I can feel you getting all determined. You can't Teddy Roosevelt your way through this one."

Against my will, I start to laugh. He could always make me laugh.

How did this happen? How, without making a conscious choice, no piece of paper divided into two columns, pro and con?

Charles squirms out of the way as I roll over on my side, bury my face in Mac's shirt and cry.

If life was a Hollywood movie this would be the end. We'd kiss and the camera would pan to clouds at sunset, a long shot of a convertible on a winding mountain road. Or there'd be a montage of scenes from our future, gray haired and smiling, walking on the beach, waving to Skye as she runs to meet us at the airport, holiday dinner with my parents, maybe even a tearful reunion with Suzanne.

However, this is not a movie; it's life, and you don't get to look away during the scary parts.

Twenty-two

January, 2001

My mother took a picture of us—Mac and me—sitting by their tree on Christmas Eve. For a while I kept it stuck on the refrigerator door with a little magnet. Whenever I looked at it I got that vertigo sensation, the way your stomach feels at the top of a cliff, the way the empty air pulls you towards the edge. Finally I took it down and put it in a shoebox in the closet, the repository for all the photos I swear I'm going to put in an album as soon as I get three weeks with nothing on the calendar.

Who is the man in the picture, this kinder, gentler Mac? In some ways he's even more of a stranger than the evil troll who lived above Alan's garage. Now he goes to therapy once a week down in Laguna Beach. It seems like a long way to go, but the therapist (Willow Maidenhair—a name I can barely say without choking) comes with an endorsement from Sylvia, so she must be good.

He keeps a mood journal and gets up at 6 AM to meditate. Suddenly he wants to share his feelings with me. He wants to focus on positive thoughts. He talks about coping strategies and avoidance behaviors.

As CM has reminded me, there's nothing inherently wrong with these things. It's just that they're so not Mac. I can't reconcile them with that little cynical edge he always had. Where did that go? I miss it.

Two thousand and one arrives with hardly a ripple. The bakery is thriving; Mac is writing—or at least trying —and he and I are stumbling together like beginners in tango class, attempting to execute the unfamiliar steps of this routine.

Tyler's departure for Greystone is a wrench. It's like when someone dies after a long illness...you know it's coming and you try to prepare yourself, but it still seems to happen suddenly, without warning.

When I offer to drive her up, she gives me a look like I'm a few sandwiches short of a picnic.

"It's not like I'm seventeen and going off to college. Besides, I need my car."

The night before she leaves I go over to her apartment, ostensibly to help her finish packing, but when I get there, all her bags, boxes and suitcases are stacked by the front door.

"Should we put these in the car?" I ask.

"No, I'll just throw them in tomorrow."

I look around at the empty rooms. "What are you sleeping in?"

"My sleeping bag."

"That's ridiculous. Just bring your suitcase over to our house and—"

"Wyn..." There's no mistaking the warning in her voice. "Thanks for the offer, but I'm staying here tonight."

She takes two bottles of beer out of the fridge and opens them. "I saved these for us."

We sit on the floor among the boxes, backs against the wall, sipping our beers and nibbling dry roasted almonds from a can.

I say, "I'm going to miss you."

"I'll miss you, too. But it's time."

I lean my head against the wall and look over at her. "What do you mean?"

"It's time for me to do something."

I sit up and turn to face her. "Do you feel like you haven't been doing anything for the last eight years?"

"No, of course not. It's just that I've never really done anything on my own."

"Nothing except run the bakery."

"Your bakery."

"I offered to make you a partner—"

She reaches over and gives my hand a condescending pat. "Can you just listen to me for a minute? Please?"

She takes a swig of beer and sets the bottle on the floor. "I'm 28 years old and I've never done one thing on my own. You've been my mother and my big sister and my best friend. Everything I've got came from you. But you know, if you were my mother, everyone would be saying, *Geez, when's the kid going to leave home?* I need to see what I can do. Without you standing down there with the big safety net." She's looking at me intently. "Do you understand?"

"I'm still going to miss you."

She gives me a five-second hug. "I'll call you and email you. Give you progress reports."

"Do you think you'll get to come home on the weekends?"

"Probably not," she says. "They keep you pretty busy. And I've never been to the wine country. There's a lot I want to see. Besides, I don't have a place here anymore."

"You could stay with me."

She emits a long, controlled sigh. "No. I couldn't."

We finish our beers and she rinses out the bottles and sets them on the counter.

"Mac said to tell you goodbye. He said to tell you he's proud of you."

"He did not."

"He did. That's what's so strange. Are you going to stop by the bakery in the morning?"

"Nah. I've already said goodbye to everybody. And it's out of the way. I want to get an early start."

"Okay. Well…" I open the front door. I know she's so eager to get on with her adventure she just wants me gone. "Have fun and do good things. And be careful. Remember to take your probiotics and get plenty of sleep and—"

"Thanks for everything, Wyn. You know…" Her face softens. "You know I love you."

It's warm tonight—for January—so Mac has grilled lamburgers and we have them in pita bread with feta cheese and cucumbers and marinated red onions. I drink a glass of red wine and he has a non-alcoholic beer which he says tastes like carbonated cat pee. Afterwards I make decaf and we linger at the kitchen table.

It looks very cozy and domestic, me sorting email on my laptop, Charles drowsing at my feet, Mac reading the paper.

I love the way he looks, sitting there with his legs stretched out in front of him. He has new reading glasses that make him look like the English Lit prof I had a crush on my sophomore year. He folds the pages vertically, like my father used to.

Suddenly he looks over at me. "Do you miss Alex?"

"What?"

"Do you—"

294

"Of course not. Why would you even ask that?"

"You're just so quiet lately. Like you're always thinking about something."

"I'm always thinking about lots of things. None of which is Alex."

After a long minute of silence it dawns on me that I'm evading his question the way he used to evade mine. So I push the computer away and I pick up my coffee cup and I say,

"I don't miss Alex. I miss you. The way you used to be."

"How did I used to be?"

"Remember the night you free climbed up to the bakery roof and cut down the sign for Ellen? That's who I miss."

He laughs a little. "Yeah. I miss that guy, too. He had his shit together, didn't he?"

I want to laugh with him, so we can pretend it's funny.

"The problem is, I'm not him anymore. I'm not sure I ever was."

He folds the paper and sets it on the table. "I wish I could explain it. This thing I have…it's so strange. Sometimes it's just a sadness…kind of intricate and rich. I can see things I've never seen before and see familiar things in a whole different way. I don't know if that's me or if it's part of the illness. Or both. I can't always separate myself from…it." He stops. "This must sound really weird to you."

I think it's the first time in all the years I've known him that he's ever seemed to truly want me to understand him, to see what he sees.

"I want you to tell me anyway."

"Other times everything just gets black and cold and empty. At those times all I can feel is anger. It isn't about anything. I'm not really angry at you. Nothing you did or said. Or if there is something, it's just a trigger, not the real reason. On a different day I might not even notice."

"When did it start? When did you first think something was wrong?"

"I don't know. I think it was happening for a long time. I just didn't realize it. If I think about it, I can remember things from a long time ago. In college. Maybe even high school."

"But you're better now. Not like you were." I feel like if I say it as a fact, he can't disagree.

"It's dormant," he says. "If it was cancer, you'd say it was in remission."

"So you think it could happen again."

"It's just a question of when."

"Isn't there anything...some kind of medication?"

He's silent for a minute, seemingly locked in some internal debate. Finally he says, "I don't want to take meds. I'm afraid it would just plane everything down to the lowest common denominator. It could make writing impossible."

"What if nothing else works?"

He comes over to my chair and bends down to kiss me. "I'll try everything. Therapy, hypnosis, eagle feathers. Herbal tea. Even meds, if nothing else helps. Just don't leave."

When he goes up to bed, I think I should go up too. Part of me wants to, but I'm hesitant. Or maybe just too tired for all the bargaining we have to do these days.

Sex used to be like spontaneous combustion. It was recreation. It was communication, bridging the gap left by a careless word. We took it for granted. Now we approach with caution, with calculation and analysis. Does he want to? Do I? Can he? Is he embarrassed? Do we have time? Is it worth the trouble?

Delusional as we are, we still pretend we can do it whenever we want. We've developed elaborate rituals to communicate ability and inclination.

The truth is, we're both afraid. Afraid of not wanting it if the other does. Afraid of wanting it too much and then disappointing each other.

I open my email program and a few messages straggle into the inbox. One of them catches my eye, makes my stomach turn over.

Alex.

It was a lie, of course. What I said to him. That I don't miss Alex. It's not as if I sit in my office doodling his name on my notepad. I delete his occasional emails after reading them…well, mostly. But I do think of him sometimes. Probably more than I should. And on bad days I feel like I was a drowning swimmer and Alex threw me a lifeline, which I batted away. Of course that's not true.

What I miss is the easiness of being with him. His openness. The feeling that I could say whatever I wanted and he would do the same. The shorthand way we talked about food and work, each of us understanding the other, no explanations required. Or maybe it was just because I didn't care what he thought of me. I didn't love him, so I didn't need to please him. Which somehow pleased him.

I pause, listening for sounds upstairs, and hearing nothing, I open the email.

Thinking of you. Rained all day, more coming. Seattle on Friday, pick up the boys and head for Hawaii. Rented a house in Hilo for a month. They're already asking about broadband and movies. Hopefully they'll get over having nothing to do but hiking and biking, surfing, fishing and sailing and the whole Pacific Ocean as their back yard. Back in Eastsound Feb 10th. Shoot me a note and let me know you're okay. A.

I type quickly.

Hey—Tyler left last week for Napa, miss her! Cheryl is working hard; I'm sure she'll be fine once she finds her feet. Just a little crazy right now. A month in Hawaii sounds like heaven. Mac is doing well. I back space.-*Mac is better. CM married her old flame Nathan on New Year's Day. They honeymooned in Mexico, are now in New York. Hope you and the boys have a great trip. W.*

I hit send, turn off the computer and take Charles upstairs.

It's February 13th and we are slammed.

Every flat surface in the bakery, including my desk, is covered with cakes and tarts, boxes and trays of cookies and cupcakes and cookie-pops—an abomination which for some unknown reason happens to be popular right now.

In addition to treats for kids and lovers, our wholesale accounts have all ordered more breads and extra pastries for their assembly line Valentine dinners. Everyone's working overtime, staying after their shift to help fill orders and tie red ribbons and lacy tags on things.

Mac and I never made a big deal out of Valentine's Day, but I've always turned an indulgent (and perhaps a somewhat wistful) eye on the festivities. However, at the moment I feel about as romantic as one of the pod people in *Night of the Living Dead*.

It's 4 PM and I'm trying to finish the delivery printouts so I can get back out front and help with packaging. Of course my computer is running agonizingly slow. Probably because I haven't defragged in months. I'm sitting there watching the little hourglass and hoping it's not going to time out when Sally comes in and hands me the mail.

"Sorry, it's been sitting by the register since noon and nobody even noticed."

"No problem. I'll be out there as soon as I get this damned thing…"
I flip through the stack in my hand, glance back at the screen just in
time to see the little blue box that says my credentials have expired and
I should sign in again. Grrrr.

I flip through some more mail. Bills, magazines, ads. The very last
item in the stack is a colorful mailer. The computer generated address
label has my name misspelled. *Winter McLeod.* I look at the words for a
minute before I recognize them…familiar and strange at the same time…

…*'Join Chef Alex Rafferty and Sommelière Paulette Riley as part of
a small, select group to experience gastronomic highlights of Europe
this spring.'*

I break the little seal and open the brochure. On the left side are
photos of Alex in the kitchen at Rafferty's, Paulette with her nose stuck
in a fishbowl sized goblet of red wine…perhaps she'll drown. There are
assorted photos of the café and one of Alex's cooking class. On the facing
page are photos of Europe, mostly France and Italy. Cozy tables, wine
caves, door and window shots with trailing geraniums, rustic buildings,
narrow streets.

The copy details how the lucky chosen few will visit not just wonderful
cafes and vineyards, but they will be the special guests of the chefs,
bakers, chocolatiers, winemakers, cheesemakers, butchers—the creative
artisans behind the exquisite food.

I turn to the last page to find a handwritten note.

*Lyn—hope you can join us! We're meeting some great bakers…
Best, Paulette*

I rip the brochure in half and drop it in the trash.

With any luck Europe will be experiencing a very cold, very
rainy spring.

At 4:30 we lock the doors and set up an assembly line in the café. I pull the shades and send Carl, our new work study baker, out for pizzas.

Forty-five minutes later there's a knock on the door and when Cheryl opens it expecting to see Carl, Mac walks in. Conversation stops for a minute while everyone acts like they're not watching him come over and kiss my cheek.

He looks around. "What's going on?"

"Um…Valentine's Day."

"Oh. Right." He takes my hand. "I need to show you something."

"Mac…I can't leave right now."

"Just for a minute," he insists. "Come on. You'll be right back. It's important."

I look around.

"Cheryl, I'll be back in a few minutes. When Carl brings the pizzas, you guys eat while they're hot. We can finish up afterwards."

"What's wrong?" I say as the door shuts behind us.

He stops for a second. "Does it have to be something wrong?"

"I just thought…I mean, you know how busy we are this week. I figured it had to be an emergency."

"It's just something I wanted to show you."

At the corner he steers me around to the right and stops. "What do you think?"

"About what?"

He points.

Parked at the curb is an El Camino. Not like the original Elky which would have been best described as a beater. This is a completely restored classic, almost a little too tricked out for my taste but unquestionably beautiful. The paint job is a pale cream, and cool turquoise. White wall tires. The bumpers look like they were spit-shined.

"Elky Two," he says, leaning over to kiss me. "I know it's tomorrow, but I couldn't wait. Happy Valentine's Day to us."

I smile. "Well, you always like to stay ahead of the curve."

I bend to look inside at the cream and turquoise tuck-and-roll upholstery and turquoise steering wheel. A sparkly blue Lucite knob graces the stick shift.

"Where in the world did you find it?"

"*Classic Truck Trader*. It's a '73...that's as close as I could get. Ready for a test flight?"

"Mac, I can't. Everyone's staying late to finish."

"You're excused."

"Yes, but I told Cheryl—"

"It's taken care of. You're cleared for take off." He opens the door. "Come on, we'll be late. Take off the apron. I don't want to be seen consorting with the help."

When he turns the key in the ignition the truck's engine purrs. There's no other way to describe it.

I can't help laughing.

He stops at the light and looks over at me. "What?"

"I was just thinking about Elky Senior. How it took fifteen tries to get it started."

"Hey, don't insult that truck. It was my boon companion."

I touch the blue dashboard. "So how come you sold it?"

The light changes and he eases into the intersection. For a minute I think he hasn't heard me. When he does speak, the emotion in his voice surprises me.

"I don't know. It was stupid. I loved that goddamned truck. That Kyle kid better be taking good care of it. He wanted it bad enough."

I notice we're heading west, towards the ocean, but then he takes a sharp turn onto a narrow windy road.

"Where are we going?"

He just smiles. "Relax. Here." He hands me a CD in a jewel case. Pop that in the player."

I open the case and lift out the disc. There's no identification on the label except SONY. I slide it into the changer and Van Morrison booms out of the speakers. "Brown Eyed Girl."

We both roll down our windows and I lean my head back.

"There's a sweater behind the seat if you get cold," he says, and I look over at him.

"You've certainly thought of everything."

He says, "You have no idea."

Van Morrison segues into the Jaynettes' "Sally Go Round the Roses."

"Wow. Haven't heard that in a while."

He nods.

The road narrows and appears to become gravel about 20 yards ahead, but before we reach the gravel he turns right and drives past a county park sign. There's a row of parking spots in front of us, delineated by railroad ties. Beyond that is nothing. Except the silver blue Pacific Ocean, with the sun just dipping in a toe. And nothing else all the way to China.

"Mac, this is beautiful. How come I never knew it was here?"

"I found it a couple years ago. I used to come up here at night."

About this time, the next song begins. The intro is familiar but I can't place it until Dan Fogelberg starts singing "Changing Horses."

My eyes fill suddenly. This is the tape he gave me when he left Seattle for Orcas Island, all the songs carefully chosen to convey feelings we'd never talked about, a story neither of us could quite believe at the time.

He reaches for my hand. "I was wondering how long it would take you."

"Where did you find the tape?"

"I didn't. I looked everywhere I could think of and time was getting short, so I just downloaded everything off iTunes and burned a CD."

"You remembered all the songs."

"Of course. The Baker's Dozen." He leans over to kiss me.

From the storage box in the bed of the truck, comes a bottle of Champagne and two glasses. "Damn, you really did think of everything."

Next he pulls out a white bakery bag and hands it to me.

"Chocolate croissants?"

"From some joint called the Bread Maven. I tried to get some of Phoebe's crescent rolls, but they're out of business."

"As they should be."

He pops the cork and fills our glasses to the top and we laugh trying to lap up the overflow, and we eat our *pain au chocolat* and we listen to the songs rolling off the CD while the sun settles into the ocean.

Tangled up in Blue, Coldwater Canyon, Cleaning Windows, Layla, I Only Have Eyes for You, That's How Strong My Love Is, It Hurts Me Too, In My Life, The Dimming of the Day.

When the music is done and the sun is gone, we climb in back with the last of the champagne in one glass. He's brought blankets.

"Are these to keep us warm or to protect the paint?"

"Both." He hands me the glass. "Remember that time…I think it was the first time we went to Orcas. We slept in the Elky in that circle of trees…"

"We looked at the stars and made love like bunnies. Plus I got the worst backache I've ever had."

"You?" He puts his arm around my shoulders and tucks me up tight against him. "I had to sleep with my knees bent all night."

"Funny, I don't remember you sleeping. Knees bent or otherwise."

He laughs softly and I finish the champagne.

"We've never really done this," I say.

"Done what?"

"Had Valentine's Day."

"I never thought about it. About a lot of stuff, I guess. Birthdays. Anniversaries."

"It's okay—"

"No, it's not. It's just…I never could stand marking things off on the calendar like that. Every date had its own baggage. I just wanted to keep my head down. You know?"

"Yes, I think so. Finally."

He reaches for an old blanket, soft from hundreds of washings, and we pull it around us against the cold breeze. It's warm, but not as warm as the feel of him next to me.

Twenty-three

Larchmont Village is my fantasy.

Sometimes I take an afternoon off and wander the streets. It's full of interesting shops in which I never buy anything, and interesting cafés in which I never eat. It's surrounded by lovely, well-kept neighborhoods where I don't live. I'm superstitious about it, like if I ever tried to actually interact with any of it, the whole thing would disappear in a puff of smoke.

One day in May I'm in Blinkers, a quirky place that sells everything from hand-knit sweaters to Hello Kitty lunch boxes, and I hear my name.

"Wynter, I thought that was you."

"Oh, hi, Sylvia." I try to sound happy to see her, but she represents reality and she's intruding on my fantasy.

We exchange a quick hug and chat for a minute. Finally she says,

"I'm about to die for a cup of coffee and something sweet. Please come keep me company at PQ."

It's impossible to say no to Sylvia.

At *Le Pain Quotidien* we sit in the back where it's quiet, and a cute girl whose blue hair reminds me of Tyler in the old days brings us steaming lattes and small, perfect pastries.

Sylvia takes an envelope of stevia out of her purse and drops a pinch into her cup. "Look at me. Low cal sweetener in my coffee, and a brownie." She laughs a little, shakes her head. "So tell me. How's Mac doing?"

"Better. He's writing. He's sleeping more. Although he had to quit taking Halcion. It was giving him nightmares. He kept dreaming that a bunch of guys were walking around in our living room. And I still don't think he's totally convinced it was a dream."

She says. "Is he on an antidepressant?"

"No. He's afraid he won't be able to write."

"Alan says his new manuscript is wonderful."

"What's it about?"

She looks at me curiously. "You haven't seen it?"

I shake my head. "He doesn't show me his stuff anymore."

"It's sort of a…mystery. About a guy who's accused of murdering his wife."

"No wonder he wouldn't let me see it."

She laughs. "He didn't do it. The protagonist. He's a musician and a heroin addict and he has to get straight and find the killer. Alan says it's very gritty. And quite good."

"It doesn't sound like his usual style."

"True. But then depression changes how you view the world. Some people are capable of using that to their advantage." She cuts a small piece off her brownie and puts it on my plate. "And Wynter. How's Wynter surviving?"

I make designs in the foam on top of my latte. "I'm doing okay. Actually I'm doing better than okay. Why does that scare me?"

She waits for me to elaborate.

"I'm not sure how to explain it. Things are good sometimes. Most of the time, in fact. We talk a lot more. We have fun together, we laugh. He's affectionate…he even made a big deal about Valentine's Day, which he never did before. But every once in a while something happens… maybe something so small…"

"Something like…?"

I take a sip of the latte. "Well, like Valentine's Day. On the 13th we were crazy at work, of course, and he walks into the bakery and insists I go outside and he's bought this restored El Camino. He's got the whole thing planned—champagne, chocolate croissants, and a CD he put together that was a copy of a tape he made for me when we first got together in Seattle. So at first I say I can't go because the bakery's so busy and everyone's staying late to get everything finished, and he tells me it's all taken care of."

I hesitate and she looks at me over the tops of her glasses.

"I don't know, maybe I just heard what I wanted to hear. He said—actually he never said it—but he led me to believe that Cheryl, my manager, knew that he was taking me out somewhere. So we go to this place overlooking the ocean and he pours the champagne and we play the music and watch the sunset and it's all lovely and romantic…and then by the time we get back it's almost 8 o'clock so he drops me back at the bakery so I can get my car. When I go in, Cheryl's still there, cleaning up and it's totally obvious that she had no idea what was going on or that I wasn't coming back to help. She was kind of upset, and I don't blame her."

"Did you ask him about it?"

"No." I look down at the untouched éclair on my plate.

"It would have been like breaking the enchantment," she says.

I look back at her. "Exactly. But it was broken as soon as I saw Cheryl. He had to know that would happen." I rest my elbows on the table and lean forward. "So why would he lie about something like that? And he could just as easily have done it the next night, which was actually Valentine's Day, and the crush was over. It makes no sense."

She finally takes a bite of her brownie. "It could have been a test. Maybe he wanted to reassure himself that he's more important to you than the bakery."

"That is so not Mac." I set down my cup. "Do you think...is he ever going to be like he used to be?"

"It's impossible to say. The most likely scenario is that he'll be fine for periods of time interspersed with episodes of depression. There's no way to know when or how long it will last." She pushes her plate away. "But one thing is absolutely critical that you understand. When he's in the grip of it, he's totally self-absorbed. He's got to concentrate on himself just to keep going. You can be compassionate and loving, but you have to learn how to distance yourself when he's down in that hole."

"Easier said than done."

"Of course it is." She looks at me sternly. "But I want to be completely truthful with you, dear. Living with a depressive is harder sometimes than being a depressive. It's like walking through a field of sunflowers that's also a minefield. It's good that you have the bakery, it keeps you engaged. Take care of you. Be with friends or family. Go to a movie or a concert. Start playing tennis again. I know it's hard. But you're strong. You can do it. And you can always call me. I mean that."

She wraps the remains of her brownie in a napkin and sticks it in her purse.

"For Alan," she says and laughs.

When I come in the back door I hear voices. I take off my jacket and lay it over the back of a chair, put my bag on the kitchen table.

In the living room, Mac is sitting on the couch with two people. The guy is thirty-something, hair fashionably spiked. Expensive looking sweater with the sleeves pushed up. The woman is very young and beautiful in that plastic celebrity wannabe way. Loads of makeup. Very short skirt, high heeled boots. Nothing as obvious as cleavage, but her spandex T-neck leaves little to the imagination.

Mac's holding a glass with about an inch of amber liquid, obviously from the bottle of scotch on the floor next to the couch. On the coffee table is a small dish with two joints, one of which is lit. Next to the dish is a ziplock plastic bag, open at the top, like some kind of marketing display, and a packet of rolling papers. So this is a sales call. The Amway of drugs, delivered right to your door.

I'm so angry the top of my head feels like it's on fire.

When Mac looks up and sees me, he says, "Hi, babe."

Babe?

The young guy smiles at me. "Hi, Wyn. I'm Rob Mayer. This is Tiffany Quest."

At least Tiffany Quest has the grace to look slightly embarrassed. I should tell her that she's keeping bad company, but I'm afraid of what might come out of my mouth if I start talking. So we all just look at each other while I try to decide what to do. When doing nothing emerges as the safest choice I turn around and go back to the kitchen, collect my things and take them upstairs.

Very quickly it seems the deal is done and I hear Mac in the hall. I'm in the bathroom brushing my hair when he comes in. He stands behind me, waiting for me to say something, but I refuse to fire the first shot.

"Why do you have to be such a self-righteous pain in the ass?" is his opening volley.

Over the last few months I've learned that the more upset and emotional I become, then the cooler, more rational and controlled he is. In this way are marital homicides conceived.

So instead of going off immediately, I say to his reflection,

"Let's define our terms. A 'self-righteous pain in the ass' would be somebody who returns home at three in the afternoon to find her husband using illegal substances in their living room with a drug dealer and a porn star?"

He sighs. "You have an amazing ability to leap to tall conclusions in a single bound. First of all, Rob's not a dealer, he works for Geffen—"

"I don't care who he works for. If he's selling drugs, he's a dealer."

"He's not selling drugs. He was buying."

I feel like I've tripped over some invisible wire.

When I turn around I can smell the scotch and the smoke on him. "So you're dealing and smoking dope now?"

"I'm not dealing, for God's sake. It was just a friendly transaction. He mentioned that he wanted some and I had some."

"Okay, so you're not dealing except just a little. But you're smoking. Why? Please explain it to me because I don't understand."

His eyes narrow. "Let's see…Because I'd like to feel good once in a while—no, not even good. I'd settle for not half bad. As opposed to hanging by my fingernails on the side of a cliff."

"…I thought—I mean, you were feeling good. Weren't you? When did that change?"

"Every day is different," he says.

"But why are you driving down to Laguna Beach every week and paying Willow a hundred and thirty bucks an hour if you're not going to do what she says?" I finish brushing my hair and fasten it back with a clip.

"You're not in any position to judge me. You can't even imagine what this is like, how hard it is sometimes just getting through the fucking day."

"I know I can't," I say quietly. "And I'm sorry. All I can tell you is how I feel. It hurts me when you're so unhappy. And it really hurts me to see you doing things that are going to make it worse in the long run."

He gives me a look that's somewhere between disgust and amusement. "Haven't you figured out yet there is no long run? There's only now, and I can barely handle that. I'm not buying any annuities."

His hair is dirty and he hasn't shaved in two or three days. I remember how good he used to look. How I used to think he smelled like pine trees, like summer.

"Mac, look at yourself. You look like a zombie."

He smiles almost cheerfully. "I can be a Prozac zombie or a pot zombie. The only difference is insurance coverage."

"No. The difference is you don't get arrested for doing Prozac."

"Actually, the real difference is pot has no side effects. And I'm not going to get arrested—"

"You don't know that. It happens every day. Do you realize that the average prison time for possession of that much marijuana is longer than the average sentence for murder?"

He wags his index finger at me. "You've been listening to NPR again."

"We could lose everything we've worked so hard for—"

"Here's where she tells me to pull up my socks and just say no."

"Oh, *stop it*. I've never said anything remotely like that."

"You don't have to say it. I can hear you thinking it. In the same tone of disgust you use for white sandwich bread."

I bite the inside of my cheek. "And what about Skye? She's going to be here in June. Is this how you want her to see you?"

"This?" He looks in the mirror, turns his face from side to side. "Have I turned into the piano player from *Reefer Madness*?"

"I can't believe you're perfectly happy to suck dope into your lungs, but you won't even try one of the anti-depressants. It could help—"

"Wyn, I can write now," he says. "I'm not going to blow that."

"You'd rather blow our marriage."

For the first time, he looks away from me. "All I can do is all I can do."

Suddenly I'm exhausted, and Larchmont Village seems very far away.

"I want you to remember something, Mac. Your own words. *I'll try anything. Therapy, hypnosis, eagle feathers. Herbal tea. Meds. Just don't leave.* Well, I'm still here."

He's already halfway down the stairs.

At 9:30 on a cool Friday morning in mid-June, Lincoln Boulevard is snarled with traffic. CalTrans is doing median work and there's a huge antique dealers' convention in Santa Monica, plus the usual volleyball tournaments at the beach, a PETA demonstration at some big leather outlet, and just general summer madness. Mac is pissed off because we gambled that this would be faster than the 405 and we lost.

We're on our way to LAX to pick up Skye, and he's been incredibly grouchy since yesterday. When I asked if he was nervous about the visit he snapped,

"Don't start projecting your anxiety on me."

Which I took as an affirmative. It's not the kind of thing he would have said pre-depression, pre-therapy, and it just underscores this nagging feeling I have that I'm living with a stranger. A strange stranger.

"We've got plenty of time," I say.

He grips the steering wheel and glares at the long line of brake lights ahead of us. "I just hate driving in this traffic."

I consider telling him that I don't know anyone who enjoys driving in this traffic, but it's probably not the right thing to say at this point.

Once we get past Marymount, things open up and we cruise the rest of the way, park in the garage, and make it to the international terminal with thirty minutes to spare.

"I need some coffee," I say. "Can I bring you anything?"

"No." He's watching the arrival times and gate numbers flip over on the schedule board.

"Mac…"

"What?" He turns impatiently when I touch his hand.

"It's going to be alright. Really. Take a deep breath."

His jaw relaxes and he nods. "Sorry."

"It's okay. I'll be right back."

I leave him in the arrivals area and go in search of espresso. Maybe I am "projecting my anxiety." I'd love to get rid of it somehow. In a way, I've been looking forward to getting to know Skye. But I'm apprehensive, too. Will she see me as an obstacle? Will she want her father to herself, resent my presence?

My feelings about her are still somewhat ambivalent. She's Mac's daughter and I want to have a relationship with her. On the other hand, she's his daughter by another woman, and I admit to a certain lingering resentment.

At Starbucks I order a mocha and nurse it as long as I dare before heading back. From 30 yards away I can see him pacing. He showered this morning, something he's been kind of lax about lately, and I noticed he took a few minutes to rifle through his closet for a new pair of jeans and a pressed white shirt. He looks younger from this distance and more the way he did in Seattle. But there's no time for nostalgia.

Skye is here, in the vanguard of passengers emerging from customs and immigration, her smile illuminating the terminal as she runs towards him, dragging her suitcase. He leans forward as if to kiss her cheek, but she's not having any of that. She drops the bag and throws herself into his arms.

I stand for a few seconds, oblivious to the crowd jostling around me, and watch them, holding each other, laughing, and I'm not surprised to feel a knot forming in my throat. I swallow hard.

Somebody has to drive.

I approach slowly, hoping they'll see me, but they're lost in each other. Finally I say, "Hello, Skye. How was your flight?"

She turns to me, still smiling. "Wyn. It's good to meet you. Again." Then, somewhat hesitantly, she moves to hug me, and whatever residual resentment was lodged in my heart melts away.

Traffic is horrendous on the 405, but they don't even notice. Good that I'm driving, because Mac spends the entire trip looking at her in the sun visor mirror while I concentrate on finding holes in various lanes to slip in and out of, letting the sound of their voices wash over me.

When I turn into our driveway she's ecstatic, exclaiming how beautiful the house is, and all the interesting plants. "I didn't really notice before, I was so nervous."

I find it interesting that these references to her first visit are totally unselfconscious, and even Mac seems pretty nonchalant about them. Or not. He's become adept at appearing relaxed, but you never know what might be roiling underneath.

In the house, Charles takes one sniff of her and becomes her devoted slave, following at her heels from room to room as I give her a quick tour. We leave her in the guest room to unpack and freshen up, but Charles declines to follow us down to the kitchen. I take iced tea and lemonade out of the fridge while Mac gets down three glasses and slices a lemon.

"Well, Charles is obviously smitten. He won't let her out of his sight."

Mac laughs. "Maybe he thinks she's going to steal the towels."

Suddenly he takes my hand and pulls me into his arms. "Thank you," he says against my hair. "I know it's not easy."

When Skye appears, she's holding a brown paper shopping bag and Charles in her arms.

"Brought you some prezzies." She plunks the bag down on the table and sets the dog on the floor.

She pulls packages out of the bag, explaining each one carefully… Manuka honey, the edible sort, not for skin care, a bottle of Kim Crawford Sauvignon Blanc wrapped in bubble wrap, a box of chocolates, a black merino wool scarf for Mac, and for me, a carved fish hook pendant.

"Here, let's put it on you," she says, looping the black silk cord over my head. "It's carved bone. The fish hook symbolizes strength in the Maori culture. I loved this one because of the woman's profile."

"Skye, this is beautiful. Thank you."

"It might darken a wee bit," she says. "That's usual."

"What do you guys want to drink?" I ask. Mac wants an Arnold Palmer.

"I'll have that too, please. Er…what is that exactly?"

"Iced tea and lemonade."

"Oh." Her nose wrinkles.

"Here, you can taste mine," he says.

She does and then smiles her understanding. "Iced tea and lemon cordial. Yes that's what I'd like, please. In En Zed, lemonade is fizzy. Like 7Up."

It's our first cultural misunderstanding.

Mac is transformed. I've never seen him so ebullient. Ever. And she clearly adores him. She solicits his opinions on everything from clothing to politics to books and music, then hangs on his words of wisdom. She teases him about the Elky, but wants to drive it. She tells him silly jokes. They jog together every morning.

They remind me a little of my father and me.

She's enthralled with L.A. We show her all the tourist stuff, Hollywood, Beverly Hills, even Disneyland. Mac takes her to Paramount where his friend Kristin gives them a tour. She meets Antonio Banderas and talks about him nonstop at dinner. Gabe takes her to his partner's salon for a total makeover and she comes home and washes off all the makeup. We go to a dance rehearsal with CM. She comes to work with me a couple of days and seems truly interested in the business of running a bakery, even more so than the pastries she inhales. We eat at trendy restaurants in Malibu and Hollywood. She insists on a visit to the Gene Autry Museum, which I've never been to, and which turns out to be fabulous. Charles abandons us to sleep on her bed. We make plans for next summer, Seattle and Orcas. And we all cry when she leaves.

The Fourth of July falls on a Friday this year and my mom wants to have us over for a backyard cookout, along with CM and Nathan, her old hippie friend Georgia Graebel and her husband, and a few couples from the neighborhood. This will probably be the last gathering at the house, because it's been bought by a young couple from Des Moines. Richard and my mother will be moving to Grass Valley in September. Funny how I hated the idea of Richard moving into "our" house all those years ago, now I hate for them to leave. I used to dread the memories living at that address; now I dread not having access to them.

The forecast is for perfect weather and I'm looking forward to an evening of food and fireworks, followed by two lazy days at home. The Maven is closed for the whole weekend—Cheryl's suggestion.

I'm in the kitchen after lunch, putting dishes in the dishwasher and packing up my contributions to the party—three desserts from the bakery—Ellie's chocolate cake, Rafe's Guadeloupe Tart and a box of lemon bars—plus my own guacamole deviled eggs in this funny little Tupperware deviled egg carrier that CM found at a garage sale. At some point I look up to see Mac, clad in his oldest swimming trunks, standing in the door to the patio, dripping wet.

"You better get showered. We need to leave in about an hour." I turn to put the pitcher of iced tea back in the refrigerator.

"I'm not going," he says.

I turn around. "What?"

"I said, I'm not going."

It's stupid, I know, but I want to cry. Instead, I say in what I hope is a neutral tone of voice, "Do you feel…okay?"

"I feel fine."

Sometimes when this happens, if I back way off, he ends up changing his mind. But I have a feeling this is not one of those times. I press my lips together.

"What will you do instead?"

"Swim. Watch TV."

Watch TV is code for drink beer till he falls asleep.

"Well…be careful not to get sunburned."

He sits in the shade at the umbrella table, staring at the newspaper, while I finish getting ready and load the car. Charles follows me out, dragging his leash.

"I'm leaving now. I guess I'll see you later."

He doesn't look up. "Okay."

When I pull up in front of my mother's house, Nathan's Prius is in the driveway. With the garage door open, I can hear music and voices coming from the backyard. I sit for a minute, recalling the last time Mac and I spent the Fourth of July on Orcas. Probably five years ago now.

We made a day of it, starting with the pancake breakfast at the firehouse. Then on to the parade of floats, trucks, bikes and the high school marching band. After that we hit the American Legion salmon barbecue, and finally ended up on Main Street at dusk, maneuvering for a spot to watch the fireworks, which were set to go off from Indian Island. I remember it was cold that year. We wore flannel shirts and down jackets, and we drank hot coffee with brandy from a thermos…

"What can I carry?" CM's standing by the car, waiting to give me a hug. She's used to Mac's unpredictable absences, so she doesn't bother to ask, but I feel compelled to explain anyway.

"He wasn't feeling good."

We look at each other for a second, then she picks Charles up and allows him a few wet kisses. "Sorry to hear it. I'll take Chas out back. Want a margarita?"

"Probably more than one."

My mother is scooping ice from the freezer into the ice bucket, and when she looks up and sees me I can tell she already knows. I set the eggs down on the counter.

"I called to ask you to bring your good ice cream scoop," she says. "Mac told me you'd already left."

"I'm sorry, Mom—"

She sets down the ice bucket and puts her arms around me. "Oh, honey...Don't apologize. It's not your fault." She adds quickly, "Or his."

"So I keep reminding myself." I pull back. "I'd better go get the desserts before they melt."

He's asleep on the couch when I get home. Two beer bottles on the coffee table and doubtless there are others in the backyard and in his office. I don't know if he really doesn't hear me come in or if he's faking it, and I'm too tired to care. After making sure all the doors are locked, I take Charles upstairs.

When I come down to the kitchen in the morning I see him through the window, sitting at the umbrella table, reading. Just where I left him. He's left the espresso machine empty of water and coffee beans, so I refill both before putting a cup under the dispenser. While it's brewing I debate whether I should sit down and enjoy my coffee or go out and attempt conversation.

"Hi."

He looks up. "I didn't know you came home last night."

"Of course I came home. You were asleep, so I didn't want to disturb you."

"Because I'm disturbed enough as it is, right?"

"You missed a good party. The kids did sparklers and we had hamburgers and toasted marshmallows and then we all walked over to the school to watch fireworks. Everyone was asking about you."

"I bet."

"What should we do for breakfast?"

"Whatever you like. I already had mine."

"What did you have?"

"Butter pecan ice cream."

"Don't you want some eggs or—"

"Actually what I want is some peace and quiet. Do you mind?"

He sleeps most of the day. I take the dog for a long walk and spend the remains of the morning cleaning out the pantry. In the afternoon I go to a movie. I make a Cobb salad for dinner. Mac looks at it without comment, fixes himself a bowl of butter pecan ice cream and goes out by the pool to eat alone. I stand at the sink, eating from the salad platter, watching him, trying to swallow my food around the knot in my throat. He's not really oblivious. He's like the boy in my seventh grade homeroom who was so dorky and knew it and always tried to pretend he didn't care.

Sunday morning I make pancakes. He eats butter pecan ice cream out by the pool, then goes into his office and shuts the door. I clean out the refrigerator and swim a few laps. I'm standing in the laundry room drying off when the phone rings. I assume since he's in his office that he'll get it.

After four rings I scoot into the kitchen and pick up the phone.

"Hi, Wyn. It's Skye here."

"How are you? What time is it there?"

She laughs. "It's 9:20 tomorrow morning. Did you have a happy Independence Day?"

"We did. My mom had everyone over for a barbecue and we watched fireworks."

"Lovely. Is Mac there? I have some news for him."

"I've been out in the pool. Hang on and I'll check."

I lay the receiver on the counter and run up the stairs.

"Mac?" I knock twice, then twist the knob. It's locked. "Mac?

No response. I knock again, harder. "Skye's on the phone."

I press my ear to the door and jiggle the knob.

"I'm busy. I'll call her later."

"She wants to tell you something."

"I'll call her later."

Resisting the urge to give the door a parting kick I go across the hall to the bedroom and pick up the extension.

"He must have gone out," I tell her. "Can I have him call you?"

"I'm going out tonight, but I'll be here all day, so…"

"You want me to tell him anything?"

She hesitates. "No, that's okay. I'd like to tell him myself." Then she adds, "I had a poem published."

"Really? How great! Congratulations. Can you send us a copy?"

"It's just a wee literary rag. I can email it."

"I won't tell him. I'll just have him call you."

"Thanks, Wyn. Hug little Scruff for me."

I fall asleep reading the Sunday paper and wake up with a crick in my neck. It's almost 6 o'clock. I sit on the edge of the couch scrunching my shoulders and turning my head from side to side. The house is quiet.

I go upstairs and listen at the closed door. "Mac? What are you doing?"

"Working."

"Why don't you take a break and—"

"Can't right now."

"Did you call Skye yet?"

"No."

I hesitate. "She was so excited to tell you her news."

"She's young. She'll get over it."

I stick out my tongue at the door.

I feed Charles, pour a glass of white wine and take it out by the pool. As soon as I sit down I smell it. I look up. His office window is open.

Back in the kitchen, I fish a credit card out of my wallet and take the stairs two at a time. I slip the credit card into the space between the door and the jamb and swipe it up. The lock clicks. The door opens about an inch and then stops against something.

"What the fuck are you doing?"

"I want to talk to you. Let me in." I grab the edge of the door and push, but it doesn't move. "Please. Just for a minute."

When I hear him stand up, some instinct prompts me to remove my hand from the door and step back. A good thing, since he leans his full weight against the door, shutting it hard. The lock snaps into place.

"You could have broken my hand."

"I'm trying to work."

"No you're not. You're sitting in there smoking dope and drinking."

"I'm not drinking."

I stare at the door, the blank white panel, imagining the crunch of my fingers. It's all in place now—anger, sadness, frustration, yes, embarrassment, too—it's all coming to a rolling boil.

"Hey, remember that story I told you about how I threw a lamp through the front window of David's house?"

Silence.

"It's true. I really did that. And I'm not above doing it again, so let me in."

"I need to work—"

"You've had the whole damn weekend to work."

"As I've told you countless times, just sitting at the computer doesn't mean I can write."

"Oh, I know. You have to be sitting at the computer at the same time I need to talk to you. That's the only way you can write."

Silence.

"If you don't let me in right now, I'm going to beat this goddamn door down with your Louisville Slugger."

I hear movement and drawers slamming, the sound of his chair rolling on the plastic chair mat. The door opens abruptly. But instead of letting me in, he's coming out. Or he thinks he is.

When he tries to push past me I put both hands squarely on his chest and shove him back with my full weight. It catches him off guard, and he trips on the old dog towel he'd jammed under the door to block the smoke. I lock my arms around his waist and we both go down on the rug. Thankfully with me on top.

"Jesus Christ, are you fucking crazy?"

He tries to push me away, but my arms are locked around him and my face presses hard into his chest. We struggle in total silence except for a few grunts and breaths. Then a feeling twists inside me, so sharp and so close to longing, that I start to cry.

He's still trying to loosen my arms.

"Stop it, Mac." It comes out as a gulp between sobs. "Goddamn you, stop pushing me away. You stupid jackass, I love you."

He goes completely still. It's like hugging a tree. I keep thinking any minute he'll put his arms around me, but he doesn't. Eventually I let go and roll away. My right wrist feels like it's been run over by a Volkswagen.

I get up and take a handful of tissues from the box on his desk to wipe the tears and snot off my face. "Mac, what are you doing?"

"I'm trying to work." His eyes are closed and when he opens them his pupils are the size of marbles.

"Show me."

"I don't have to prove anything to you."

"Oh yes, you do. To me and to Skye."

He gets up slowly and sits in his chair. I drag one of the wing chairs over and sit facing him. The air in the room is obnoxious with pot smoke and there's a pill bottle on the desk. "I want you to tell me what's going on."

He turns his head to one side. "I'm sick of this."

"Of what?"

"Everything. You going off to your mother's for the whole damn day and half the night—"

"We were invited to the Fourth of July party. We said we'd go—"

"No. Your mother asked *you* and *you* said we'd go. You didn't ask me if I wanted to go. You know I hate that kind of shit."

"What do you mean, you hate that shit? My mother adores you and you always get along with Richard—and CM and Nathan—"

"Nathan bugs the crap out of me. He's so fucking full of himself. Mr. Broadway—"

"Oh, stop it. Nathan's a cream puff and you always said you liked him—"

"It was just an excuse to be gone all day."

"Don't be ridiculous. I wanted you to come with me."

"You think I don't know what you tell your mother and CM and God knows who else? I'm not stupid."

"Nobody thinks you're stupid. Least of all, me. Mac, I love you—"

"As long as I'm behaving. As long as I don't upset you. Don't say weird shit. Don't embarrass you—"

"Where are you getting all this crap? You're the one who decided at the last minute that you didn't want to go. What was I supposed to do—stay home and watch you drink beer?"

"You didn't give a shit if I went. In fact you were hoping I wouldn't."

"It's really amazing how you know everything that goes on in my mind."

"Believe me, you're not that hard to read."

I rest my elbow on the desk and practice flexing my wrist. "What are those pills?"

"What's that got to do with anything?"

"What are they?"

"They help me concentrate."

"Dexedrine?"

"Ritalin."

"And this is supposed to help?"

He looks at me, then away again.

Charles chooses this moment to peek around the corner of the open door. He spots his old towel, gives it a sniff and starts to fluff it up. I smile automatically at his ability to wander into a war zone and settle down for a nap. Either a happy dog or my smile or the combination of the two is apparently unbearable.

His face changes...not just the expression, but the physiognomy. I can actually see it happen.

"Get the goddamned dog out of my office."

I look at him for a minute. "Mac...I just wish you would—"

"Go ahead. Tell me what you wish I'd do and I'll put it on my list."

I pick Charles up and pause for a second in the doorway. "I wish you would call your daughter."

Twenty-four

The rest of July is a black hole. It's not like before and he doesn't leave home...I almost wish he would. He spends hours staring at his computer without typing so much as a word. He swims a lot and takes very long showers. Our water bills are astronomical.

He doesn't go out, he doesn't read. He doesn't talk much. Even when Skye calls, I can hear the distance in his voice. I worry that she won't understand, that she'll think he's mad at her or doesn't care. Once or twice I think about calling her myself, but as mapmakers once wrote in the uncharted corners of the known world, *Here be monsters.*

And then in August with all the advance warning of a piano dropping from a skyscraper window, he makes an appointment with the psycho-pharmacologist recommended by Willow and comes home with a prescription for Prozac. I suspect that it's more about his being unable to write than the fact that our marriage is hanging by a thread, but at this point I'll take what I can get.

He takes 20 mg of Prozac every morning, and at first he seems to improve. Then he gains twenty pounds, can't sleep and loses all interest in sex, which makes him nearly as depressed as before. The psycho (as Mac refers to him) assures him that this is common and that a bit of experimentation should smooth things out.

He changes the time he takes the medication, then the dosage. When neither helps, he adds Nortriptyline, which restores libido, but makes Mac a zombie who can't work, or run or swim or do anything, really, other than sex. Delete Nortriptyline, add Wellbutrin, which works fairly well for a while, then edges him towards anxiety. He paces, bites his nails to the quick, compulsively checks cell phone and email, worries if I don't come home when he thinks I should, yells at Charles every time he barks, which is often. He does lose some weight because he runs about five miles a day.

September brings the attack on the World Trade Center. Horrifying images and choked voices. The eerie silence of empty skies. At the bakery I turn up the radio and we all—staff and customers, delivery service people and security guards—stand in mute shock listening to NPR. I call the house but Mac doesn't answer the phone, and when I get there I find him asleep in front of the TV while footage of the plane hitting the second tower plays in a seemingly endless loop.

The doctor decides to wean him off Prozac, but he gets impatient and starts skipping doses. The result is an unpleasant withdrawal effect called "brain shock," which he describes as a cross between electric shock and vertigo. He also begins having lurid nightmares about falling out of a plane or being held under water.

By mid-November he's cleared of Prozac and starting on Atomoxetine, the next attempt to fend off the dark side. The doctor says it's commonly used for ADHD and secondarily for depression. Possible side effects could include loss of appetite, which Mac doesn't see as a negative, and irritability, which, God knows, is nothing new, and something called QT prolongation. This has to do with abnormal heart rhythm and it worries me, but Mac wants to try it because the psycho says it should help him focus. And so it begins again, with forced optimism and crossed fingers.

The first Friday in December I come home early. A winter storm has moved in from the Pacific, the kind of weather Charles loves. He probably has genetic memories of his ancestors out herding sheep on the moors in the bone-chilling English rain. All I want to do is get a pot of soup going, make some kind of bread for dinner. I'm looking forward to sitting by the fireplace afterwards with a glass of wine.

I thought he'd be working in his office this afternoon, but the house is cold and dark. I turn the thermostat up and try to ignore the infinitesimal seismic shift. He's at the library. Or at Office Max buying a toner cartridge. Or maybe he went to have coffee with Gabe, who's become his "asshole buddy" (an old Southern expression, Gabe assures me.) They're both off alcohol at the moment, so they meet a couple of times a week for coffee.

I gather what I find in the fridge and start chopping onions. While they're slowly sweating in olive oil, I chop carrots and celery, part of a red bell pepper, tomatoes, potatoes and zucchini, adding each vegetable as I finish chopping. Except the zucchini, which I don't like cooked too much, so I save it to throw in at the last minute. I grate a chunk of Parmigiano-Reggiano into a dish and toss the rind into the soup pot, stir together the dry ingredients for cornmeal biscuits. I've been pointedly ignoring the clock, but now I allow myself a casual glance.

Six-thirty. I wander around the house looking for clues. No note on the bed or his desk. The library card is in the Chinese porcelain dish on the hall table. There's nothing written on his calendar. His gym bag is in the closet. Alan and Sylvia are on a Caribbean cruise.

I talk to myself. Don't weird out over nothing. It's only six thirty. He's been working hard. Cut him some slack. But the dead air space in my chest tells a different story.

The year has been difficult in so many ways. At times I've thought of leaving, but then we have a few good days and I tell myself it's going to be fine, I just need to hang on. I try not to show him my fears. I don't call his cell if he's twenty minutes late meeting me. I don't ask where he's going or with whom, or when he'll be home. I don't remind him to take his meds or go to his appointments. I try to monitor his moods without being obvious. I avoid asking how he slept. I want to know all those things, but I can't ask. I have to wait till he volunteers the information. And for the most part, he eventually does.

At seven-fifteen I call Gabe and leave a voicemail. *If Mac's with you, tell him dinner's ready and I'm giving his share to Charles.*

A few minutes after eight the phone rings and I make myself not snatch it up on the first ring.

"You guys eating dinner?" It's CM.

"Not yet. I'm making soup. What's up?"

"Nathan's got four tickets for Lion King Saturday night. You want to have dinner and catch the show?"

"Um…sure. Sounds great. I'll just check with Mac and get back to you tomorrow."

"I was thinking we might try that new place in Westwood…I think it's called Degas or something. Some painterly name."

"Okay. Sure. I'll let you know."

We hang up. Five minutes later she calls back.

"Is everything okay?"

"Yes, yes."

"Are you sure? You sound kind of like somebody's standing on your hair."

"It's just…Mac's not home. Yet."

"Where is he?"

"I don't know."

"Well, you know what this town gets like when it rains. Traffic's probably a bitch. Have you tried calling him?"

"No. I don't want to be paranoid."

"Right. Well, he's probably sitting in traffic. Maybe his phone's dead. Could be a lot of things. I wouldn't worry too much. We're home all evening. Call me if you want later on."

"What are you going to do, take the bloodhounds out?"

"No, Ms. Smart-Ass. I'm just going to be your ever faithful, long suffering best friend who puts up with you when nobody else will."

I exhale. "I know. I'm sorry. Thanks for that."

At eight thirty I call his cell. I leave a message, still trying to sound casual. *Hey, it's me. I made minestrone. Call and let me know when you're coming so I know when to put the biscuits in. Be careful driving in this stuff. Love you.*

Nine-thirty. Ten-thirty. I'm no longer in denial. Something's happened. It's just a question of what. I don't want to consider the possibilities. If he was okay he'd have called me by now. But I'm paralyzed. I don't know what to do. The soup is cold, under a slick of olive oil. I put it in the fridge. I cover the biscuit ingredients and set them in the pantry.

Upstairs I turn on the 11 o'clock news on the bedroom TV and settle in with Charles, pretending that I'm not watching for the story of some hideous multi-car pileup on the 101. God, where is he? At midnight I go in the bathroom, open the medicine cabinet to retrieve my toothbrush and find myself staring at the amber plastic bottle that holds thirty capsules, a month's supply of Atomoxetine.

I take down the bottle and open it, pour the contents into my hand. Fifteen orange and yellow capsules. I turn the bottle to read the label. The prescription is dated November 1st.

There are two possible interpretations for what I'm looking at. Either the prescription was filled before he actually needed it, or he hasn't been taking it every day. I try to remember what he's been doing for the last two weeks. Why the hell didn't I notice? I've been so intent on not nagging, not spying, not questioning…could I have missed something?…some sign that things were veering off track. But where is he? I can't start calling everyone I know and asking if he's there. It's after midnight. Shit. I'm going to kill him. If he's not dead.

I try his cell again and get voice mail again. I don't leave a message.

I fall asleep about an hour before I have to get up. The rain has stopped but the sky is still low and gray. I brew a double espresso and go through the motions of feeding and walking Charles. I pull on jeans and a turtleneck, put Charles in the back seat and drive to the Maven.

Cheryl has become an adept reader of my moods, almost as good as Tyler. I feel like the wicked queen, making my employees skulk around trying to stay in my good graces or risk being beheaded. In any case she sees that this is not the morning to tell me about personnel problems or suggest that one of the floor mixers should be replaced.

I head to my office, get Charles settled in his secret hideaway, and sit at my desk trying to compose myself for the day ahead. I boot up the computer.

The problem is not knowing whether to be furious or frightened. Is he in trouble? In a hospital? Lying in a ditch? Is he drunk? Strung out on something? Or just hunched over his computer somewhere? Why doesn't he call?

What I really hate is that I'm not even supposed to get mad at him because HE CAN'T HELP IT. IT'S NOT HIS FAULT. IT'S THE DEPRESSION. YOU CAN'T BLAME HIM. Okay, damn it. So who do I blame? When I want to pick something heavy and heave it through the front window, whose fault is that?

Somehow the day passes. It's not until four o'clock that I realize I haven't eaten since breakfast. I feel cold and shaky. There's about an hour before the after work crowd starts dropping by to pick up bread for their dinner, and with our new schedule, the kitchen is closed but the fournil is busy. I go into the prep area and make myself a tuna sandwich, take it to my office and start checking email. I try not to expect a message from Mac, but I'm still disappointed not to find one. I make a half-assed attempt at answering email, eat two bites of my sandwich and then pillow my head on my arms and doze off.

I startle awake when Cheryl comes in.

"Wyn, are you okay?"

"Just tired. I didn't sleep much last night."

"Why don't you get out of here?" she says. "I can take care of closing."

I look at her tiny frown. "Maybe I will. If you're sure…"

She jerks her head towards the door.

To fill the silence I turn on Joni Mitchell full blast. That's why I don't hear the door until Charles goes on full battle alert. I know it's not Mac. He'd come in through the garage. But maybe…

Gabe is standing on the porch, droplets of water in his hair, smiling hopefully. He hands me a plastic shopping bag full of books.

"Hey, darlin'. Mac wanted to borrow these."

My vision swims. "Have you seen him?"

"No." He steps inside, closing the door behind him, and pulls me into a damp hug. He smells of some expensive cologne and he holds my head gently against his cashmere sweater.

"I haven't seen him since yesterday morning when I left for work."

"I'm sure he's okay."

"No, you're not."

He sighs. "No, I'm not. But I'm bettin' on it. Meanwhile, how 'bout I cook you some supper?"

I shake my head. "I've got a pot of soup in the fridge. Please stay and have some with me."

I take the dry ingredients out of the pantry and mix up the cornmeal biscuit dough, cut it into squares and bake them in a hot oven to Gabe's obvious delight. It cheers me somewhat.

I eat a couple of spoonfuls of soup, but Gabe cleans his bowl while Charles sits attentively at his feet, waiting for crumbs.

"Honey, are you starvin' this puppy?"

"He'd like you to think so."

He holds a piece of biscuit down to Charles, who looks at me for the go-ahead.

"Okay, but just one bite."

Gabe laughs as the dog hoovers the food neatly off his fingertips. "I do believe he has better table manners than my cousin Ned."

"Have some more soup. There are more biscuits in the warming oven."

"I wouldn't say no to that. You just sit still and try to eat something, Wynter. I can get it."

He's just lifting the lid off the soup pot when the phone rings. I almost turn over my chair in my rush to get to it.

"Good evening," says an unfamiliar male voice. "Is Mr. McLeod in?"

"No," I say.

"Do you know how I can reach him?"

"This is his wife. Can I help you?"

"Well…" He clears his throat while my fingers fumble with the button on my sweater. "Mrs. McLeod, this Sgt. Ruskin, Santa Barbara County Sheriff's Department. I was wondering if maybe his car had been stolen? Or maybe he loaned it to a friend? Silver 2000 BMW coupe?"

My throat is totally dry. "Not that I know of. Why?"

"Well…" He pauses again. "We found the car abandoned on a side road off Highway 1 south of the city. Keys in the ignition, several items in the trunk, including a laptop computer and a denim jacket. When was the last time you spoke to your husband?"

My teeth clamp down on the inside of my cheek. "Yesterday morning."

"Did he say anything about going to Santa Barbara?"

"No. He didn't."

"Okay. Well, we've impounded the car. We'll be investigating further. Can you give me a physical description?"

"He's forty-three. About 6'2", sandy blonde hair, green eyes."

"What was he wearing when you last saw him?"

"Jeans and a sweatshirt. I tried his cell phone but I got voicemail. I left a message for him to call me."

"If you hear from him will you contact me please? The number is 888- 988-0998. Is this number the best place to reach you? Is there a work phone?"

I give him my cell number and hang up, not looking at Gabe.

I say, "His car was abandoned near the beach south of Santa Barbara."

He replaces the lid on the soup pot. "How 'bout we take a little ride? Grab that puppy dog."

For a while there's no sound inside the Alpha except the gentle swish of windshield wipers. Charles curls up in the tiny space behind the seats and goes to sleep.

"You know, depression's an ugly thing," Gabe says. "Sneaky, too. It takes over your head without you even knowing till it's too late."

"Are you speaking from experience?"

He nods, keeping his eyes straight ahead. Headlights slide past us.

"Twelve years ago when I came out it was quite the hometown scandal. I was engaged to a lovely young lady from a very prominent family. All lined up to go into her daddy's business. We had season tickets for Ole Miss football games…hey, no laughin' now. That's a pretty big deal where I come from."

"So, what made you decide to come out then?"

"I didn't exactly decide. I sorta got caught with my britches down. So to speak."

"I see."

"With a lovely cousin of my lovely fiancée."

"Wow."

"Yeah, darlin'. Wow. Within a very short time I couldn't get arrested in that town. Actually I was probably lucky her daddy didn't shoot me. No jury in Mississippi would've convicted him."

"Your family…?"

"Cut me off cold. Friends too. Even one or two that I knew were in the closet."

I turn to him. "Really?"

"Yeah, darlin'. They had no plans to come out and they didn't want to look guilty by association."

"So then what?"

"So I packed my belongings and drove out here to Never-Never Land to finish my *roman à clef.* But I didn't know a solitary soul and I was homesick as hell and felt guilty for screwin' up my life and my family's good name. Well…semi-good."

"So you got depressed."

"Yeah, but not right away. First I made a few friends, Alan took me on as a client…he actually sold my book. Things were looking up, as they say. And then, lady, the bottom dropped out."

"After you finally got your life together?"

"That's the way it works sometimes. See, up to that point I was too busy surviving to be depressed. But I think it was always there. Waitin' to sneak up behind and tap me on the shoulder."

"What happened?"

He sighs gently. "I was a classic case. Sleeping for days on end. Not doing anything when I was awake but cryin'. I was s'posed to be revising my book, but I couldn't even read, much less write. I was a damn mess. Then I started self-medicating with bourbon so I could work a little bit. But I was goin' through two bottles a day. Eventually got myself a bleedin' ulcer and ended up in the hospital."

"How did you get well?"

He doesn't answer right away. He turns down the wiper speed. Then he says,

"That's the thing, darlin'. I'm not well. I'm better. But it's somethin' that's always gonna be with me. Mac too. You can see it in other people right away. It's like how two combat vets recognize each other."

"But I don't think he saw it in you."

"Yes, I believe he did. That's why he never liked me much. He saw that in me and he knew it was in him. And it scared the livin' shit out of him. Pardon my French, honey."

The trip, of course, is futile. We drive up and down along the beach in the pouring rain, then head for the police station. Sgt. Ruskin has gone for the evening, but the desk sergeant on duty takes Mac's name and my description of him and the car and goes down the hall into another room.

After several minutes he's back.

"Your husband's been located, Mrs. McLeod."

Gabe's hand on my elbow steadies me.

"He was apparently staying at a Travelodge Motel several blocks from where we found his car. When he returned to the beach and found the car was gone he called us. He picked up the car about an hour ago." He gives me a measured look. "Is everything alright?"

I have so many questions I can't think where to begin, but I don't think the Santa Barbara County Sheriff's Department has the answers.

"Yes, it's fine. I was just worried." I try to arrange my face into a smile. "Thanks very much for the…everything."

When I get in the car I almost sit on Charles, who's migrated to the passenger seat. I put him in back, but as soon as I've buckled the seatbelt, he climbs over the seat and settles on my lap.

"Good man, Charles." Gabe reaches over to scratch behind his ears. "You know, my granddaddy always used to say you get one great dog in your life and one true love."

He turns the key in the ignition and lets the car idle for a minute while I nod and stare out the windshield.

On the way south, we stop at the Travelodge and Gabe goes into the office.

"He checked out a couple hours ago," he says when he comes back. "He's probably gone home. In fact, we probably passed each other on the highway."

Mac is standing in the hall, reading the mail, eating a biscuit and drop-ping crumbs everywhere. He says, "Where have you been?"

It catches me off guard. "Where have I been? Where have *you* been?"

"Working."

"Working where?"

"The Travelodge in Ventura."

I'm very nearly speechless. "Do you know how long you've been gone?"

He looks at his watch. "About thirty six hours, give or take."

"Did it never cross your mind that I might wonder where you were? That I'd be worried? I left you several messages."

"I turned off the phone."

"The cop said your laptop was in the trunk. How could you be working?"

"Ever hear of paper and pen?" He waves a handful of damp, ink-smudged, wrinkled pages under my nose."

"Why did you leave? Why couldn't you work here?"

"I just felt jumpy. I needed some peace and quiet."

"Mac, I don't even know what to say. I was frantic. With the rain and everything, I worried that you were in an accident."

"Well, as you can see, I wasn't. Have we got anything else to eat?"

I slam my purse on the floor. "What is wrong with you? You disappear for three days and all you can say is have we got anything to eat?"

"Two days. Two and a half." His eyes are flat and dull.

"Have you been taking your pills?"

"Yep."

"Really? Why are there so many left in the bottle?"

"No idea. Maybe you put them in there so it would look like I wasn't taking them."

I pick up the phone. "We need to call Willow—"

He grabs the receiver out of my hand and slams it down. "I have appointments. Next week. Everything's fine. I feel great."

He turns and walks into the kitchen. I pick up the pile of yellow legal pages and look at each one, front and back. They look like jabberwocky.

I should disengage right now. Just walk away. Go take a hot bath. Do something constructive. But I can't. I'm furious and exhausted and frustrated. And completely helpless, which makes it worse. Not only can I not help him, I can't even have a good screaming fight with him about it because he's speaking Remulac.

So instead of doing the intelligent thing, I take the pages into the kitchen where he's drinking a beer—another bad sign—and I hold them out to him.

"This is what you're working on?"

"Correct."

"What is it?"

"What would you like it to be?"

"I don't think what I'd like it to be is important. You're the author."

"It could be any number of things. Which is the beauty of the piece."

"You shouldn't be drinking that, you know."

He looks at the bottle as if this is news to him. "Why not?"

"The doctor said not to drink alcohol when you're taking that stuff."

"Well, this tastes a hell of a lot better than Atomoxetine, so I think I'd rather drink and stop taking pills."

"I think you've already stopped taking them. Haven't you?"

"Of course."

"Why?"

"Because they don't work."

"I know they're not perfect or wonderful, but they were making things just a little easier."

"For you, maybe. Not for me. I can't work, I can't think. My hands shake all the time. You want to know why I left the car? Because I was afraid I was going through the guard rail."

"I'm sorry. I'm really sorry it's like this—"

"Bullshit. All you care about is whether I'm taking the fucking pills. Add one, drop one, reduce this, increase that, wait six weeks and then start all over and in the meantime I wander around like the undead."

"We just have to keep trying until we find the right—"

"What's this we shit? I don't see you popping any meds."

"If we keep going like this I will be."

"Great. Then you'll know what it's like."

"*Mac!*" I wad up the yellow pages and throw them at him. "If you didn't just quit taking your meds, you wouldn't be going through this."

"Let me explain this to you. Again. When I take the pills, I can't write—"

"So is that the only thing you care about anymore?"

"What do you want? Should I go back to being a bartender? Would that make you happy?"

"Yes! It would. I liked you as a bartender. You were happier; you were a lot nicer. As of now, you seem to think being a writer entitles you to act like an asshole."

He reaches past me to pick up his keys off the table.

I take a deep breath. "I'm sorry. I didn't mean that. I'm just so upset I can't even think. I don't want to argue anymore. We can talk about it tomorrow. It's late and we both need—where are you going?"

"I don't know."

In bed, I curl myself around Charles, lulled by the warmth of his little body and the soft drone of his breathing. When my shoulder gets sore I turn on my back and lie there with eyes open in the dark. At dawn I get up, brew myself an espresso and turn on the computer. I Google Liv Keppler and get an amazing number of responses. There's a private mail box, but there are two other addresses listed—one in Santa Monica and one on Starlight Canyon Drive in Hollywood. I'm betting on that one.

I've always found driving in the Hollywood Hills annoying and confusing, but at this moment I'm preternaturally calm. It's a gorgeous Sunday morning, cool and sharp, air washed clean by the storm, clouds dispersed. Hardly any traffic. I only have to double back once. The street sign has been knocked down and when I come back around the corner I spot it lying in the mud.

It's easy to find number 10899, easier still because my husband's car is sitting about half a block down the street, a ticket flapping on the windshield. It's almost a relief.

I look over at Charles and he looks back at me. Sensible little dog that he is, he doesn't try to jolly me out of it. I pull into a driveway and turn around, heading back towards Sunset.

Sometimes it happens that you know the exact moment when everything changes, when you run out of excuses. When compassion fatigue sets in.

For me, this is that time.

As divorces go, ours is pretty civilized. Certainly more so than my first, which dragged on for several years, full of acrimonious wrangling over finances. Neither Mac nor I have the heart to fight over anything; nor do we have a lot to fight over.

The dissolution of us takes place in a conference room instead of a courtroom, with a clerk instead of a judge. When the brief proceeding is over I fully intend to say something to him. Something to gentle the landing, to close the door without slamming it. But I put my papers in a file folder, say good bye to my attorney Elizabeth, and turn around to find the room empty.

Twenty-five

O
n a rainy spring morning, I drive up to St. Helena for Tyler's graduation. CM offers to go with me, but I know Nathan's coming that week, so I let her off the hook. If the truth be told, I'm just glad to get away. From Luna Blanca, even from the bakery. Life has slipped into a different gear lately; it feels as if I'm standing still and things are moving around me.

I've just had the Volvo in for a tune up and new brakes and James gave the car a rueful look.

"How much longer you planning to drive this baby?" he asked, chewing the frayed toothpick that's forever in his mouth.

"As long as I can," I said.

"Pretty soon it's gonna need a new clutch. Gonna run you about a grand. Probably not worth putting that much into it."

"Well...I guess I'll drive off that bridge when I come to it."

He grinned and shook his head.

What I didn't say because it seemed kind of silly—although, being a car guy, he'd probably understand—is that this car seems like the one constant in my life. The smell of it, the feel of the driver's seat's worn leather, the shiny black shift knob under my hand...those are the things that comfort me. Yeah. It's down to that.

My mother and Richard have a condo in Sherman Oaks, but they spend most of their time in Grass Valley. CM jets back and forth to New

York, stockpiling frequent flier credits for a planned trip to Tahiti this fall. I still talk to them all and see them occasionally, but day to day, it's pretty much the bakery, me and Charles.

Strangely and unexpectedly, Cheryl has become a godsend. The emotional connection that I had with Tyler isn't there, but in a way, that's a good thing and I have no complaints about how she runs the bakery. Sometimes people surprise you, the way they grow into a situation. And without being intrusive or nosy, she's helped me through some rough patches.

So far, Tyler hasn't said anything about coming back. In fact, Tyler hasn't said much about anything for a while. During the first term she called every couple of weeks, but that tapered off, partly I assume because she's busy, and partly because I didn't feel comfortable talking to her about Mac. Since that was pretty much all-consuming for me, we didn't have a lot to talk about beyond what was going on at work. Even her interest in the bakery seemed to wane after a while as she got more involved in her classes and her externship at an elegant restaurant in Monterey.

It's almost lunchtime when I turn off Highway 101 and head east into Napa. At Mustard's Grill I order a half-pound hamburger, which is worth every penny of the fifteen dollars it costs, and I eat the entire thing, including every crispy French fry without feeling a shred of guilt. Hopefully we'll have a late dinner.

It's been years since I've been in the wine country. I think last time I was with Husband Number One. I drive slowly—too slowly for a lot of people driving behind me—but I refuse to power through this lovely place, so I pull off from time to time to let them fly past. Yes, it's touristy and crowded, but I still love cruising the two-lane highway through the lush valleys. I love the fields with the wild mustard growing between the grid of vines, the swags of mist festooning the surrounding hills, the wineries with their stone entrances and manicured lawns.

When I check into my B&B, I congratulate myself on my choice of lodgings. I chose Livingston House based on a brochure one of our customers showed me when she heard I was coming up here. I booked it mainly for two reasons—one being the location, just a couple of blocks from downtown St. Helena and a five minute drive to Greystone. The other reason was the gorgeously understated interior of the place and its eclectic collections of art and books. Too many B & B's in the valley are over-decorated Victorians with their print wallpapers and canopy beds and ornately carved armoires—cute, cluttered and—to me—claustrophobic. When I saw the photo of the sunny downstairs room with a tile soaking tub and steam shower, I was hooked.

I call Tyler's cell phone and leave a voicemail that I've arrived and then I climb into a hot bubble bath, already regretting that I'll only be here two nights.

Eventually the water cools and the bubbles dissipate. I push myself up and out of the tub, shivering, wrap up in the French terry robe, and lie down on the bed, intending to check tomorrow's forecast on the weather channel. Two hours later my buzzing phone wakes me.

"Wyn! I've been trying to call you for the last hour. Where are you?"

It takes me a minute to figure out the answer. "Um…the hotel. B&B. Inn. Whatever. Sorry, I fell asleep and my phone was set on stun. What time is it?"

"Six-thirty. We have a 7 pm dinner reservation. Can you be ready in ten minutes?"

I sit up, yawning. "Sure, if you don't care what I look like."

"I don't. See you in a few."

A quick look outside reveals a steady drizzle, so I put on my good jeans, a pair of leather boots and a cotton sweater, pull my travel raincoat out of its stuff sack, and proceed to the parlor to wait for her. Makeup be damned.

At first I don't see the person standing behind Tyler. Then while we're hugging I find myself looking into a pair of soulful dark eyes, and I suddenly know I'm looking at the reason why I haven't heard from her lately.

She grabs his hand and pulls him towards us. "Wyn…" She actually blushes, a first for my Tyler. "This is my…friend…János Herczeg."

He takes my cold hand in his two big, warm ones and kisses me on both cheeks.

"I am so glad to finally meet you," he says with just a whisper of a mysterious accent. "You are all this girl talks about."

The way he looks at her when he says "this girl," melts my heart.

"I'm very happy to meet you, too." I smile. "And I'm so glad Ty has a friend whose name I can pronounce."

He has a big, friendly laugh, and Tyler rolls her eyes at me. "You'll get used to her weird sense of humor," she says. Then she actually hugs me again, without any prompting, and we go off to dinner.

The next morning Ty picks me up after breakfast and takes me on a tour of Greystone. When I walk through the huge arched stone entrance I have a sudden flash of déjà vu.

"What?" she says.

"I just realized this is the old Christian Brothers winery. I was here years ago with David."

"Well, it's changed a lot," she says. "Come on, I want to show you everything and we don't have much time."

We visit the tasting bar and the chocolate kitchen, the store and the demo kitchen. On the second floor the old barrel room, now the winemakers' hall of fame, is being set up for the graduation ceremony. The teaching kitchen, with its gleaming banks of Viking stoves and stainless steel counters, moves to a complicated rhythm all its own as teachers and students and guest chefs bustle around getting food ready for the celebration dinner. At one point I glimpse a guy in a white chef's jacket who—at least from the back—looks like Alex. My reaction is instantaneous and visceral.

In her car on the way back to town, I lean my head against the window and sigh. "This is beautiful. I'm so glad you got to come here."

"Me too." She laughs. "And if I hadn't, I never would have met János."

"I really like him, Ty. He just seems so…real." I give her a sly smile. "Nice buns, too."

She pulls into a parking place on Main Street. "Let's have a quick coffee before I take you back."

We get double mochas and sit at a marble counter facing the street.

"I like this place," she says. "Doesn't it remind you of Queen Street? Just the feel of it."

"It does." I look over at her. "You look different, girlfriend. Like you've got the world by the tail."

She looks right back at me. "Happy. Wyn, I'm so happy. I had no idea love was like this. Oh, God, don't cry."

"Oh, shut up. I'll cry if I want to. As Lesley Gore said." I dab at my eyes with a napkin.

"Who?"

"Nevermind."

We sip our coffee silently for a minute; then she says, "I…um… wanted to talk to you about my plans."

My stomach dips. Last night I learned that János's parents live in San Francisco and I'm envisioning him taking a job there. Marriage. Babies. Only seeing Ty on Thanksgiving or when they bring the kids to Disneyland.

"Big or small?" I ask.

"Big or small what?"

"Wedding."

She laughs so hard she nearly falls off her stool. "We're not getting married," she says. "Not right now, anyway. My god, we've both got loans to pay off. János wants to take his wine degree before he even looks for a full time job. And when he does get a job, it will just be to get enough experience to open his own place. Then, who knows?"

"You mean…I thought you'd want to be together."

"Oh, we do," she says matter-of-factly. "And we will. We'll have to commute at first, of course. But we'll work it out."

Suddenly I feel very old and out of it. "So…what plans are you talking about?"

"Work," she says. "The bakery. You said I could come back. You haven't changed your mind, have you?" A small frown appears, then vanishes into a smile.

"Oh, God, Wyn. Don't cry."

It's mid-afternoon and the Grill on the Alley is pretty quiet. It's late for lunch, too early for happy hour. I've just come from a post-surgical appointment with the orthopedic surgeon and I'm in a lot of pain, but I can't take oxycodone on an empty stomach and I don't want to drive all the way back to Luna Blanca with no relief.

I'd like to eat at the bar, but having one arm immobilized in a sling makes climbing up on a stool somewhat of an undertaking, so I let the host show me to the booth back in the corner on the right, my second favorite place to sit. He helps me get my good arm out of the ugly warm-up jacket I was instructed to buy for post-op wear.

"What did you do to yourself?" the waiter asks.

"Threw a no-hitter. Too bad it was just spring training. Looks like I'm out for the season."

He nods. "Shoulder, huh? Rotator cuff, I bet. I had that a couple of years ago. What can I get you?"

I order the Caesar with chicken because I know it'll be quick. I'd kill for a margarita, but they don't go well with oxycodone, so I ask for iced tea. As soon as the waiter brings the bread basket, I slather a piece of sourdough with butter, wolf down a couple of bites and pop my pill. Then I lean my head against the back of the booth and wait for the pain to fade.

Since the surgery I've had to sleep sitting up with one of those contraptions everyone had in college for studying in bed—a wedge-shaped pillow with arms. Looks like a chair with no seat. Interestingly, they were called husbands. They work fine for reading in bed, but for sleeping, not so much. Every time I doze off, my head drops forward, sending a sharp pain down my upper arm. So now, as soon as I lean my head back, I start drifting away.

"Wyn."

When my eyes flutter open I nearly choke. My ex-husband (the actual male, not the pillow) is standing beside the table. The shock of seeing him for the first time in over a year combines with the drugs to make me feel faint.

He frowns. "Are you alright?"

I nod. "Just stoned."

The waiter appears with my salad and greets Mac like a cousin. "You want a table or you sitting at the bar?" he asks.

There's a brief awkward silence and then I hear myself saying, "You can sit here…if you want. If you're not…"

"Thanks," he says and quickly scoots into the booth opposite me. I have a sudden flashback to our first dinner together, at a wonderful old-time Italian place in Seattle called Lofurno's. I had a Caesar then, too. But asking for grilled chicken on it probably would have caused the chef to fall on his meat fork. That night we sat across from each other in a wooden booth, eating and talking and listening to music into the early morning hours.

The waiter brings a Martini and sets it in front of Mac.

He's a little thinner than I like to see him and his hair is cut very short, which makes him look boyish, except that the gray is more noticeable. He's wearing jeans, a T-shirt that probably cost more than any one item in my closet, and a luxe gray sport coat.

I wish I had a glass of wine right now. It always makes me sociable. Whereas drugs simply make me drugged.

He looks at my arm. "Finally had to get it fixed."

"The biceps tendon was almost severed when they got in there. So now I'm in therapy for probably a year and it hurts like hell. The only upside is good drugs."

He laughs. "What did they give you?"

"Oxycodone. That's why I had to get something to eat."

"You didn't drive over here?"

"Of course I did. How else would I get here?"

"You shouldn't be driving around while you're on that stuff. And how can you drive stick?"

"I swapped cars with Cheryl today. I probably won't have any transmission left when I get the Volvo back."

"So are you still in the apartment?"

"No, I just moved into a townhouse a little north of Luna. Well, I'm in, but this…" I look at my shoulder… "is making the unpacking phase a rare pain in the butt. My mom came down for a few days, and put away all the basic necessities, but I've still got cartons all over the place and I don't know where half my stuff is."

The waiter reappears with my salad and a steak buried in shoe-string fries. "Anything else for you two?"

I look at Mac. "Did you order that?"

"I'm a really boring guy. I don't have to order."

He smiles at me and for a moment I flounder. "Look," he says, cutting the meat precisely, "I'm leaving tomorrow for Orcas for a week, but when I get back, I'll come over and help you get things put away."

I feel suddenly awkward. Did he think I was hinting? "Oh, don't worry about it. CM said she'd help me when she comes back from New York."

"I'll do it," he says. "I'll call you when I'm back."

Flustered, I change the topic. "Are you going up there to write?"

"No, I'm going to crew for Alex in some race. Up to the Gulf Islands. We'll spend a couple nights on Salt Spring and then work our way back."

"Sounds like fun." My mind rolls over the subtext. Ex-husband and former lover going sailing together? If only I could be a fly on the gunwale. But they'll probably do the guy thing and talk about sports and the stock market.

"Yeah. It's been too long since I've been on a boat. I'm really looking forward to it." He pauses. "I have some other news…*December Light* is in post-production."

"Oh my God, Mac! That's wonderful. Congratulations."

"I can't believe it yet. I kept thinking something would blow up and the whole thing would be back in development hell."

"When will it be released?"

He frowns. "We're trying to time it a little closer to balloting for the Oscars."

I look at him and he bursts out laughing.

"Admit it, you bit."

I laugh too. "Only because I'm on drugs."

He puts some fries on his bread plate and nudges it towards me, not bothering to ask if I want them. He knows my weakness.

"How's everything at the Maven?"

"Oh…good. I was actually thinking about doing pizza."

"Pizza."

"Well, you know…like gourmet pizza. Thin crust, wood fired oven…"

His eyebrows lift. "You really want to make pizza?"

"No." I sigh. "I really just wanted an excuse to put in a wood fired oven."

"Because…?"

"Because wood fired bread is so unbelievably wonderful."

"Would you take out the Bongard?"

"No. I couldn't do the volume of bread I need in one brick oven. It would just be like my midlife crisis red convertible. Anyway, it's not practical." I sit for a minute, reminding myself of all the reasons why it can't happen. "Not enough space, too much money. No place to stash the wood. Re-training all the bakers…"

"Why don't you just put one on your patio at home?"

"Yeah, the homeowners' association would be all over that like grilled cheese on Wonder Bread."

"Oh, I bet you could wear them down." He laughs. "Tell you what, you get it approved and I'll build it."

"You don't have time to fool around with brick ovens."

"Sure I do."

"Besides, what's in it for you?"

"A percentage of the product. I'm serious." He looks directly into my eyes. "Think about it."

"Okay, I will. Soon as I get off drugs and I can actually think."

We finish our food and sit talking. He tells me he's going to New Zealand again to see Skye. They're planning to hike the Routeburn Track. He tells me about his therapy with Willow. He's actually had two phone conversations with his mother. He says he's off medication and while he still has black days, he'd rather feel what he's feeling—good or bad. I guess I can understand that.

We don't talk about the rest. About the divorce, the slow, painful disentangling of us. It seems dishonest in a way, but maybe a bit of dishonesty is what's called for in order to move forward and still be good to each other.

By the time *December Light* is distributed, he's not only helped me unpack my household goods, but he's fixed my garage door opener— twice—and installed a doggy door from the kitchen to the patio for Charles. I've given him my Lakers tickets a couple of times. We've had lunch twice for no particular reason.

Then one day he phones to ask if I would cater desserts for the *December Light* release party at a small theater off Sunset. After I've said I'll be happy to do it, he drops the bomb. The film's producer, Kristin French, has moved into the Luna Blanca house with him. Somehow I find it possible to say,

"Good, Mac. Good for you. I'll look forward to meeting her."

Christmas Eve, 2004

My mother wanted me to spend the night at the condo, and I suppose I should have, since I'll be going back tomorrow afternoon, but I prefer to sleep in my own little house. Plus she doesn't like Charles sleeping on the bed. So, after many admonitions to drive carefully, keep my doors locked and don't make eye contact with other drivers, Charles and I depart with my mother's CD of Handel's Messiah blasting out of the sound system (to keep me awake, she says.) As soon as I leave their complex, I turn it off.

After an evening's laughter, conversation and music with my mom and Richard, CM and Nathan, Tyler and János plus me and my date Charles, what I crave is silence. The great thing about being paired with a Corgi is he never contradicts my opinions or gets drunk and flirts inappropriately or tells boring stories about his herding days. He doesn't remind me to signal for a lane change or warn me that the light three blocks away is turning amber. In short, he's the perfect companion.

I love driving my new car—actually a pre-owned Saab convertible. It suits me, in the same way the Volvo suited me. More like a companion than a utility. I turn down my street, filled with…not happiness exactly. More like contentment. Or comfort. More at peace with my life than I've been in…how long? When was it…the last time I didn't have to think about breathing? Two years? Three? No, longer than that. It's shocking to realize that it was probably sometime in the late nineties. Maybe since—

That's when I see it. Parked in front of my house, shimmering under the streetlight like a mirage. Elky 2.

Mac's at the wheel, window down, his arm resting on the door frame. A thin plume of smoke trails up into the night sky. I pull up next to him and put down my window.

"I thought you quit smoking."

His grin still does funny things to my stomach. "New wheels?"

"My birthday present to me. What are you doing here?"

"I was just in the neighborhood and I thought I'd stop by and wish you Merry Christmas."

"Where's Kristin?"

"Melbourne."

"Australia?"

He nods. "Working on a picture. Were you at your mom's?"

"I think I've just been insulted. For all you know, I could be coming home from a hot date."

"If you had a hot date, you wouldn't be coming home. And your mother would cut you out of the will if you missed Christmas Eve dinner."

"True. You want some coffee? I also have some of Tyler's amazing chocolate hazelnut torte."

"I wouldn't say no to that. Since I gave up Scotch, chocolate's my new vice of choice."

I hit my garage door opener and he pulls into the driveway behind me.

I find my French press in the pantry and brew a pot of decaf while he walks around my house and Charles follows, nipping at his heels, trying to herd him back to the kitchen. Finally he bends down and picks up the dog.

"Hey, Chuck, it's Christmas. Take the rest of the day off."

He settles Charles on his cushion by the back door. "New couch?"

I open the fridge and stare into it for a minute, then focus on the cream pitcher. "Slipcovers."

"Looks nice." Back in the living room he studies the art on the walls as if he's never seen it before. He flips through a book, picks up a tin box with a silver and turquoise concha on the top, looks inside and, finding it empty, turns it over to read the artisan's signature.

"This is cool. Where'd you get it?"

"CM got it for me in Santa Fe."

"I always wanted to go there," he says.

"Really?"

I don't remember him ever saying a word about Santa Fe. Or anywhere, actually. I guess I always assumed that with all his wandering, he'd pretty much been everywhere he wanted to go.

When we sit down across from each other at my table, the easy stream of conversation that's carried us this far seems to dry up. I take a sip of coffee and burn my tongue.

"Talked to Alex lately?" he asks and I look at him sharply.

"Is this a trick question?"

"Just wondered." He takes a bite of the torte and pronounces it *intense*. "He emailed me a few weeks ago. He wants to go up to Whistler in March."

"Sounds like fun. Will you go?"

"I don't know yet." He stirs a heaping teaspoonful of sugar into his cup. "It's been a long time."

"Since you went skiing? Or since you saw Alex?"

"Since I saw you," he says. "What was it, October?"

"At the Bean Tree."

"Right. You were with that asshole."

I laugh. "Greg's a perfectly nice guy. Just a little OCD."

"Are you still with him?"

I feel my face color. "I was never exactly *with* him. We had dinner a couple of times. Just friends."

Silence. Then we both start to talk at the same time.

"Go ahead," he says.

"I was just going to ask how you are. How are things going? What are you working on?"

"Things…" He sits back in his chair. "are going fine. I'm working on a book. Non-fiction."

"About…?"

"Rock climbing at Yosemite. Sort of a history. Stories about Chouinard and Galen Rowell and some of the guys who pioneered clean climbing and free climbing."

"Guys? Were there no gals involved?"

He laughs. "One or two. Liz Robbins. Sibylle Hechtel…"

"What made you decide to do nonfiction?"

"Kristin and I did some climbing up there last summer…beginner stuff, but it was scary. I just started wondering what it would have been like climbing those big granite walls when nobody'd really done it. At least not that way."

He sets down his fork. "I need to ask a favor."

"Sure."

"Don't say that till you know what it is." He pauses. "I want you to be the executor of my estate."

I stare at him.

"I decided to make a will—"

"But you're…not old."

"I'm also not young. It's mainly because of Skye. I want to be sure if anything happens…she's taken care of. Would you do that for me?"

"Of course, but…I mean, why not just make her the executor? She's an adult."

"Yes, but she's not a U.S. citizen. Technically. I talked to my lawyer and apparently there's some weird shit about me having to acknowledge paternity under oath before she was eighteen. When you start wrangling over those kinds of things, the lawyers end up with all the money. And it's irrelevant anyway since she's never expressed any interest in living here."

"What about Kristin?"

"I'd like you to do it. If you're willing."

I nod. "Okay. Of course."

He drinks some more coffee. "And there's…one more thing."

I laugh. "I said I'd do one thing, not two."

He smiles, but his expression changes. "I want to be cremated—"

"*Mac*…what are you talking about?"

"And I want you to scatter my ashes up on Orcas. In the ocean."

Goosebumps rise on my arms. "Why are you doing this?"

He reaches over to touch my hand. "It's just something I want to get settled and then I can forget about it. Will you do it? The ashes. I want *you* to do it. Personally."

We sit looking at each other.

"Will you?"

I can hardly make words come out. "Yes, if that's what you want… I just…are you sure nothing's wrong? You're not sick or anything?"

"No." He says it lightly. "Nothing's wrong."

"What if I die first?"

"Then you're excused." He smiles. "Sorry to spring it on you like this. I just want to get it done. I'm meeting with the lawyer right after the first. I'll send you copies of everything. Thanks for…doing that."

He finishes off the dessert in three bites. "Compliments to Tyler."

I smile. "Yeah, she's damned good. It's great having her back."

"She still hate me?"

"She never hated you."

"Sure she did. Probably still does." When he puts down his cup and looks directly at me, my heart contracts. "I don't blame her; sometimes I hate me, too."

"Don't say that."

"Why not? It's the truth. As I recall, you were always pretty big on truth."

There's a sudden heaviness in the air like a drop in the atmospheric pressure before a storm.

He says, "I hate what I did to you. To us."

"I don't think of it as something you did. It was just something that happened. I was…I didn't handle the…situation…very well either."

"Liv wasn't there, you know."

"What are you talking about?"

"That night I came back from Santa Barbara. I knew she was in New York, but I knew where she kept a spare key. I just went over there to sleep."

"It wouldn't have made any difference."

"I know. That's why I never told you."

"So why are you telling me now?"

He shrugs. "I guess I just wanted you to know."

"Well…" I get up and take my cup to the sink.

I hear the scrape of his chair on the tile and then his hands are on my shoulders. It's like brushing a live electric wire. How strange that after all this time and everything that's been said and done, there's a part of me that would still like to slip my arms around his waist and lay my face against his chest.

Instead I turn around and take both his hands in mine for a second. I look straight into his eyes. "We can't do this."

"Why not?"

"Because I can't. I wouldn't survive another break up."

"What if—"

"Mac, don't. Please. It's too complicated. It's like some beautiful, intricate machine. You take it apart, some little piece gets lost, and when you try to put it back together, it never works like it did before."

He seems about to counter with some other point, but then he just smiles and kisses the top of my head. "Okay."

He lifts his jacket off the back of the chair and I walk him to the door.

"See you next year," he says.

When he's gone, I sit down at the table with his empty coffee cup and chocolate smeared plate. I think I would like to cry, but my reservoir of tears is empty. At the bottom there's only a sadness that settles into my heart like a hard little stone.

Twenty-six

Mac

He hates March. Even in Southern California, it's mostly ugly. Normally rain doesn't bother him that much, but today it's blowing in sheets across the patio, making the pool look like a gray pincushion. He's been trying to write for the last hour, but his mood is ugly, too. When the door opens and Kristin comes in carrying two steaming cups, he gets this hollow feeling in his gut. Like when something's about to happen in a movie.

Don't go in the basement!

She puts down a cup of hot chocolate on the desk. "How's it coming?"

"Slow. Thanks."

"Why don't you take a break and talk to me."

She's wearing a new sweater, sort of a pale lavender that's beautiful with her dark hair. She's got earrings on and she smells great. From the looks of it, this isn't going to be just another skirmish.

She sits down facing him across the desk and studies him for a minute.

"You know I'm turning forty next month."

"Yes, I know."

"I was thinking I'd like to do something special."

"We could go to Paris." *Nice try, McLeod.*

"I'd like to get married."

His heart sinks. Here it is again. The thing that won't die and can't be killed, ignored or even run away from. Like *The Terminator.* Where's a good hydraulic stamping machine when you need one?

He tries a smile. "What's your second choice?"

"There is no second choice."

He turns in the chair, and the pain in his back strikes like a snake. "I told you two years ago I was never getting married again. Didn't you believe me?"

"Yes, I know you told me. I did believe you. But things change, Mac. People change. I thought that if we lived together for a while and it was really good, you'd see that getting married wouldn't be such a horrifying thing."

"It was never a horrifying thing. I'm just not wired for it."

"Do you love me?"

"Of course. Apparently that's not enough."

"*Of course?*" She laughs. "How incredibly romantic. You really know how to wow a girl."

"I'm sorry. I thought we had this all straightened out a long time ago, but I guess I was wrong. Kris, I don't know what to tell you, except I don't plan to ever get married again."

She takes a breathy sip of the hot cocoa and he notices her hand shaking as she sets it down. He feels like a shit.

Her gaze is clear and very direct. It's what makes her a good negotiator. She says,

"You know what I think?"

Answering those kinds of questions is rarely a good idea, so he waits her out.

"Ever since I moved in here, there have been three people living in this house. You and me and Wyn. I think on some level you still believe she's going to come back."

"This has nothing to do with her, except that I screwed that up so badly I have no desire to repeat the experience."

She ignores what he just said and proceeds with her own game plan. The mark of a pro. "You know I'd never ask you to break off all contact with her. I know you guys are close, and that's truly okay—"

"No, it's not okay. And let's don't go there."

"I like Wyn. As ex-wives go, she's great. She's always been really nice to me and I think she genuinely cares about you, but I can tell you right now she's not going to—"

"Kris—" God, she's like a pit bull.

"If you want to have lunch with her once in a while or help her out with something at her house, I have no problem with that."

He hates himself for what he's about to do, but she's left him no choice.

"What about sleeping with her? You have a problem with that?

That stops the juggernaut. She frowns...puzzled but not yet panicked. "What?"

"Because I have, you know. At Christmas when you were in Australia."

Check and mate. And yes, I'm a bastard.

Her face is blank. She swallows. "No. You didn't."

"Okay, I didn't. But I wanted to. I tried to. She wouldn't."

She looks at him for a long minute, clearly puzzled. "If you didn't sleep with her, why did you say you did?"

He looks away. "I don't know. I just wanted you to forget about getting married. It's not possible for me."

"Well, you get your wish." She actually smiles. "And I guess what I'm giving myself for my fortieth is a new house."

He sits forward. "You don't have to leave—"

"Of course I do." She stands up. "While I still have a few shreds of my self-respect left."

July

The house is quiet.

He'd gotten used to hearing Kristin, her voice low and clipped, punctuated with an occasional dry laugh, talking on the phone to New York or London or Sydney or Toronto nearly every Sunday morning. It was her time to catch up with various projects scattered around the globe. Even after four months, he sometimes still expects to hear her.

He supposes it means he misses her or at least that he's lonely, but he's satisfied that the relationship reached its inevitable conclusion. He's seen her once, at a restaurant with a group of people and he'd felt something...a sort of recognition, like driving past a house where you once lived. She smiled and waved at him then went back to her conversation. So like her.

It's only been a few weeks since her brother-in-law and his two sullen teenagers had finally come to collect the rest of her things, and he's already forgotten what was in the empty spaces left scattered throughout the house.

She's a beautiful woman, no doubt about that. Intelligent, capable, funny. Lovely in bed. But even before the final face off in the dusty street at high noon, he'd suspected that things were drawing to a close. His regrets aren't so much that it ended, more about the way it ended. He'd been honest with her from the start, but she seemed to feel betrayed, humiliated. Maybe that's how women always felt about the end of an affair. Somehow you were responsible, not just for what you said, but also for how they heard it.

Wyn, on the other hand, had been content to accept things as they were. She never seemed to care about making it legal...at least at the beginning. Ironically, he then had decided he wanted to marry her. Muddy Waters nailed it.

The blues is what happens between a man and a woman.

He pulls on shorts and a T-shirt. Eight A.M. and already in the eighties. He makes himself an iced espresso and takes it out by the pool with the Sunday *New York Times*. He remembers all the Sundays he and Wyn spent out here with Brownie, him with the *NY Times*, her with the *L.A. Times*, which she loved passionately and defended hotly against his disparaging comments. He's suddenly overcome with a nearly unbearable longing for her, the wild and willful hair, the scent of bread, the feel of her skin.

He finishes his coffee, goes upstairs, drops his laptop into the computer bag, puts on his hiking shoes, throws a towel and flip flops into his gym bag and gets in the car heading northeast to the mountains. To a beautiful little lake where he can hike and swim and work and come back this afternoon before the worst of the traffic. On the way back he'll call her. They can have dinner at that little French place she likes.

They'll talk. He won't push. Not like Christmas. That was stupid. He'll have to be more careful. It won't be an easy sell; she can be incredibly stubborn. But he can be incredibly persistent.

Ideally she would move back here. He never imagined he would feel so attached to a house or stay in one place for so long. But they could always sell it, buy something else. Maybe closer to the beach, farther from L.A. Or, if she insists, they can maintain separate places. They could still be together even if she doesn't want to live with him. Given their history, maybe that's the best idea. Friends with benefits. It doesn't matter. Nothing really matters except being with her.

There are only a few cars in the lot when he comes down off the trail. He's winded, which pisses him off. He needs to start swimming every day again, get back in shape. Even considering the heat today he's sweating too much. Well, a quick swim to cool off, then start back before the surge of returning weekenders clogs the freeways. He strips off his shirt and throws it in the trunk with his walking shoes. Then he grabs his towel and heads for the little wooden dock. He steps out of his flip flops and lays them carefully on the towel, zips the car keys into his pocket and stands for a moment looking down into the clear blue water.

He's thinking of her when he dives.

PART THREE

AFTER

We don't receive wisdom; we must discover it for ourselves after a
journey that no one can take for us or spare us.

—Marcel Proust

Twenty-seven

September, 2005

After the memorial, after the estate business is done and the personal effects distributed, after Skye has left, I place myself back in the bakers' rotation for the first time in a very long time. I work the early shift because coming in alone and letting the place fill up around me is easier than inserting myself into a room full of people. I congratulate myself for holding things together, satisfied that I've metabolized the sadness and completed most of my obligations.

That's when the wheels come off.

I get my period two weeks early. It lasts for three weeks. Sometimes my heart races for no discernable reason. I have night sweats and I can't sleep because I'm afraid I'll stop breathing. I go to the doctor. He authorizes a battery of tests and finds nothing. It's stress, he says. Or…it could be peri-menopause. He suggests hormones. I decline. He offers a course of Prozac and I stare at him, grasping at a fragment of memory. I tell him no thanks.

I'm suddenly clumsy. I stumble. I drop things. I forget things. Not just where I left my keys or why I came into a room. I forget names of people I know. I forget words. Like book. And telephone. I forget to pay bills. Small problems appear insurmountable. The flat tire I once would have changed myself causes me to sit in the car weeping until I remember that this is why I pay the Automobile Club $200 a year.

I obsess. My thoughts wander down strange paths; anything can set me off.

A passing thought of Skye—she blames me for his death, although she stopped just short of saying it. I know it's not true. People don't die from love except in Child ballads. And God knows, Mac was no Sweet William. But that last medication he was taking...one of the side effects had something to do with heart arrhythmia or something didn't it? And I was the one who pressured him to take it, wasn't I? And then I left him anyway, right?

An email from Sarah pops up in my inbox, reminding me of the outrage I felt that her husband had left her to deal with the cancer on her own. But didn't I do the same thing? Didn't I leave Mac because I couldn't cope with his depression? So why is Sarah's husband a heartless bastard and I'm (as CM assures me) brave and strong?

Christmas Eve when he came to see me...was it just a coincidence that he'd decided to make a will? Or did he suspect something was wrong? Why did he suddenly feel compelled to tell me that Liv was out of town the night he went there? He just wanted me to know?

In October a couple from New Jersey makes a full price offer on the house, pre-empting everyone else that's looking at it. Thanks to the insanity of the California housing market, the shabby little Tudor cottage that Mac and I paid $400,000 for and spent seven years fixing up is now selling for a million, two.

There are complications of course. It never goes like those ReMax ads on TV where everyone is smiling. The inspection has revealed a problem with the roof. Mac was always convinced that roofing companies would say you needed a new roof when all it needed was a patch. Now it appears the roof must be replaced and the buyers want a $20,000 allowance.

My first impulse is to say forget it. I'll fix the roof and then put it back on the market.

Nancy Holland, our agent, says, "If you want my advice, Wyn, it's going to be a lot easier on you to just give them the allowance and let them have the work done. By the time you get a new roof put on, we'll be at the tail end of selling season."

"Surely the way the market is, we won't have trouble selling it. Besides, it's not my decision."

She looks longingly at the pack of cigarettes sitting on her desk. "You just never know what the market's going to do. And when the monsoons hit, that roof could become a real headache for you. You might want to mention that when you talk to Skye."

I email Skye and get no response. The couple from New Jersey want an answer yesterday, so I telephone. Gillian answers, sounding harried.

"Hi, this is Wyn. I'm calling to speak to Skye about an offer on the—"

"You'll have to ring her mobile," she says. "She's got a flat in Wellington now."

"...house. Okay. Well...thanks."

"Cheers." She hangs up.

I call the number I have in my contacts and after many rings an anonymous female voice invites me to leave a message. I leave my work, home and cell numbers and wait.

Nancy calls me on Thursday morning.

"I haven't heard anything," I say before she can ask. "I'm sorry. I've emailed and phoned, but she hasn't responded."

Nancy sighs. "The offer expires at 6 tonight," she says. "Can you give it one more try? It would be a shame to lose it just because we can't reach her."

I look at the clock.

"It's 5 AM there. I'll call her in an hour and get back to you."

An hour later Skye picks up her phone and mumbles something unintelligible.

"Skye, it's Wyn."

Silence, then. "Christ, what time is it?"

"I know it's early, and I'm sorry, but I need to speak with you about the offer on the house."

Another silence.

"The what?"

"The house. I emailed you three days ago. Some people made an offer on the house. It expires this afternoon, so I need to know what you want to do."

"What time this afternoon?"

My patience snaps. "I need to know now, Skye. It'll take till this afternoon to get the process started."

A sigh or a yawn. "Okay. Give me half a tick."

She sets the phone down and there are rustling, thumping sounds, a male voice, then she comes back on and listens silently while I read her the salient points of the offer—price, terms, closing dates—and tell her about the roof. When I finish, she says,

"I see. Well, okay."

"You want to make a counter-offer?"

"No, let's just have it done."

"Alright, then, I'll call Nancy."

"Sweet as. I'm going back to bed."

"Skye…"

"What?"

"I have to fax you the offer and you'll have to sign it and fax it back."

"Now?"

"As soon as you can get to a fax. And you'll need to email me or call me with the number."

"I will." And she hangs up.

I'm doing the job I said I would do. It's for Mac, not for her. Still, a "thanks, Wyn" wouldn't have been out of place. Is it too much trouble to say goodbye before hanging up? Is having any kind of relationship with her asking for too much?

I replace the receiver in its cradle, brushing off my floury fingerprints.

July, 2006

It's been a long week.

I had an excruciating blind date with Nathan's newly divorced squash partner, who, in the middle of dinner at the Border Grill, burst into tears and started telling me how his wife left him for another woman. Then one of the bread bakers quit abruptly and now two people are out sick. I've been working a double shift because I'm reluctant to ask anyone else to do it. The good part is it keeps me focused on bread, on baking.

In the cool, gray light just before dawn, I'm enveloped by the familiar smells of wheat and yeast and coffee, the hypnotic rhythms of Bach, the radiant warmth of the ovens. And the dough—its resilience and the pebbly texture of whole grains against the palm of my hand—that's when I feel safe. And most myself.

That's when the borderline softens, becomes a permeable membrane letting me pass freely between past and present. I might be Jean-Marc's apprentice at the Boulangerie du Pont, washing bowls and pans, shaping clumsy beginner's loaves and learning to make *levain*. Or working nights at the Queen Street Bakery in Seattle with the ever-obnoxious Linda, teaching Tyler to bake, experimenting with different flours and tecniques, testing, searching for the ultimate loaf of bread.

Of course there is no such thing. Or maybe there are many ultimate loaves, not just one.

But even more troubling than hassles at the bakery and scarier than the thought of blind dates, is the fact that Charles is sick. He's not coughing or barfing or anything obvious, but he's pretty much stopped eating, which for a Corgi, goes totally against the grain. When I put down his supper dish, he sniffs disinterestedly, takes a halfhearted nibble, then lies down with his chin on his paws. I try sprinkling grated cheese on top, then a few dollops of pumpkin, spoonful of peanut butter, all his favorite things. He manages to hoover off some of the good stuff and leave the rest. I buy a different, very expensive brand of kibble, but he turns up his nose like it was old broccoli.

So tonight we have an appointment with Dr. Karen, who took over Chuck's veterinary practice when he retired. She's one of those people who doesn't just love animals, but seems to communicate with them on some cellular level. Probably because she doesn't relate well to her own species. She looks like the kind of girl who carried a briefcase in high school, tall and skinny, wispy brown hair forever escaping from her long braid, serious expression, not given to wanton smiling. I don't think much of her bedside manner, but Charles adores her. Today, however, he seems indifferent even to her charms.

She takes his temperature, listens to his heart and lungs, checks his mouth, nose and ears. Then she looks up.

"Would you mind going outside for a minute?"

"Me?"

She sighs. "Unless there's someone standing behind you."

That scares me. "What's wrong?"

"I just want to be alone with Charles for a minute. Do you mind?"

I pace in the waiting room, watching the staff clean up and leave, one by one, till it's down to the receptionist and me.

"Can I get you some water?" she asks. "I'd offer you a cup of coffee, but by this time of the day it's usually like India ink."

"No thanks."

She gives me a weary smile. "It's natural to be worried. But Karen's the best vet I've ever known. And I've known a lot of 'em. Why don't you sit down and watch the aquarium or something?"

Just as I ease into a chair, the examining room door opens and Karen calls me back in.

"Sit," she says. As if I was a patient.

I obey, gripping the edge of the plastic chair, prepping for the worst. "What's the matter with him?"

"What's the matter with you?"

I give her my most annoyed look. "Nothing. What do you mean?"

"You know, Wyn, Charles is totally dependent on you. You are his world. He mirrors your feelings, your thoughts, everything. I don't know you very well, but I do know Charles. He's totally stressed out. And I believe it's your stress that's doing it to him."

I fold my arms. "So what am I supposed to do—put him on Prozac?"

"I don't know what to tell you about your problems, but until you get your life under control, here's what I suggest. Sit down with Charles every day, twice a day if you can. Touch him and talk to him. Tell him you love him. Tell him you're okay, just going through a hard time. Tell him everything's going to be alright. Can you do that?"

"Okay. Of course. But what about the not eating?"

"Try not to obsess about it. He picks up on the anxiety you project at every meal time. Just put down his dish and walk away. He'll start eating when he gets hungry enough. If he doesn't, try him on rice and chicken broth. Call me next week."

She sets Charles on the floor. He gives her one quick glance before he runs to my side, and I nearly lose it right there in the examining room.

I drive home and sit on the patio with a wine spritzer and my laptop, checking email. Nothing from Skye.

I emailed her yesterday because it was already today in New Zealand, a concept I only understand intermittently. I haven't heard from her since we closed on the sale of the house, and that communication consisted of an email that said,

Wyn—thanks for your help. Skye

Lately I've wondered how she was getting along, whether she's decided what to do with her inheritance, if she's still with Trevor and if Gillian's still on the farm. Once or twice I started to write an email, but halfway through I began to feel like my questions would be seen as intrusive, so the messages are still sitting in my drafts file. I shut down the computer.

It's seven P.M. and the air is warm and still. Charles ate some of his dinner tonight, but now he walks in restless circles, scratching and pawing at his towel. Maybe there's a fire out in one of the canyons and I just can't smell it yet.

I lean my head back and close my eyes and before I know what's happening, tears are sliding out from under my eyelids. I can't seem to make them stop. Soon I'm sobbing great, heaving sobs, trying to catch my breath. I sit forward and lean my forearms on my knees. I bite my lip, I clench my fists till my fingernails leave half-moons in my palms, but it will not stop. What the hell is the matter with me? Am I having some kind of nervous breakdown? Or is it just that it's been one year and tonight, for whatever reason, I finally understand that he's gone? He's not just in a different house with another woman. He actually no longer exists, and it feels like a hole in my chest.

Suddenly I remember the little green bottle of Valium that's been lying untouched at the bottom of my underwear drawer for over a year.

An hour later I'm feeling better. A bit muddled, but calm. The sobbing has stopped, leaving me with a scratchy throat and swollen eyes. I lie on the chaise lounge, too exhausted to eat. Thank God I'm off tomorrow. When the last light is gone I lock up and head upstairs to bed. The Valium has made me drowsy, but every time I close my eyes they flutter open.

Eventually I fall asleep, and it truly is like falling. Or diving maybe. A long, slow pitch into a cold lake, somersaulting through clear water, going on for so long, I want nothing more than to hit bottom.

It feels like I've only slept a few minutes, but the room is pearly gray and the clock says ten till six. Charles lies on his side against my legs, snoring softly.

And Mac is sitting on the end of my bed. For whatever reason, this is not alarming to me, or even surprising.

He grins, the familiar slow grin. "Is this a bad time?"

"Of course not. Are you okay?"

"Not too bad. Considering. How about you?"

"Fine. Except I miss you. More now. Why is that?"

"Yeah. I miss you, too."

I hesitate. "What's it like? Being dead…"

"Takes some getting used to."

"Was that you in the parking lot at Gelson's?"

"No." He laughs.

"He sure looked like you. I should have gotten his phone number."

"Listen," he says, abruptly serious, "I need to tell you something…"

"What?" My hand tightens involuntarily on the blanket.

"You need to drive the truck more. It's not good to let it just sit in the garage."

"Oh. Sorry. I didn't think about that…"

At that moment my alarm goes off and I reach over to silence it. When I roll back down on my pillow, he's gone.

When the brain fog clears, I get up, reaching for my terrycloth robe, pulling it around me as I go barefoot down the stairs with Charles right behind me.

I flip on the garage light.

The Elky sits undisturbed, its turquoise and cream paint covered with a fine, nearly invisible layer of dust.

I let Charles outside, scoop some kibble into his dish and go back upstairs to shower and dress. In the bedroom, the secondary alarm has gone off and the radio is playing. I stop in the doorway, listening. It takes me a few minutes to recognize the song, haunting and familiar.

Baker's Blues.

I enter the bakery through the front door because everyone else is in back, and slip quietly into my office. I close the door behind me and boot up my laptop. When I hear the discreet tapping, I don't bother to say come in because I know who it is and I know she will, no matter what I say.

Tyler opens the door just enough to stick her head in.

"What the hell are you doing here? You're supposed to be off today."

"Thank you. I know that."

"Can I come in?"

"I think you already are."

She's balancing a tray, which she sets on the desk. Double shot latte, extra hot. Festival Scone. Clotted cream. The scent makes me forget I had breakfast at home.

"My jeans are getting too tight."

She sits down across from me. "So? Charles doesn't care, and he's the only male that ever sees you naked."

I ignore her, take a sip of my latte and break off a piece of the scone. It's still warm from the oven, with crunchy edges, full of tiny bits of dried fruit, toasted pecans and candied lemon peel. I dip a corner into the clotted cream and take a bite. It nudges my mood thermostat upward.

"I needed to get out of the house—"

"Pretty pitiful that all you could think of to do was come to work." She leans forward, resting her elbows on my desk. "It's summer. The sun is shining. The birdies are singing. The waves are crashing. Why don't you put the top down and go for a ride? Why don't you take Charles to the park? Maybe you'll meet a single stockbroker with a female Corgi."

"If I could interrupt the comedy monologue for just a minute...? I came in because I wanted to talk to you about an idea I had."

She helps herself to my latte and makes a face. "Eeeuw. Burned milk fat. I need to give Tiffani a refresher course in latte 101. So talk to me."

"I've been thinking I might go up to Orcas for awhile."

"Seriously?"

"I need to get some work done on the house. Scatter Mac's ashes…

"And check in with the hottie chef." She gives me a wicked grin. "I mean, as long as you're going up there anyway."

"Alex and I are good friends."

"Of course." She nibbles the inside of her cheek. "When are you going?"

"Well…here's my thought. And if you don't think it's a good—"

"Tell me already!"

"I decided that there's really no need for both of us to be here all the time. Except for the holidays, maybe. So if we block out November and December that leaves ten months where we could switch off being here. What would you—"

"Yippee! I love it!"

"So I'm thinking I'll go up to Orcas next month and come back in October. Then you can take some time off after the holidays. Or whenever. I mean, we can basically divide up January through October however we want. What do you think?"

She sits back, smiling, and props one foot on the corner of my desk. "I think the longer I know you, the less annoying you are."

Twenty-eight

I'm halfway under the kitchen sink, trying to locate the shut-off valve for the water purifier when the front doorbell chimes twice in quick succession. Charles leaps into action and I bang my head on the cabinet frame trying to intercept him.

By the time I get to the door he's scratching at it, barking like a dog possessed. I pick him up and open the door.

"Hello, little scruff. Knew it was me, did you?"

Skye is standing in the door way, her trusty roll-aboard on the ground beside her. She looks very different from the young woman who came to L.A. for her father's memorial service last year. Her face is thin and washed out looking with hollows like bruises under her eyes. Her hair is pulled into a dirty ponytail and her clothes are wrinkled. She turns to wave off the taxi idling in my driveway.

"What were you planning to do if I wasn't home?"

"My next stop was the bakery."

Charles squirms in my arms, so I hand him off to her and she cradles him like a baby.

"It's good someone's happy to see me," she says while he licks her face.

"I'm happy to see you. But I hardly ever lick my visitors. And I'm shocked. What are you doing here? Why didn't you call me?"

A faint smile hovers around her pale mouth. "I was afraid you'd tell me to sod off."

I take her arm and pull her inside, shutting the door. She sets Charles down gently.

"May I use the loo?" she says, already heading for it.

Charles stands sentinel in the hall till she comes out and they join me in the kitchen. She's washed her face and combed her hair and put a little blush on her cheeks.

"Sorry to just drop out of the clouds on—are you moving house?"

"Am I what?"

"Moving house." Her glance takes in the boxes stacked in various corners. "Are you leaving here?"

"Oh." I laugh. "I'm going up to the island. For a while. The house needs some work…"

She walks directly to the fireplace where the tin box is sitting on the mantel. She lifts the lid slightly, then lets it back down, says nothing.

"Are you hungry?"

"Famished. Airplane food is so foul."

I peel off half a dozen strips of bacon and lay them in a skillet.

She puts away two BLT's and a glass of Pinot Noir, followed by a large piece of Rafe's lemon tart that I brought home for my dinner while explaining that she's come to the States for school. She's been accepted into the viticulture program at UC Davis.

"That's pretty impressive. Mac would be proud of you."

"Thanks," she says, finally pushing the plate away. "I'm excited. It's something I've always found rather gripping."

But I keep studying her. She doesn't look like somebody who's excited. She doesn't act like somebody who's about to embark on a "gripping" course of study.

"Could I have a lie-down?" she says abruptly. "I didn't sleep on the flight and I'm totally clapped out."

"Of course. You know where the guest room is. Um…I was just wondering…how long you might be—"

"Orientation is Thursday morning, so I'll fly up Wednesday. Is that okay?"

🌿

It's nearly 8 P.M. when she wanders into the kitchen wearing a nightshirt and black leggings. I'm in the middle of organizing bread files.

"Feeling better?" I ask.

"Yes, thanks."

"How about some tea?"

"Yes. Thank you." She sits down at the table and pulls her knees up under the nightshirt while I fill the kettle and put it on the stove, get down a mug and locate a box of Earl Gray.

"Sugar? Milk?"

"Yes. Thank you."

I'm starting to think that's all she's going to say.

"Wyn…I'm sorry about the glass."

I turn with the milk carton in one hand. "What glass?"

"The one I broke. Last time."

"No big deal. It was an accident."

"No, it wasn't."

I close the file box and put it back in the pantry, unsure how to respond. She gets up again and goes to stand at the French doors, then comes back to the table. I sit down across from her.

"So you came all the way from New Zealand to apologize for breaking my wineglass a year ago? You could have just emailed."

"I wanted to talk to you."

Tears brim in her eyes, and a few trickle down. She produces a pale blue handkerchief from somewhere. Most American women in their twenties probably don't even own a handkerchief.

"God, I'm sick of crying. Why am I so bloody stupid?"

"What are you talking about? You're not stupid." I touch her hand.

Instead of pulling away, she puts her other hand over mine and begins to weep soundlessly but steadily, like an open faucet.

"You don't know," she says almost in a whisper. "You've no idea."

The kettle whistles and I disentangle myself gently to fix her tea. The hankie is proving inadequate, so I pull a dishtowel out of the drawer and set it on the table with the mug.

"Why don't you tell me."

"It's too embarrassing."

"I've done my share of embarrassing things. More than my share, actually."

"Mac would be so…disappointed in me."

"After everything he went through he'd gotten to be pretty non-judgmental. Besides, he loved you very much. I doubt you could do anything that would—"

She blots her face with the towel. "Oh, yes. Yes, I could. And I've done it."

"I think I'll have a cup of tea myself." I turn on the kettle again, get down another mug.

She wipes the table where her tears have fallen.

"It's the money," she says after I sit down. "It's gone. Well…most of it."

I have to clamp my mouth shut for a few seconds. Then I ask,

"What happened?"

"Trevor…his divorce was finally granted. We decided to—we were opening a restaurant. In Wellington. It was… We wanted…" A few more tears spill onto the table. "We wanted it to be the best…a place that people would come to from everywhere. We were going to be married there…before the opening…so it needed to be…beautiful. We bought the tables and leather chairs. We had a bar built with a granite top and…the fine linens and china. And wonderful art and beautiful crafts, all from local artists. We hired this chef…

"We hired him away from another place because he was the best. So we had to pay him a lot. We had to put his first year salary in a special account. In case anything happened."

She presses her lips together. "We hired servers. We hired a bartender… Elise. She used to work at this posh club in Auckland and she was very up on all the new drinks and she had lots of friends in Wellington. And she's quite…pretty. I knew we were spending too much money…"

"All yours, I assume."

She looks startled. "Yes. Of course. We had no record, so not many suppliers would extend credit. Trevor was paying child support, so he had none to spare." She tips her mug and stares at the tea and I wait.

"I knew we were spending pots of money, but I thought we'd be earning it back soon, and Trevor kept saying that's just the way it is when you're opening. You can't skimp. Everything has to be dead flash or people lose interest before you even get started."

Of course he did. The prick.

She takes a breath and lets it out slowly, seeming to shrink in the chair. "I was supposed to be planning the wedding and he was taking care of the restaurant. I wasn't paying enough attention to all the things he was…embossed menu folders and…then one afternoon I came home early from meeting with a wine agent and found him with Elise." Her eyes darken. Just like Mac's did when he was angry. "In our bed."

"I went completely berko. I screamed and threw things and... she ran out with hardly any clothes on and someone called the police...it was awful. You know what he said? He said I was acting like a child. It was just his last fling. Before the wedding. I should think of it like a bachelor party.

"I told him to get out of my flat. And I had new locks put on that same evening. And then... the next morning..." She takes a deep breath. "I rang the accountant. And he told me exactly what we had left. And it wasn't enough to...it wasn't very much."

"When did all this happen?"

"It's been about a fortnight."

"Does your mother know?"

She looks at the ceiling. "I had to tell her. My cousin is my solicitor. It would have got back to her and then she would have been totally furious. Which she is anyway."

I drink my tea and keep silent.

"I know I shouldn't have run away. But I had to. I threw my mobile away so no one could ring me. Trevor's on the line every five minutes and Derek's threatening to come and re-arrange his face and my mother's calling and lecturing and...I was about going mad. Colleen, my cousin, said I could leave and she could start the legal process...of course I'll have to go back at some point, but maybe by then I'll be able to think. I'd already been accepted at Davis for spring, but I hadn't sent a deposit, so I called them and they said I could start fall term." She dries the last few tears from the ends of her eyelashes and looks at me. "Today was supposed to be the wedding. Or yesterday in En Zed. So, you see, I couldn't stay there."

"Do you need money?"

"No," she says quickly. "I've enough for my first year's tuition. Then, if my marks are good, maybe I can…"

She folds her arms on the table and pillows her head on them. "God, I don't know what's going to happen."

I smooth back the dirty, lank hair and resist the impulse to tell her everything will be alright.

Charles sleeps with her and when I come downstairs in the morning the two of them are sitting on the couch. She's still wearing the night-shirt and leggings, now decorated with dog fur, but she looks somewhat more animated.

"Were you able to sleep?" I ask.

"Amazingly. After my nap and my body clock getting all jumbled, I thought I'd be tossing all night."

"I forgot…do you eat eggs?"

"In case you didn't notice, I eat anything that doesn't bite back. I'd have made coffee but I couldn't seem to find the pot."

"I don't keep it out because I usually just have a double shot."

While we're eating scrambled eggs and toast, I say, "I have to go to the bakery for a few hours to catch up on some paperwork, but I could drop you at the mall or the beach. Or you could come with me if you like."

"Thanks, but I think I'll just stay here with Charles. I've got some paperwork of my own for school that I have to hand over tomorrow when I arrive, plus some…legal stuff to send my cousin. Do you by chance have a fax?"

"No, but there's a Kinko's less than a mile down the road. You can either walk down there or we can go when I get home. I won't be late."

She finishes her coffee. "Actually a walk sounds lovely. May I take Charles?"

"Of course. Just don't take his leash down till you're ready to walk out the door or he'll drive you crazy in the interim—Oh...I almost forgot. There's a box. The cleaning service found it when they were getting the house ready for the buyers. I don't know how we missed it before, but you might want some of the things. I'll bring it down for you before I go."

When I leave, she's pounding her laptop at the kitchen table and Charles is sitting at her feet, watching her like she was a movie about dog food.

The house smells the way I want heaven to smell. Skye's in the kitchen and Charles is asleep in a puddle of sun.

"I hope it's alright. I found some things for veg soup and I made scones."

"It's better than alright." I set my purse on the counter and hang up my jacket. The box of Mac's stuff has replaced the laptop on the table.

"Did you have a chance to look through that? Do you want any of it?"

"I want all of it." She turns down the flame under the soup and peers into the oven to check the scones. Then she walks over to the box and opens the flaps. "His journals are here. And some books about music. And some photos. He wasn't keen on snapshots, but there are a couple of him on a boat and one in some pub. And this is my favorite." She holds it out to me.

The hammered copper frame, a gift from my mother and Richard, is distinctive; I know exactly which photo it holds. Mac and me at the summit of Mt. Constitution on our first trip to Orcas sixteen years ago.

My first thought is to hand it back without looking, but instead I hold it with both hands, rubbing the tarnished copper, blackening my thumbs. We look so young. So utterly and happily unaware of the future. A gorgeous

180 degree panorama spreads out behind us and we're only looking at each other.

"If you want it, I understand," she says.

"I have a copy up at the cottage," I lie. "You keep this one."

Our dinner is soup and scones—true Scottish style scones—light, delicate, not too sweet. I tell her to call me if she ever wants a job as a baker.

"Of course, you'd have to work with Tyler."

"She's not such a bad lot. She and I are actually alike in some ways."

"What ways?"

"I think we both feel if something's gone wrong, there must be someone to blame." She looks over at me. "I...was going to take the ashes. When I left last time. Except I couldn't find them."

I smile. "They were in the truck."

"How did you know?"

"I didn't. I went out there after you went upstairs. Just to sit for a while, and I left them there. I guess it's stupid, but I thought he'd like to be there."

"You loved him, then."

"I did. And I do."

"Will you take them to the island now?"

"Yes."

"I keep thinking of things to tell him or ask him." There's a charged pause and then she says, "Do you believe in God or reincarnation or anything?"

"Occasionally."

"My girlfriend Angela, she's a bit woo-woo...Uncle Rory used to call her the Faerie Queen. She's always talking about Mac being my 'spirit guide.' Looking after me. Now really…can you imagine Mac in full angel regalia, hovering about?"

I can't quite prevent a smile. "Mmm…no. But you know, every now and then I get this very strong sense of my father. It's funny, sometimes I can't even picture his face clearly, but—"

"What about Mac? Do you ever…have a sense of him? Because I want to. I so want to, but there's nothing."

"Maybe it takes a while." I drink some wine and set down the glass. "I had this dream…He was sitting at the end of my bed. We were having this sort of everyday conversation…like *how are you? I'm fine.* Then he said he had to tell me something. "

She's very still; almost holding her breath.

"He said I should drive the truck more. Not let it sit in the garage."

She smiles. "God, sounds like him. Drive the truck more. Did he say anything else?"

"No. My alarm clock went off and that was it. I thought about it for days. I wanted to tell someone, but I couldn't think who. To be perfectly honest, I think everyone's tired of dealing with me."

Her eyes lock on mine with sudden recognition. "That's exactly how it is, right? Nobody wants to know. Trevor wasn't interested. Kristin won't talk about him. My mum doesn't care. You're the only one I can talk to about him. I miss him so much. Does it get any easier? Will I ever get over it?"

I pick up our dishes and take them to the sink, run water into the bowls and stand for a minute, watching the tiny debris of vegetables rise to the rim and spill over.

"Did he ever tell you how we met?"

"He said you used to come in the pub where he worked."

I laugh. "Yes, but that was later. He didn't tell you about delivering the firewood?"

"He never said much about Seattle."

I turn to look at her, to see him in her face. "I wish you could have known him then."

"What was he like?"

"Amazing. So handsome. So smart. Interesting. Interested in everything. And funny. We used to laugh so much."

"So...it must have been difficult when he started...when he got depressed."

I fill the teakettle and put it on the stove.

"Yes. Incredibly. Unbelievably."

One of the bulbs in the hanging lamp has burned out, so I bring the automatic lighter and two candles to the table. The flame jumps, falters, catches. I light the second candle off the first.

"You keep trying to see the person you love. You're so sure he's still in there somewhere. You know none of this is his fault. But..." I sit down and look at her. "that doesn't make it any easier to live with."

She says, "I'm sorry."

We sit for a few minutes without talking. Then she smiles.

"About the firewood, then?"

"Well...it was fall when I moved up there, and it was starting to get cold at night. I discovered that this cute little house I'd rented had no heater. Just a wood stove...so I called and ordered a half cord of wood and this guy came to deliver it...and he looked awful."

"Awful?"

"He had really long hair. Long, wet hair, filthy baseball cap, grungy clothes. And he smelled like dirty socks. Of course he was delivering wood all day in the rain, but still...I told him later he looked like the psycho killer handyman…Anyway, then he offered to come in and show me how to use the wood stove—"

"Did you let him?"

"Do I look that stupid?"

The kettle begins to whistle, and her head falls back and she laughs, a true laugh.

We spend the evening at the kitchen table. When the tea is gone, I brew another pot; when the candles burn down I get two more. I tell her the stories I thought I'd forgotten. Our first dinner at Lofurno's. How he drove me to the hospital in the snow when I had appendicitis. I tell her how pissed off I was when he left for Alaska, the song he wrote about the bakery closing, "Queen Street Gentrification Blues," the night he climbed up to the roof to cut down the bakery sign for my partner, Ellen. Even the disastrous dinner with Suzanne.

I talk till I'm hoarse and I've run out of candles and we're both awash in tea and red-eyed from laughing and crying and not sleeping. Now I'll spend what's left of the night going to the bathroom, but it's worth it, the way she hangs on every word. It's suddenly clear to me that this is all she really ever wanted. Not an analysis of his depression or a blow-by-blow account of our disintegrating marriage. She just wanted to know about her father. Who he was and how he lived in the time before she met him.

Wednesday morning she's up, showered and dressed before I even put feet to floor. I fix myself an espresso and find her sitting on the patio, combing out her hair like windblown silk. Her suitcase waits by the door.

"I wish you didn't have to leave so soon."

"I'll come back if you'll have me. I can't fly home for every school break."

"Maybe you could come for Thanksgiving."

"I'd like that."

Charles runs out, flopping across her feet in a futile bid to prevent her departure. She combs her fingers through his coat.

"Lovely, isn't it? The way animals make you feel adored, even after you've completely stepped in it."

I pull up a chair and set my cup on the umbrella table.

"Think of it as getting a lot of prerequisite bad stuff out of the way early. So you can move on."

"Yes, the question is move on to what."

"To everything. Your life. Your right livelihood—"

"If I even have a right livelihood."

"Of course you do. You'll find it and it will become your anchor. You won't be able to imagine doing anything else."

She laughs. "So why is it that everyone tells me I'll find someone else, and you tell me I'll find work?"

"You will absolutely find someone else, too. Someone wonderful. But work is where you find yourself. That comes first."

We both smile at the same moment, and she leans over to put her arms around me.

Twenty-nine

By 1:20 P.M. I'm leaving Anacortes on Washington Highway 20 spur, driving west along the water towards the ferry terminal, windows down, CD player blasting "Hotel California." The Orcas ferry doesn't leave till 3:30, but the lines are long on summer afternoons, and I'm taking no chances. When I pull up to the ticket booth, I turn off the music.

The agent casts an approving glance down the length of the Elky and smiles. "Nice ride," she says. "Where to?"

She runs my credit card, tells me to get in Lane # 5 and adds, "You've got a little wait, but it's good that you're early. We've been running full all day."

I park the truck and clip Charles' leash to his collar, even though he clearly feels it's unnecessary, and we head over to the snack bar. Then with a latte for me and a paper cup of water for him, we head for the narrow strip of beach where people are walking their dogs. Even on the hottest summer day the breeze carries a freshening chill, and today I can just make out the ice cone of Mt. Baker through the haze. Cormorants perch on pilings, spreading their wings to dry, gulls and terns call and dive and soar.

While I watch the birds, Charles scrutinizes a pair of retrievers and a Daschund puppy, investigates various items, alive or otherwise, littering the strand. He's going to smell like seaweed or worse for the rest of our journey, but today I don't mind. I reach in my jacket pocket for my phone to take a picture of him and then realize I left it in the truck.

I'm tired. Even Charles is tired, and he hasn't done anything but ride shotgun for four days. I could have done it in three, but we both like to get out and stretch every few hours, so we probably hit every rest stop between L.A. and Portland. And now, after four days, here we are… where the road ends.

It came to me after Skye left for Davis…the idea for a road trip. I was planning to fly up to have a look at the house and scatter Mac's ashes. But why not drive the Elky?

It's been a good trip in spite of a few small glitches—I'm embarrassed to say I ran out of gas on the 17-Mile Drive. Our motel in Eureka was the scene of a high school soccer tournament awards banquet and a bunch of teenagers partied all night long. We had to have the wheels balanced in Eugene. Nothing terrible, but I'm ready to be on the island.

By the time Charles lets me know he's ready to head back to truck, the ferry lanes are full, and cars are lined up from the toll booth back towards the highway. It's easy to spot the Elky by the little cluster of people—mostly guys—standing around checking it out. A few of them say hi or just smile and say "nice truck" before they drift away. If I was a guy they'd want to hang around and talk cars, but they probably imagine—correctly—that I don't know anything about the mechanical stuff. Or maybe they think the man who owns the truck will be showing up soon.

I rub Charles down with his old towel, he hops in ahead of me and we settle in to wait. In the distance I can see a ferry just clearing Fauntleroy Point on Decatur Island and, even though I know it's too early to be ours, the sight of it causes something to rise in my chest, like bubbles in a glass of champagne.

Then I notice the blinking light on my phone announcing a missed call. When I punch up recent calls, the top number jumps out. Rafferty's Café. I sit and look at my phone till the display goes dark.

For the last few weeks I've debated calling Alex. He is, after all, a good friend. It would be perfectly natural to call and casually mention that I'll be on the island for...awhile. And yet...I'm reluctant to stir things up. I don't want any expectations—his or mine. Or maybe I've just been afraid to find that my imminent arrival elicits only polite disinterest on his end. In any case, I'd already made up my mind to come. So I postponed the call. And the longer I waited, the more impossible it seemed. And then I was leaving, and it seemed not only impossible, but pointless. I'd be there in four days. I figure whatever we need to say to each other will be said in good time. Or not.

But now the little blue light on my phone is blinking at me insistently. I look at Charles and he returns my gaze noncommitally.

Before I can start over-thinking it, I hit the call button.

When he answers I say, "Did you know I was thinking about you?"

"No. But I was hoping. Actually, I was just calling to give you some news."

My heartbeat slows to a thud and I wait, expecting to hear that he's getting married. Or selling the café and moving to Hawaii.

"I'm going to be a grandfather."

"*What?*"

"Yeah. That's what I said when Dustin told me."

"Wait. I thought Dustin was starting Stanford this month."

"Chris—his girlfriend—is pregnant. Both mothers are having a meltdown...I just got back from Seattle last night."

"Oh…" I sit for a minute, picturing the slender, serious boy who delicately lifted sheets of pasta out of the machine, now a young man with a baby on the way.

"I was trying to talk them into waiting till Christmas break to get married. They're both eighteen, so they're going to do what they want…"

"Which is…?"

"Get married, go to school, have a baby…like, *oh, no problem.*" He sighs.

"So, Alex, what were you doing at eighteen?"

"Working the line at some dive café in the International District. Getting drunk, getting stoned." He sighs again. "Getting married."

"And you made it through okay."

"That's still up for debate. I just didn't want him to be stupid like I was. He had everything going for him. Which is what I told him."

"I bet that made him feel good. Like he was a has-been at eighteen."

"Yeah. That's when he told me to fuck off."

"Well, I have some news, too."

"Like what?

"Um…the ferry."

"What ferry?"

"Anacortes. That's my news. I'll be there about five."

"Why the hell didn't you call me?"

"How about I buy you dinner—"

"Damn it to hell, Morrison."

"And I can tell you about my plan to make bread up here in the summers."

"How does that work?"

"We can discuss it at dinner. Okay?"

The silence is long.

"Okay," he says finally. "But I'll cook."

"Geez, Alex, don't you want to relax?"

"Nah. Park on the street and come around to the patio door."

"There's just one problem…I've got Charles with me."

"Who?"

"Charles. My dog."

"Does he eat burgers?"

"Medium rare, no salt. But can he come in? We've been on the road four days and I hate to leave him in the truck."

There's a pause and then the laugh I remember so well.

"He won't be the first illegal in my kitchen."

At 4:45 in the gold and blue afternoon the M/V Elwha bounces in slow motion against the Orcas Village ferry landing and the ramp clangs down.

Charles is standing on his hind legs in the passenger seat, nose pressed against the glass, watching people scramble to their cars. When I put down my window to inhale that peculiar, specific combination of fresh salt air and diesel fumes, the sounds wash in along with it— the noise of car engines turning over, people talking, laughing, music. The atmosphere is electric, like a party about to happen.

After the pedestrians are cleared—the hikers, cyclists wheeling their bikes, a few guys wearing their kayaks on their heads, then the motorcycles—finally the AB removes the blocks from the tires of the car in front of me and the driver edges forward. My turn. I release the parking brake, let out the clutch, and follow him down the ramp, joining the parade on Horseshoe Highway.

I drive slowly, drinking in the familiar winding road, lined with blackberry brambles, wild sweet pea vine and delicate umbels of Queen Anne's Lace. We dip into shadow, then rise into a bright meadow where horses graze. Past the farms of Crow Valley, past the golf course. The ramshackle barn painted over each spring by successive graduating classes from Orcas High School, layer upon layer, till it seems the paint is all that's holding it together, an archeology of hopes and dreams.

Now the road begins to climb, and the blue water of East Sound is suddenly visible through the trees on our right. Nose out the open window, Charles is gathering in the island scents. I reach over to rub that little white patch on his chest.

"Here we are, Charlie. I think you're going to like this place."

September

The campsites are empty now, and the air is still except for a few gulls, swooping and diving. The high bank above me is thick with Madrone trees. He always liked their twisted red branches and peeling, papery bark.

A sudden shadow of motion between boulders catches my eye—otters! Two of them. I get just a glimpse of their pointed little tails as they disappear into the water.

I sit on a half-submerged rock, pull the tin box out of my daypack and set it next to me. Inside is the plastic bag of "cremains." It doesn't look like ashes, more like coarse sand, granular bits of gray, black, white, brown.

So, Mac.........here we are, saying goodbye again. As many times as we've done it, shouldn't it be getting easier?

I unzip the top and stick my hand in, withdrawing a fistful. Look at it. Rub it back and forth against my palm. I've always imagined that we all possess something tiny but indestructible at our core, an essence. Like the germ of wheat. Whatever that essence may be, it's not here. How could this handful of grit ever have been Mac? His eyes, his smile, his voice.

I tilt my hand over the water and open it. The heaviest bits sink, the rest floats on top in a little mass, jostled by the water's motion but reluctant to disperse. Some of it clings to my skin.

Another handful.

You know I wouldn't change anything, don't you? If I had to choose, I'd still choose being with you. No matter what came after.

I lose track of how many times I repeat the motion.........gathering, sifting.........until suddenly the bag is nearly empty. There's a tightness in my chest, a knot stuck in mid throat, a voice in my head. Oddly, the voice isn't Mac. It's Gabriel Kenmore Cleveland.

You get one great dog in your life, darlin', and one true love.

All due respect to Gabe's granddaddy, I'm not sure that's true. And even if it is, don't you still have to go on as if every dog is your one great dog and every love is your one true love?

The wind gusts, chilling me through my jacket. I shake out the bag over my hand, close my fist and plunge it into the icy water. I sit there till the cold begins to burn and my fingers grow numb and stiff.

When I finally uncurl them, the pain makes me cry.

Acknowledgments

While I was doing research for Baker's Blues, I kept thinking about that Nietzsche quote, "And if you gaze long enough into the abyss, the abyss will gaze back into you."

There were a lot of mornings when I woke up with an unfocused sense of dread, of sorrow, of regret. I didn't know why, I only knew how I felt. Call me a slow learner, but eventually I realized that I was spending my days reading books about depression, talking to people who were depressed, trying to imagine what it would feel like. And after a while, in a very small way, I began to find out.

This is not to say I experienced anything like full blown depression--simply that I now have a profound respect and empathy for people who do. And also for the people who live with them. So I'm grateful to the writers of those books, and the people who shared their stories with me on the depression message boards. And the people who live with depressives and somehow manage to hold things together.

I owe thanks also to Jo-Ann Mapson, trusted writerfriend (yes, it's one word) and first reader, and her husband Stewart Allison, who designed the beautiful cover, for their help and encouragement in bringing this book to life.

For educating me in great detail about wood-fired bread ovens, I'm indebted to my friend Stewart Brittner, whom I've never met in person, but with whom I've exchanged many an email.

Thanks to Susan Thomas, my best foodie friend, who's never too busy to talk about the intricacies of bread and baking. Okay, any kind of food, really.

And of course to my husband Geoff who still makes my world go round.

About the author

Armed with a degree in journalism and a short attention span, Judith Ryan Hendricks worked as a journalist, copywriter, computer instructor, travel agent, waitress and baker before turning to fiction writing. Her work has been translated into 12 languages and distributed in more than 16 countries. She lives in New Mexico with husband Geoff and dog Blue.